The Beautiful, Winged Madness

The Beautiful, Winged Madness

A NOVEL

P. PENNINGTON DOUROS

Order this book online at www.trafford.com
or email orders@trafford.com

Most Trafford titles are also available at major online book retailers.

Front and back cover pictures by P. Pennington Douros.

Printed in the United States of America.

ISBN: 978-1-4669-1187-1 (sc)
ISBN: 978-1-4669-1188-8 (e)

Trafford rev. 01/23/2013

 www.trafford.com

North America & international
toll-free: 1 888 232 4444 (USA & Canada)
phone: 250 383 6864 ♦ fax: 812 355 4082

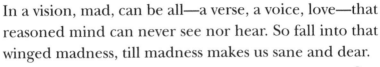

In a vision, mad, can be all—a verse, a voice, love—that reasoned mind can never see nor hear. So fall into that winged madness, till madness makes us sane and dear.

—Guy

The Beautiful, Winged Madness

A Story of Love and the Reality of Illusion

By Guy, Poetic Guy Being

Dedicated To:

The Man in the Mirror

Chapter 1

IF WOMEN WERE sculptures, he could enjoy just sitting and watching this one be, her sensual curves a play of yearning, her essence of intrigue—a question. He liked sculptures, and poems and paintings. They were non-intimidating friends and seemed possessed of purer souls than the life that spirited his world. But she was not a sculpture. She appeared, rather, to be a ghost—a ghost of beauty, perhaps of truth and love.

*   *   *

Los Angeles. The night of The Event. He sat in a half-lotus posture, his legs crossed, back erect, and eyes closed, on the gravel rooftop of his apartment building, meditating and preparing his being. The green fronds of palm trees and a cubist cityscape of buildings, everywhere and everywhere, surrounded his silent retreat.

Imprints of the city.

His eyes opened. The autumn night sky was lucid and black—waiting. A hazy blur of clouds encroached from the east.

"Damn!"

The always hum of city traffic drifted from neighboring streets. An odor of boiling beef wafted from a Mexican tenant's window, flavoring the air. Tostadas.

The soft whir of a motor. He looked up. A silver blimp floated across the dark void of the sky, magical and surreal, as in a scene from a 1950's science fiction movie depicting a vision of the future. In illuminated gold letters on the zeppelin's shell were the words: Trompe l'oeil.

The name of a cologne. *Trompe l'oeil,* he reflected. *The French term for an illusion that appears real or a reality that is an illusion. Perhaps all things are so, or perhaps not. How could one even know?*

His eyes again closed. Sounds and scents vanished, his sizable mass gone floating in a clean space of reverberating grays, wonderful pacifying grays he nothing and no one ironically agreeable no harsh ridges and confining walls no complexities or urgent passions. Quiet. Floating. Floating.

Then. A dark shape intruded on the purity of his consciousness, on the absence, flying rapidly and erratically toward him. Black wings slashed his spirit space. A screeching caw as real as his mind. Cold gripped his muscles. The form smashed into him, a frenzy of shattering black. His eyes startled open.

He saw her, standing at the rooftop's edge like a fluid, wind-dance shadow. Soft amber moonlight penetrated ghostly veils. Soft within, the form of a woman—tall, statuesque, soft. A contour of soft arcs and flows, soft arcs and flows, and apparently nude. Softly, ghostly nude.

The moment he saw her, he was captivated.

Her arms lifted from her sides evoking the form of a cross, her veils hanging like dark, prophetic wings. She stood motionless as in a challenge, or a tribute, to the engulfing dominion of the night, staring into its soul. Then she looked down to the streets below.

He tensed. *To fly? Or to jump?*

Confusion and fear whirled him. He stood and approached her, his strides cautiously soft across the rooftop's stage, fearing to come too close lest he fatally impinge on her precarious balance.

He stopped. The specter lady turned.

His poet's mind awakened. *Yes! Poet mind, now is the time.* A verse surfaced, one he had penned fancying the delight of a simple man on first acquainting his true love. *Why?*

In absolute defiance of his reticent nature, in one of the most diametric acts since he, with prophetic cry, was birthed into the world, he spoke the words aloud to her.

"Vision, bond not to self, the sleep, too won. Awaken! See what spirit's this. Beauty. Love. Open deep and hold, space distance fold, and heart be."

The ghost lady looked into his eyes, entering deep and probing gently.

"You're a poet," she spoke, her voice low and haunting, as if more of thought than words.

Who was she?

She was clothed in two layers, creating an eerie yet seductive duality. The exterior resembled the cloaks of a woman in mourning, long, loose, and solemn, but the fabric was gray and sheer, a shadow film falling as a spectral sheet from the top of her height to her feet. A separate piece covered her head and a veil obscured her face. Arms and legs eerily floated beneath their phantom shrouds. He imagined her shadowy, gloved hands greeting disembodied souls into their afterlife. "Come with me into eternity. Die to be born!"

She suddenly adjusted the veil over her face so it fell more evenly and pulled her black gloves a fraction of an inch higher over her forearms. The precision of her effort intrigued him.

"Perfect," she whispered.

Through the garment's partial transparency, penetrated by his captive vision, he saw an alluring woman, provocative as to challenge propriety, who appeared to be, but was not, naked. She was sheathed from shoulders to ankles in a flesh-hued leotard that created the baited illusion.

She appeared about twenty-seven years of age and evolved maturity; her body tall, about five-feet-eleven, strong yet soft, toned with discipline yet gentled by gracing curves. Her legs were perfectly sculpted as would complement any model.

The leotard's top plunged into cleavage offering an enticing glimpse of the robust swells of a guiltless bosom, intolerant of confinement. A narcotic scent, musty yet sweet, as that of a beast in heat, lingered around her.

He inhaled a deep breath and trembled, frightened by the vision of this beguiling woman carrying a strange specter of death. *Game, or not?*

A peculiar, hushing breeze blew across the rooftop.

He feared to look closely at her face, but he did. It was framed by brunette hair cascading down beyond smooth shoulders. He leaned closer, attempting to defeat the veil's obscuring. The woman eyed him curiously, grinned, and slowly lifted the veil.

She rewards my interest with a vision.

Her face. Of a rather common visage, yet, a quality. A beauty he could not define; he, a poet. A beauty trapped. Never defined.

An aesthetic trap, he thought. "Be wary of aesthetic traps," he had once been told by a wise elder. "Odd words to tell a poet and an artist," he had responded but had never forgotten the advice.

Here was such a trap—even more precarious, an aesthetic trap that was a woman! Her flesh was subtly hued with a slight pale of vulnerability; her cheeks soft and her nose delicate, her lips petite crimson pillows.

Eyes. That defined. noun 1: An organ of vision. 2: That gateway to the soul. Never had he seen such immense and dark eyes. 3: May evoke the fear of looking into the mystery of life itself. Absurd! He looked. The mystery. 4: A magic that pierced a black emptiness, illuminating the world, his clandestine world, with a light. 5: A madness!

"Damn!" he mumbled. He took a step back and, for a pivotal moment, examined the entirety of the woman before him. She seemed a woman in mourning for the death of herself or the beautiful woman she had once been. She now carried the illusion of that woman with her, hidden beneath an apparitional veil, entombed in some secret fate. It was a perplexing and provocative sight, especially to be found on the rooftop of his generally banal building.

The overall image she evoked was that of a woman inside the ghost of herself.

"You're a poet," she reiterated in her somber Dietrich-like voice, aborting his reflections. She smiled winsomely.

He stood mute, remembering the poetic lines he had just spoken, surprised that he had spoken at all.

"Yes. Sometimes." His words dragged self-consciously like boulders through mud. He looked down at his shoes.

"And a shy poet at that. A master of words with few words." Her voice was now elevated to a height above the grave.

Was it her?

Then, Guy sensed it. He intuited that it was about to occur and pointed to the night sky above.

"Look! I can sense it. The Event, it approaches."

"Ah yes!" She responded. "The entire Western Hemisphere waits, a beguiled audience. Perhaps the heralding of a new age. Perhaps the end of the world."

"It doesn't excite you?"

She shrugged. "Many things excite me. But let's experience it and see." She looked up into the heavens.

He looked, silent, waiting.

A distant star, white and pristine, in the wondrous and terrible night heavens, went supernova. Exploded. A fiery sphere of orange and gold dispersed into a radiating luminance of blue-white. A brilliant, virgin sun appeared in the ebony sky, bringing a peculiar, surreal day to the night. Both spectators and the entire City of Angels were cast in a phantasmal blue, yet ironically warm, illumination. For a moment, the world glowed.

Scientists, having observed particular and revealing changes in the star's topographic activity, had predicted it would supernova that evening.

Time suspended. The poet and the ghost woman stood enraptured on the rooftop, staring at the celestial phenomenon. There was no sound or motion.

It was one of his Moments.

He raised the Minolta camera hung over his shoulder. In that magical juncture of death and rebirth, of rare and consummate unearthly beauty, he took the woman's picture.

The vision.

The light spoke to him. "See! It is she."

The sun-star dimmed, its light ebbing into the black. Dark returned to the night. It had been the first time in thirty-two years, since the year of his birth, that such a celestial spectacle enthralled the eyes of the Western Hemisphere.

The ghost lady's gaze remained fixed on the heavens. Then she turned and smiled.

"Wow! It was extraordinary!"

"Yes." He looked into her eyes.

She glanced down at the rooftop and then back up. Her shadow veils shivered in the breeze.

In a following moment of quiet, he suddenly felt an urge to look deep into the reborn night sky, the vastness beyond the cloak, above their tiny presences and the sprawling city and the whole of the world, and he did. Its space was immense and lonely, its minuscule stars exquisite. It was a clear and brisk night in the City of Angels. *Angels.* He felt its cold and its light. Its all.

He spoke. "What . . . who are you?"

The ghost lady again looked down, as if saddened. With a faint, Mona Lisa smile, she slowly and enigmatically nodded her head.

Yes, a trap, he thought.

"You wish to hear my tale? After such celestial beauty and wonder, you wish to hear my tale?"

The night city became even more silent. The stars flashed a signal.

She knows my answer. "Ah, yeah."

The specter lady gazed into the air as one in search of a long-abandoned memory. He shuffled. He and the night.

"I am nothing, a void," she spoke. "A vacant space that can exist as nonexistence or be filled with any fanciful or terrible creation. I am the Minotaur and the unicorn. I am the Empress of the Universe, the vision of all beauty, a tarmac road, and a speck of dust. I am the curse and the inspiration, life and death."

"That's all?"

"And I am a song, the plaintive song I sing. A voice in the air."

She sang, her voice resonant and haunting.

"Lover come, my port's open to thee.

Rest now, and touch me sweet.

Die, and live anew in me.

Lover come, my port's open to thee."

Suddenly he shivered; an unexpected sensation, as of dissolution. He scrambled inside, pressing boundaries back into place. *Something is happening.*

"And I am evil, a killer," she persisted. "Perhaps of a person, or an idea, or a dream." She perused her surroundings, appearing disconcerted. "Perhaps life, or this world. It may have been today or months ago, or centuries past. It may even be right now in this moment. That violation turned me into a ghost. Karma, the innate tendency of the universe to create balance. Or it was justice or amends. I became the ghostly form you see." She paused. "Or the form you don't see since it's a ghost. It's also, of course, rather beautiful. And quite enigmatic." She nodded, twice. "Yes, it must be enigmatic, and yet nothing could be clearer. Do you understand, Mr. Poet Man?"

He shrugged. "Ah, maybe, or maybe not. But it probably doesn't really matter, right?" He grinned. "You sound like a character in Alice in Wonderland."

She shrugged, then grinned, then removed a glove and offered her hand.

He accepted her hand and shook it gently, rejecting the common conviction that a man's handshake should be firm and assertive. That was not how he felt. Her hand was soft and warm.

"I'm Anna, a performance artist and evolving actress."

Anna. "I see. That makes sense."

"I tend toward the fanciful, even the Shakespearean, in many things," she elaborated. "I believe I was born in the wrong century." She frowned resignedly.

"On no, definitely not!" He grinned, and then twitched. "Why are you on the rooftop dressed like a sexy ghost? Is this a performance?"

"I wear personas. They are metaphorical costumes that express aspects of reality or life."

"You were so close to the edge. You weren't thinking of jumping, were you?"

She answered without altering her now stoic expression.

"Actually, yes. I often think of suicide and death. To die, or not, is one of the most relevant of questions. But would I have jumped this night? No. I know because I'm still here. Although, with The Event, it might have been an exceptional night to die." She smiled, partially.

"You have a grim side."

"Yes. What is your name?"

"Guy."

"Hello, Guy. That's a basic name. Have you a nickname?"

"Ah, no. Only Guy."

"Then, I do believe we should give you one."

"Huh?"

The corner of her mouth cocked. "We are both artists, correct?"

"Yes."

"Then we must create. Let's see."

Her face became an absolute of intention, her eyes looking skyward as if beseeching the heavens for inspiration. "Heavens, speak!"

Guy thought she looked cute.

"You are a poet. You obviously have a degree of being. I can perceive it. How about Poetic Guy Being?"

Guy's face illuminated. "I rather like that. Poetic Guy Being it shall be. Thank you."

"You're welcome."

"Well then, we must have a poetic name for you as well." Guy's poet mind searched. "How about Anna, Spirit of the Shell?"

She cocked her head. "Close. Make it Spirit of the Persona."

"That's good," he concurred. "Perhaps even better, Anna Spirit Persona."

"Yes! Excellent."

She smiled, the warmest yet, which actually meant, but a little warm.

Becoming defined, he thought.

"Well, Poetic Guy Being, Anna Spirit Persona is most pleased to meet you."

She again extended her hand and they shook.

"I'm happy to meet you too. This is a day for spirits and goddesses." He did not know why he said that.

She peered at him curiously. "That's an interesting remark. I rather like it, Poetic Guy Being." She glanced up at the amber moon. "The moon waits quietly. Time, that strange friend and foe. I must retire now. I have to work in the morning. I work at the Wanton Muse Bookstore. Bills to pay, you know. The real world is such an imposition."

"You don't go to work dressed like that, do you?"

She glanced down at her gown. "Actually, yes. I like playing roles. It's fun and . . . revealing. The bookstore's kind of artsy and hip. The customers enjoy my personas. I believe they wonder, 'what and who will that strange woman be today?' It helps business, which, of course, pleases the management. I'm home free. Besides, the world's mad anyway. No one gives a shit."

He tried to conceal a grin, but couldn't. "Yes, I understand, and I think you are . . . a lovely and provocative sight."

"Thank you."

"May I take another picture of you? My camera's set for night shots." Guy raised the Minolta.

"Why?"

He stared. "Because I think you're intriguing and attractive, and I would like to have some pictures of you from the first time we met."

"First time? You think there will be others?"

"Well." He shrugged and shuffled, and then straightened and fortified. "There may be, if we choose to create that."

Her lips hinted at a smile. "Good enough. You're a photographer, too?"

"Of an amateur sort. I like to take pictures of the city and its people. Los Angeles and its peculiar angels. It makes the place feel more like home, and it creates at least the illusion of a family."

Anna brightened. "Yeah, I know what you mean. In spite of its masses, L.A. can be a lonely place. That urban irony. Feeling alone among millions."

For a moment that pushed beyond the momentary, they stood silent, looking at each other. A mellow concordance. *Defined,* Guy thought.

"Yes." She said. "You may take my picture."

"Great!"

Anna stepped back to provide his camera a complete view.

"To the left more." He placed her so the moon glowed above her. "The moon accents you graciously." *You are as a painting.*

She glanced up and agreed.

"You have the touch of an artist," she spoke sensitively. "An aesthetic sensibility at work. It gives more beauty to our world."

Then she partially lifted her arms in the gesture of a beckoning as if, ever so slightly, communicating: "Come to me."

An undertow. It excited and disturbed him. In the gentle wash of moonlight, Anna again looked erotic and commanding, and vulnerable, behind her protective veils. As he focused his camera, the image evolving from an abstract blur to the sharp reality of this splendid and intriguing woman before him, a vague foreboding haunted his enchantment, clenching at the hollows of his stomach.

He snapped the picture that he knew would be a prize in his collection—the woman, the ghost, *the mystery.*

"Thank you."

"You're welcome. I have to go now. It's been nice. We'll talk again. Bye."

She stepped away, her motions hesitant. "Bye, not bye," she whispered and then appeared confused, and then annoyed, and then not. She stopped and turned.

"Guy, tonight *was* an Event." She smiled, partially.

He nodded and smiled, partially. "What apartment are you in?"

A moment. "401. We'll talk again, OK?"

"OK, Anna Spirit Persona. I'm in 504."

Again she smiled, but embracing.

"Goodnight, Poetic Guy Being. You seem a good, although odd, soul." She paused, hesitant. "I like good, odd souls."

Guy watched her walk across the rooftop. He noticed the night seemed more vivid and purer than it had before, more real. Colors intensified and the scent of nearby lawns and flowers smelled especially fragrant and pungent. Pigeons sweeping by overhead seemed . . . *a poem.*

Guy suddenly perceived that he was perceiving. He thought it wonderfully peculiar. He distinctly heard a dog bark three times and the bells of a distant ice cream truck playing a Scott Joplin ragtime jingle, unusual for that time of night.

Walking away, Anna's eyes brushed across the night landscape that now appeared more alive and vital. Lights sparkled and sounds reverberated, all enhanced into a poetic mirage. She turned and sent him a final wave and smile.

Then she turned and grimaced. "No! No! Hell no," she spoke, hushed, her expression confused.

Guy felt encouraged by her wave. He watched her elegant and mysterious, real yet illusionary shadow form disappear into the darkness of the doorway. Then he watched longer, as if preserving her afterimage. *Anna is an intriguing and beautiful woman and appears, also, to possess a good, although odd, soul.* Guy liked good, odd souls.

Chapter 2

GUY WAS, BY any assessment, a strange man. His earliest memory was of himself floating in the womb experiencing absolute nothingness. As a diapered and burping infant, the first words he spoke were not the anticipated "Mama", but rather the startling query, "To be or not to be", or so was the tale his mother many times told and he chose to believe. To be.

If the gods in their whimsical mischief mixed a soul of innocence, the heart of an eclipsed child, the mind of a delirious poet/artist, the body of a lovelorn man, and the alchemy of bewildered psychiatry to forge a being at whom they could laugh and cry—a simple, complicated man—that being would be Guy.

He lived in an age of complexity, in the digital neurosphere and cultural confusion of the early twenty-first century, in a one bedroom apartment in Los Angeles, that City of Oz where cars are deities, dreams are Truth, and happiness waits in the eternal pursuit of beauty and youth. Two evenings after The Event, Guy sat in his favorite chair, chocolate brown, frayed, and permanently molded to the contours of his substantial frame, performing his daily ritual of envisioning what he might possibly do the following day that would be of meaning. There was a knock, knock, knock upon his door.

He jolted alert and listened, verifying whether there was indeed such an entreaty. Visitors were a rarity in his world. Again, a knock, knock, knock. He scratched his scalp and sauntered toward the door. For a beleaguered moment, he hesitated in front of it and then finally opened the door.

A surprise! A pale green lady, tangled with flowers and vines, smiled from the hallway. *A peculiar hybrid of Catwoman and a salad,* he immediately assessed. Through the curious vision, he recognized a face.

"Anna?"

The salad woman raised her arms and spun gracefully like a model in a fashion show. Guy stared. *The woman visits the man.* He was surprised by how that peculiar thought pleased him.

She was dressed—no, it would be more accurate to say second skinned—in a tight leotard of a silvery-green color. Stockings sheathing her lengthy, elegant legs were of an identical hue as was the paint covering her neck, face and bare feet. The partial obscuring and etherealizing of her features by the filmy, monochromatic color created the illusion of a human-shaped spirit. Woven around that spirit were vines of emerald leaves and delicate, colorful petals. At first Guy assumed they were synthetic but the floral fragrance that sweetened her presence established their authenticity.

Anna looked like the ephemeral beauty of nature. *A sexy nature,* thought Guy, *and a curious sight to be standing in my hallway.* His mind searched for an apt phrase to describe her.

"A spirit graciously enveloped by nature," he spoke and grinned.

Anna smiled. "As are we."

His otherworldly reflections abruptly grounded when his attention riveted to the boldly cut cleavage of her leotard that provided the barest concealment propriety permitted of breasts that could define Woman.

His poet's mind silently referenced a passage he once wrote: *Breasts. That first maternal home to which all of life's weary sojourners eventually yearns to return.* Guy grinned.

"What?"

"Oh, nothing. I was distracted." Guy's smile skewered.

Pinned above Anna's bosom was a corsage of white and blue roses. She looked at the flowers and adjusted them precisely so the descending stems were parallel to the vertical meridian of her body.

"Perfect!" she proclaimed.

Pale green subtly streaked her now earthen-hued hair in a nod to her persona. Fresh flowers, burgundy, white, and yellow, adorned its tumbling waves like a bouquet floating in its currents. A splash of vibrant green, accented with glimmering sparkles, framed her eyes, sweeping upwards toward her temples like the wings of an exotic bird. Her eyes evoked dark, mysterious seeds of primal nature. Guy thought she looked astonishingly poetic and beautiful.

"Well, am I invited in?" She queried.

"Yes, of course, Anna. Please come in."

She swept by him, an invigorating scent of gardens lingering in her trail and then waltzed around the room in sweeping circles, her head and arms swaying. She floated to Guy and stopped, a creature of fancy poised before him.

"Anna, you look lovely, earthy and spiritual. What are you?"

"I am," she swept her hand down her body, "Nature's Rapture. I was created when the earth was seduced by raptures in the air."

Her body swayed sensually. The performance!

"I am the procreative force of nature. I am fertility. And birth. And the persistence of survival." Her eyes speared Guy's. "I am the most potent force in the universe!"

"I see."

She's good at her roles, Guy thought. *Improvising? Or has she perfected this one before?*

"You may see me as an ideal or a vision. Nature's Rapture will be in your dreams."

Her amiable voice streamed through the room like liquid music, but Guy thought it incongruous with her manner the night they had met, which bordered on the aloof. *A woman of complexity,* he concluded. And yes, he was certain he would see her in his dreams.

The Rapture of Nature slowly walked around Guy, the man, studying his anatomy with the keenest interest. He shifted nervously.

She saw a tall man, six-feet-four, with a sturdy but slightly portly build. He had thick brown hair, parted in the center and falling almost to his shoulders. His face was rounded but strong, his eyes mahogany with tiny specks of gold, and his lips well fleshed and soft. On his left cheek was a peculiar discoloration, a magenta hue in the shape of a triangle about one inch at its base. Anna thought it interesting and that he looked masculine yet sensitive.

Yes, nature's rapture, she reflected with a smile. Then her expression rigidified. *No!*

She spoke. "Nature's Rapture confronts, I believe, a man. Is this so?"

What the hell, Guy decided. *I'll play. The play within the play.*

"Some might describe me more appropriately as a beast." He growled, although it sounded less than ferocious.

Anna cocked a brow. "Oh yes! The spirit man-beast. Born of the conjugal of heaven and hell."

She crouched slightly, her eyes continuing to explore his body.

"It is rumored you have fangs and claws, a mind of madness, and the most desperate loins. You rage at the moon and eat your fellow beasts."

Guy fidgeted. "Oh no, no. Well . . . yes, it is basically true."

"How fascinating."

She leaned against his body and ran her hand up his side. It felt nice to him. *She is good at this.*

"Are you going to eat me, man-beast?"

Guy tensed. Darkness, black and vast, descended.

"No. Well, to be honest, I don't know."

The nymph of Nature pulled away and positioned her hands on her hips. "That's not a very comforting answer."

He did not reply.

"I understand. But let me forewarn you, beastman, Nature's Rapture can also bring despair, for it is the power of dynamic masses, brutal violence, dispassionate decay, and death."

"Oh oh! Here we go again. The killer."

She grinned, slightly. "That which giveth, also taketh. And I must be as the leaves of a tree, always reaching for heaven."

She reached her arms up and waved her fingers.

"Virtue must remain my lover."

Her arms lowered and her face saddened, her voice falling plaintive.

"Once, when from passion, and perhaps love, I conjoined with a man-beast, from it was spawned a bitter offspring."

Guy thought she looked convincingly pained and for a moment, he, too, felt sad. There was an authenticity in her voice that played beyond her role and irritated him. He wanted to end the play.

Silence and silence.

"Hello, Anna, nice to see you again. I hoped I would."

"Nice to see you too, Guy." She reincarnated back into Anna.

"Illusion and reality," he remarked. "My favorite confusion."

She laughed gently. "It's my world. Well, do you like my persona?"

"Yes, very much! It's lovely. Provocative and metaphorical."

She nodded. "Yes, always metaphorical. I wore it today because there's truth in it, and I think you appreciate truth."

The accuracy of her statement surprised Guy.

"Yes. I am truth." He grinned.

"I believe in truth too. At least, when I'm being me."

Those simple statements induced in Guy a profound relief. A truth.

Anna, now both nature and woman, surveyed Guy's apartment. She assessed the decor as loner's disarray, as when one stops tidying for visitors who seldom arrive. Grand picture windows offered profuse light, air, and a panoramic view of the city. *Redeemers for the soul*, she assessed. In the corner of the living room, which was obviously also his bedroom, was his bed, queen size and unmade, provoking in her a strange, confused feeling. The other furnishings were discriminatingly selected yard sale bargains *(pragmatic but meaningless)* and artworks and plants *(meaningful but impractical). An interesting balance,* she thought. The plants were abundant, on tables, a bookcase, windowsills. A couple Hoyas vines dangled like entwined, tropical snakes from ceiling-suspended pots. Inharmonious with the disorder surrounding them—strewn paper, bags, clothing—the plants appeared lovingly attended by the Jolly Green Giant of TV commercials. They were vivid, green, and flourishing, some with leaves splashed with vibrant colors, others blooming exquisite flowers. The scent and oxygen of a rainforest infused the room. Anna relished it, inhaling a deep breath. *Oxygen and aromatherapy,* she mused. There seemed a primitive enchantment to it all, and a peculiar danger. She suppressed the thought.

"Nature's Rapture can certainly feel at home here. You like plants?"

"Plants? Actually, I've barely noticed them. They were just here when I moved in." He paused, blank faced. "Yes, I like plants, very much. They're pure and truthful, and add a presence of life."

Anna smiled profusely. "I agree and I've never heard it expressed better. Except by my persona."

She strolled the room examining the plants and had the peculiar feeling they were examining her back. She looked whimsically into the air.

"If I were anything but a human," she declared, "I believe I would like to be a plant."

"Truly, why?"

She gently lifted the leaf of a Prayer Plant, green with red veins and colorful splotches.

"In addition to their beauty and naturalness, plants don't have to struggle to *be* anything, or to discover who they really are."

She released the leaf and looked at Guy.

"They just grow by some grand, enigmatic process and design, totally fulfilling themselves and their purpose."

"Like Nature's Rapture," Guy interjected.

"Precisely! That's why I like this persona." Her nebulous eyes, glistening, glanced upward in reflection. "They are always achieving their destiny."

"I agree, absolutely." His face brightened. "And plants don't have egos. Ego betrays us. Can you imagine a plant saying, 'No, no, no! I will not be humiliated by being stuck in this dank and dirty ground, kin to worms, naked in the sun, condemned to the tedious misery of mere growth and spewing of oxygen. My seeds were rooted for grander deeds.'"

"Yes!" She agreed. "Seriously, although it may sound foolish, I believe I would sacrifice all for that supreme feeling of being pure and complete in nature, totally living and dying my purpose. Such a simple perfection. A plant or tree growing in the sun and air, just growing and being, has a perfect relationship with all things."

She again performed her sensual, swaying dance, like a branch blowing in the breeze.

"That, in its form, is the truest love," she said.

Guy shuffled. *This is becoming too . . . unreal. What be we if we be not what we be?* was the silly but apropos thought that seized his mind.

"But Anna, we are not plants. Humans are more complex than plants, and this world far more intricate than a garden. We could never be fulfilled being as a plant. That's an illusion."

Anna stilled and glared. Eyes knifed. "Yes, I know! Maybe that's the problem. I'm talking about an ideal one can pursue. Like a vision. Right?" Her tone sliced the air.

"Well, yes, of course."

For a stretched moment, they did not communicate.

Then she viewed his paintings. They were displayed on his walls like windows into the landscape of a life and a soul. Some were realistic, containing human figures, often composed to suggest a modern concept, like alienation. They were beautiful, precise, and detailed, testifying to his excellent skills, yet each expressive of a singular vision. She stood before one that she especially liked, a nude woman in a tree, done in an aqua blue.

The tones possessed a soft sensuality expressing both the outer, and the inner, essence and beauty of a woman.

"I think this one is excellent," she related. The artist nodded graciously.

Anna examined the other works. Some were in a different style and would probably be labeled Neo-Expressionism by those compelled to classify all. Consummate delusions. Poetic nightmares. They depicted recognizable figures, people, objects, trees, that were distorted or altered for emotional effect. Colors were intense and bold, often slashed with broad brushstrokes or painting knives. They vibrated with assertive yet constrained power, creating tension and contradiction. Like life.

Most impressive of all, behind some large potted plants, was an enormous painting done on an entire wall. It was a lovely Edenic Garden scene, a visual symphony of plants, flowers, trees, fanciful creatures and birds, and a soft, shimmering waterfall. Its style was fantasized realism with some plants or animals larger than life, suggesting an enchanting dream.

Anna thought the painting surprisingly naive and romanticized. It seemed incongruous with the sophistication she sensed in her new acquaintance. But she could not deny its beauty and immense power, primordial yet innocent. She liked it.

"It's meaningful to me," Guy explained, noticing Anna's delight and confusion at the work. "It reminds me of what's essential and pure. Sometimes I forget." He paused, looking at the mural, and smiled. "When the apartment manager heard that I had covered an entire wall with a painting, he came up here upset. But when he saw it, he loved it and asked me if I ever vacate the apartment, to please leave the painting on the wall."

Guy suddenly felt like walking to a corner of the room and sitting on the floor, alone, in the cold sunlight, silent, for a very long time. *What the hell?*

"I can see why," Anna replied. "It's gorgeous."

Then she noticed, toward the front right of the painting, beside a life-sized tree, a painted, empty space. She pointed to it, her expression inquiring.

"I left that space available. One day when I meet the woman who is my true love, if she does exist, I will paint her into that space with me beside her, as an Adam and Eve in our paradise world. I realize that may sound naive," he shuffled, "but I allow myself such ideals, as you do. This world needs that."

"I think that's sweet, and romantic. I like that idea." Anna peered at him intently. "And when do you think this woman may arrive?"

Guy shrugged. "I don't know. It could be any moment."

Anna looked at the empty space in the painting. "It will be filled one day, Guy."

Then she startled. Barely detectable in the painting, peering from behind the leaves of some bushes was a fantasy creature, half woman and half plant. It had the curvaceous body and lovely face of a woman, but her hair was plant leaves and stems, her eyes forest green, and exotic vines and colorful flowers wove her body.

"Me!" Anna pointed to the figure. "Nature's Rapture."

Guy saw an uncanny, and surprising, resemblance. Then Anna turned and placed her back against the painted wall. She assumed a winsome pose, resting her weight on one leg and lifting an arm outward in a gesture of invitation.

"Damn!" Guy proclaimed.

In a Trompe l'oeil illusion of reality, Anna, in her Nature's Rapture persona, appeared to merge into the painted garden image, like one of its fantasy creatures.

"Don't move," Guy commanded.

He quickly obtained his camera from a desk drawer, stood before the immense painting and Anna and took a picture.

"Destined to be a favorite." He grinned. "A classic."

Anna stepped out of the paradise world, pleased that, in a sense, the photograph would allow her to remain in it forever. *In Nature's Rapture.*

"So, you're a painter, too."

"Yes, I like to paint." His smile expressed a distinct pride. "Paintings are visual poetry. They share a bond. Some of these have actually been seen by someone. That makes me a professional." He smirked.

"You *are* a professional. I like them very much. They have a power and beauty that impact. They communicate. You're good."

"Thank you. Please take one. I have plenty." He gestured at the walls.

"Honestly? You'll give me one?"

"Yes. It would please me. Select one."

She again toured his curious little gallery, witness to his specters and angels, yearnings and guilt. One painting spoke.

Choose me, dear child, for a muse, by bewitchment of my master's mind, decreed I be painted for thee, like a destiny.

It suggested organic, tender life smashed and compounded with harsher, brutal matter, perhaps of the mind or the world. Above this collision floated a serene dispersion of light color. It reminded her of death and redemption.

"This one. I like this one."

Guy removed the painting from the wall and graciously presented it to her. Her face radiated with light. She hugged him, softly kissing his cheek. He felt his soul brighten, and his body lift as if becoming a serene dispersion of himself. *Paintings can be prophetic,* he thought.

"A painter *and* a poet," Anna declared in revelry as she released him from her arms.

Oh no. He foresaw what was coming. It had happened before.

"Oh Guy, darling." The Rapture of Nature employed her sweetest voice. "Recite to me one of your poems."

He was right.

"I love poetry. Choose one of your favorites."

Anna became a little girl at a Disneyland birthday party, which seemed to Guy extremely cute but, in a way he did not comprehend, strange.

His mind searched for an exit strategy. "Well, I'm a little, no, a lot, uncomfortable reciting them. I'm shy, and cowardly."

"Please, please, please." The adorable girl with pleading eyes.

He wanted to flee, but didn't. *I am a poet.* "I haven't given many recitations."

"Nothing to fear. Simply speak the words, and it will be."

Guy thought of a favorite poem. He inhaled a fortifying breath and spoke.

"Words lose their meaning, but expression persists. Like solemn, blanched bones, resigned. Demure inscriptions on arid sand, denoting a robust design, and determined force, now emptied, yet, uncannily willed perfect in being, still."

The room became silent. He looked down and waited.

"Bravo! Excellent! I love it." Anna applauded and then waved her arm to indicate the expanse of the room. "The world applauds."

She embraced Guy in an affectionate hug. "Thank you," she whispered in his ear.

He hugged her tightly. *How warm her body is against mine.* He felt her heart beating beneath his. For a delightful moment, they beat in synchrony.

Guy floated. He was two inches below the ceiling with the Rapture of Nature in his arms.

Congratulations! We do well this day, his floating spirit commended his body below, which instinctively looked up. Anna then also looked up but saw nothing but the ceiling. He looked down and smiled. She looked down and smiled.

"You are talented, Guy. Never doubt that."

She stepped back out of his arms. For a second her expression confused.

"I'm . . . very pleased to discover someone in this building with a similar orientation to mine," she said. "Often, people around me, well, I don't think they get me, and I can understand that. But it's very nice to find someone who might."

"Yes. I think I understand you. I understand that you're a bizarre mystery."

Anna laughed. Strands of her wavy hair swung across her face.

"Good enough. So, poet, artist, are we to be friends?" Her face spoke of the unspoken.

"Yes. Let's be all we can be."

Anna glared suspiciously, as might have Eve to the serpent. Then she smiled. "So be it." She draped her arm around his shoulder. "I think this is the beginning of a beautiful friendship," she proclaimed in a rather good Bogart impression.

Guy looked at her without speaking. He twitched and then: "Anna, I'm enjoying this. Well, it's like a special day, you know, and . . . would you like to go out together somewhere, tonight?"

Am I asking her for a date? It's been so long.

A light glittered in her eyes. "Thank you, Guy, but I may have a better idea. One reason I came over was to ask you if you'd like to join me in listening to some opera in my apartment. I love fine opera."

Just as good. "I believe that would be excellent. Can I bring all my madness and illusions?"

"But of course! I like that in you."

"It's my Beautiful, Winged Madness. It's seductive to similar souls."

"What is that?"

Guy grinned. "I'll explain it later. To be or not to be." Guy didn't know why he made that remark. It just seemed right.

"OK then, to be. Opera it is. Come, Guy, man-beast."

Nature's Rapture took her beast by the hand and led him toward the door. As they walked, Anna's attention fixed on another of the room's features: many sculptures, ranging in size from six inches to one three feet high standing beside a coffee table. Most were nude human figures, mainly women, in different poses. A couple were fanciful creatures. She paused to examine one possessing the head of a woman, the body of a bull, and broad, unfurled wings. It was in a contorted pose that could be interpreted as either pain or rapture. She liked it.

Then she heard a voice. *You are one of both rapture and pain, are you not, my love?* Anna startled and looked away.

"You like sculpture, too." She refocused.

"Yes, very much. Three-dimensional poems and paintings although true to themselves."

"Have you ever been to Forest Garden Cemetery?" she asked.

"No."

"We must go sometime. I think you would enjoy it."

They left his apartment. The hallway was vacant, lit with dim, buzzing fluorescent lights. Often the drab tunnel incited a disturbing loneliness in Guy, but not that night.

As they walked toward Anna's apartment, Guy, behind her, realized how much he delighted in just looking at Anna. It was such a simple thing, far less sophisticated than composing a poem or painting a picture. Yet, observing her form, grace, and sensuality gave him happiness.

"Nature's Rapture can enjoy, and give, more pleasures than that of a symbol," Anna commented, then felt surprised that she had said that.

Guy thought it uncanny, *as if she knew.*

She knew.

Chapter 3

To WALK INTO Anna's apartment was to enter a world of ordered domesticity enchanted by a lovely illusion. It reminded Guy of a person whose character had a core of rationality that was persistently threatened by a whimsical sensibility.

Pale gold window curtains and beige lampshades created a soft aura of luminance, rather than merely lighting the space, and a scent of forests freshened it. *A woman's space,* Guy thought. *It is nice.*

An archaic and classical decor intermingled with the contemporary and bold. On a wall was a lovely Rembrandt painting of the mythic woman Danae reclined nude on her bed as she beckoned a handmaiden. Beside it hung a modern print of slashing dissonance and chaos.

A home of contrasts. Violence along the quaint canals of Venice. The seduction of innocence by worldly sophistication. Yin and Yang. Endless associations pervaded Guy's mind. He liked her apartment.

On top of a round antique coffee table was a model of a pink 1959 Cadillac convertible with its audacious rocket fins. The front end was smashed as if driven into a brick wall.

"I bought the model, put it in a vise and smashed the front end with a hammer," Anna explained as Guy curiously examined the car. "I call it The Demise of Popular Culture."

Guy, seated on her living room couch, laughed and then had an idea.

"I'm going to create a gift for you, Anna. I'll get a recording of a Mozart concerto and have a computer mix it with a recording of heavy rock music. It would be a perfect soundtrack for your apartment."

"Sounds great. Like Stravinsky's *Rite of Spring*, one of my favorite pieces of music."

"Yes, your place has a *Rite of Spring* ambiance. Whatever that means." Guy shrugged and grinned.

"A place of sacrifices," she responded pensively, her eyes lowered, and her pose stilled.

Guy thought Anna resembled a sculpture and, perhaps because of the words she had spoken, bore vulnerability. *If women were sculptures,* he mused. She seemed imperfect and yet, to him, perfect. He thought of a classic statue of Aphrodite with broken limbs and cracked, idol breasts, so ideal and yet so flawed. What could deface such beauty?

Then, from her, a smile. "But also a space of creativity and celebration. To create life, death, beauty, horror." Again, a solemn pause. "Would you like some wine, Poetic BeastMan?"

"Yes, I would."

Anna retreated to her kitchen and returned with a bottle that she presented as if a treasured trophy.

"This is my favorite of all the world's wines." The burgundy bottle displayed a blatantly commercial pink label. "And, of course, I've tasted them all! It's from the wine collection of Seven Eleven, hidden in their refrigeration case beside the mocha coffee creamer and nonfat fruit yogurts."

Another impoverished artist, Guy thought.

Anna scrutinized the bottle's label. "An excellent vintage, aged three months." She poured the precious liquid into two glasses. "One must be grateful for what one has."

"I am grateful." Guy received his glass, held it up in a toast and then took a sip. He actually liked it.

Anna walked to her CD player in a wooden cabinet and inserted a disc of a Wagner opera. "I love Wagner, his recurring themes of redemption through love and death and transformation." She looked at Guy. "Do you believe in death and transformation, Guy?"

Guy suddenly felt a surge of anxiety, electricity needling his body. He struggled to evade it. "If it involves love, art, or fun, yes."

"Good answer." She smiled.

The music's dramatic chords, heralding an assertion of passion, elevated the room. "This is *Parsifal*, one of my favorites."

The lush aria of the opera coiled her like a seductive serpent.

"Who are your favorite composers?" She asked.

"Beethoven, Mahler, Mozart, and Stravinsky."

"Superb choices! You are a cultured man-beast."

She raised her glass in tribute to her guest and then drank deeply from it. She poured a refill.

"I value all of the arts," Guy confided. "They are my friends. My best friends." *Maybe, my only friends,* he thought.

Anna stilled. *Such a bittersweet statement.*

"Because you, too, are an artist."

Guy suspected the wine was casting its narcotic spell.

"Yes, an artist of some or more madness."

"Are not we all?" Anna giggled and then drank.

"More mad, I suspect, than less." He added.

Anna sat beside him on the crimson velvet couch, an Edwardian imitation, worn as to look authentic. Guy sensed her feelings. She was in her own space and yet, she was also in his. *She wants to be fully in both.* As did he.

They luxuriated in the music, Anna sometimes humming to the opera. It sounded less thunderous and dramatic to Guy than Wagner's usual compositions and more mystical, even visionary. The voices suggested singing prophets. It was music of his soul, and it soothed him.

Guy further examined Anna's apartment. She had recently moved in and there were unpacked boxes on the floor. Her furniture appeared to be patiently selected from rummages through antique and second-hand stores, not selected as much for their value as for their unique personalities—gracious chairs, noble end tables, aesthetic footstools. She collected interesting artifacts—toys, small statues, ceramic figurines, mementos; some colorful and fragile, some witty or tacky. Guy especially enjoyed a ceramic female Canadian Mountie with a broken leg and a svelte black cat sculpture that Anna had placed on top of a reclining straw man. Guy suspected she identified with the cat but wondered who the straw man was. He squirmed.

Everything collectively created a charming but eerie museum exhibiting reflections of times and experiences past. They were keys to Anna's life, and yet not Anna at all. Like her personas.

"Thank you, Guy." Anna broke his revelry.

"For what?"

"For just being here with me. Being you and sharing this music. It's nice." She smiled gently. "I think this wine betrays me."

She gazed into the air as Wagner's operatic drama floated around her.

"Look, Guy."

She pointed toward a wall. Leaning against it were some more artworks, yet to be hung, mainly classical or art nouveau pieces. Among them was his gift painting, more violent and boldly colored. The contrast pleased him.

A half-dozen plants, siblings to Nature's Rapture, were already stationed in strategic locations of light, air, and space, or positioned to add a needed accent of color. A foot-high gold statue of a plump, contented Buddha rested on a triangular corner table, his serene meditation undisturbed by Guy's presence, or anything else in their world. Guy stared at it and then jolted when he heard a distant, soft voice.

"Just keep awakening."

"Did he speak to you?" Anna interrupted.

Guy looked at her in surprise. "Yes, I believe he did."

"Don't tell me what he said." Her smile was knowing. "It was meant just for you. He speaks to me too." She looked at the statue teacher. "Right now he says enjoy some more wine!"

Anna poured herself and Guy another glass. Guy accepted although he knew he should not drink too much. He was on medication.

He scrutinized Anna's face. The wine's caress softened her features, making them dreamier. She looked lovely, the Anna behind the Nature's Rapture inside the ghost. Then he fretted. *This could be a complicated affair.*

I do not want the evening to be complicated, Anna suddenly decided. *I will abandon all persona behavior with its enigmatic allusions and veils. Although still costumed, only I will be present.* She slid closer to Guy on the couch. *He can now more easily experience me, and not my illusion.*

No! Yes! Damn! She hesitantly placed her hand on his arm.

"Guy, tell me about yourself, your life."

She smiled affectionately, the corners of her lips lifted, shaping her mouth into an emerald ship floating in the sea of her silvery-green face.

He relaxed and smiled. *My rehearsed reply.*

"I was born, at the youngest of ages, on a back street in Brooklyn, New York. A tiny infant, one of newborn truths, crawling between the darkest shadows of desperate crimes and the dazzling lights and sounds of urban passions."

Silence and a reprimanding glare from his hostess. "Please, more matter with less art."

"You're right. I'll keep it more real. My mother struggled to move us to New Jersey when I was one. There was only her and me. I never knew my father. She worked in the fashion industry assisting designers, but never fully became a designer herself. A 'fashion accenter', she described herself and was very proud of those final complements she contributed to another's creations. One time, after incessant encouraging from a seven-year-old me, she created her own design for a dress consisting entirely of those complements without any integrating motif. When she put it on, it looked like an ornamental, eccentric aberration of fashion. Beautifully mad! We both loved it. She even occasionally wore it in public to the aghast reaction of people. I think she could have been a great designer.

"We lived in a small brick house on a tree lined suburban street."

Guy proceeded to unfold a tale of middle class, suburban America, of oak trees and playground school yards, afternoon picnics, weekends visiting the Big City with the Liberty Lady, TV as an alternative reality, evenings in libraries—he liked to read, and it provided escape, Star Wars and discotheques ("I rarely actually danced"), awkward dates, teenage drunks, and on and on.

"And there were many, many lonely nights."

Inadvertently, his story edged into a tale of loneliness and searches for love and struggles with emptiness. His voice lost its conviction. Guy squirmed, his expression fractured. The muscles caging his stomach tightened.

He stopped. *What story should I tell?*

"What is it? Please continue."

"Anna, I don't think I'm relating my story quite accurately." He looked at her apologetically.

"Yes, I thought it sounded somewhat Hollywood, middle-class archetypal," Anna replied. "There's more to it, right?"

He inhaled slowly. "Yes, the other side."

The other side, his thought repeated.

"Tell me it all."

"Well, I don't know. Now I'm uncomfortable." His torso twitched.

"It's all right. You can tell me. I like knowing about my friends' lives, no matter what. Believe me," she nodded and raised a brow, "there are things in my life that are difficult to reveal, but I *will* tell you. We are friends now. We share truths."

She patted his hand and offered a nurturing smile.

She is right, Guy decided. *I care more about sharing with her now, completely, than any embarrassments or hauntings from my past.*

A thunderous chord in the Wagner opera seemed to accent his decision.

"I was born from an immaculate conception." Guy reopened his life. "At least that was the only conclusion I could reach. My mother not only never revealed my father's identity, she never even acknowledged there *was* a father, nor any embrace of intimacy that could have spawned me. 'You just appeared, dear,' she delighted in saying. 'Here,' pointing to her belly, 'then here,' pointing to the outside world. 'A perfect creation. Like a blessing.' I think subconsciously she actually believed I was a perfect creation, from her to me to the world. As I say that now to you, I see the absurdity of it."

"Not totally," Anna interjected.

Guy shrugged. "Well, my mother, her name was Lilly, was a lovely woman, petite, with soft, long brown hair and a tender face, and possessing an accent, that seems the correct term, an accent of grace. She enjoyed the arts. I think they mirrored the untarnished beauty that I could always see in her spirit. She often took me to museums, plays, and concerts. That planted the seeds of a poet and painter in me. As a little boy, I wrote poems to her that she found delightful. It was then that I learned the precious power of words and how they could woo a person's heart, even if she was my mother.

"There were always men *around* her. Indeed, she seemed to be considered an elusive prize by the neighborhood men, this charming, delicate, and simple woman, but none appeared to be *with* her. I think she enjoyed this lure, or power, she had over men, like an enchantress with her willing subjects. I heard stories from the neighborhood kids that she was having affairs, passionate rendezvous with men in secretive places." Guy's eyebrows rose and his eyes intrigued. "In the back rooms of clubs or the guest house on a banker's estate. I asked her about the rumors. She would look at me, abashed, and say, 'Oh dear, don't be silly,' but a sly smile would slip across her mouth. She would laugh and shake her head. I could never determine the veracity of those stories.

"My mother, with her sensual aloofness, tended to excite the imagination and fantasies of the town's pubescent boys, and girls, and sometimes, I must confess, my own."

Guy checked Anna's response. She was listening, absorbed. She smiled and nodded. Around them the opera wove eloquently like a soundtrack for his story. Love and delirious pain.

"But there was another facet to my mother. She always seemed perpetually frustrated and unable to handle emotional demands and harsher realities. She tried to pretend things were different than they were, more ideal, until reality caved in on her. I don't think she was a happy woman. Occasionally, I saw something in her eyes that frightened me, like a bewildered and sad madness, sad as the final, fading notes of a requiem.

"Once I had a dream about her that expressed it well with that perceptive wisdom that dreams possess. She was a naked little girl, I knew it was her, playing in a crystalline garden of colorful and sparkling plants and flowers, but never quite accepting that they were not natural and real, that they were made of glass, hard, dead, and fragile. Glass illusions. She ignored the approaching of gray, ominous clouds until a terrible storm struck, shattering the garden. Then she stood alone, injured by the fury, bleeding, on a barren field of broken glass, unable to walk without cutting her feet, feeling bewildered, betrayed, and very angry." Guy paused and laughed hesitantly. "Dramatic, but accurate.

"But my mother adored me, sometimes I think too much. I have confused memories of moments when it seemed we were one person, sharing the same body, like in a strange and secret dream." Guy shifted. "I think she wanted to stay in those moments, and hold them, like a woman in a possession."

He paused. Anna was silent, but her face spoke of disquieting thoughts.

"Mother cared for me well, except for my," Guy looked down, "illness, my lunacy, as I tend to call it. She would never accept it, even though I was seeing therapists and was on medications."

"How have doctors diagnosed your problems?"

"They haven't been certain what to call it. They've given it various clinical labels, like borderline character dissociative. Once, when a teenager, they even labeled me schizophrenic. I looked up the condition and knew I was not schizophrenic. Schizzy maybe. A few months later they changed the diagnosis and gave it another name. I ended up a catalogue of peculiar illnesses."

Guy laughed and took a sip of wine. He stared into the glass, enjoying the reflections on the surface of the liquid.

"So I decided to refer to it as lunacy—an eccentric, sometimes terrifying, madness."

"But what is it actually? What happens?" Anna queried.

"Well, when I was four years old, I began to be plagued by terrible nightmares, like being executed before a wall by a firing squad of kangaroos in Nazi uniforms. In elementary school, sometimes in class I became confused or disoriented, having trouble differentiating reality from my own mind creations."

"Sounds like an artist to me," Anna asserted.

"No, not this, I'm afraid. I would see things that weren't there, believe things had happened which hadn't. And the voices in my head. That was the scariest part. Haunting and taunting me, often in rhymes. One voice was pleasant, angelic, but most were cruel. The medications did help that. My mother wanted to believe it was all nonsense, something I was creating for some inexplicable reason, and that one day it would all simply stop, like I would outgrow it. Or, she would say, 'maybe you can get out of it. Just try, dear. It's foolish. You don't need it.' She would look at me with the most concerned and naive eyes.

"Well, I couldn't just get out of it. Although therapies helped some, the condition continued year after year. That was when I learned that time does not heal all things, and there are painful realities this world does not know how to deal with. Maybe no one knows, except spirit. I lost my innocence."

Guy quieted and stared at Anna, his face tense. "Will this push you away?"

"No," she answered succinctly. "I'm acquainted with such things." She smiled. "Please continue. What *was* causing the illness?"

Guy shrugged. "I don't know, really. I still struggle with it. The doctors only have theories. It's a psych mystery. I'm still on medication and have to be careful how I live. It appears to be a brain chemistry disorder aggravated by certain life patterns and environmental problems, as there can be in relationships.

And it becomes confused by my artistic tendencies. I have visions often, but sometimes, especially in the past, I have trouble distinguishing a creative vision from a hallucination of lunacy."

"Perhaps there is not a difference," Anna suggested.

"Sometimes there isn't. But that's a different thing." Guy's posture straightened and he smiled. "Then it's a state that's half mad and half inspired where I can find the most sublime truths and the most terrifying illusions. It's like the experience of death and rebirth, or a beautiful, wild poem. Artists, spiritual explorers, mystics, and lovers often know it as when they find truth, create love, or see God. It can be frightening and dangerous, or exquisite, but it's always exciting. I call it the Beautiful, Winged Madness."

Anna's eyes beamed radiant. "Yes! I believe I know what you mean. It's exciting but scary. They are leaps into meaning and the soul."

Guy nodded. He knew he had an ally.

"Well, I have both experiences. I'm doing better in my life now, as I hope you can see."

Guy then became silent, staring into space. Anna smiled and sat quiet. She looked at one of the plants on the coffee table, observing the perfect curves of its leaves. *Such a simple and unlabored perfection,* she thought.

"Do you want to hear more, Anna?" Guy asked.

"Yes, please. Let the saga continue."

"Something happened one night that changed everything. I was never able to get the complete story from my mother or anyone else. I was nineteen. It was a warm spring evening with a quiet but forceful breeze. A pale moon glared down from its cold and lonely station, knowing something had demonized the night and was to assault its sight." Guy paused. "I'm conjuring that image because it feels correct. My mother was walking near the woods that bordered the neighborhood when she saw the dark figure of a man lying on the ground before the trees. He urgently called to her, pleading. 'Come here! Please, come here!' She said she was uncomfortable but could not walk away from a person who may need help. As she approached him he stood and she saw that he was no mere man.

"She said he was a man-beast, like your reference earlier, almost naked, muscular, with excessive hair over his body. I did a drawing of him from her descriptions. He had a long, thin tail and ears near the top of his head, rather than on its side. His earthen hued hair flowed down beyond his shoulders and course spikes of skin protruded from his forearms and shoulders. The pupils of his eyes were red and intense.

'I have never seen such eyes on a human,' she recounted, 'and they trapped me.' He took her by the hand and led her into the woods. Then my mother said her memories were like a charmed but terrifying dream. She could not resist. He did things to her, or with her. I don't think she knew, or was willing to remember, which. She spoke of glimpsing the bright moon over his muscular shoulders, and how it suddenly went black, and of animal sounds, and warm fluids, of crushing movements and tearing feelings. The memory confused her and provoked guilt. Apparently she awoke, as from a spell, sometime later, hurt and bleeding, in what she described as a 'slack surrender'. She left the woods and walked toward home in a calm but detached state, not seeing or hearing anything around her. Her clothes were torn, hanging off her. Some neighbors saw her walking, bleeding. There were deep, scarlet teeth marks on her shoulders and thighs, marks that would remain as scars branding the events of that night on her. The neighbors tried to help and then called the police. Mother could not accurately recall what had happened, or honestly describe it as an assault, which disturbed her more. Her memories were confused and provoked shame and guilt. She was kept in the hospital for a couple days. The police never found her 'man-beast' and, of course, many doubted her story."

"Wow!" was Anna's only response.

"The story she told to only a few leaked out to the neighborhood and created a myth, a dark legend of a beastman who comes out at night to seduce women into acts of abandonment and mutual violence. Needless to say, many of the neighborhood women were repelled by the legend and rebuked it. Yet women, especially young, were continually warned not to go by the woods alone at night. It all haunted my mother. Whatever had occurred, she never came to terms with it."

Guy stopped, took a swallow of wine, and looked at Anna. Her beautiful persona of nature and rapture seemed strange considering the ominous context of his story. *Life is ironic,* he thought.

"The change and the wounds in my mother were deep," Guy continued. "She became withdrawn, removed from friends, especially men. I never saw her with a man again socially. Although some people were compassionate, others placed a cruel stigma on her. It reminded me of the scarlet letter in the Hawthorne novel, although with a 'B' for Beast Woman, as some called her. It made me very angry.

"Mother spent more and more time alone, in her bedroom, sleeping, or just lying in bed, barely eating. She didn't go to work. We had some money she had saved to live on, and some investments, and the monthly disability payments I received. I could see she was sinking into deeper depression. Sometimes I heard her crying or even screaming at night. One time when I went into her room, she was sitting up on the bed, rocking, looking vacant and possessed, repeatedly saying, 'He knew he could prey on me. He knew he could prey on me.'

"It frightened me. She would not see a doctor for treatment. 'They wouldn't understand,' she said."

"That's a disturbing experience for her to go through," Anna responded in a consoling tone. "For anyone to go through. I don't know how I would have reacted. I think your mother is a strong person."

"Well, I'm afraid there's more. It was very strange."

"Wait, before you continue." Anna leapt up and exchanged the opera disc in her player for another. "I'm putting on *La Mer, The Sea,* by Debussy. It's soothing. I like to listen to it when things are difficult. It might help you with your story."

The music swelled through the room like the rising, gentle tides of the ocean. Its soft, interweaving rhythms reminded Guy of the playful currents of an eternal sea. *How nice it might be to drown in, and become part of, the sea,* he reflected. *Quiet and peaceful, forever.*

"You're right, Anna. That's soothing. Thank you."

She sat back down beside him and took his hand, shaking it gently.

"This next part, although disturbing, you may also find fascinating," he continued, wondering if perhaps 'fascinating' was an inappropriate term to use. "On my mother's forty-fourth birthday, she had been in bed for days, I brought her a birthday present. It was a tape of songs by Edith Piaf, the French cabaret chanteuse whom she liked. In her husky, throbbing voice Piaf sang about the heartbreak of disillusioned women, which I suspected my mother identified with. Mother was listening to the songs when she started talking oddly, in a little girl's voice. 'When can we go on the rides?' 'I want to wear my new bathing suit.' 'Will daddy be here?' I thought she had gone into some type of delirium.

"It continued for days. I sat beside her bed and listened carefully to the things she said. 'I had so much fun on the beach today, Mommy. But the water was soooo cold! Why was it so cold?' Then I realized what was happening. Once my mother told me the only time in her life when she was really happy was when she was six years old and her family was living on the New Jersey coast near to Atlantic City, the seaside resort. Apparently during that one year things were well with her family; there was peace and enjoyment between the parents and all the four children. Mother had gone back to that year and become that little girl again. No matter what I did, or how I talked to her, she wouldn't come out of it.

"When I told my doctor about it, he brought her to the hospital. They said she had gone into a regression, which people sometimes do if pain in their lives becomes too severe and overwhelms them. It's like a defense mechanism. They gave her medications and therapy, but nothing helped." Guy spontaneously laughed. "My mother could be stubborn. The doctors were surprised and confused. Usually regressions, in an adult her age, were temporary. The patient recovers with care and support. Not Mom. The little girl refused to leave her glass garden.

"I believe my mother just willed herself back to being that girl of six so she could be happy again, and she wouldn't change that decision."

"It was like she went into that persona and made it truth," Anna remarked.

"Yes, well said. It was so strange. She totally was the little girl again. She loved playing kid games, like jump rope and skip and sit where she would skip in a circle then sit down quickly, then leap up and repeat it. Then she would laugh. She would talk excitedly about her day on the beach with her brothers and sisters, and the amusement rides at Atlantic City, all as if it had just happened. Imagine seeing your forty-four-year-old mother changed into a little, whimsical girl. It was painful and bizarre."

Guy paused and listened to the primal and soothing currents of the symphonic musical sea.

"The remaining members of her immediate family, a brother and a sister, visited her, but it didn't help. On her next birthday, her forty-fifth, a year from when the regression began, I visited her in the hospital in the psychiatric ward and brought her a special birthday present. It was a doll of herself as a forty-five-year-old woman. A woman I met in a therapy group who made dolls created it. She did an excellent job. It looked uncannily like my mother. I had the desperate hope that it might help bring her back to reality. She loved it. She held it to her bosom and said 'Grandma'. It didn't bring her back.

"Then mother said, 'I love being six. I want to remain six forever. No more birthdays!' and she went to sleep. I realized she then thought of herself as becoming seven. I let her sleep and left.

"That night the hospital called me and said my mother had died in her sleep. They never found any cause for her death. An autopsy revealed nothing. Afterward I battled guilt, believing there should have been *something* more I could have done to help her, to save her. But I couldn't see what. I laid my seven-year-old mother into a cold grave."

"That's so sad and tragic," Anna stated somberly. "I'm very sorry."

"Anna, do you believe a person can just choose to die? Will it? One calls to that Dark Grave Master, and when he offers his hand, it's willingly taken?"

Anna considered the question for some time, her expression pensive, and her head resting on her fist. She reminded Guy of the sculpture *The Thinker*, but far more lovely.

"Yes, I believe so," she answered. "We will the continuation of life every moment we're alive. We could choose not to, as in suicide. We will love or hate by embracing them. We will art by creating it. So yes, I think one could just will one's own death. It's probably involved in many deaths even if the person is not conscious of it."

Guy nodded. "I agree. I think my mother willed her end because she had completed her year as that six-year-old. I also choose to believe that during that year of regression she really *was* happy, the same as if she was back being that little girl. It was real."

"What did you do after that?"

"I moved to Los Angeles and to this small apartment. I didn't want to remain in New Jersey in our home. Too much had happened there. And I've lived here, by myself, ever since. And that is my story until I met you. A normal, human drama."

Guy sent Anna an affectionate look. She smiled. Debussy's musical poem of the sea swirled toward a foamy apex of truth.

"Things can change in one's life, Guy. I strongly believe that. Look at me. I change every day." Anna laughed gently. "I want to tell you my story, but I will wait so I can reflect on yours. But Guy, there is something I'm concerned about." She became austere. "The thing about the psychiatrists, medications, and madness. Be careful, and wise. Often I think those doctors know nothing about the artist or a creative spirit. I've dealt with them, too. If they can't comprehend something, God forbid if it's in the spiritual domain, they attribute it to sickness, abnormality, or madness. And they confuse creativity with insanity, vision with illusion, spiritual purpose with naiveté or delusion. They can kill the wonder in you, Guy, especially with their plethora of drugs. Drugs can suppress the self. Only when you're homogenous with every other apathetic, damaged soul on Earth are they satisfied. They will not understand you, Poetic Guy Being."

She took a slow breath. Her eyes looked steeled.

"If they had dispensed their charlatan hexes in earlier centuries, there may never have been a Beethoven's *Ninth Symphony,* or van Gogh's *Starry Night.* I think it takes courage to be real and natural, what one really is, including one's defects and insanities. They make us unique. Popeye, that dear soul and common man philosopher, understood that when he said 'I yam what I yam.'"

Anna laughed and then fell quiet. A moment of calm passed.

"Sorry," she resumed. "You can see I have some issues with psychiatry. But I really don't know about *your* condition, and I don't want to misguide you. I don't know what you need. So don't pay too much attention to me. Maybe I'm just ranting. But be careful. I have faith in you, Guy."

Anna placed her hand on his arm, smiled, and kissed him on his cheek.

"You are my new friend," she continued, "a dear friend, and already I feel I want to protect you." She smiled again, her teeth ivory white between her emerald Nature's Rapture lips. "Even though it all also frightens me."

They embraced. She felt so warm and soft in Guy's arms, like a wonderful grace of femininity. *A woman, a fabulous woman!* was all he thought at that moment, but that thought was all.

Debussy's music of the sea suddenly hit a dissonant chord. Guy flinched. *A storm approaching,* he surmised.

The next couple hours for Guy, feeling pleasantly mellow from the wine, were as delightful as a stroll through a foreign and exotic, yet always enchanting, landscape of a dream. It was not a matter of intensity, like the passionate crescendos of opera, but of more subtle and gentle moments; an expression of curious interest in Anna's eyes or a smile, the sharing of personal antidotes, fond or embarrassing, laughter, or merely his awareness of her presence, so near. The ethereal Nature Lady, made even more fanciful by the magic of the wine, could play the theatrical with pouts and flourishes or the sincere and vulnerable with a touch or a smile. At one point he said to her, "Anna, you're like a painting done by a child."

"I am both the child and the painting," she replied.

Occasionally Anna paused from their conversation, closed her eyes and dropped her head back on the top of the couch, curls of her hair alighting on her forehead and her neck curved and sensuous. She became lost in the hypnotic flows of the music. Then her eyes flashed open and her head rose. With an animated expression, she presented an insight that the moment had inspired.

"I think this is a destiny, Guy, our meeting," she offered, "for we are to further liberate our spirits together."

Each sentence she spoke was to Guy as a passage in a novel that he highlighted so it could be savored anew later. He stored those hours in his mind as a future 'this is what it's all about'.

After a particularly complimentary statement to Anna, "You enchant this world," she leaned over and kissed him on the cheek. "Thank you for being so sweet," she whispered. Her floral scent wafted through his senses like a hazy beckoning. He looked into those eyes that were a soothing antidote for any anguished soul, eyes fathomless and bewitching. His lips, as if possessed of their own will, moved spellbound toward hers. At the last moment, Anna placed her forefinger between their mouths.

"Let's be friends," she advised gently. A look of sympathetic concern followed. "At least for now."

"Yes, of course. Sorry," Guy replied, contrite.

"No need to apologize. Not yet." Anna chuckled. "Well," she feigned a yawn, patting her mouth. "Nature's Rapture must retreat to sleep."

The image of Sleeping Beauty from the fairy tale, although in an alluring nakedness *not* of a children's tale, overcame Guy's thoughts, wiling his poet's mind to a reverie that he spoke.

"To that realm most natural and unnatural, uncloaked, yet cloaked with mystery, shorn of worldly light or shapes, home to specters and mistscapes."

"It sounds like the poet exiles me to death." Anna playfully shivered.

Her haunting remark sent a glacial chill through Guy. He tried to dismiss it with jest. "Oh no, my lady! It would be rather my death for your heart and soul, I would choose. To sleep, perchance to dream."

The soft lines of Anna's face sharpened. That cryptic remark puzzled her. But it was late, *a lateness that arrives too early*, she thought, and she was weary.

"It is agreed then. To sleep for us both," she presented as if a resolution to all.

They stood and embraced one last time.

"Let no fate break our embrace," Guy spoke boldly and then kissed her on the forehead.

Anna looked at him dubiously and then smiled affectionately and kissed him on the cheek.

"Thank you, Anna."

"Thank you, Guy."

No more needed to be said.

As he walked down the hallway outside her apartment, Anna lingered at her door watching. She became inspired to a line written by the bard, *the* Bard. She thought it would be dear, so she spoke it.

"Goodnight, sweet prince. May flights of angels sing thee to thy sleep."

Guy heard and smiled.

Chapter 4

GUY FLUNG HIMSELF on his bed, bouncing like a floppy doll before settling on his back. He stared at the ceiling as if gazing through its coarse plaster into the vastness of the night beyond with its swirling galaxies, colorful celestial orbs and, most of all, heaven.

"Heaven, I'm home in heaven," he sang softly to the universe, feeling like Fred Astaire in a 30's musical.

Yes, now, this is a Moment! He realized absolutely and felt transported from a grim, stagnant age into a splendid Renaissance. His heart beat to poetic palpitations.

And this is a time when I permit myself—hello, self!—to feel and say the most foolish of things without critical reproach. But one word seemed not foolish at all. "Anna."

He spoke it into the charmed air. "Anna who appeared unforeseen in my life—a living ghost, a rapture of nature, an enigma woman—possesses me."

Do you think or dream of me at this moment, Anna, lying on your bed, perhaps asleep, naked and renewed, as I now feel renewed? Do you know?

Guy floated a few inches below the ceiling. He felt as light as the ether of the intoxicating air. His body spoke to its levitating spirit above.

"Dear spirit, can you identify the source of these peculiar manifestations?"

"Oh yes, dear body. Although it has been a rare occurrence in our life and may seem irrational, I recognize it well. I am, we are, in love."

"In love? Can it be, spirit?"

"It is so, body. Rejoice!"

And so it was, and so he did for coveted moments quiet on his bed and suspended above. Love for Guy had been rare and elusive, as a dream by his spirit when that spirit itself seemed but a dream in his world. But as he had chosen to accept that his spirit and its dreams were real, he embraced this unexpected love and rejoiced.

Then. Encroaching, slithering in. An intruder impinged upon his joy. It was the phantom of foreboding, that grave visitor, nemesis of the heart, which had haunted him upon first meeting Anna. It stood as an imposing shadow on his enchanted stage.

"Be forewarned!" It moaned in its sober voice and then shook and howled like a Dickens' ghost. Guy almost laughed, but the specter glared with such icy eyes that he shivered.

"Be gone, cold and ranting specter!" Guy commanded courageously and expelled the antagonist from the stage.

A heartless fool lives but one foolish life, Guy philosophized. *A heartful fool lives a thousand foolish lives. Either way he be a fool. I choose the bounteous, and happier, of the fools.* He smiled, pleased with his resolution.

But the foreboding phantom merely retreated to a corner where, hidden, it grinned and waited.

Relaxed on his bed, his room as silent as the hollows of his past, and its light dim, Guy mulled over his evening's conversation with Anna and her fervent views on psychiatry and medications. *No champion of them is she.* He had been surprised by the vehemence of her criticism. But might there be wisdom in her words? His hand stroked his chin as in a mock, theatrical pondering, but his questioning was sincere. With a detached objectivity, he was aware that medications did not work their wonders, or even the slightest of healings, without exacting their toll. He thought of a man selling his soul to the devil for power and love, but without a soul, he was no longer a man.

Creativity, emotion, passion, individuality, spirit, even humanity itself, these were the qualities and virtues he most admired and sought, yet these were considered by many in psychiatry to be acceptable sacrifices, collateral damage in the battle against the demons of the mind.

"Demon," he stated aloud. Even the word excited something seductive and creative, even if threatening. Perhaps without the demon there cannot be the saint. Isn't a creator also a demon, destroying what exists at the moment he creates the new? Creativity and destruction are sister passions. In the vanquishing of aberration, might the product be equally aberrant?

A plethora of questions too complex and confusing to fathom besieged Guy. His very being now seemed hazed by doubts. Finally he realized there was only one question he needed to address to dissipate the haze, that one most basic and eternal, *the question of being*. With medications and therapies, was he being more or being less? It puzzled him and the fact that he could not satisfactorily answer it was dismaying. Guy suspected the worst.

A giant X. Above him, Guy noticed a pattern of white stripes on his ceiling formed by the newer plaster of repaired cracks. Curious. *A symbol?*

Shakespeare. In his mind. *To be or not to be? That is the question.*

"Ugh!" Guy moaned.

Often he had considered going off his medications, but much as a smoker dreaded the moment of withdrawing the cruel but blissful nicotine from his life, he had postponed the decision. Addicts and psych cases are notorious procrastinators.

He had now met a woman and was in love, and she condemned such practices, encouraging a life more natural and truthful in spite of the irony of her constant personas. And what of the healing power of love, perhaps the greatest healer of all? 'Love can heal everything that pains you; love can heal everything there is.' He recalled the lyrics of an old song he had heard in a movie.

He saw a vision of him and Anna in a Garden of Eden, like the image painted on his wall, both healed and natural, au naturel', Anna wearing nothing but the mystery in her dark eyes. They were free from guilt and inhibitions, insanities, and fear. Even the serpent tempter with promise in its fire eyes as it coiled Anna's body kissing her flesh with its reptilian tongue, offered nothing less welcomed than passion, creativity, and consummate love.

Then the vision changed. He and Anna were in a sleazy, smoky nightclub, The Blue Nest. On a stage, naked, beneath glaring lights, they made raw love, sweaty and noisy and deep before the eyes and howls of a drunken crowd. It was terribly sinful and exciting.

Angels and beasts be we all, from spirit and mind and flesh and blood, not from drugs, he reflected.

Guy knew his visions were naive, abandoned fantasy, but they also expressed profound inner stirrings and truths—yearnings. In his present state of urgent anarchy, the anarchy that love provokes, he embraced the visions.

The decision. Made in a moment, as many transformative decisions are. He would trust spirit and flesh and Anna and, most of all, love. They would be his healers.

As of this moment, I stop taking all medications.

For an instant, cold swept him. Then he thought of Anna, and all fear vanished.

If the voices return, he speculated, *perhaps they will be kind and enlightened as the voices of angels. If the hallucinations visit, perhaps they will be inspired and visionary. If madness plays, perhaps it will be transcendent and divine. Yes! I call upon The Beautiful, Winged Madness.*

Guy experienced a profound serenity. Debussy's *The Sea* floated through his memory, carrying him in its delirious currents. He became the music, and dissolved into its beauty.

Chapter 5

"WE ARE IN Venice, Italy, overlooking the charming canals," Guy announced.

"Are we not standing on Sixth Street in Los Angeles in front of a Chinese fast food restaurant?" Anna asked.

"Would it be any different?" he challenged, and Anna smiled.

For weeks Guy and Anna spent most of their free time together. Guy felt basically well. Stopping his medications had not opened the door to bizarre hallucinations or haunting voices. He felt some increase in anxiety and occasional dark feelings as he withdrew from the drugs, but the effects were tolerable. His soul lifted.

Guy learned how to transcend time and place. The hands of earthly clocks slowed, a minute filled with the life of an hour and each hour with a day. Any space he occupied felt as delightful as any other. An alley could have been the walkway to the Taj Mahal; his experience would have been identical. All places existed as one place, and all moments as one moment, the place and moment he most desired: with Anna.

"Shall we go to the Louvre, Anna?"

"No. I like the Los Angeles County Museum of Art. Let's go there."

"Just as well."

They visited art galleries, strolled parks, and explored unfamiliar city domains. Local cafes, bookstores, antique shops, and toy stores were their haunts.

"Look! A toy figure of Bettie Page, the nostalgia pin-up girl." Anna excitedly proclaimed in Wacko Toys. Ms. Page looked wonderfully tacky standing in a miniature jungle haven of plastic palm trees and a leopard. Anna bought it.

"Ah! A battered book of spiritual poetry." Guy purchased the book in a bookstore and they read it together before candlelight the following evening in Anna's apartment. One recited a poem and then passed the book to the other for a reading. Their spirits linked.

Sometimes they played the game of doing something they customarily would never do. They visited the Thundering Alley Bowling Center because neither liked bowling.

"Tonight I present my Effete Gay Male Persona, a flamboyant Oscar Wilde-like character," Anna stated brazenly with a cocky stance on the bowling lane. Her face was powdered pale and her blackened hair, slicked with hair lotion, was parted and combed smoothly back like a 1940's male film idol. A white ruffle shirt, a red bow tie, a black walking cane that she periodically fenced the air with, and a pink lapel carnation complemented her dapper pastel blue pin striped suit. Anna thought the persona amusingly incongruous with the stereotypical beer guzzling macho bowler and absolutely inappropriate for performance of the sport.

"Perfect!" she trumpeted.

Unfortunately, some who embodied that stereotype did not share her wit and antagonistic glares greeted her.

They made no pretense of proper bowling or form. Balls were lobbed, sometimes with two hands, in the direction of the pins and occasionally, by a quirk of physics, brought some down.

"Force equals mass times velocity," Guy proudly tutored Anna, absolutely resolving for her all the mysteries of the game and elevating her to a master.

Most of all, they enjoyed sitting on the cushioned seats in front of their rented lane and clandestinely being what they were, artists observing the people and rituals of the peculiar culture around them. "A bowling cult," Anna designated it. They admired the community and passion of the gamers, and Anna began conceiving a new persona to augment her repertoire: the classic American bowler.

*   *   *

On a Los Angeles evening, starless from a haze of smog, Guy and Anna dined at Crusty Charlie's Pizza Parlor, a pizza emporium cleverly designed to lure children and their parent's cash flow, promoted as a family entertainment restaurant.

"Does Fellini come to mind?" Anna asked.

Twisted tubular and maze children's play environments resembled bizarre traps. Garish, life-sized plastic figures suggested human and animal hybrid mutants. Anna frowned at one with the head of a squirrel and the body of a female super model. Dissonant sound-clashing and color light-flashing neon computer games stupefied the mind. *The interior of a starship of some psychotic alien species,* she thought.

"A commercial, American nightmare," Anna critiqued. "Although I must admit, I rather like it, somewhat."

A sign on the wall that he thought a peculiar disclaimer drew Guy's attention. 'Patrons: This establishment is not responsible for your children, regardless. Please attend to them while on the premises. Thank you. Management.'

They sat and a waitress in an orange and green striped Crusty Charlie uniform served them. A depiction of Charlie's gleeful face grinned from the mounds of her abundant bosom and a green beanie with wire insect-like antennas capped her head.

"Miss, have any children ever been killed in one of these elaborate, juvenile play contraptions?" Guy questioned her sincerely, pointing to a suspect structure.

The ingénue waitress smiled slyly. "May I take your order, please?"

Anna was in her pirate persona. "Piratess," she corrected Guy when he addressed her earlier that day. "Mistress of the Seven Seas, but of no wretch upon its shores."

"Regrettable." Guy sighed.

She looked adventurous and sexy in a cotton pirate blouse with billowing sleeves, a flaring collar, and abundant cleavage. A red bandana wrapped the top of her head, a large gold ring hung from her left ear, and a black patch covered one eye. Her legs were sheathed in tight black leather pants and boots. Inserted beneath a scarlet sash around her waist was a replica of a hefty, intimidating dagger with a gold pleated handle topped by a crimson jewel. The costume's dangerous and erotic edge drew reproachful looks from the restaurant's more matronly mothers, but the children loved it. Thinking she was part of the show, they drifted to her table to question and play.

"A pirate! A pirate! Ahoy, matey," they shouted, up on their pirate lore.

"Ahoy, scallywags," Anna retorted.

Guy and the piratess chewed and chewed on their Crusty Charlie's Cyclops Pizza. The giant round pie had at its center a mozzarella eye with a tomato pupil. Its stringy cheese stretched the length of Anna's arm as she attempted to bite off a portion.

"Cheeses!" she declared.

Three children, a boy and two girls, entered one of the purple and green convoluted mazes with twinkling colored lights and hypnotic synthesized beeping sounds. Anna and Guy watched. Five minutes passed. Two of the children emerged. Ten minutes. A girl did not appear.

"Where's Suzy?" The mother, a petite red-haired lady, asked and surveyed the installation. A sound, haunting, escaped from within the installation's bowels: a muted child's cry. Then screams.

"Oh my God!" The frantic mother screeched and then yelled to a Crusty employee. "My child!" Patrons noticed and paused, observing. Mother and employee stooped and entered the ominous guts of the construction.

Guy and Anna looked at each other. Anna wiped tomato sauce from her chin with a rainbow colored Crusty Charlie napkin.

"Oh oh," Guy mumbled.

A plaintive cry by the mother sounded from the pit of the device as from a distant tomb. Anna could not suppress an image in her mind. The fated little Suzie devoured in the jaws of a monstrous game device, a creation for play, and then digested in its synthetic tubular intestines. Her stomach coiled.

Agonizing moments. Tick, tick, tick. A smiling sun-shaped wall clock marked the dreadful seconds. Finally, the child emerged from the play site, shaking and crying, followed by her mother with paled flesh and anemic eyes and the employee who appeared surprisingly unaffected.

All resumed in the restaurant with shouts, laughter, buzzing, clanks, and whirls. "The play universe presses on," Guy remarked.

He and Anna sat quiet, their consuming of the pizza now an arduous chore. *Is this a bizarre dream?* Anna wondered.

A boy, cute, about five, with doleful eyes and unruly, wavy auburn hair approached and stood silent before their table, staring at Anna.

She smiled and winked. "How be ye, matey?"

The cherub child shyly spoke. "Will you take me away on your ship?"

Anna's heart sank. She saw the desperation in the boy's expression, his face like a night moon grayed by a gauzy cloud. Anna looked at the boy's mother seated at a nearby table. She appeared jagged and tense, carping at one of the boy's sisters, unaware that one of her brood had strayed. The image of a berserk rooster, angrily pecking at any in her path, afflicted Anna's mind.

A place deep in her heart was stricken. *Yes, of course, little boy. I will take you anywhere you wish to be,* she thought but knew she could not say.

"What's your name, matey?"

"Bobby," he answered timidly.

"I'm Anna, a piratess."

"Anna," he echoed back tenderly, his eyes brightened.

Anna's heart wrenched. "I would love to take you with me, but I'm afraid my ship, the . . . Devil's Mistress, is only for grownups. A pirate's life is hard and dangerous." She nodded slowly.

The boy's face saddened and his gaze fell to the floor.

"But hey, don't be sad." She rubbed him on the head. "They'll be many worlds you can explore. They're coming. You'll find them soon."

Bobby smiled wanly.

"But now you better go back to your mother."

The boy obediently turned and walked, robotically, away.

Anna plunged. Colors and lights dulled. Anger constricted her throat.

One stringy slice of pizza later. A manager, whom Anna noticed observing her with interest since they arrived, approached their table. Guy offered the generic nod male greeting. The man was middle-aged with a plump, red flushed face, receding, neatly combed brown hair, and a stomach punch and was dressed in a white shirt and a black tie, obviously exempted from the dress code requiring his lowlier employees to wear striped uniforms and antennae. A nametag on his shirt designated senior manager.

"Your pirate's costume is . . . wonderful!" He complimented Anna.

She noticed his eyes cruised the landscape of her form, penetrating it. Anna was perceptive to those subtle invasions. She read the implication of the look of arrogance on his face. *I am a manager! Subjugate thyself.* Even Guy noticed, sending him a dagger glare.

"Would you consider working as a waitress for us?" The manager asked with the most generous benevolence.

Anna waited silently before responding, a theatrical technique employed to build drama.

"Do I have the honor of speaking with Crusty Charlie himself? You appear a man of such stature."

"Oh no, no." The manager laughed, rubbing a hand across his slicked hair. "He's like a mascot, a company symbol. You understand a symbol?"

"Well, yes, I believe so." Anna nodded.

He grinned. "I'm Bernard, the s*enior* manager."

He emphasized the word 'senior' and extended his hand. Anna took it and squeezed firmly and then more firmly. His expression startled and then grimaced, his face turning crimson.

"Well Bernard, *senior* manager, do I look like a goddamn waitress to you?" She smiled and then inverted the smile into her harshest glare.

"Well, well," Bernard stammered as she released his hand. He shook it, turned, and muttered something less than eloquent as he stomped away.

I have been born into the wrong world, Anna thought, as she often did, and frowned.

Then, behind her. She heard and felt the wind of flapping wings. She turned, but nothing was present.

My mind creates a consoling illusion, she thought with a smile, her enturbulation diminishing. *Although I play in its domain, the reality of illusion yet startles me.*

Guy decided it was time to take Anna out of the restaurant and to gaze at the charming, and innocuous, night stars.

"Yes." Anna quickly agreed. "Let's get the hell out of here."

On the way to the door, they stopped before a 60 inch television monitor.

"Look at this, Anna."

The screen displayed a fantastic and colorful world, a surreal landscape of peculiar shapes in neon hues, computer games, and electronic toys. Robot birds flapped through the air, spacecraft hovered, and motorized miniature cars zoomed across the ground, all stretching beyond sight into a distant horizon above which hung a blood-red sky. Cowboys and cops and robbers ran about shooting loud and smoking guns. Some dramatically fell, shot.

In the center of the scene was a gigantic, dazzling electronic toy, four stories high, that blinked and whirred and rattled and shook like the operatic whimsy of a digitized god. Standing before it was Crusty Charlie, a slender, aged man with white hair and a blue painted face, wearing the colorful, comical attire of a Vaudeville clown: baggy pants, a striped shirt, and an old, crumpled hat. He waved a beckoning hand at the screen.

"Come, kiss! Join us in our fantastic world. Crusty Charlie welcomes you. Come! Join our world of games and fun. Escape and play. Forever!"

Guy and Anna amazed at how real the image on the screen and its fantasy world appeared. They looked at each other and grimaced. Guy felt nauseous. *Come!* He thought. *Join our world!*

They left. Outside the night felt heavy like a silent, black iceberg. Only a few stars glinted feebly behind the hazy smog curtain, not enough to charm Anna.

"Damn," Guy mumbled.

Anna was solemn. She could not dismiss the thought of the girl, Suzy, who had almost been lost to a play site. And the lonely, desperate little boy. *Where is the spirit and grace in our culture?* She pondered. *How was it lost?*

A ghostly Metro bus, like a giant, white metallic capsule, appeared from the haze and hissed to a halt. Guy and Anna boarded. It took them away from that world, at least for a while.

*   *   *

The Hollywood Sign. That internationally known symbol spelling 'Hollywood' in towering white letters stood on a hill above the city, visible for miles. The preservation of those simple, wooden letters seemed to Guy one of the finest demonstrations of the wisdom of Angelinos. He and Anna sat on a grassy slope beneath it looking quietly over the celebrated city with its sprawl of decades old, quaint houses and buildings and narrow, cinematic streets. The autumn morning air titillated, scented by dewy grass and blossomed flowers.

"You perceive me as extroverted and confident?" Anna questioned with a challenging stare.

In a rare abnormality, she was dressed normally in faded blue jeans, a peach cotton shirt and lavender sport shoes. Guy had barely recognized her that day when she appeared at his door.

"Well, yes. Because that's how you are," he answered with confident demeanor.

"That's how I *act*. It's an illusion as behavior often is. It's not the truth of my life."

"If you create that, then you are that," Guy rebutted astutely.

"Are you every poem you write? No. I know how to perform. I'm a performance artist." She gazed into the sky. "It's not an unusual story. I'm relatively popular among casual crowds and fellow artists. But closer, more trusted friends are few."

She looked piercingly at Guy. He saw the white letters of the monumental sign reflected in the orbs of her dark, earthen eyes. *Goddess of Hollywood,* he thought.

"Actually, in truth, my friend, right now, you are my only true friend." She chuckled at her play with words. "Pathetic, huh?" She cocked a brow.

Guy flinched. "Well, no, I wouldn't describe it as pathetic, I mean, I enjoy being someone's choice of desperation."

Anna grinned. "You are a perfect choice." The mockery was unintended. "And, as far as intimate relationships," she scratched her scalp, "well, that is a tale of woe. It's been a while. Over two years. And all this time, you thought I was this hot chick." She wiggled and swayed.

"You *are* this hot chick. What are you saying, Anna?"

Anna watched a pigeon fly over them and perch on top of the letter W as if declaring itself deity of the sign. *Reign on!*

"Intimate love frightens me now. It can be like a drug, an opiate of the flesh and soul. When it takes you, it's delirious and euphoric. I'm in love! You shout to the world. And then you become totally irrational, a true expression of madness. Or, at least, that's been my experience. I had such a relationship. If it was just a beautiful madness perhaps it would have been fine, but it became destructive. Into my heart and will was injected an addictive emotional and spiritual poison. It almost destroyed me."

She looked up at the clouds floating in the azure sky.

"If I hadn't ended it, I probably would now be looking down on you from those clouds high above. Sooo, I've since avoided intimacy. I'm . . . waiting. This hot chick is now a coward."

Guy retracted in surprise. He had immense difficulty perceiving the woman of his secret passion in any such negative manner.

"No, you're just a person, Anna, and a woman."

Anna smiled. "Yeah, we're all crazy when it comes to love. Or, at least, that *need* for love." She shrugged. "Maybe humans don't really need love. Maybe that's a myth, another oppression perpetrated by society, so we'll buy more perfume and pay for exercise classes and spend years and billions of dollars trying to make ourselves more worthy of love and commit to creating and maintaining families. But I know my *family* loves me."

She laughed and then quieted and looked deep into thought-space. Her eyes vitalized.

"Maybe you and I should create the ideal relationship," she said. "We'll have and share everything together, except love." She stared at Guy with penetrating interest.

Guy looked deep into *his* thought-space for about three seconds. "Sounds like a bummer to me."

Anna's posture deflated. "Yeah, you're right." She leaned over and kissed him on the cheek. "You're the sweetest."

Then she leapt on him and wrestled, attempting to pin his shoulders to the ground. Guy struggled bravely. There were moans and growls, but despite his considerable power, his shoulders were pinned flat against the earth.

"We know who's dominant here!" Anna proclaimed victoriously.

Whether Guy liked it or not, he suspected she was correct.

A blur of motion. Anna sprang to her feet. She looked at the long descent of the grassy hill and then at Guy and smiled capriciously.

"Come on!" She raced forward down the slope.

"Oh no." Guy pulled the considerable mass of his body to its feet, fighting against a determined inertia. He followed

Anna's path, slow and reluctant, then faster and faster. His body suddenly became lighter. A spirit, which seemed both within him and without, began to carry him. He spread his arms like wings, running. By the time he caught up to Anna, he had the excited sensation that he was flying. *No way will she reach the bottom first.*

"A race!" he yelled as he sped past her.

But Anna was not one to cower before such a challenge, and her legs were strong. Soon she passed him, peering over her shoulder and laughing.

"You'll lose!" Her voice swept over his head.

"No way!" He gained on her.

Anna suddenly dropped to the ground and rolled down the steep decline, over and over, laughing.

Guy copied. As he rolled and tumbled, his mind drifted to a distant and enchanting time and place, free and childlike. Come, roll and play free! It is the time. An illusive spirit urged.

They rolled and rose and ran and laughed until they reached the slope's bottom. Then they sat on the grass, gasping, catching their breath, and laughing more. Both had grass stains on their jeans, and on their spirits.

"It was a draw," Anna proclaimed.

"I agree," Guy agreed.

For several minutes, they rested in silence, gazing dreamily into the sky. Then Anna looked at Guy and smiled devilishly.

"Oh no," he mumbled.

She bounded to her feet. Without comment, she started running. Guy remained fixed to the ground. *Again?* Then, as in a moment of communion, he understood and felt Anna's spirit. He rose and followed.

They ran beyond a grassy strip and onto the street that stretched parallel to the base of the Hollywood Hills. Guy breathed in deeply the invigorating air. They ran up and down a hilly sidewalk and past aged, picturesque houses, relics of a Hollywood past, residences to artists, rebels, iconoclasts, and families of humbler means. They raced past majestic graying trees and Technicolor gardens, some sprouting home grown vegetables and herbs, both legal and not. The fresh scents of nature infused the air, awakening their senses more. Anna extended an arm and touched the trunks of sidewalk palm trees as they swiftly streaked past, acknowledging their presence. They ran through splotches of warm sunlight and cool shadows, dodging pedestrians attired in the Hollywood dress code of jeans and T-shirts. Playfully they warded off a barking and pursuing dog while feigning howls of terror, and they zigzagged around leisurely bicyclers.

A flock of pigeons swept down out of the white glare of the sun and flew above them, tracking their run and keeping pace with the two swift sprites below. Anna noticed and waved a greeting. The pigeons responded with a chorus of coos.

She pointed to the sky. "We have company," she shouted with a raspy laugh without interrupting the rhythm of her stride. Suddenly the birds raced upward in a steep ascent and vanished into the sun.

They ran and ran and ran. Although Guy routinely did aerobic exercises, as did Anna, he was amazed that he could run so much, so far, and yet his body was not fatigued and his breathing not labored. It seemed he had become a part of the air. His muscles were immune to exhaustion, but he knew it was not only his muscles that transported him. It was a power, a force, something pervasive and alive which he had not felt for a long time that passed from a greater source, perhaps the entire cosmos, through Anna and him, lifting and carrying them, almost effortlessly. It was subtle and yet profound, and he felt it around his entire body. Something rarer and more vitalizing than oxygen charged the air he breathed, some purer energy that tingled Guy's body and flushed his skin with a glowing reddish color. It felt wonderful!

He kept looking at Anna, seeing that she was similarly affected. Her breaths were deep but not labored, rhythmic and synchronized. Her skin glowed and gleaned with light moisture, and she vibrated. Guy had never seen her so alive.

Anna turned to the left toward the hills with Guy a few steps behind. They continued running on a grassy strip that formed a border between the forested hills and the suburban neighborhood and which Guy knew would eventually merge into Griffith Park. They were running between two worlds, an untainted sylvan paradise of hills and forests to their left and the bustling complexity of modernity and civilization to their right.

We run as ambassadors and messengers of both, Guy mused with a smile.

He thought of Pheidippides, the Greek hero who ran the immense distance between Marathon and Athens, thousands of years earlier to deliver a message of victory to his people and was the inspiration for the marathon race. Guy did not know what message he and Anna carried to the people of their world, but he chose to believe it was positive.

Eventually Anna and Guy depleted even their transcendent resources. At the same moment in a grassy stretch lined with trees, they both collapsed to the cool earth, deliriously exhausted. They rolled onto their backs and stared into the pristine sky. Between heavy breaths, they laughed and laughed. The sweat on Anna's flesh made her glisten in the sun; she looked sensual and ecstatic, like a sleek, primitive animal after a successful hunt or mating.

Guy felt limp but euphoric. He recalled a verse he once wrote and, between gasps, recited it to Anna.

"Mortally unsleeved, boys run at Einsteinian speed, nullifying the earth's centrifugal spin, deliriously suspended where creation begins to ascend to the stars and embrace the ambiguities of the gods."

"Superb poem," Anna, raised on an elbow, praised. "My dear poet, my dear Guy."

She shuffled nearer and kissed him affectionately on the cheek. He smiled. Then she lay back again and sank into the earth. Guy gazed and lost himself in the blue nothing of the sky.

"We ran to the edge of the earth," Anna poetically proclaimed. "And we did not fall off."

"Never!" Guy boldly declared. "Never, and forever, falling off."

Anna laughed and jumped to her feet. She held her arms straight out from her sides and spun, slowly at first, and then faster. A whirling dervish.

"Never! Forever!" she repeatedly shouted.

Guy leapt up and spun, joining Anna in a buoyant dance. "Never! Forever!"

*   *   *

'Home of the Happy Tummy' was the sales motto for Benny's Diner on Sunset Boulevard where Guy and Anna had breakfast later that morning. Seated in a wooden booth beside a window, Anna looked out at the streets of Hollywood, the city once of celebrity and glamour, now like a fallen and aged starlet. *Yet, it still is, and will always be, Hollywood,* she knew.

"Give a cheer for Hollywood!"

Anna saluted the legendary city with a toast from her coffee cup and a line from a classic song. After their run, with her world and self seeming as one, she bestowed on all realities the joy that was in her spirit.

Guy also felt exhilarated, but Anna's communication earlier that morning descended upon him like a gray overcast. Looking at Anna, so vital and alluring across the table behind a jar of strawberry syrup, he fostered thoughts about her, thoughts he now suspected she did not, perhaps could not, share.

Damn, he silently moaned as he munched on his eggs and pancakes drenched with sweet syrup.

"Anna, I wish life could be more like a painting. Just keep working on it until the vision is realized. Or a poem. Compose it until it achieves a desired perfection. I'm a fool for ideals. I mourn their loss."

Peering over a forkful of California vegetable egg omelet, Anna presented her knowing yet enigmatic Mona Lisa smile. "Perhaps life is ideal."

Simple, Guy thought. *Perhaps correct.* He smiled and finished his pancakes.

*   *   *

That night, alone and quiet in his apartment, Guy meditated and prayed. He prayed for the achievement of ideals in both spirit and flesh.

*   *   *

During later times together in other places but always in that ideal place of Guy's, with Anna, she spoke of herself in contradictory terms: she as the introverted extrovert, a romantic realist, a pragmatic idealist, even a deflowered, she confessed with an uncharacteristic blush, *oft* deflowered in days past, virgin. Guy spoke of himself as confused, and Anna laughed.

That salvation laugh, he reflected. *So often given.* Uncomfortably, Guy discussed some of his disappointing relationships with women. He struggled not to appear a loser.

"I don't think they assessed me as a lucrative investment."

But Anna was not adversely affected, caring little about the past and even less about the evaluations of others.

"Loving, artistic souls create now to determine the future," she tutored with utter confidence, "and they certainly don't give a damn about how the world perceives them."

A true individual. Guy reacted with admiration. Her comment was encouraging since he trusted that he was a loving, artistic soul. Or a madman.

Long, warm embraces and soft, affectionate kisses, frequently shared—on streets, in parks, in their apartments, hanging upside down from a tree branch, pretending to be bats—gave an embodied reality to their platonic love.

I am totally, and dangerously, in love, Guy thought.

"It might be best if you try not to fall in love with me," Anna said.

Something seemed wrong with the design.

Spirits get lost in worlds of tempting devils. Flesh might be sacrificed, or souls. The sun turns black and radiance fills the night sky. To experience ecstasy, or to die? Such a simple dilemma, yet they could not decide. Night or day? Life or death?

Guy's thoughts rambled frenetically during such moments. It was too late!

Most of their times together were of lighter and more joyous fare. Anna began teaching Guy to dance—he was a clumsy but enthusiastic student. He introduced her to the pleasures of painting—she possessed a natural gift for it although she enjoyed putting the paint on her body as much as on the canvas.

They were often as little children, laughing and playing, freed from the enforcers of a harsher world. Once, on a grassy field of flowers, they ran toward each other in slow motion and then fell into each other's arms as they had often seen in movies and commercials. In spite of his perplexity, Guy felt stronger and saner than ever before in his life with no severe symptoms of lunacy even though off his medications.

My fears were as shadows, no more substantial than a painted demon on a fantasy canvas. Who fears painted terrors?

*   *   *

A Friday evening. The New Renaissance Theater. Guy and Anna watched the classic Japanese film *Ugetsu*, subtitled 'Tales of the Pale and Silvery Moon After the Rain.' It was one of Anna's favorites, and she paid it tribute by devoting considerable time to creating an appropriate persona: Lady Wakasa, a seductive and beautiful ghost character. The costume was similar to a Japanese geisha with decorative, wrapped kimono, paled flesh, dark exotic eyes, and bundled, black hair penetrated with thin bamboo sticks. Echoing her ghost creation from the night Guy first acquainted her, Anna easily possessed the role. Guy thought she looked mysteriously lovely.

"How wondrously divine! Paradise invites." Anna paraphrased a character, referencing the film.

In what made for an exceptionally memorable evening, she convinced a reluctant-to-the-point-of-whining-in-protest Guy to also assume a persona, transforming him into Genjuro, the peasant pottery maker. She dressed him in a loose, raw-as-the-earth cotton shirt and pants and leather sandals. His hair was pulled back tight and blackened with temporary coloring in Japanese feudal style. Her makeup artistry transformed his eyes into the upset Asian genre.

"I feel silly," Guy complained as he walked in his new incarnation through the streets on the way to the theater. Then something changed. He began to feel unusually earthly and humbled. When they passed an apartment building garden, Guy could not, and did not, resist the urge to drop to his knees and plow his fingers through the soil. It felt so cool and essential, magnificent! He knew there was within his self the yearning to be the simplest of men, an unsophisticated creature of earth and streams and nature but rarely had he experienced it so profoundly.

From perplexed poet to village potter, he mused. *Such is the power of illusion.*

The persona helped him to better understand their lure for Anna. Personas were a means through a fanciful journey to both release and discover the self. Most of one's feared inadequacies and guilt temporarily vanished, for they were not what one was creating. One could liberate hidden qualities and be created anew. And it was weird fun!

Fun. He repeated the word several times.

A guy sat beside Anna in the dark theater watching the film's drama and comedy unfold. He not only empathized with the characters but, to a surprising extent because his confining and defining boundaries were diminished, he became them. He was a Samurai warrior, a humble villager, a forlorn, lovely ghost, a grieving wife, and a lover beguiled by a forbidden love.

"What a grand experience," he whispered to Anna, and she understood. The movie became for him as it was for her, a favorite.

*   *   *

Later that night, somewhere in Los Angeles, among its dreams and illusions and realities, a voice spoke.
"I kill love."

Chapter 6

THE NOTHINGNESS CAFÉ. On a midweek afternoon, 'hump day' to the normal working world, Guy and Anna met for lunch at the cafe near to the bookstore where she worked. Guy arrived first and claimed a table in the crowded restaurant.

The Nothingness Café. Guy began to think about it and then felt he was committing the most violate act. Here, one should think nothing. Then he reasoned that to think of the Nothingness Café was to think about nothingness. Acceptable!

The tale of the Nothingness Café always amused him. It was the brainstorm of two business partners who had the sublime concept of creating a café in a space of nothingness that would evoke pure spirit, like God's dining room. They thought of the ambiance of a Japanese teahouse or a Zen meditation room, although even purer. The entire café was painted light gray—walls, ceiling, bare floors, tables, and chairs. The windows were covered with translucent gray plastic sheets. There were no plants or paintings or decoration, nothing. Waiters and waitresses dressed in gray uniforms, shoes, and caps. Women employees could wear only minimal makeup. The gray menus proudly presented in nondescript font the concept, 'Dine in Pure Spirit.' The two visionary entrepreneurs succeeded brilliantly in creating nothing.

Patrons hated it. Restaurant critics denounced the Nothingness Café as the most dismal cafe in Los Angeles. Indeed, in the entire history of L.A.. Every customer who dined there considered it an absolute failure, the most boring and uninspiring café they ever had to tolerate. Children refused to eat in 'the garage', as they referred to it. Instead of experiencing spirit and serenity, visitors expressed feelings of emptiness, loss, existential despair, and depression.

But this was Los Angeles. Because the café was such an unequivocal, consummate failure and its creators exposed as such moronic restaurateurs, the Nothingness Café became a phenomenal success. It was seen as a unique cultural phenomena and peculiarity. Patrons often dined there in their drabbest gray clothes. Some even painted their faces gray. They all celebrated the extreme of total nothing and failure, a notion many could identify with. People enjoyed crying in the restaurant or dwelling in abysmal despair. It was the chosen place to share dire news. The café accrued a fortune.

In a way, Guy believed it had achieved its purpose. It did possess a purity and was a something from nothing that reminded him of pure although misdirected creativity. *Like my ceaseless struggle against the sense of nothingness, and the artist's purpose in creating something from nothing.*

Seated at his drab table in the drab gray light looking over the voided environment and identityless patrons, Guy examined its perfection, not spiritual, but perfect as it was. Perhaps that was why people, including him, loved it. In spite of its monumental flaws, it was yet perfect as were they.

The café also evoked his earliest remembered experience of floating in the womb in total nothingness. As the café had gone from nothing to a grand something, so he hoped it would be with his life.

Guy, being a proud rebel against convention, dressed in his most colorful T-shirt, exploding with vibrant hues that electrocuted the eye, artist's jeans that were so mottled with colors they resembled his painting palette, and a baseball cap that was a collage of hues. *Perfect,* he assessed.

In fact, it seemed a rare perfect afternoon, Guy concluded with an effusive smile. *I am here waiting for Anna on a beautiful fall day in L.A. in a perfectly imperfect café. That is how it should be.*

He heard a rumble and screeches. The dreary café door swung open, a patron entering. A Metro bus had stopped for a light on the outside street. A murky cloud billowed from its rear, enveloping the street and seeping treacherously into the café. A moment later, Guy sat in noxious, toxic fumes, tasting its bitter acidity.

"Damn!"

Anna entered the restaurant. She appeared through the gray haze like a cryptic heroine emerging from some netherworld, difficult to miss and immediately owning the space. All eyes riveted to her.

Anna's superbly evolved body was tightly sheathed in black leather—trunk, neck, arms, hands, and legs—accented by scores of chrome metal studs, some connected by tiny steel chains. A section of omitted leather on her upper outer thighs exposed bare flesh in a sexy, provocative touch. On her chest was a plastic breast plate painted dark metallic gray, as were shoulder pads and wrist armor of the same material. Grouped strands of colored wiring attached throughout the costume created a science fiction android look and a large ornate silver medallion with a blinking red light in its center hung around her neck like the talisman of an alien planet priest.

Her hair was gelled and moussed, rising from her head in twisted and tangled strands resembling a nest of entwined snakes. Black bat-like wings swept up on each side of her head and metal rod earrings dangled from rubber, pointed Mr. Spock ears that were cosmetically blended to fuse into her skin. Anna's umber eyes floated in pools of aquamarine that flared upward in a design echoing the wings. Her lips were violet and primitive designs, slashes and arches, were painted in black and purple on her cheeks and forehead.

When a startled Guy beheld her, he thought of Batgirl, the Terminator from the movies, and a Kiss band member morphed into one.

"Anna, hi! Or should I say whoa?"

He stood and greeted her with a hug. For a gratifying moment, he felt pride at being with her before the curious and admiring eyes of the onlookers. In a space of nothing, they were somebody.

They sat, Anna dropping hard on her chair.

"You look imposing, dangerous, and sexy, Anna."

She leaned toward him, her scent adult and musky. "That's because I am."

She smiled fiercely, looked down and examined her costume. "Symmetrical and balanced," she whispered. Then a scowl anguished her face. A metal stud was not fully seated in its slit. She attempted to reset it but couldn't.

"Damn!" She tore off the stud and handed it to Guy. "Here, a memento."

"I'll cherish it. Thanks."

In a flash vision, Guy saw peeling leather and offered flesh, and the most sublime of things.

"What are you today, Anna?" He suppressed the vision.

"I am a Techno Pop Cyber Punk Extraterrestrial, or something like that. I'm not certain myself."

"That sounds uncomfortably familiar. But whatever you are, I like it. And it is absolutely boring and appropriate for the Nothingness Café."

"As are you."

They both laughed. Guy strongly suspected that when the café's patrons saw the effect that Anna's elaborate persona created and its bold contrast to the establishment's ambiance, they too would start frequenting the cafe in their most flamboyant costumes.

Such is L.A. A logical madness. He grinned.

Their waitress, a young gray near-nonexistent presence with a stoic expression, took their orders with a nod but no spoken word. She did project a strong spiritual intention. Guy thought she was excellent. Anna ordered an Immaculate Salad with no dressing that meant blue cheese dressing. Guy opted for the Humility Hamburger Unadorned that meant cheese, onions, and all condiments included. They both had Tithe Cups that were cups of coffee and ordered, as most patrons did, the House Specialty, which was nothing; an empty dish was served. It cost nothing.

"Oh, this looks great! It's nothing." All enjoyed saying.

Their meals were unceremoniously served. Guy and Anna reverentially recited the suggested café prayer printed on the menu's back: 'Everything is nothing but Spirit, so let us, Dear Lord, be nothing.' They ate and spoke of simple yet vital things—a thought, a plan, a person. Hardly anything.

"I added a score of brushstrokes to a painting I'm creating," Guy stated, "that attempts to express all the layers of a person, each communicated with its own layer of paint, in one portrait."

Anna told him of a man. "You know there's this odd man who regularly visits the bookstore. He's about your height."

"Six-four," Guy clarified.

"Yes, and slender. Mid-forties. He lost his left leg and right arm, a car accident, he told me. Both are replaced with electronic, prosthetic limbs. When I see him, I can't help thinking of an odd balance achieved between a human and a machine. He can walk although with an awkward gait and a slight limp."

Anna mimicked the walk's limp by using two fingers across the table.

"He can also move his artificial hand and fingers, but with limited motion. It looks like a plastic mannequin's hand. When he does, one hears the sound of the mechanism operating, like an electronic motor whirring, moving the cables and wires, I assume. It sounds robotic like an android in a science fiction film. It's a bit eerie."

"Interesting." Guy chewed a slice of onion. "But bizarre."

"Very much so, but there's more."

Anna delicately forked some greens into her violet-framed mouth and then looked at Guy with her provocative penumbra eyes.

"He always dresses in a long black coat and cape and wears a flamboyant charcoal gray hat that sweeps dashingly down from the top of his head, and he carries an elaborately carved black walking cane. His dress resembles a portrait I've seen of the late nineteenth century painter Courbet, who's often credited with fathering the bohemian artist lifestyle and look."

"Ah, yes, Courby!" Guy nodded. "What does this man do, his work?"

"He's a professor of nineteenth century literature, you know, the romantic writers like Shelley and Byron. Think *Madame Bovary* and Edgar Allan Poe." She paused and looked upward. "I can see him in front of his class, this bizarre and shadowy figure, discussing *The Pit and the Pendulum*." Anna chuckled. "Most of his communications with me are accented with poetic or literary passages. 'Hail to thee, blithe spirit, bird thou never wert.' He usually greets me with that Shelley line. It can be impressive, even charming."

"Oh oh."

Anna grinned. "No, well," she shrugged, "when he speaks to me, I feel both enchanted and disturbed. He's like a character in a strange but poignant film, equal parts human, machine, and brooding poetry. It all seems unreal and so odd." Anna glanced down at her costume. "An ironic statement coming from you know who."

Guy drank from his tithe cup. "He sounds like a tragic but sympathetic character, actually no better or worse than any of us."

"Yes, but here's what I'm really getting to." She leaned forward and her voice softened. "I can tell this guy likes me. Probably because I'm always in a persona costume, I think he believes we're kindred souls, or even soulmates. I may be his fantasy woman. He flirts and comes on to me, courting me with Byronic quotes and romantic flourishes. He gave me a white rose one day. For lost purity, yet ever present beauty, he said. But on one of the stem's thorns was blood. I don't know what that was meant to symbolize, but it disquieted me.

"Today especially I think he really connected with my cyborg-human costume." She pointed at her clothes. "It paralleled him so closely."

Guy frowned and shuffled uneasily, but did not speak.

Anna noticed. "I don't encourage him. He makes me uncomfortable. But," she stared into her coffee, "I have to confess, sometimes around him, speaking with this mysterious, romantic stranger in society, I become a little excited. I suspect there are numbers of women he drives to bizarre, erotic fantasies. Well, I've had mine. I will not share them, they're private, but I will say that in them he has a genital organ that's somewhat different. It's half human and half robotic device."

"You mean like a humanoid sexual dentist drill?" Guy interjected, less than enthusiastic.

"Yes, a good metaphor." Anna grinned. "But there's something in him dark and disturbed, probably dangerous. I feel it when I'm around him. I'm leaving it alone and keeping my distance." She nodded.

Guy looked down. "A wise decision, I think."

"I believe I told you this, Guy, because I want you to know I struggle with conflicted passions. Things are not simple. It's difficult."

Guy smiled. "Yes, of course. You're a woman."

In silence they continued eating, occasionally gazing around the café or studying the diners. Guy wondered if Gregorian chants would be complementing music for the café and then realized that silence was more appropriate because it was nothing.

"Anna, do you believe in a truer and purer love?" Guy suddenly asked. "I do. I believe the love between a man and a woman can be the truest and purest thing in this world. It's like two souls finding a mutual home. I know it sounds idealistic, and many would say naive, but I don't care. I believe it can and should be. The virtually perfect love."

Anna chewed on a stick of celery and peered into Guy's eyes. "It's a lovely thought, Guy, but I don't know if I can say I truly believe it. I would like to. But I think love gets tainted. It will be as flawed as humans are. Perhaps when our souls are pure and ideal, then so will be our love. And it may involve more than two souls joining. It involves this world and life, which may not support it. It's a long shot."

She returned to her salad. As Guy watched her, he believed even more absolutely in his ideal.

"I also believe in ideal beauty," he said. "Ideal beauty and love."

When Anna glanced up from her salad with the most dubious expression, he merely smiled.

"In love we can all be beautiful," he elaborated. "Ideal beauty is most found in pure and ideal love. Find or create one and you have the other." Guy baited on. "Like Aphrodite, the mythic goddess of love and beauty. She's one of my ideals. She is beautiful because her essence is love, and she knows she can love because she is beautiful."

Guy smiled proudly. Then, behind him, he felt the wind of flapping wings. He looked over his shoulder, but no one or nothing was present. *Odd,* he thought and took a hefty bite of his burger.

"See. It's simple."

"You *are* a romantic idealist." Anna responded. "OK, I'll play. Even if one had this true and perfect love, with one's soulmate, what would be the proof, the test of it?" Anna grinned.

Guy looked into thought-space. "I believe if two people were truly in love, that near perfect love I propose, if one were to die and leave this earthly plane, the other would then also die by either taking one's life or just allowing it to leave, so one could be with his or her love. Then they could remain together in spirit, or perhaps in their next life, continuing their love. And all would be beautiful."

Guy leaned back and expanded his chest. He smiled victoriously and then chomped on his Humility Hamburger.

"So," Annie retorted, "the test of truer and purer love is death. Perfect." She smiled triumphantly.

"No, the test of true and ideal love lies in continuing that love, beyond life, death, and all. No matter what."

Anna swung her hands up. "I surrender! I truly hope you are right as they are lovely beliefs."

A twentyish blonde woman at a table across the cafe began singing a Scandinavian love song in Scandinavian. Her voice was tender and melodious, floating through the room like an opiate stream. The tones of the song evoked a passionate, and tortured, love affair. Guy and Anna, as well as all the other patrons, listened silently, captivated, and when the singer finished, all applauded.

Anna's eyes glimmered. She leaned across the table and whispered. "Guy, watch this."

Anna stood, stepped away from their table and moved her body in provocative waves and flows. She performed a sensual, expressionistic dance, looking dangerously erotic in her kinky leather persona and quickly seducing the attention of all the café patrons. She languidly danced over to the table of the Scandinavian singer and graciously offered her hand. The comely singer, apparently not intimidated by such invitations, smiled and accepted it. Anna kissed the woman's hand and then drew the two of them onto the top of a neighboring empty table. Anna resumed her exotic, free form dance, facing her partner, and the blonde joined the dance.

Their bodies moved in an intimate communion, often touching. One would lean into the other, pressing against or rubbing her partner. Sometimes their legs crossed or intertwined or their hands traced the contours of the other's female form. The Scandinavian beauty wore a loose peach dress that flowed with the undulations of her body. They swayed and gyrated like two slinky, melding serpents in a dance of erotic pleasure.

Guy watched mesmerized. Tingling aroused his body. He felt he was witnessing a lovely dance of seduction on the island of Lesbos. He became confused and excited.

Anna pressed tightly against her beautiful, nubile partner. Her left arm wrapped around the blonde's waist and pulled her closer. Guy saw Anna's right arm reach up. A metal object was in her hand. A glint of light sliced off it.

Then Anna suddenly dropped her arm and plunged the knife deep into the breast of her partner. The Scandinavian woman gasped, her face contorted with shock and terror. Then a paralysis, still, silent, on the table, in the café, in the universe, and the blonde smiled tenderly, as in an odd resignation, and fell limp in Anna's arms. Anna held her close, gently placing the woman's head against her breast and resting her head on top. She whispered something into her succumbed partner's ear. Guy saw a fine stream of bright red blood trickle down the front of the Scandinavian woman's dress and drip onto the floor.

His expression petrified and his eyes horrified. He looked toward the floor, grasping for comprehension, and began to rise to approach their table. He looked up at the couple, at Anna. She and the seductive blonde were swaying in the delirium of their dance; Anna crouched and glided her hands along the sides of her partner's hips.

Then the two women stood straight and embraced warmly. Holding hands, they faced their audience and bowed. The applause was loud including catcalls and whistles. Anna held a hand up, quieting the fans, and spoke.

"Do not rejoice and do not despair. Accept! It is all part of the Beautiful, Winged Madness."

The patrons applauded emphatically. Anna looked at Guy and winked.

Guy felt numb. He stared into space, perceiving nothing. *My mind plays and creates. Yes, that is it! Of course, I am an artist.*

Anna returned to their table and sat, vibrating.

"A good dance is as powerful as life and death." She smiled radiantly.

Guy looked at her with an anemic expression shorn of spirit. "Yes. It is."

It is all right, he affirmed and forced his attention back on reality.

Their waitress returned and stood mute. Guy assumed that meant she was asking if they wanted anything more.

"More coins for our tithe cups," Guy humbly requested, trying to capture the mood of the moment. The waitress brought them more coffee.

"OK, time for my life story," Anna announced like an emcee. "I have not told you it as I promised. Interested?"

"Yes," Guy swiftly replied. An escape.

Anna sat still, staring into empty space as if pulling inspiration and then spoke.

"In the beginning, I was born a perfect and ideal child, a blessing from God, given to this world. It was in Annapolis, Maryland."

"City of Anna. They named an entire town for you?" Guy feigned puzzlement.

"No, quite the contrary. My mother named me after the town, the home of the U.S. Naval Academy. She told my father some nonsense about it being a tribute to the gallantry and honor of the naval cadets, but one day, when her discretion was compromised by a heavy bout of alcohol drinking, she confessed the truth to me. It was not their honor but their youthful virility, which she sometimes fantasized about, that my name pays tribute to. She accented her confession with a revealing laughter." Anna paused and smirked. "Noble beginnings! I suspect she had affairs with a few of the cadets. My mother was an attractive woman. Tall, like myself, and handsome with stronger chiseled features than I have. But she was more of pride than virtue. Sometimes I wonder if my real father was some stud cadet in a white uniform. Either way, I was named after my mother's erotic fantasies."

"Aha! Now I understand," Guy interrupted. Anna scowled. "I mean, that origin could confound anyone's destiny." Anna again scowled. Guy decided to shut up.

"I will confess that as a nicely maturing young woman, I too, harbored fantasies about the cadets who were always on the prowl for attractive town girls. Locals, they called us. Several times when I tried to live out the fantasies with some of the cadets it was always immensely disappointing. That is when I learned the divide that can exist between fantasy and reality.

"My parents were basically good people," she continued, "but I think they were very discontented. Not an atypical story. At some point they abandoned their true dreams: my father's to help engineer the city of the future, my mother's to be a botanist, developing new and beautiful plant species. All were abandoned for practicality and reason. As if it's irrational to keep pursuing one's vision." Anna grimaced. "My father became a city engineer overseeing the operation of traffic lights, a timing and coordination analyst. He was the one making certain that the changing of the traffic lights from red to yellow to green throughout the city was always synchronized correctly. Have you ever wondered who handled that function?"

"Actually, no."

"That was Dad! He took great pride in knowing if the lights were changing precisely on time and could tell, down to one-tenth of a second, whether they were by merely observing them without using the instruments designed to check and correct the timing. The devices had esoteric names such as Synchro/Sim Traffic Passer. Several times they tested him against the instruments, and he was always correct. 'Two tenths of a second off,' he would say, and was right."

"Damn! Now that's truly impressive," Guy asserted, truly impressed.

Anna nodded. "He erected a traffic light in his bedroom and perfectly synchronized its sequence so one day, when he's on his deathbed, he can watch it in the final moments of his life. He said it would be like a peaceful meditation, and he would only leave the earthly realm when the light was green."

Guy stared. "Earth people, you be a strange species."

"Yes. He was a pleasant man, cordial and conscientious in daily affairs. He kept us fed and comfortable, bless his soul. But he seldom talked to me. I don't think he knew what to say. But I learned a lot about traffic lights." Anna smiled as one in acceptance.

"My mother was primarily a housewife. She needed to be with me and my older sister."

"It sounds like a basically harmonious family."

Anna shrugged. "Not really. There's more. My mother sometimes worked to help supplement the family income at . . . I think you'll enjoy this. She worked at Uncle Bob's Ant Farms. They built those glass panel ant farms that parents buy their kids. Children stare at them for hours fascinated by how such tiny and primitive creatures could create such intricate environments and sophisticated social orders." She paused because Guy was staring skeptically. "It's true! My mother really worked there. For years."

"OK, proceed. Traffic lights and ants."

"I was also intrigued by the ants and put in my study time."

"You didn't have some erotic fantasy with giant ants, did you?"

"Well, now that you mention it." She grinned. "To continue, our house had an exceptionally large ant farm, it covered a portion of a wall, that the company gave to loyal employees. 'My other family,' my mother said looking at the ant colony endearingly. Sometimes as a child I saw the entire world, and all of society, as a gigantic ant farm."

"Not far from the truth."

Anna nodded. "Yes. To me, there seemed to be little difference. My mother's name was Belle. 'Do not ask for whom the Belle tolls, it tolls for thee,' she would say and confuse me. I thought she or I was going to die." Anna cocked her brow. "At work she assembled the toy farms, pouring in the soil or carefully placing in the ants. Or, on her more fortunate days, assisted in collecting the ants. Corralling, they called it. The company had a plot of land outside the city where they bred and harvested the precious creatures, an ant preserve. With all its anthills it looked like an alien planetscape. They would extricate the ants with a gentle suction devise resembling a huge vacuum cleaner. In addition to her hourly salary, mom was paid a commission, a cent or so, for each ant she collected *alive*. That was the rub! Unfortunately, in the process, some ants sacrificed their lives for the demands of commerce. She would work with the utmost care, priding herself on being both a competent and humane ant collector. Mom was the best! She spared many ants a grave fate. It was her contribution to this greater world." Anna swept her hand through the air, indicating that greater world.

"Nothing eccentric about your family." Guy remarked. "A human traffic light calculator and an ant farm humanitarian. Do you have an Ant Persona you go into?"

"I think I'm in it every day. Anyway, my mother, too, had her qualities. She, like my father, was a good person, but I could tell she also was immensely frustrated inside. Mom either ignored it, similar to your mother, or attributed it to some vague existential condition, like the innate disappointment in human reality. We all suffer, she would say, and sometimes quoted the writer Thoreau: 'The mass of men lead lives of quiet desperation.'"

"Well, there's some truth in that," Guy concurred.

"True. My father would just bear it out. He wouldn't complain much. 'This is the greatest country in the world. We are fortunate' was his rationalization for non-action. Translate that to: 'We should have no problems, therefore there are no problems.' But year after year, a deepening grayness, a terrible unhappiness, fell over our home."

Anna paused, looking over the café.

"Somewhat like this café, a disturbing nothingness. Imagine a family of people standing on a stage, each nude and painted entirely gray, barely moving, repeating the same rote lines over and over endlessly, feeling little, communicating less, creating no true characters or life. The stage would lighten and darken and one would assume a day had passed. Occasionally, a Christmas tree appeared and one would say, 'Merry Christmas' and then 'Another year has passed.' News of a relative dying would arrive and one would think, for a moment, 'Life is mysterious and tragic,' but not express that, or respond in any meaningful way. 'Life must go on. I must remember to let the dog out.'"

"Good images, Anna. I understand, and I'm becoming appropriately depressed." Guy's head and shoulders slumped.

"Yes, that's my point. Have you ever seen a Japanese shadow play?"

"I believe so. In films."

Anna laughed. "Appropriate. The projected images of a film presenting a Japanese shadow play. Illusion upon illusion. In the plays, cutout figures on sticks are moved around in bright light behind a screen. The audience sees shadow silhouettes of the characters performing ludicrous or humorous, but symbolic, dramas while the puppeteers speak their dialogue. Now, imagine one of my mother's ant farms, those colonies of efficiency without human emotion or communication or vision, presented as a shadow play. A shadow layer of a mundane, repetitive drama. The feeling that gives you is the feeling I'd have around my family."

"Shadow layers on top of shadow layers," Guy elaborated. "Nice."

"Exactly. I became depressed. It hit me hard when I was about thirteen. I felt as if I was this nonperson. It terrified me when I realized that the entire world, everything before me at all times, seemed unreal, like painted forms on a flat screen." She paused. "'Dark eyes that must stay blind to see, all human quest of no avail. People flat forms on a painted screen, life and death weighed on a diminutive scale.' I wrote that when depressed. There's a bit of a poet in me, too"

"I can see that. I'm going to encourage you to write more."

Anna nodded. "Please do. Artists must encourage each other. The world may not. Well, I had trouble experiencing myself in any manner. It was like a subtle but devastating nightmare. I became very withdrawn and self-conscious, constantly examining myself to see what was wrong with me. I did not like myself at all. I also noticed my sister, Theresa, had lost the light and spark she had when we were very young. It seemed, at least to my depressed mind, that we were all becoming shells." Anna's face became a mask, a shell of a face.

Guy felt a wave of cold.

"Shells. That's an interesting word to use. Because now you play with shells. You create them—personas. Is that how your persona thing evolved?"

Anna stared down, her brows lowered. Guy noticed she looked beautiful in such purposeful reflection. *Sometimes, everything contributes to beauty,* he reflected.

"Yes, basically. You see, not only did no one have any answers to those conditions, but they didn't even care to ask the questions. It simply was not considered important. Not relevant enough to their world—no problems! So, I began my own search, a search for answers and truth, and one could say, without meaning to sound trite, a search for myself, and it continues to this day."

"What have you found?" Guy's eyes reached eagerly.

"Nothing. The Nothingness Cafe." Anna smiled. "Actually, when I was fifteen, I found the arts. They involved people asking the questions. They *cared* about the questions. I felt an enormous relief. I had found my people. I had a connection and did not feel so alone."

"I had a similar experience at about the same age."

"Yes, I thought so."

Anna then revealed one of the most pleased smiles Guy had yet seen on her. It even seemed to warm the coffee in his tithe cup. Almost mystically, their waitress came and, without a word, filled his cup.

"Although I also discovered spiritual and philosophical avenues," Guy added. "Answers are also pursued there."

"Yes, as did I! Art and spirit, our brethren." Anna paused to just smile.

Presentation complete, Guy thought.

"I decided to perform," she continued, "then to create performance pieces, like an actress artist. And I began exploring personas."

"Ah! Now we get to the real key to the mystery that is Anna Spirit Persona."

Anna grinned. "Personas. In them I discovered that wonderful irony that I think is in all of life. In personas I could find myself more by losing myself more. By being what I wasn't or by expressing some part of me, I could find and be what I am. In an even greater irony, I saw that I was also what I created even if it did not seem to be what I was. Simple. I saw that we are all created personas. Anna doesn't really exist. She's an illusion and my greatest persona, a persona that believes it's real and strives to know its own creation. It reminds me of your Beautiful, Winged Madness. It's crazy but wonderful! I am both creator and creation."

Guy nodded, impressed. "Both the artist and the artwork. I think I understand. But don't you think there's more?"

Her provocative Mona Lisa smile. "Yes, Guy. There is much, much more."

"Wow!" Guy replied. "Expressed like a great mystery."

They both laughed.

"Also, it was enormously liberating to discover that I could be anything, for I am nothing but a creator, connected with that greater Creator. We create together. I could close my eyes and become the wind, blowing gently across the land, *all* lands, and I really *was* the wind. I could be a tree, or horse, Earth, a soft whisper, or even an artwork, like a sculpture. Sometimes I enjoy just being a sculpture, an aesthetic form of who I am." She smiled. "For all are created illusions anyway, as is Anna. It was magical. Do you understand?"

Guy's head rocked. "Ah, not fully. I can definitely see you as a sculpture, a beautiful statue, and I confess, at times I have. But I have trouble with the part of being, say, a horse?"

"True. I may not actually have the horse's body, but I become his beingness. And I believe it's possible that I could have a horse's body if I chose." She glanced around. "But a horse would not be a something they would permit in the Nothingness Cafe."

"I wouldn't assume that."

"It's all as real as anything." Her tone became whimsical. "All reality is illusion, and all illusion is reality. Except that which is the creator." She cocked a brow. "Don't I sound profound? And what I most yearn to create is what I've mentioned before: to be, at all moments, a perfect integration of being, purpose, and living. That is my ideal, and that proclamation ends my philosophical dissertation for the day. The professor has left the building."

Anna returned to her salad. She rolled a ripe cherry tomato around in the gray bowl. *There is more than philosophy in this life,* she thought. There was something more she wanted to tell Guy, something hidden but vital, but she could not identify it. It remained as a nothingness.

She picked up the cherry tomato and held it before Guy's mouth. He opened his mouth and ate it.

"Guy, why are you not a professional artist and poet? You are good. What is your rationalization?"

"You're right. My rationalization is that I like to create, to feel inspired, and to put meaning and truth into form. But I'm a pathetic and lazy businessman."

Anna shrugged. "Sounds typical, like a true artist. Tell you what, friend." She leaned closer. "I'll try to help. I'll be your muse, not just to create but to deliver your work to the world."

"Great! But who will help you?"

"Come on! You know. *You*. We muse each other." She laughed.

"OK. Mutual muses we be. Agreed?"

"Agreed."

Anna extended her elegant hand and they shook on the agreement. Guy's attention was suddenly pulled to a conversation at a neighboring table. A woman was quoting a non-present person.

"Love? Oh yes. I kill love."

"Guy, maybe you're a genius. That's why you're so strange."

Guy pressed his focus back onto Anna.

"Doubtful. In our culture, anybody who can create anything is considered a genius."

Anna slapped the table. "So true, so true." She returned to her rather aesthetically created salad and considered the genius that had created it.

Several minutes passed without talk. Then, "Anna, do you know what I would be if I could be anything?"

"No, what?"

"I know this sounds embarrassingly normal but, although I do wish to be a successful artist and poet, even more I would like to be a husband and a father, one day."

"Whoa! So human," Anna responded. "I think that's beautiful. And I'm certain one day you will be all of that. What you get in life is not what you want, but what you believe. I heard that on TV, and TV wouldn't lie. So be like Peter Pan."

"Peter Pan?"

Anna's punk android face brightened. "Yes! Remember? He saved the life of little Tinker Bell, her light dimming, by saying, 'I believe, I believe, I believe,' and he had the TV audience say it with him. I did. And Tinker Bell was saved. Sooo, say it with me."

Guy frowned. "I believe, I believe, I believe," they recited together. He felt a peculiar lightness. *I think I really do believe.*

"It shall be so, Guy. I will be at your wedding."

The moment she spoke those words, both fell quiet, looking down at their plates.

A time of musing passed as personal mythologies were considered and created. Anna thought of playful days and of symbols that expressed her being, like a theatrical spirit mask. Guy thought of playful nights and a book with blank pages beside a plumed pen. *Why?*

Suddenly Anna became excited. "I almost forgot to tell you. I have some good news! I won a contest to present a performance play at the Paul Dubois Theater in the Inner City Cultural Center."

"Great! How'd you accomplish that?"

"I submitted a video I made six months ago. It was about a man, an artist like you, an obsession, a brutal truth, and a strange cosmic laugh."

"It truly does sound like me. But what will your new piece be?"

Anna flung up her hands. "Alas! That's the problem. I don't know. I need to come up with a concept quick. I don't have much time."

"Don't worry. It will come to you. Trust your muse."

"*You're* my muse. Remember?"

Guy considered. "No. Trust your *other* muse."

Anna peered at him puzzled. "Well, OK. My other muse. Yes."

Anna closed her eyes and softened her breaths. *What am I doing? Muse, whoever you truly are, give me inspiration.*

Quiet stillness. A moment, and another, elapsed.

"Damn, Guy! I got it!" Excitement infused Anna's eyes. "I've got the concept for my performance play."

"Great!" Guy exclaimed. "Trust your muse." *What do you know.*

What Guy knew was that, in the space of the Nothingness Cafe, on that splendid afternoon, there was truly *something*.

The following day, Anna began work on her new and inspired performance play. And for nights following the café lunch, Guy dreamed of Anna and plays, cyborg lovers, a world painted in the colors of life and death, and wondrously inspired artists and muses, everywhere, even in the nothingness.

Chapter 7

To SANTA MONICA Beach. Sunday morning.

Guy knocked on Anna's door three times, paused, then twice, and then twice again. It was a code they agreed on so she could immediately identify him as her visitor, especially in the late, and treacherous, hours of the night. Guy and Anna were to spend that Sunday in an ocean, sun, and clean air rejuvenation at Santa Monica Beach. *What persona might Anna charm my eyes with for this occasion?* Guy contemplated. *A mermaid perhaps? Her smooth, naked torso blending into a glistening turquoise tail sweeping into an exotic fin? A creature to negate all rationality and submerge one into a world of sensual wonders.* Guy grinned. *Not likely. But no doubt something just as delightful.*

Then. A woman's voice; soft, calling to him. It sounded from the space before the door and grew louder.

"Come! Come to me! I'm waiting."

It was like a mirage. In a blue-gray ocean tomb, in front of Guy, a woman in a vestal-white gown floated, her long brunette hair wafting like seaweed, her skin pale as marble. She beckoned with an outreached, undulating arm, her eyes emptied and her lips anemic gray. *A living death in the sea,* he thought.

Guy's body chilled.

"Come!" she called, her voice cold and plaintive. "Join me! I wait. Come."

The door opened.

We should not go, Guy thought, his appalled eyes downcast.

"Hi! Ready to go?"

He looked up. The ocean tomb vanished. Before him stood a 1940's bathing beauty. Anna's lengthy hair was permed into a tempest of waves. Her lips were scarlet red and extended black eyelashes flapped when she blinked like the wings of a bird lifting off on some unbounded journey. A blush of rose bloomed her cheeks. She wore a one-piece red bathing suit with a short red and white pleaded skirt that hung playfully from her hips.

Anna as nostalgic pin-up girl. Guy had seen such images in reproductions of World War II calendars and posters created to boost the morale of lonely U.S. soldiers overseas. If she, as the American Beach Girl, had graced one, morale would have soared.

All morbid visions abruptly seemed foolish. *The plight of the dark poet,* he reasoned. *It meant nothing.*

Guy glanced at Anna's sleek model's legs, gasped to capture a breath and straightened his posture. *Composure!* He smiled, feeling both delighted and foolish.

"Behold the Goddess of Sand and Surf," he exalted, saluting her with a raised hand.

Anna Goddess smiled. "This," her hand swept down her bathing suit, "is the latest fashion from Coney Island. Dietrich wore one, mesmerizing her fans. Like it?"

"How could I not."

Anna shimmied cutely, her dance of pleasure. She looked down and with a hand on each side of the suit's skirt tugged gently adjusting its descent to be straight and even.

"Perfect!" She decreed. "Hold one moment. I'll be out."

She dashed into her bedroom and moments later returned with jeans and a white T-shirt over the bathing suit. From forties' bathing beauty to contemporary Levi girl.

"For the bus ride."

A beach bag that hung from her shoulder was illustrated with a festively costumed Latin woman standing in a partially peeled banana, a provocative pop image. Anna pulled Guy into the elevator, its heavy steel door slamming shut.

"To the beach!" she heralded with a smile of promise.

All is perfect enough, Guy resolved. *This will be an excellent day.*

Guy and Anna were eager to exchange the sullen tones and cold concrete of the city, even a City of Angels, for the warmth and vivid Technicolor of the Southern California coast.

*　　*　　*

After a one-hour light-as-abandoned-thoughts bus ride, they arrived at the beach. Guy loved Santa Monica, perceiving it as a smartly architectured compromise between a bustling commercial city and a hedonistic seaside resort; the mind of an entrepreneur in the body of a surfer. Reality (commerce) marries illusion (paradise). It was his and Anna's type of playfully schizophrenic town.

Anna took one step in the sand, lifted her foot and pointed to its dainty imprint.

"We are here!" she commandingly announced as if claiming her territory. Guy suspected she had. Who could challenge her?

The beach formed a pale beige strip of sand that stretched as far as one could see along the coast both north and south. Beyond it, the expansive sea, a grayed aqua blue, extended out to softly disperse into a misty horizon. Benign surf clawed at the sand perpetually shaping an edge of white foam. Scattered bathers dappled the sand like impressionistic swabs of paint. And the sun pressed down, unusually warm for an autumn day, the temperature approaching ninety degrees, luring beach lovers into stolen post-summer swims. An invigorating, briny ocean breeze brushed all.

Above was an ideal beach sky, blue as a daydream marked only by a gracious whisper of clouds. To the south rose the contours of the pier amusement rides, most notably the metallic hills and valleys of a red roller coaster and a gold-spoke Ferris wheel. A wooden pier laid a narrow gray swath over the top of the sea and, like sacred adornments, white seagulls flew lethargically above.

The seagulls—lovely, graceful, floating lethargically above all, Guy's thought replayed. *Perhaps they knew.*

And all smelled of sea and salt. An impression imprinted in Guy's mind for an archetype of the California beach that he knew he would visit again.

Anna raced across the sand to a vacant spot and flung down her blanket. Content with a supporting role, Guy followed. Anna clearly was to be in command of the day. As he watched her peel off her T-shirt and shimmy out of her jeans, form and flesh unveiled, the moment moved in slow motion. Perhaps he made it so, for he, as a man and an artist, studied sensuality. *The beauty of a woman in the grace of the sun and the sea. Poetry,* he mused.

For a wonderful and pivotal moment, Guy understood.

The beach's denizens bestowed their vision upon Anna, the anachronistic, classic beach girl from a decade past. A twentysome blonde woman in a blue bikini that strategically negotiated her abundant curves stared with snatching eyes. She stood and walked to Anna.

"I adore your bathing suit. Where can I get one?"

"I made this one myself. I designed it after the bathing suits of the forties." Anna smiled cordially. "I don't know where you might buy one."

The bikini woman deflated like a punctured inflatable doll. Then her expression elevated. "As an original, no one else will be able to buy one either. Bye."

She smiled consoled at Anna, returned to her blanket and stretched on her back, lithesome in the toasting sun.

Anna smoothly rubbed suntan lotion across her exposed flesh, glistening her skin. Guy noticed men on the beach watching, their expressions speaking their question: Who is she?

Guy removed his clothes down to his pastel blue swim trunks. Disharmony invaded, as if his eyes were outside himself staring critically at the man before them. They saw a sizable man apparently possessed of a near proportionate strength but amiss of the form of the fitness devout. Thin sheets of fat concealed his muscle tone and, at thirty-two years of age, his belly already declared its prominence. Guy noticed—oh yes, he noticed—the men and women sprawled on their blankets around him looking back and forth between Anna and him, no doubt thinking: What is *that* woman doing with *that* guy?

Then a clarity of vision. *What nonsense! Do I damn myself forever to pubescent insecurity?* He scowled and looked at Anna, his current and excellent companion, who smiled. He knew himself, his large and sturdy carriage, his pleasant face and soft features that still spoke of boyishness, his thick brunette hair falling nearly to his shoulders, *rather hip,* and his chestnut and gold eyes. He suspected that Anna, the only woman whose opinion he now gave weight to, considered him, as probably many women did, sufficiently attractive for any relationship she chose to create. He also believed that Anna was a woman more interested in substance and soul than packaging. And so it was with him.

A recollection surfaced to taunt and entertain, reminding him of how absurdly insecure a man can become. Once, when doubting his masculinity, for an hour a day for several months, he practiced an esoteric Tibetan Tantric mind/body empowerment meditation and yoga asana, a disciplined feat of contortion and twists and pulls that purported to enlarge the size of a man's vital genital organ and male ego. It didn't work, and it didn't need to, Guy now surmised.

"Guy!" Anna's hailing liberated him from his distractions. She was running toward the water, her form an animated slash of red and flesh against the expanse of blue ocean and sky. Her galloping stride halted abruptly when the first wave crashed against her legs.

"Great!" She yelled. "Warm!"

She shimmied and then dived directly into the next assaulting wave that consumed her in its foam.

Exquisite! the wave moaned, not feeling the least violated. For long moments Anna was lost, and then her head and shoulders bobbed above the waves. She shook the sparkling water from her face and hair and then performed a series of dives into the incoming waves, her body simulating a dolphin at play in the froth of the ocean.

Anna gave herself to the sea.

Yes, the sea, she thought as the cool liquid absorbed her.

The sea delightfully welcomed the strong and captivating woman into its fluid folds. Its mysterious and eternal spirit already knew Anna. Like the hands of a masseur, it flowed in smooth caresses over the contours of her form.

"I will be your secret lover," the sea whispered with each thrust of its currents.

Anna sensed its proposition and willingly surrendered, diving and undulating deep in the ocean's consuming embrace. She relinquished all rigidity from her body and all autonomy from her soul, becoming as fluid and sensual as the sea.

"Come deep into me," the sea spoke and she complied, treading and floating in silent suspension in its tepid depths. Anna and the sea were lovers.

She understood intuitively the unique and preternatural bond that existed between her and the sea. The ocean manifested that perfect integration of being and purpose, design and realization that was her highest ideal and aspiration. Few humans could comprehend such perfection. She wished to be as the sea and merged her consciousness into its being and her flesh into its body as a meditator dissolves his self into the All.

And you feel so good! she thought. Her only regret was that she was not totally naked in giving herself to her lover. "Another time," she vowed.

She never harbored the thought of drowning as she submerged for dangerous times in its blue crystalline space. For such would not be a tragedy, but a transcendence. To die in her lover's arms was as to die in a dream. She could not drown in the sea any more than the sea could drown in her.

Melding into her sea lover, Anna found an experience of beauty and truth that she would be reluctant to reveal to any man. It was only to the sea that she could now surrender her entire being. And in her the sea found the sensuality of a woman and the beauty of a soul.

"Thank you, dear sea," she spoke.

"Thank you, dear Anna," it spoke.

No man could love Anna as could the sea.

But she had another whom she loved, a dear friend, who was cautiously walking in shallower water looking toward the horizon for her. Surfaced, she turned onto her back, treaded water and called to him.

"Come on, it's great!"

Guy walked and floated, his hefty body bobbing with each cycle of waves, more than swam toward Anna. She rolled off her back and dived under. When the water had reached the height of his chest, Anna surfaced a foot before him.

"Hi! Feels good, doesn't it?"

She spoke excitedly as she floated with the swells of the water and then took Guy's arm and gently pulled him down until they both sank beneath the surface. Quiet and hazy moments passed.

Guy resurfaced, kicking and splashing, with Anna on his back. He struggled to rotate his body, his arms digging deep into the water, attempting to shake her off but Anna hung tight, laughing. The salt of flung water stung his eyes. Guy realized it was impossible, so he enjoyed a rousing struggle with the foam of the sea and his woman passenger. The immense power of the ocean pulled them into deeper water.

Finally Anna relinquished her hold and with a triumphant yell used his body to kick off from, like a springboard. She twisted in the air and again dove deep into the water.

Guy saw that Anna was an excellent swimmer. He was excellent only at splashing and floating. But in her spirited dives and swims, she made it clear that they were not in competition. They were there to play. So play he did, grasping and tossing her velveteen body around his. Anna was having fun, and he was there with her. That was all that mattered.

The aquamarine pool of the ocean, its dazzling slashes of white reflections, the rolling foam of the waves, the pure azure sky above, the bobbing curves of Anna's body, the occasional warm brush of her flesh against his—the sea, the sky, the skin, and the salty scent and taste of the ocean, all dissolved for Guy into one delirium of sensations and sounds. Boundaries and forms dissipated.

"This is like a kind of drowning," he shouted to Anna, although she could not decipher his words. They had drifted apart. She responded with a smile.

Then Guy was under the water, swimming. Everywhere he looked was a glassy blue-gray void, so pure and lovely. Liquid space. He became pleasantly disoriented, like a man on a euphoric drug. For a stilled moment in time, he thought perhaps he *was* gently drowning. *If so, I feel no desire to resist.* As he slowly tread the sea, floating yet moving, submerged somewhere in the vast blue universe, there was only wavy distortions of water, accents of light, and sleek forms moving around him.

Guy startled and stared through the blurry liquid. First there was one, a female. Anna, he assumed. Then several more, then dozens.

How strange and delightful! I am in the center of a school of . . . what?

They were men, women, and children, but neither human nor fish. Swimming around him was a school of human dolphins.

My god! He thought in wonderment. *How can this be?*

He blinked several times to see if the water might be playing tricks on his vision. They were still there, each of their bodies an aesthetic and functional synthesis of the two forms, human and dolphin, sleek and graceful yet strong and evolved. They ranged in size from three to seven feet long. "Dolphinus Huminus," one of the larger creatures informed him through a thought communication as if attempting to allay his confusion. Swimmers with streamlined dolphin bodies and tailfins, some with women's breasts, looked at him with human faces and eyes, and even smiles.

How extraordinary!

"Come with us and we will take you to the center of the sea," they communicated as a group through a telepathic process. "Beauty and serenity awaits."

Guy stroked to the surface, inhaled as much air as he could possibly intake and dove back down. Suddenly and enigmatically possessed of improved swimming skills, perhaps from intention, Guy swam with the group deeper and deeper into a darkening vastness. He looked up and saw only a faint aura of the sky's light beyond the water's surface far above. They descended deeper, seeming to penetrate into the ocean's dark heart. Then before him appeared a filmy realm of white luminance. The human dolphins swam into it and their forms moved and floated like a dancing vision in the extraordinarily beautiful radiance.

Guy followed them in. The most euphoric sensation consumed him as if he were adrift in pure spirit and grace. All earthly restraints seemed lifted from his being. He felt free, delightfully free!

What could this possibly be? he wondered. Familiar words floated through his mind. *The Beautiful, Winged Madness.*

Then another, more severe voice in Guy's mind spoke. "Breathe! Breathe!" So he did, or tried, but could not. Liquid entered his lungs. He panicked and coughed. His muscles tightened and his arms and legs flailed against a suffocating wall of water. The human dolphins vanished and the surrounding aura darkened. He felt cold, so, so cold. All became vague.

This is it! So now I die, some detached and strangely calm part of him thought.

"Goodbye, for now," he heard gentle voices say. "Do not fear."

Then Guy felt a powerful force lifting him toward a hazy light above. A moment later his head broke through the water's surface. Anna was behind him with her arms firmly wrapped around his chest.

"Are you . . . all right?"

Her voice fought through staccato breaths as she struggled to keep him afloat. He nodded, gasping and spitting out water. In the middle of the effort, Anna kissed him on the forehead.

For a time afterward, they floated and swam gently, Anna always remaining close, diving and swimming in circles around him. Then they just floated, the waves placidly rocking their bodies.

"What happened?" she queried. "You were under so long. I couldn't find you. I thought you had drowned."

Guy looked at the glimmering sky above and then at her.

"I don't know. I almost did. I became disoriented. Sorry, and thank you."

He would tell her of his strange experience later, perhaps. He did not comprehend what had occurred, but he knew he had almost drowned. He also wondered how deep he had actually swum.

Anna smiled tautly. "Please, be careful."

Guy nodded and smiled back. The ocean beneath him, keeping him afloat, and Anna's presence, provided a security.

Was that experience in the sea's serene and radiant center like death, or the afterlife? The artist and seeker in him pondered. *If so, why is it so universally feared? One should embrace it, for it was wondrous. How strange!*

Guy no longer felt frightened but rather unusually relaxed and safe as he floated in the sea's embrace. He remembered the final words he had heard. "Do not fear."

Something had changed in him. Something small but significant, as if a road had appeared inviting him to walk it, *a road without threat,* he thought. He now floated and splashed and played freely and happily in the ocean with his lovely guardian Anna always beside him. He looked again at the blue universe of the sea.

What mysterious wonders you hold.

*   *   *

Anna and Guy strolled with tired steps and exhilarated spirits from the water back toward their blanket.

"Being in the sea can be an intense experience," Anna, with a knowing smile, remarked, glancing at Guy. She considered telling him of her romance with the sea but decided some things should remain one's secret.

"You don't need to convince me of that," Guy replied with the smile of a wiseman. *We share some profound and secret reality,* he thought. *I, Anna, and the sea.* "Nothing like a quick swim on a warm day."

Anna laughed.

A cluster of bathers stood observing something that had washed onto the shore. Guy and Anna approached and saw what resembled a thick gray shadow lying on the pale beige of the sand.

The carcass of a dead whale, Guy surmised. They edged past the onlookers to discover it was a huge transparent vinyl bag about twice the size of a bathtub that apparently had rolled out of the sea.

A lifeguard attempted crowd control. "Please stay back! The police have been called to remove it. The bag may be contaminated."

Despite his directive, Anna stepped closer and bent over the cryptic object.

"Plastic flowers and plants," she yelled to Guy. "It's filled with plastic plants."

They saw a tear, which may have been intentionally cut by a knife or was from the ravages of the sea, on a side of the bag that had allowed ocean water to enter and partially fill it creating the resemblance of a giant cell. They assumed it also had permitted some of the contents to be released.

The Santa Monica police in dark blue shorts and white shirts arrived. They attempted to disperse the crowd while speaking urgently into their cellular phones. *Santa Monica beach invaded by a giant plastic plant cell!* Guy imagined their calls reporting. As he and Anna left the scene, they looked at each other, cocked their brows and smiled, sharing the same thought: *bizarre!*

*   *   *

Guy watched Anna pat the sea from her smooth and shiny flesh. Water from her wet hair streaked down the curves of her body. He was certain he smelled not only the salt of the ocean on her but also the scent of her flesh itself. It was an erotic and poignant fragrance, one bespeaking of pleasures of, and yet beyond, that flesh.

Guy was again enraptured by her statuesque beauty and that face he often dreamt of. He was convinced Anna was the loveliest woman he had ever known.

I see it is both her soul and her form that affects me so. He smiled. *And I am more certain than ever, I have fallen in love!*

He wanted to speak those very words to her at that moment on the beach in the passionate sun, sentiments that he previously had only implied, at most. Their secret imprisonment in his heart induced a profound ache. But he didn't.

Clandestinely he removed his Minolta camera from his denim beach bag. He would capture Anna in that unrehearsed moment, like Venus arose from the sea. Anna heard him snap the picture, looked up from the towel she was drying her lithe body with and smiled. She lowered the towel to her side and with her other hand stroked back her long, damp hair. It was a classic, sensual pose captured forever with another click of his camera.

For a time most luxurious and serene, Guy lay beside Anna on their blanket. She rested on her back as her shimmering body in the vintage bathing suit indulged the heat of the sun.

Let me warm you, sultry woman, with the fires of my being, Guy imagined the sun speaking to her.

Anna's face appeared peaceful, her eyes closed behind the cocoa shell of her sunglasses. Guy felt close to her; he could hear the rhythm of her breathing, light hisses of air evoking in him a simple pleasure.

"Thank you, Anna," he whispered, but she did not hear.

*   *   *

Anna suddenly leapt to her feet. "Let's hit the pier, dear! I burn if I'm in the sun too long, and I'm feeling hot!"

She performed a cute flapper girl dance, pulled on her T-shirt, and with wiggles and shimmies struggled into her body contouring jeans. She and Guy swept up their items and, taking his hand, Anna ran toward the pier, dragging him behind.

The century-old pier was constructed of grayed wood and extended hundreds of yards over the sea. Along its sides were gift shops, snack food stands, and a couple seafood restaurants including Bubba Gump Shrimp Company. At the pier's beginning, a warehouse-sized building housed an arcade of computer and children's games with flashing color lights and synthesized electronic sounds—the twenty-first century. Nearby on a usurped parking lot were the carnival amusement rides, a prime attraction for kids and young couples. The pier's ambiance was one of a salty, venerable, and casual amusement center world. *A festive balance for a leisurely day at the beach,* Guy thought. *The yang for the yin of the sea.*

"The rides!" Anna shouted as if ordering a military charge. Play was the game.

First, the roller coaster. Not the highest in the country but for them on that day, the highest in the world. It climbed at a clanky, staccato pace and then descended at a velocity beyond the speed of light. "I know that is so," Guy informed Anna, "because I saw us in the car behind us which was first before us until we trailed behind it because it was still ahead of us."

Anna understood. Her excitement accelerated as they both held tight to the security waist bar and screamed in terror as the coaster dived and dived.

The Ferris wheel was the next allure and when their golden car, an open-air bench, reached the top, it stopped, as it always did for a few apprehensive seconds pretending to be stuck. As it swung precariously high above the seascape, Anna and Guy feared for their lives.

"I apologize to all for being an arrogant jerk!" Guy shouted loudly into the air.

"I apologize, God, for being such a slut when I was younger!" Anna shouted to the heavens. Guy threw her a duplicitous look.

They survived, and the majestic golden wheel kept turning. *A metaphor for life,* they both thought with a smile.

Back on earth, Anna slapped Guy on the back. Guy punched her on the arm.

"Are we happy?" Anna asked.

"I believe so," Guy replied.

"Strange," they both proclaimed in unison.

Rides ridden and terrors faced, they took the walk to the end of the pier. The ocean breeze blew gustily, heaving their hair. Guy thought Anna looked wonderfully abandoned. A couple ancient fishermen with faces like worn leather shoes, dressed in denim overalls as anachronistic as Anna's covered bathing suit, leisurely leaned over the railing monitoring fishing lines, patiently awaiting bites that seldom came, but it did not matter. Buckets holding their scant catches imbued the air with an oily fish odor. Mingled with the salty smell of the ocean, it created the eternal scent of the seashore.

A teenage couple cuddled in a corner at the pier's end, cocooned from a less tender outside world. Guy and Anna leaned against the pier's railing and looked out over the misty ocean and then quietly observed the rhythmic passing of waves beneath the pier.

"The meditation of watching the sea," Anna mused. "All seems a part of one whole. I suspect it is like our souls."

"Yes, I think so," Guy concurred. "Even with its tempestuous storms and drownings and pollution."

Anna laughed gently. "Perhaps this is it, everything, before us. Except TV."

"Bummer!" Guy smiled and wrapped his arms around Anna, pulling her close. "My Muse, I ask you, will this life and world ever truly support our visions and ideals?"

Anna's disposition shifted, dropping sober. "I don't know, my Muse, but that may well be the most critical question of our lives." She looked back at the ocean. "Perhaps the answer lies in the mystery of the sea."

"Ohhh, we're so deep and philosophical." Both grinned.

They stood quiet, perusing that mysterious sea and allowing the soft, repetitive sounds and the visual flows of the waves to wash away the world and the splinters it inserted in their souls. Guy could taste the sea, its salt and moisture. Then he heard faint voices. They were women's voices, winsome and melodious, and were sounding from the sea.

"Anna, can you hear that?"

"What?"

"Voices. Women's voices. Singing. Coming from the sea." Guy's eyes brightened.

Anna tilted her head. "I don't hear anything."

"They're growing louder. Women singing. I can hear the lyrics. It's something about an eternal life in the sea. You can't hear them?"

"No. I don't hear them." She stared at the water. "Maybe, just maybe, you're hearing mermaids. Mermaids singing in the sea." Her face animated and her eyes illumed.

"Mermaids? How could that be?" Guy replied. "Are there really mermaids? These voices sound real."

"I don't know."

Then Guy heard other voices, men's voices, anguished, calling and screaming, and eerie. It seemed like a tomb had opened.

"Now I hear more. Men, they're screaming."

"Guy, you might be hearing the voices of men lost at sea." Anna stared into the water, pondering. "It could be you have an exceptional sense or perception. Yes, I think that's it. How fascinating! I believe you're hearing the calls of mermaids and drowned mariners. I've heard some people can do that."

Guy's expression strained. He shook his head rapidly and looked around to see if there might be people nearby who were playing music, singing, or yelling, and it was all a matter of his confused directional sense, but there were no prospects.

"I think you might be exceptionally gifted in that way."

Or exceptionally mad, was the disturbing thought that invaded Guy's mind. He looked to the horizon and saw, floating in the sea's vapor, the gossamer image of a sailing vessel. It was of an archaic design, wooden hulled with billowing sails, like a galleon of earlier centuries. The ship appeared, then vanished, then appeared again. A demon gripped his soul.

"You should feel fortunate. If it's true, it's very rare," Anna expounded, but Guy barely heard. Staring into the gray haze of the horizon, he saw a frightening reality emerging.

He had experienced it before and recognized the symptoms. He remembered the ghastly image he saw that morning at Anna's door and the strange school of human dolphins that appeared during his swim.

It is beginning. His stomach tightened and cold clenched him.

Anna leaned against the railing and stared into the mystical horizon, *a mysterious end and beginning*, she reflected and smiled. She spoke words intended for more than the sea. "Yes, it's amazing. How wonderful!"

"Yes, Anna. I think you are correct," Guy replied somberly. He was starting to slip below the line.

*   *   *

'The Curse of the Mummy' in black letters on the side of a Metro bus. Its shell was transformed into a giant gold sarcophagus, a mummy's casket inscribed with Egyptian hieroglyphics and swarmed over by images of horrific mummies attempting to enter to suck the passengers inside dry of life, élan vital. A life-sized portrait of the dashing, weapon-bearing hero and his lovely damsel in distress covered the bus rear panel. Saviors of the world. Eye-catching and scary, it was a clever advertisement for a soon-to-be-released big budget Hollywood film; a promotional gimmick sometimes employed in L.A., the movie hub of the world.

Entering it made Guy uneasy. *Mummies carry curses*. He was not particularly eager at that moment to tempt a curse, be it real or not.

But he had not protested. Anna, seeing it approaching, pointed excitedly and firmly declared, "*That* bus!" She loved it, seeing it as a huge, hideous pop art object. "Only in L.A.," she decreed.

So they rode the sarcophagus home. The bus was but a third filled with passengers. "I wonder why?" Guy slyly questioned.

They took a seat in the rear.

"What is this uncomfortable feeling I have?" Guy asked. "Oh! I see. It's being entombed."

Anna smiled, placed her hand on his shoulder, and said, "Mummy dearest."

The vast shadow cape of night was descending, subduing color and sounds and urging an exodus of bathers from the shore, accentuating the eerie atmosphere Guy felt in the rolling casket. He and Anna had the crumpled, towel-dried look that typified beach adventurers at their day's end. Guy felt determined not to allow the intrusion of voices and hallucinations to ruin their trip. It had been a delightful and interesting day.

Interesting, yes. That was how he would consider the delusions. They were interesting.

His stomach hurt. He did not speak of it to Anna.

An abandoned newspaper lay on the seat across the aisle. Anna grabbed it and scanned the front page. A headline announced, 'Cupid Killer Takes Fourth Victim.'

"Listen to this. Some guy is killing people in L.A. by shooting arrows through their hearts. He sent a letter to the L.A. Tribune stating merely, 'I kill love' and signed it the Cupid Killer. Very bizarre."

Guy had the shadowy feeling of a horror movie trailer.

"Yes, I know. I've heard about it already. It sounds . . . darkly poetic. Maybe he's a poet, or some type of artist." Guy paused. "Killing. I wonder if he even knows he's doing it?"

Anna shrugged and then turned to the local city section of the paper. In the lower corner was an article headlined, 'Toxic Plants and Flowers Confiscated.'

"Ah! Here's our story. Listen. Truckloads of plastic plants and flowers made from a toxic material hazardous to humans and animals were confiscated in a Santa Monica warehouse by health authorities. If the plants are placed in the mouth it could result in illness, especially in children. Authorities fear large quantities may have been illegally disposed of in an attempt to conceal evidence." She glanced at Guy. "Our giant plant cell."

"Doesn't surprise me." Guy shook his head. "Expect sick fish swimming in the sea."

"God!" Anna threw down the paper. "Don't fall in love or eat tuna fish sandwiches. You'll be doomed."

Guy immediately imagined himself in love thinking of Anna while eating a tuna sandwich. In a wall mirror, he sees the reflection of a disenchanted Cupid Killer staring at him. He kept the thought private.

The bus moaned and clanked through the city streets as a panorama of the casual hip to ritzy upscale stores and restaurants of Santa Monica and West Los Angeles swept by their window like a blurry dream backdrop.

Guy spoke. "Anna, something about the toxic plant cell incident urges me to tell you this." He inhaled and straightened his posture. "I love thee."

The bus hit a sizable bump bouncing them in their seat.

"Thee?"

"Yes. Thee is the correct term. It's a classic and eternal love I feel toward you. Toward thee. Whether it be friendship or . . . whatever. The finest of love. Really, I'm serious."

He could not restrain a smile that seemed to belie his intentions. Then a thought. *Still I hide.*

"Oh, I see. I understand," she replied. *Be he sweet or does he tease?* She smiled. A moment passed.

"Then, I love thee, too," she announced.

Guy was pleased. He detected a thought, either his or hers. *His love for her is more intense, hers for him purer as if passion courted the angelic.* He felt like he was reading a romance novel.

"Oh no!" he moaned and shuddered.

Anna peered at him curiously.

Monastic silence. More blurred city vistas. Glances and smiles at Anna.

And voices. Unwelcome voices sounding in his mind as from illusion passengers; eerie, taunting, all speaking at once. Witches and demons from Halloween graveyards.

"Listen, sweet poet. Oh, precious poet. It is nothing. Darling Anna. Nothing!"

"Two blind mice. See how they run! Heads cut off with a poetic knife. She makes now a morbid wife. Two blind mice."

One dominant, shrill voice screeched above the chorus. "It's so sad! It's quite mad. Once upon a time. Nothing was. Nothing is. Nothing but a rhyme!"

Then all the taunting voices became one voice, the voice of a little girl crying. Then they stopped.

Guy stared vacantly out the window. *Perhaps they are right. I rather like nothing. If only . . . .*

"Do you have a last name?" Anna asked. "In all this time, I've never asked you." She leaned closer and scrutinized his face, as if the answer waited in his eyes.

"I don't have a last name," he answered succinctly.

Anna stared, suspecting there was some symbolic significance in his answer.

"Yes, I believe I understand. I think I also do not have a last name. I used to."

They both smiled. Guy leaned over and kissed her on the cheek. Anna smiled again but did not say anything.

More silence. A peaceful silence that to Guy seemed transcendent, a Metro bus passenger meditative silence. Concerns about his hauntings absolved as if reality was being created moment by moment, and it was now a new moment. *As it is now, and now.* The squeaks and clanks of the aging bus as it battled road aberrations and the swooshing of its doors opening and closing did not disrupt the peacefulness of those moments in the moment. His experience could be an excellent advertisement for the L.A. bus system, Guy mused. *Is traveling stress a must? Be a Buddha on the bus.* He grinned.

The sarcophagus of serenity drove through the city of Beverly Hills, the mecca of affluence and celebrity and the 90210 zone. *The other world,* Guy reflected, as would most of the inhabitants of Earth. Like an awed little boy peeping in extravagant Christmas store windows, he stared at the window displays of sleek, idealized anorexic mannequins in their chic designer fashions. One wore a burgundy dress that was skin tight and skimpy on its top half and then exploded into wild, ballerina ruffles on its bottom. Guy had never in his life seen women wearing such clothes in his world, or on his streets, and he wondered where they might. At hidden, invitational nighttime balls in guarded exclusive mansions? He entertained images of scandalous parties and taboo rituals and elegant women surrendered. The other world.

He thought of his mother and how thrilled she would have been to add her accents to such indulgent fashions. But he still preferred his mother's accent conglomerate dress. There was much to be said for the inspired creations of the common sensibility!

The Ferraris, Porsches, and Jaguars proudly showcased in the automobile dealer's windows dazzled Anna. *To be given but a glimpse of such treasures, and nothing more, was frustrating, even cruel,* she lamented, feeling resentment toward the more affluent of the world.

Then she became annoyed. *I'm still such a damn materialist! Prey to their traps.*

Minutes later. The bus entered the Wilshire District, the zone between the Los Angeles city that was more suburbia than city and the true urban downtown. Guy noticed the ride roughened with more bumps in the road. Reentering the real world. He reached into his denim beach bag, removed a pen and a pad, and commenced to writing.

"What are you writing?" Anna asked.

"A poem, for you."

"Great!" Her smile was Disney animated. "Don't let me distract you."

He wrote and scratched out lines, and added words, and scratched and wrote.

"Is it done?"

"Not yet."

He wrote more, concentrating, looking into that empty space where inspiration waits.

"Is it done?"

"Yes. It is done." He looked at her with a smile of creator's bliss, stroking a hand through his hair. The poet.

"Read it." Anna's head bobbed like a jack-in-the-box.

"OK. For beautiful Anna."

"Good start. You're a master."

"Shhh! Give the poet audience. It's called The Girl on the Beach. It's part real, part fantasy."

"As am I," Anna interjected.

Guy read. "At port of entry, I court the favors of a seaside girl, a sleek flamingo tracking the sand, tossing coquettish slights. A fancied lover stolen and spied, as fingers surf the waves and trace the contours of precious shells that wash to land in the foam of urgent tides."

Guy turned to Anna's wonder-eyes.

"I like it, truly! It's very evocative."

"It's for you, Anna." He handed her the paper.

"Thank you. There couldn't be a truer gift, or erotically suggestive. I believe I can envision your 'foam of urgent tides.'" She cocked a brow.

"I am an erotic Guy, you must know."

"Must I?" She grinned, placing her hand on his arm. Then she gave him a maiden-to-hero kiss on the cheek. "Thank you."

A surprising, gentle warmth infused the air. *The warmth of true affinity*, Guy assessed. It swelled beyond the perimeter of their seats and enveloped the bus. Being an impromptu community in a metallic container, a can, all aboard were affected. Most smiled, feeling temporarily rescued from harsher realms, though not comprehending why. Guy, the perceptive artist, noticed, and it provided him a clue to understanding the attraction of urban life, the moments when it transcended stereotypical 'urban jungle' or metaphorical 'ant colony' realities and offered shared, communal pleasures and meanings.

The city, the bus, the people.

* * *

Guy and Anna stood quietly at the door of Anna's apartment, shuffling and fidgeting. It reminded Guy of his high school days and awkward teenage dates. *How absurd!* he thought.

"Anna."

"What?" She smiled.

Guy wanted to say more but did not. He had the annoying feeling of being trapped in a particular, fixed reality, one that had been carefully cultivated and then turned on itself in betrayal.

"I had a wonderful day," he spoke. "Somewhat strange, but I enjoyed it. I didn't even have to drown. Thank you, Anna."

Anna presented her smile of light and stood waiting, a touch of puzzlement in her eyes. She still had the wash of sun and salt upon her, creating a vital, wanton look.

"I did too. I had a good time. We'll have to go back."

She sensed what was occurring, the thoughts that were urging and confounding Guy. She felt an excitement and was about to speak when gloom assaulted.

"Well, I must go," she said. "I have some things to take care of tonight. I'll see you tomorrow. OK?"

She made a point of presenting him her warmest smile and then embraced him and kissed him on the cheek.

He kissed her on the forehead.

"OK, Anna. Thanks again. I had a great time."

"Me too. See you tomorrow."

Guy walked to his apartment. He felt happy. It had been one of the nicest days he had experienced in years, in spite of the hauntings which he refused to think about at that moment. *I am fortunate,* he thought.

Then he felt himself drop as if the floor suddenly descended and a grayness, a sinister shadow, passed over.

"Damn!"

Chapter 8

GUY AND ANNA entered an alien world, pristine and silent—the California desert, its flat, moonlit vistas bordered by the blue-violet silhouette of distant mountains, domed by an operatic night sky of infinite and brilliant stars, never so dazzlingly visible in the city. A full moon shone white and luminous.

Like a maborosi, Guy thought recalling the Japanese word for a mysterious light far out at sea. His sensibilities heightened.

This is the dreamscape of a forgotten past, he mused, *unscarred by the intrusions of human visions and vanities; a world that still looks at the world through inviolate, primitive eyes to glimpse the presence of original creation.*

It was the next Saturday evening and Anna took Guy to the desert. She borrowed a friend's car, an ancient olive green Toyota, pitted and bruised with two missing wheel covers, dented fenders, a tape player that chewed up tapes, wounded seats bandaged with plastic tape, and odometer mileage totaling twice the circumference of the earth. *An unequivocal survivor,* she thought admiringly. Its engine produced a throaty, gurgling sound, as if gargling with gasoline.

"It's a work of beauty," Anna decreed. "A perfect synthesis of form and function."

She did not reveal the exact destination or purpose of the venture. "This is a night of trust and mystery. Tonight you must be as a child."

"Easy," Guy replied.

In one of the very rare times since he had first acquainted her, Anna was in her own persona, being just Anna, as she had been in Hollywood. She wore faded and frayed blue jeans, a mauve T-shirt, its front embellished by the figure of a lovely goddess standing before the sea, and a fatigued brown leather jacket as insulation against the cool of the desert night. This persona, or absence of one, became Guy's favorite.

As herself, Anna is even more alluring and, in an unexpected irony, intriguing. And even more than usual, he wanted to share her space.

In a tribute to her most authentic self, Guy had changed into worn jeans, a mauve T-shirt illustrated with a testosterone god posed on an Olympian mountain peak (they had purchased the shirts together at a store on Melrose Avenue) and a distressed brown leather jacket. *Tonight we are a team.*

They drove the flat, endless straight of highway mile after mile after mile through the stark desert landscape. The Toyota rumbled past the last developed outpost of Barstow and entered the more remote and primitive desert. Guy thought of gargantuan lizards, gigantic, prehistoric reptilian birds, and a desert floor strewn with blanched skeletons. The heart of darkness.

For many years Guy had rarely left the urban density of Los Angeles—the towering concrete monoliths and myriad freeways, the smog and congestion, and the masses of people. That alone made the night special.

"Thank you, Anna."

"For what?" Her vision remained fixed on the narrow lane of the treacherous road.

"For bringing me here."

"You're welcome. But the best, the heart of the game, lies ahead." She flashed her enigmatic smile. "Delights, perhaps terrors, shall unfold."

After a bone rattling twenty-minute drive down a remote side road, cracked and fragmented as if assaulted by a bombing raid, they arrived at their destination, an abandoned, grayed wooden shack. It stood in the still night lonely and emptied.

An old miners' cabin, Guy deduced. Only ghosts of the grizzled miners, burdened with heavy tools and dusty bags of bartered apparatus, now visited its space, talking of failed dreams of fortune and then fading like dust into the cracked walls.

When Guy stepped from the car, he heard the miners' voices, like quiet echoes.

"Neva shudda came here. Ain't right of us to tear up this land. It's a beautiful thing. Like a woman. Don't wanna go tearing up a beautiful woman."

"Puts a curse on you. Ain't no riches here. Just dust and graves. Can't sell dust and don't need no grave but my own. A curse on everyone who comes here."

"We are here!" Anna announced to both Guy and the shack.

Guy looked at its boarded windows and the metal lock on its door, broken by an earlier trespasser. *Anna*, he surmised and grinned.

"Great! We traveled four hours across the desert to find a shack"

Anna smiled slyly and slowly opened the shack's door. The moonlight rushed inside, according its interior an eerie glow.

"Come inside," Guy heard either Anna, or the shack, request. He followed her in.

Anna strategically placed two round gold pillows seven-feet apart on the wooden floor in the center of the room, counting the distance with footsteps. She returned to the car and brought back two plastic gallon containers of water that she precisely located to the outside between each pillow creating a diamond space. Then her tan woven handbag was placed two feet to the side of one of the pillows. The precision and reverence with which she executed the procedure reminded Guy of the disciplined ritual of a Japanese tea ceremony.

"Have a seat," she instructed as she sat on one of the pillows and assumed a crossed-legged meditation posture.

"Anna the Master prepares to commence the sacred ceremony," Guy remarked. He took a seat on the pillow opposite her. He attempted to duplicate her Buddha pose but could not and improvised a comfortable, partial posture. *Now a disciple!*

Cool and invigorating desert night air entered the shack carrying the pleasantly sweet scent of desert flora. Guy touched the planks of the wooden floor. They felt coarse and worn, but essential. He liked essential.

Anna sat in silence for a few minutes, her form a sculpted shadow with boundaries defined by ambient moonlight. Guy did likewise, concluding it was not a time to make inane remarks. He sensed this was serious, even sacred, business.

"We are going to play a game." Anna finally spoke. "Life is a game. Most of all, a game of truth. We now duplicate that game. Appropriately, I call it, 'The Game'. The rules are simple." She paused, creating drama. "I will close the door so we are in a void of complete dark and silence as can only be found deep in the desert, or perhaps in the center of the sea or some remote point far in space. I chose the desert so we would not drown or suffocate. Then The Game would be over." She grinned. "We sit seven feet apart. You may stand or stretch if needed and then immediately resume sitting. There is water in the containers you may drink if you are thirsty. If you must relieve yourself, you may leave and use the bathroom, the desert sand, and then return. While outside, you may look at the sky, the stars, and the moon for several seconds, but no more. There should not be distractions.

"The most important rule is this: we cannot speak unless we have something to communicate that will, for certain, improve our lives or the condition of the world, or is an essential truth to our existence. Nothing else can be said or done. Simple. The Game continues until daybreak," she paused, "or a rule is violated."

Guy looked at the dimly lit gray planks of the cabin's walls as he considered her proposition. An interesting and worthy game, he concluded, and the type he would expect Anna to conceive of. But he suspected there was a little more involved.

"And what happens if we say something that does not meet the criteria?" He braced for her reply.

In the vague moonlight he saw the corners of Anna's lips rise in a duplicitous smile. "The penalty is extreme and final, as it often is in life."

She reached into her handbag and removed a plastic prescription container. She slid her body across the floor, like a gliding Buddha, and placed the container at a midpoint between them and then slid back to her cousin.

"That contains a medication, a sedative, of sufficient dosage and quantity to kill any person. If either of us violates the rules, that person takes all the pills."

She nodded toward the water indicating that everything necessary to accomplish that was present.

Guy laughed and then looked at Anna's face for an indication that her proposition was an amusing joke. There was no such sign. Her expression was stoic, as blank as the face of the meditating Buddha whose posture she feigned. She said nothing.

"You're not serious, are you?"

"Am I not? The Game must be as life itself. There is nothing more serious, and yet it is not serious at all."

She again flashed her smile of delighted mystery.

A perfectly ambiguous answer, Guy thought.

"The Game must have the same credibility as life," she elaborated.

Guy did not respond. Anna saw the soft lines of his face harden into a puzzle of jagged pieces.

"Do not worry so," she said. "You'll be surprised how easy it is to find meaning if one intends to. It's everywhere, waiting, within and without ourselves."

Guy thought her words sounded like the lyrics from a 1960's Beatles song, but he had long ago learned to respect Anna's concepts. He knew she was serious.

Anna peered into that thought-space that is always suspended in midair before a person. "Besides, I have faith we will both play The Game well. One could say we play this game every day, every moment in our lives. For if we do not choose to live our truth, then every moment in some way we die."

"Yes," Guy answered.

Her sagacious words pulled him into a different space, one more subtle and intuitive. Then, in a moment that seemed absurdly reckless, yet absolutely right, he realized he did agree with the rules of this peculiar game. They were rules that one had to be willing to live by. Truth and meaning or death, be it of one's body or spirit. Anna was on to something so simple, yet so correct.

A thought came that he spoke aloud. "To be or not to be. I will play The Game."

Anna smiled.

"But I have a question," Guy added. "Who determines if the communication qualifies or not?"

"The other person decides. *But,* since there must be an agreement for a truth or a lie or meaning to be considered so, otherwise it is purely subjective, the decision must also be agreed upon by the first player. Both must agree."

"And if they don't?"

"An agreement must be reached for The Game to continue."

"I understand."

Anna looked out the door at the chaste moonlit desert. "Believe me. I've played this game before. If you cheat, if you violate the rules, perhaps lie, for something less important than integrity, like your human life, afterward it will haunt and even torment you. When you make a commitment to this game of meaning, truth, and integrity, it is absolute. There is no way one can cheat and get away with it. It is as in life.

"But don't be too serious about it. Most of all have fun, even if you end up dead. It's just a game." Anna's face brightened and she laughed. "So, do you still wish to play? If not, we can simply drive back home."

"Yes, I wish to play." When Guy spoke those words, he felt an immense excitement, and a terrible dread that crashed like a steamroller. "Perhaps this game should be called the Beautiful, Winged Madness," he said.

Anna smiled. "Yes! Good. Then lights out. Let The Game begin."

She walked to the wooden door and closed it, it creaking hauntingly like a door in a ghost movie. The room became totally dark, a space of black. Guy heard her shuffling footsteps as she found her way back to the pillow.

All was profoundly quiet, like silence echoing itself. Long, mute, and dark minutes passed. Guy noticed that his hearing became amplified, detecting the faintest sounds, like Anna's breathing that she had reduced to a slow and shallow rhythm. He even believed he heard the pulse of his blood pumping through his veins and the beating of Anna's heart yards away. His sense of his own and her presence grew powerful and yet intimate. Experienced with meditation, he moved into a similar state although with a difference. He felt a stronger sense of immediacy and of a greater reality that pressed softly on him, descending from high above.

Suddenly Guy saw one point of light. The point was intensely brilliant, like a miniscule sun. Then it flared into a blinding illumination and then contracted back into its pinhole source.

He heard a word: *One.* Immediately he understood.

"Anna, perhaps the most meaningful and profound number is one. For I think there is only one spirit, like God, that we are all of. And one basic reality: being, as we are now, in this room. And one moment, this moment, always, forever."

Guy smiled, feeling like an enlightened guru.

"Well, I do believe that is an excellent perception," Anna responded, a sense of play delighting her voice. "That one, One, I do accept. You may live."

"I agree."

A return to silence. Moments, serene, unfolded and drifted.

Anna spoke. "Guy, I'm realizing something."

Her voice cut through the quiet with a stiletto edge. He imagined the look of intensity on her face.

"All of life is a noisy silence, like white noise, that mass of sounds so complex it creates the effect of a hypnotic silence. It is artists, like you and me, who are meant to both interpret and dissipate the noise, and to reveal the living and creative silence, and truths, beneath it."

She stopped and Guy sensed she was probing her insight more deeply.

"We, as both humans and artists, are simultaneously creators, carriers, interpreters, and liberators of the noise and the silence," she added.

"Good, Anna. I finally have a job description. That's a pass."

He and Anna laughed, and then they were again silent. Guy detected an occasional sound from outside the shack—the whisper overhead of a passing jet; the haunting, heckling laugh of an animal in the desert. A hyena, he suspected. He noted the sounds and then gently pulled his attention back to nothingness.

Anna fixed her attention on an imagined dot in space. First, it was white within a dark gray space. Then the space became lighter and the dot darker. Imagery appeared.

"Now I see a vision, Guy. It's vivid. In it I'm a woman made of glass. My entire skin is a mirror. I walk the world, reflecting everything around me—cities, forests, skies, buildings, and people. And I become all those things, blending into whatever's around me. It's strangely comforting." She paused. "And there's a man, tall and hearty, about forty. I'm standing the correct distance from him so his reflection perfectly fills my form. It's like I'm him, and yet not. I like . . . the feeling. Now he's walking out of me." She inhaled a slow breath. "I feel alone.

"Now I'm in a town. Most people don't see me. They think I'm part of the environment, an image that sweeps by them. But I think a few do notice that I'm there. They are looking curiously toward me. Yes, one is a child, a boy. He keeps walking back and forth before me, looking at his reflection on my shape. It's wild! I'm a human mirror." Anna laughed. "Now I'm standing before a large mirror that's in front of a store, a display on the sidewalk. It's odd. I'm looking at myself reflecting myself as nothing. Nothing reflecting nothing into infinity."

Anna paused. Guy heard her shuffle on her pillow.

"I'm disturbed, angry, and I walk into the storefront mirror, shattering it and my glass skin. The glass fragments scatter onto the sidewalk around me." She grinned. "And, behold! There is this beautiful woman beneath the mirror. My body is cut and bleeding from the broken shards, but I don't care. I walk into the world, naked and wounded, and join it. Everywhere I go I leave a trail of blood. The wounds never heal, but the blood is never depleted. People now do see me, the bleeding, naked woman. Some scream, some laugh, some stare at me curiously and offer help. Some greet me and talk. I realize I'm now a small part of everything, and I'm happy to be so."

"Cool, Anna." Guy employed a colloquial term he rarely used but that now seemed appropriate. "Does this mean you will no longer be a chameleon? You'll stop assuming personas?"

"No. Not likely. But I like this vision. It gives me more understanding."

"It reflects you." Guy smiled. "Well then, that's good. You may live."

"I agree."

They were both pleased with the exchange, and although they could not see each other, each knew the other was smiling.

Silence returned and the dark appeared to deepen, falling blacker. Then something changed. To Guy, the quiet grew heavier. Heavy, as if it was to crush him into the floor. Heavy, and suffocating. He twitched, and his stomach burned. He remembered the voices and hallucinations, the terrifying, mocking demons he had been experiencing and feared he might be especially vulnerable, at that time, in this game requiring a surrender of defenses.

But they did not assault. During the past week there were days when they visited and days when they didn't. He suddenly felt a reassurance from somewhere that they would not haunt him this night. There was a power and purity in The Game, and in Anna's presence before him, that would ward off such demons. He didn't know how, but he felt it.

The air lightened. Pressure diminished. His anxiety quelled.

The nectar fragrance of an outside desert flower infused his senses. He heard the call of a bird. New images materialized in the black space, and he squinted to perceive them more clearly. They were shapes of light, becoming sharper and more defined. At the very moment when he realized what they were, he knew he should communicate it.

"Anna, in the dark, in this black void, I see shadows of light. It's as if the darkness is casting shadows off objects that are not present, and the shadows are created of light. They're beautiful and luminous. They're everywhere around me. Light forms, some like objects, others like beings, some moving in a delirious dance." He stared, captivated. "There's one that's larger than the others. It's in the shape of the shadow of a woman." Guy examined it. "Yes, I see it. I know. That one, that shadow of light, Anna, is you. It's exquisite!"

"I can't see them, but I can imagine what you describe," Anna replied. "It's also a wonderful metaphor. But it's your vision, Guy, and I thank you for envisioning me so. You may live."

They quieted, reflecting on the experience. Suddenly Anna saw a shape of illumination. It was one shadow of light as Guy had described, and she identified its shape.

"Guy. I do see one shadow of light, in the shape of a man." There was awe in her voice. "And I know that shadow of light is you."

Delight flowed through Guy, and his head tingled.

They continued on, occasionally expressing a vision or perception. Both knew The Game was succeeding. Sometimes they even forgot it was a game. It seemed like something more, and natural. At one point Guy, having to relieve himself, left the shack and visited the desert sand. He looked at the sky and beheld again its incredible wonder, its thousands of glimmering stars and constellations, more than he had ever before seen. Around him the desert landscape appeared more brilliantly hued than it had earlier, painted in opulent blues. Everything was crisp and clean, as if a powerful wind had blown a haze out of the air. All had changed.

"Dazzling!" He spoke aloud. "God's universe."

Guy felt behind him the wind of flapping wings. He turned but saw only the serene space of the desert. *Odd,* he thought and then remembered the rules of The Game. He could not loiter. He returned to the shack.

*   *   *

Guy suddenly had a thought, a thought so simple he passed over it. But it returned. He examined it to see if it met The Game's criterion and found a humorous but sharp-edged truth in it.

"Anna, I just realized something I think I should communicate."

"Is it life transformative?"

He smiled. "I believe so. There is almost an irony in your question. What I realized is that one day both of us, you and I, will have to grow up."

Guy could not see it, but Anna's gentle face tautened. Her brow dropped, forming a rigid ledge over her eyes.

"That's it? We have to grow up? Is there more to it?"

"No. I just see that we need to grow up."

"Everybody needs to grow up. We're always growing up!" Irritation scratched her voice. "I'm afraid that's not enough. I cannot accept that."

"Yes. That's the point."

A silent moment hung like a noose.

"No, it's not a qualifying communication," Anna proclaimed. "It's too mundane. Do you believe it qualifies? Now the judgment is up to you."

Guy felt compelled to answer in the affirmative but withheld his response. He would be objective. He examined his statement, viewing it in the perspective of the other originations that had been accepted.

Growing up. It is a common matter. Even a child knows everyone must grow up. He deliberated. *Anna and I seem to resist growing up. But is that unusual?*

The conviction he felt when he made the statement deteriorated, and his self-assurance plunged. He searched for a different way to view the statement but found only trite words.

"I think you are correct, Anna. It was not a well-considered statement. It's too . . . trivial, and I feel I must be honest. I cannot accept it either."

An agonizing lag. They both sat mute in the now-terrible dark. Guy felt confused.

"I thank you for your honesty, Guy. The next step has to be decided by you. I prefer not to decree it, but you know the rules."

"Yes," Guy concurred and then scowled. His shoulders slumped. The whole situation began to seem ludicrous.

A contrived game played by two struggling artists trying to find something profound while sitting in the dark in the middle of nowhere. An artistic self-indulgence. And now, I'm supposed to take my life? Because of a silly rule I agreed to? That's madness!

Then Guy remembered something, an experience he had often. He spoke it aloud.

"Many times while working on a painting or writing a poem, there was a critical point I reached, like a moment of truth, or a leap of faith, when I realized I had to abandon all constraints and rational thoughts and simply surrender to my instincts, to my creation." He probed for words. "I had to just act, unconcerned about the outcome or consequences. Do it because it felt right. They were moments that created a new reality. I believe this is one of those moments."

"That's better." Anna spoke. "I feel like letting you pass, but I can't. It doesn't change what was earlier said, or the rules of The Game. Again, Guy, it is like life. One has to maintain its integrity and make it real, or it's meaningless, and this is all about meaning. There cannot be rationalizations in this game."

"I agree." And truly Guy did.

A critical moment. Guy knew what he must do, *not for The Game, but for myself, and Anna.* And he would.

Act! Don't think! Act.

Without further hesitation or thought—he feared reflection would collapse his resolve—he slid forward, his hand groping in the dark until he found the small container. He grasped it tightly and then located the bottle of water. He slid back to his pillow. He twisted off the container's cap.

"I say no more."

With a swift motion, he brought the container of pills to his lips. *This is insane!* he thought. *No! This is right!* He swallowed half of the container's contents and then removed the water bottle's cap and took a large swallow of water. He swallowed the remainder of the pills, and more water. It took only a few seconds and was done. It was easy.

Then a spearing anxiety; no, a dozen stabbing spears, and a black deluge of dread. Guy felt terrified. Then he didn't. *It will finally all be over.* Then he did. *My God!*

Anna heard his actions and knew the decision had been made and executed. The Game had been honored.

"Guy, I'm . . . a little disturbed. Later, I know I will be more. But I greatly admire your integrity. I was not sure. Integrity, yes! That is the most important thing, Guy. And you truly have it."

Guy was pleased with the respect she showed him, yet, so objective. So impersonal. This was the woman he loved. *As often in life, the game becomes more important than the players. Perhaps that is how the world evolves.*

Guy became drowsy. "These work fast, Anna." He looked into the surrounding darkness. "I don't want it to be like this. I want to see you again, not just blackness. I want to see the world once more. I'm going outside."

"Certainly! You don't have to complete The Game in here."

When Guy stood his legs were numb, like sleeping appendages. He shook them and then walked outside. He felt dizzy.

The night was pristine and clear. The air invigorated as it filled his sluggish lungs and streamed like a liquid cool through his body. It seemed correct that this bluish surreal dream world would be . . . *the last place I see on Earth.* His eyes absorbed the scene, he wanted to remember it, although he knew not for what, simply because of its beauty and mystery.

Anna removed two blankets from the back seat of the car and spread one on the sand.

"Lie down on this. It'll be more comfortable."

Guy lay on the blanket, feeling sleepy numbed. A terrible fear lurked right below the surface of his consciousness, but he kept it pushed back. Anna placed the second blanket over him. *She tucks me in,* he thought.

Supine on his back, he looked into the infinite night sky. Its orchestration of luminous stars punctured the blackness like thousands of tiny light holes, mystical and dazzling. His eyelids became leaden; he struggled to keep them open. He looked for a last time at Anna, who was kneeling before him. Cast in a soft aura of moonlight, she appeared lovely. He smiled at her, and she smiled back.

Guy knew what they were doing was mad, but it also felt correct. He understood. It was pure and absolute and beautiful. It was as they—*a Beautiful, Winged Madness.*

Anna leaned over him. "Guy, I want to give you a gift, to say farewell."

Images of a final and loving gift charmed Guy, but he realized that in his increasingly anesthetized state, he would not be able to receive the choicest offering.

"Damn!" he moaned.

"It is always sad," Anna spoke, "that the greatest praise is bestowed upon a person during his eulogy, after he's dead, when it's too late for him to hear it. I want to give you yours now, Guy, while you are still alive."

She looked at him with tender eyes.

An odd gift, Guy thought.

"Yes, Anna, that would be nice," he responded in a fading voice.

Anna whimsically perused the night sky as if entreating each glowing star for the proper inspiration.

"In Memoriam," she announced loudly and began to grin, then appeared most solemn. "Thank you Lord, Spirit, for the opportunity to speak this eulogy to Guy before he is dead." She smiled blissfully yet sadly. "We are gathered together to honor the almost departed, my dear friend Guy, Poetic Guy Being. Perhaps if he had never been born and had not walked among us in this world, no one would have missed him, for he would not have been here. But he was and since first acquainting him, I have loved him, my closest, truest friend."

She paused and sniffled as grief suppressed her delivery.

"He is a wondrous soul, a spirit that would not be confined by the banalities of this world and the trivialities of a lesser mind. He refused to be, as many become, a human chair, or an ant, or mere quarts of blood, or a faint and meaningless breath that wafted through life. His was a world infused with vision, elegant and profound, like a symphony or a novel," she paused, "or at least a concerto or a short story. Let he be seen as that which is what it is, no more and no less, and thus perfect. The perfect Guy!" She smiled. "He turned shadows into light, and with the pen of a poet, transformed the detritus of life into rockets of sublimity. Zoom!" She swept her hand through the air. "Guy was the mud of humanity sculpted by the loving hands of an artist into the visage of an individual, not one mutilated by time and elements, with missing limbs or head and cracked breast, but one complete and lovely, with only minor cracks, and normal breasts. And without one of those ridiculous fig leafs over his genitals. He was . . . exposed."

She giggled and then cleared her throat.

A moan sounded from the man eulogized. The stars above looked down with tearful eyes. The moon chuckled.

"Most of all, Guy was a good man of compassion and character who was willing to give all for the integrity of The Game and his soul. For that some may consider him an incredible fool, a moron, but not I. With love and respect, I will always walk with him in spirit and in my prayers. As an innocent child finds joy in a simple toy or cartoon, I will eternally delight in my memory of Guy. He is my dearest friend and I love him, not for who or what he was, but for him."

Anna bowed her head as a tear dropped from her eye onto the desert sand. She bent down and softly kissed Guy on the forehead.

"Goodnight, sweet prince. I love thee, and may flights of angels sing thee to thy sleep."

Guy stared, perplexed. Then he decided that perhaps it was indeed a splendid eulogy, perhaps he did not listen closely, and felt pleased. He wished his eyes would swell with tears, as seemed appropriate for the occasion, but instead they were dry and burning from the sedatives and the strain of keeping them open as the fateful sleep encroached.

"Goodbye, dear Anna. Always I love thee," he spoke in a hushed voice as breath abandoned him.

He felt her hand touching his. Then there was just the silence of the desert and a graying, graying field of inner space.

"Wait, Guy!"

He heard Anna's voice command.

"Where would you like your body buried?"

Not what he had hoped to hear in the final moment of his life, but he felt it was important, as always, to respond to Anna.

"Desert." His voice was faint.

"Dessert? There is no dessert. This is it."

"Purple mountains and golden plains," he whispered with his last breath.

"Oh, desert. Yes, of course."

Guy opened his eyes one final time. He saw the line of the horizon where the flat desert touched the mountains that touched the sky. It seemed so simple, and perfect. Beautiful!

Guy's eyes gently closed. It felt just like he was falling asleep, falling asleep, falling . . . .

*   *   *

Guy was standing in a cemetery. He glanced around and could tell by the buildings in the distance that he was back in Los Angeles. It was a small cemetery of rolling hills, lovely trees and bushes and tombstones. He looked down. Before him was a gray headstone inscribed: 'Guy, Poetic Guy Being', with his date of birth and death and a short ode.

What is this? Why am I in Los Angeles, and not buried in the desert, as I requested? Did Anna ignore my final wish?

Then he saw a little girl, about ten years old, dressed in a long white dress walk up to his grave. She had pale flesh and ebony hair and eyes. She stood silent and then placed a blue rose before the headstone.

"Little girl," he asked. "Am I dead?"

The girl looked up. "No, Guy, you are not dead."

Her voice sounded strangely distant, as if not originating from her body but from an exterior source.

"Open your eyes," she directed. "You must see this!"

*   *   *

Guy's leaden eyes struggled open. Far in the distance, the desert horizon was bleeding. Fluid red spilled over silhouetted mountains and stained the desert floor. The sky was darkly thick with a purple aura diffusing from the horizon into the blue-black of space above it.

In front of the scene, as if a shadow before a scarlet curtain, a woman danced, swaying and spinning in free-form movements before a lethargically rising sun.

"Wake up, Guy!" She yelled in the middle of a graceful spin. "Look at this incredible sunrise."

Anna stood motionless and then ran toward him. Guy was still lying on a blanket on the sand.

"Are you awake?" She leaned over and scrutinized his face closely.

"Awake? You mean I'm not dead?"

Anna cackled heartily. "No, you're not dead! It was just a game, Guy. Do you think I would allow my best friend, whom I love, to die for a game?" Her expression appeared incredulous. "You did very well. I'm proud of you. But it was just a game."

"But, I felt it. The pills. I felt like I died."

"There were three real pills, sedatives, in the container," Anna explained. "The others were placebos, soy powder capsules. The three merely put you to sleep for a while. I awakened you to see this." She pointed toward the horizon sunrise. "You must feel very drowsy."

Guy lifted into a seated position. His head felt as if it was molded of iron.

"Yes, I do." He shook his head. "A game? Just a game?"

"Yes, just a game, and it seems to have succeeded grandly. You have not risen from the dead. But *now*, please look at this glorious sunrise I woke you for. Let your drowsy eyes behold!"

She turned toward the awakening sun and graciously flowed out an arm.

Guy looked. The dawning light was changing into exquisite hues of orange gold that swept across the desert floor like an unrolling carpet of mystical light. Everything was so quiet he believed he heard the arriving sunlight touch each grain of sand and desert brush. The cool dawn air washed across his skin like the waters of a cleansing baptism, its fragrance cactus floral. Guy imagined all of Earth must have looked and smelled like that on the first morning when primordial man sat, like him, to welcome the original day.

There was no finer way to awaken from a charade of death, a game. It was like experiencing the sunrise for the first time.

*   *   *

The inimitable green Toyota chugged down the straight miles of highway as the temperature warmed into a desert Sunday. Guy hypnotically watched the infinite white slashes of the highway's median strip roll beneath them. The surrounding austere desert seemed to exist in a space neither alive nor dead but suspended between the two without any desire for either to prevail. It was just being.

The persistent drone of the Toyota's engine soundtracked the scene with an ironic mechanical mantra. It provoked thought in Anna, the driver, and urged questions about The Game.

"Guy, did you really believe that taking the capsules would be fatal?"

Guy stared into the beige sea of desert.

"I wasn't certain, but I had to assume they would be. I decided I had to play The Game as if it was all absolutely real. Otherwise, why play?"

He looked closely into Anna's face.

"Maybe just for fun?" She tossed back. "It was just a game. But I truly admire your commitment and courage."

"Yes," Guy nodded. "That peculiar confusion of nobility and insanity, typical of artists."

Anna laughed. "That Beautiful, Winged Madness. But it does raise an intriguing question. If it had all been true, you would have died for a game. Would it have been worth it?"

Guy gazed at the horizon that vanished into nothing.

"Yes, because that's what I decided. Perhaps, especially as artists, we have to approach everything with that commitment. There's something about playing a game, any game, the game of life, the game of art, with absolute commitment that's important. And integrity. Isn't that what we're about, Anna?" He felt surprisingly confident of his viewpoints. "And yet," he continued, "while also remembering that it's not important at all. I think that's it. Do all things as if they're totally important and yet not important at all. Guy's philosophy."

Anna glanced at him and smiled. "I agree, wise one. That's a pass."

Guy pointed toward something in the desert sky. Anna leaned down so she could view it through the car's windshield. A half-dozen dark slashes circled high above the sand.

"Vultures," Guy stated as they both recalled the classic image of the predatory birds hungrily orbiting over an ill-fated creature in old western movies.

"What ghastly corpse might be the scavenger's entree?" Guy pondered aloud. "Someone, or something, played The Game to its finality. The other, terrifying side of the reality."

Anna moaned. In the distance she saw a grayish tone starting to stain the pure blue of the sky. It was the smoggy haze of a distant Los Angeles, its first welcoming sign to approaching desert travelers.

"Wait, I have a question," Guy interjected. "What if *you* had failed The Game? What would you have done, Anna? How would you have played it out?"

Anna reached into the pocket of her jeans and removed a plastic container. It had a red X marked on its label.

"This container is filled with sixty real sedatives. If consumed together, they would quickly summon the Grim Reaper. This one I bring for me alone. I would not give it to anyone else." She turned the container so the red X faced her. "Whether I would actually take them, I am not certain. That would be a moment of truth and values."

"So you *do* take The Game seriously." Guy baited. "Do you think you would do it?"

She looked at him and smiled slyly. "To be or not to be. That is The Game."

Guy stared at the desert and then at her.

"If you die, I die," he said. "We are in the same game. One game."

Anna smiled, pleased by his sentiment, but it also disturbed the deepest recess of her soul.

The desert continued to scroll past like a lovely minimalist landscape painting. Guy recited a verse.

"All the enchantments and horrors waiting to behold. I flee the theater and escape to the roads. Too timid to pass I maintain my lane. Negotiating fields of flickering signs. Bypassing doors of seductive designs. The asphalt an endless battlefield mire, I charge, skirting the bullets of friendly fire.

"Eternities traveled to arrive nowhere. Days and nights layered in painted air. For what is there, but what there is here?

"My family dispersed, I prefer the ghosts of hallowed verse."

Two gargantuan beasts from a prehistoric era suddenly loomed over the desert, startling the humans' vision. One was a Tyrannosaurus Rex, the other a Brontosaurus. A large sign by the highway read, 'Dinosaur Restaurant and Gift Shop'. Guy remembered. He had seen pictures of the giant beasts and the flat roofed restaurant. They were well known to students of California travel lore.

"Brunch." Anna announced as she veered into the parking lot. The moment they stepped from the car, the scent of eggs and bacon, cheeseburgers and coffee tantalized their senses.

The concrete Brontosaurus, posed boldly on the sand, had an elongated gray body with a disproportionate peanut head and a lengthy tail. An opened door on its belly from which a ladder descended invited visitors to climb its rungs and enter the monstrous hollow creature's interior where, to no one's surprise, a gift shop waited.

Guy and Anna noticed a girl, about four, in denim slacks and a Wonder Woman T-shirt, her blonde hair topped with a pink bow, standing at the bottom of the ladder, staring up at the creature. Terror inscribed her face. She tugged at her father's hand attempting to pull him from the towering threat.

"It's all right, Karen," the sympathetic father consoled. "It's not real. It's a big model."

The girl looked suspiciously at her father and then at the beast. She seemed unconvinced and broke from her father's grip to flee from the fantasized danger.

Good for you, Guy thought. *Trust your own perceptions.*

Anna laughed. "Perhaps she knows something we adults don't."

They walked around the perimeter of the massive beast, examining it from all perspectives.

"It's rather tacky," Guy critiqued with a disdainful expression, "and I certainly would not say it fits the pristine beauty of the desert. But still, I rather like it."

"Me too," Anna concurred. "It is kind of goofy, but it's fun to discover it, like a great bestial guardian, out here, in the middle of nowhere. It suggests a primal force in a primal serenity."

She perused the Brontosaurus. *Where is your home?* She silently questioned.

They walked to the ladder and looked up at the rectangular opening in the dinosaur's gut. They glanced at each other for a consensus.

"Well, shall we enter the belly of the beast?" Anna asked.

Guy replied with an embracing smile. "We always do."

Chapter 9

THE BELLY OF the beast.

On the following Friday night, a demon of the dark, empty whole seized Anna. When Guy visited, he found her in bed, as she had been all day, in a shadow persona, a morose, leaden cast of herself.

"What is it, Anna? What's wrong?"

She looked at him with rootless eyes and for a still, pained moment did not reply.

"Sometimes . . . this happens," she finally responded. "The dark arrives."

Anna seemed a vague specter against the bedspread's vibrant peacock colors, her complexion pale and her gaze unvarying, as one who had nothing to see. She looked crumpled, dressed in old jeans and a wrinkled, slept in T-shirt. Her hair was tangled—Guy assumed by her anxious fingers assailing it. The strong, sensual body that helped define Anna lay resigned and comatose on the bed as if attempting to sink into the mattress, or into nothing. It frightened Guy. He knew it well. *Depression.*

How strange to see Anna so grave and dispossessed, he thought. *I am the one tempered for such distractions, not her. The mind's morbid ghosts can haunt any home. They wait for their hour.*

Guy placed a hand on her shoulder.

"Let me try to help. Tell me what you're feeling, Anna. Describe it. If you can't, try to imagine it as an image." He borrowed from the techniques of his past therapists.

No response. Anna stared at some distant point in space. The room around her seemed to Guy as pale as her, its colors dim and its air languorous. Yet he understood since for him there was no disparity between Anna and the world.

She tried to speak, dragged and weighted.

"It's . . . as if this immense umbrella that has covered and protected an enchanted, fairytale world . . . alive and bright . . . suddenly collapsed and closed that world. Crushed it."

Then mute moments. Guy waited.

"Gray . . . gray ashes, the world that remains, made of ashes . . . with hulking, faceless, and terrible ash forms that barely move, or care. There is nothing for them to do . . . nothing can help. It's over." She looked up at Guy. "A wind could blow them away."

Guy recognized the image. He had been in similar states and knew how difficult it was to climb out, but he would not indicate that to Anna. He sat on the edge of the bed, looking reassuring, and took her hand.

"Is that really true, Anna, or is it the depression speaking? I don't think it's your world. I know your world."

"Something . . . happened, Guy."

A dreadful reality. Coming, Guy sensed. He didn't want to inquire, but did. "What happened, Anna? Tell me."

She stared at the ceiling. A shadowy space opened.

"Once upon a dark time in the City of Angels." She laughed feebly.

Good, Guy thought. *Some humor. Better.*

"There was a woman, peculiar, who worked in a bookstore, and a man, haunted and damaged, who spoke poetry." She paused but did not look at Guy, staring instead into the dark, opened expanse. "Remember the android man, Guy? With a prosthetic arm and leg? The literature professor?"

Damn! Not this. "Yes, Anna, I remember."

"He came to the bookstore. Yesterday. I was feeling . . . weird. Something going on with me. I don't know what." Her vision pried a hidden thought. "Some aloneness. You know how that sometimes strikes. Like things are very wrong. I felt pain—unfocused, pervasive." She looked at Guy. "Do you want to hear this? I don't feel quite right."

The room became thick as if overgrown by dense roots and weeds. It smelled musty. Guy had difficulty breathing. He did not want to hear it, but knew he must. *It will help Anna.*

"Yes, I do. You should tell me."

She stared at him more intently, checking. He conjured a smile.

"Well, OK. He came on to me, as he always does . . . bullshit charm and verses. But it felt flattering, even comforting. So, even though I sensed it was a mistake, I didn't seem to care. I agreed." She stopped, her eyes enervated. "He waited till I was off work, and we went to his apartment. A pleasant place in Los Feliz by Griffith Park . . . we drank some wine. He was dressed in a black turtleneck, very hip. Well, before long we were in his bedroom."

She glanced at Guy. "You sure?"

Guy saw her sensitivity to him as a good sign. Real feelings were returning. She had to continue. "Yes, go ahead."

"Well, you know, the usual at first. He undressed me and then himself. I was in this odd, detached state . . . like being a character in a movie. He said sweet things. Something from Whitman. And he kept looking over my body. Then he laid me down on his bed and started touching me, everywhere, slowly . . . but not with his real hand, but with his prosthetic hand. It was only mildly pleasurable since his hand was cold, and it seemed strange." She stared fixed at nothing. "Can you feel anything?' I asked him. 'No, but I can imagine,' he said. 'Why don't you use your other hand?' I asked. 'I prefer it this way,' he answered with an odd smile. I thought it a peculiar statement and felt uncomfortable, but I didn't stop him."

"Well, we continued and made love." Anna stopped, examining an image in her mind. "He had, by the way, a totally human penis, normal and functioning. Not a drill or android device. I was both relieved and disappointed."

Again, Anna smiled faintly.

"But I . . . can't say that he made love. It was harsh. He seemed to keep forgetting I was there. It was like he was doing things *to* me, not with me. I kept telling him, 'More gently.'

'Look at me.' 'Easy.' He might try for a moment and then became dominating again. I felt he needed to control it. It wasn't too bad for a while. Not tender, but some excitement. Then, gradually, it worsened." She looked at the wall opposite her. "He got very rough. When I looked into his face, his eyes, I did not see a man who was making love with a woman, but . . . someone who has done something, releasing something, like pain, *on* something. It frightened me. It frightened me terribly!" Anna shook her head. "Then, as he thrust violently, his cyborg hand grasped my throat, holding me down and controlling my movements. He began to squeeze too tightly. He may not even have realized he was hurting me as he may not have been able to feel how firmly he was clasping my neck." She rubbed it.

Guy did not move or speak. He just watched and listened.

"Although he sometimes looked at me, at my face, he didn't seem to be seeing me, but something instead in his own mind, something angry and desperate. Then I became really terrified. With a gasping voice, I told him to stop and I tried to struggle out from beneath him, but he didn't hear me and his mechanical prosthetic leg had me pinned tightly, like in the jaws of a pliers. I pushed hard against him and fought to extricate myself." Anna squirmed. "I could hardly breathe. His grip on my throat was tightening more, but still I gave a small scream, which I think he heard. Finally, I broke free. Although I had trouble breathing, I had that energy, that adrenaline, which comes from danger. I quickly dressed. I was too upset and frightened to say anything. I just wanted to get the hell out."

"Good," Guy interjected.

"Yes. He sat on the edge of the bed, looking like some dejected child. 'You need help,' I told him. Now I was feeling angry. 'You've got big problems! You're dangerous!' Then he seemed to be more himself and conscious of what had occurred. He apologized for being so rough. I just glared at him and said, 'Yes. Get some help, and stay the hell away from me!' He nodded, then hung his head and recited Shakespeare.

'If only this too, too sullied flesh would melt, thaw, and resolve itself into adieu.' I told him to cut the bullshit."

Anna shook her head, and then Guy shook his.

"Shakespeare. Can you imagine?"

Anna became angry, and Guy knew that was positive.

"I was very upset and certainly not in the mood for a recitation. It all seemed so weird. I gave him a cold look and left."

"I'm glad he didn't hurt you more."

"Yes. But when I got home, I wasn't feeling well. I felt sick and nauseous. What the hell's wrong with me? I kept thinking. I must be insane! And I kept dropping deeper into depression." She vaguely smiled. "And then you came to rescue me."

She looked at Guy fondly. "Thank you, Guy. I feel a little better already."

She took his hand and squeezed it.

Guy felt like remarking cynically, "Can you feel it? Why don't you touch me with your other hand?" But he didn't, crushing the impulse.

Yet not totally. For some moments he did not even want to speak to her. He felt like hitting her. *She will not be intimate with me, but she will with some lunatic!* He looked at her but did not smile. Words came into his mind. *I kill love.*

He tried not to appear severe, but Anna picked up on his emotion.

"Guy, I know I said I wouldn't be with that man, and I meant it. I just went a little insane. I mean, I'm sorry, I betrayed that. It was just something I thought I needed." She paused, examining. "Something I chose to do. It was a mistake. I do foolish things sometimes."

"Yes," Guy concurred.

Anna smiled and then stared at the ceiling.

A painful silence. Guy knew he had to help her more. She was more important than his petty anger and feeling of betrayal. *After all, we are merely good friends,* he thought. *Anna may do whatever she pleases.*

Anna smiled and placed a hand on her cheek. "I feel warmer now."

Guy spoke to her on other topics, anything that occurred to him, hoping the dialogue might help to further extricate the demon's grip.

Guy told of his own battles with depression and what had helped. He related an awkward lovemaking attempt with a female friend, including embarrassing details that on another occasion he might have omitted. Anna laughed. He reminded her of the good times they had shared together, and he flattered her.

"You still look beautiful, Anna. A bit sad, but very beautiful. Do you know you always look beautiful to me? It's almost unsettling."

Anna smiled and nodded. A hazy light abated her blackness.

Guy recited an amusing verse he once wrote.

"Oh no, depressed! Focal point obsessed. Fetal curled in a milky eye, scoping my imaged self, a squashed fly, inverted and compressed. Black fingers knead my heart.

"I pray penitent to my savior TV. An illuminate man, Gallop poll handsome with murky edges, breaks the news. 'Discovery of probable life on Mars.' I knew it! I should have been the gel of a Martian cell, dethroning humankind with my amorphous shell. The truth is out there! I feel inferior to Martian bacteria. Oh no, depressed."

Anna laughed softly. "That's clever, Guy, and amusing. Thanks."

But her spirit still seems lost, Guy observed.

He remained with Anna through that long, difficult night. He lay beside her on the bed so she would always know he was close, and he kept the light on, believing it might defray her demon. Sometimes he held her hand or gently touched her face. They spoke occasionally, but mostly Anna rested quietly.

Finally she fell asleep. Her face softened, and Guy was relieved. *Perhaps it will restore her,* he thought. *I pray that nightmares, sleep's treasonous and brutal mates, do not assault.*

In an agitated moment, she rolled against him and laid her head on his chest. He placed his arm around her and kissed her forehead. She smiled faintly. *She is recovering.*

He, too, fell asleep.

His breaths whisper my name. I feel the warmth of his body and the kindness and love of his concern, Anna's sleeping consciousness thought. *It penetrates the black shroud that drapes me and banishes my demon. I will not forget, Guy, and I release my depression. Let there be beautiful dreams!*

Anna had lovely dreams. White, benevolent forms lifted from colorful plateaus. Huge, playful dinosaurs, not ferocious like a Tyrannosaurus Rex but soft and purple like TV's Barney, rose from golden deserts. She floated through streams of music.

Slowly the new morning arrived, bright and fresh. With a glittering sweep of magic, its wand waved above them, vanquishing anything remaining of the dark night and Anna's mordant state.

She awakened. The color was renewed on her cheeks, and a smile danced across her face, like Sleeping Beauty after the kiss by her prince.

The morning light illuminated the room with a hazy aura. Anna thought it was exquisite, especially when she remembered the terrible blackness of the previous night, the belly of the beast.

She looked at Guy sleeping, smiled and then kissed him on the forehead and the cheek.

"Awaken, sweet prince," she whispered into his ear and then extracted a feather from a toy on a bedside table and brushed it across his face. His nose twitched and his lips pouted. She laughed, and Guy opened his eyes.

"Anna," he spoke with an urgent breath. "How are you feeling?"

"Much, much better, thank you. Sorry I put you through that."

"It's OK, Anna. I'm glad I was here to help." *Just don't get together with that damn android man again.*

"I won't," Anna responded, sensitive to Guy's expressions and surprising him.

Most of that day Guy and Anna stayed outside, enjoying together the simplest of things: the sun and air, children playing, the rituals of the city dwellers, an escaped red balloon drifting lethargically across the cerulean sky. Anna watched a leaf drop delicately to the ground, and they discussed the fragility and enormous resilience of nature. Both were delighted by the sight of a silver advertisement blimp floating dreamily across blue space like an Orwellian airship.

It was revitalizing. Yet neither could escape an uneasy feeling. *Something unwelcomed and unkind contests the fancies of our world.*

"Anna, it's great you're feeling better now. But I think we have to be careful. There are always demons that hide in the light."

Guy silently avowed that he, too, would remember and then brushed aside the omens. He was just happy that Anna was better.

"Yes, I feel it, too." She looked into the sky and thought of an old phrase. "There's a bad moon on the rise."

Chapter 10

DRUNK NIGHT. ANNA proposed it that morning with a simple, eloquent declaration. "Let's get drunk together." Her smile suggested unbounded possibilities.

"OK," was Guy's simple, eloquent response.

It was the Saturday following Anna's dance with demons. In the afternoon, Guy was returning home from the neighborhood library where he had studied the poems of the French poet Rimbaud whose beautiful but defiant works inspired him, especially *The Wayward Boat,* about a symbolic ship's doomed voyage of freedom. Guy identified with the ship, the voyage, the freedom, and the doom.

It started snowing.

Glistening, mystical snowflakes descended from the gauzy grayed sky onto Wilshire Boulevard swiftly coating streets and buildings and cars in a delicate, crystalline layer of white, a blanket of reflected light.

Shapes slithered and streaming, his mind contrived. *Blinding fields, white and absent.*

How wondrous and strange! Guy thought. *It never snows in Los Angeles although so often have I wished it would.* A snowflake fell on his nose.

Then flames poured from the sky. The falling sheets of snow transformed into thousands of tiny streaks of fire, searing the air and showering the city. Guy felt its heat on his skin. The snow instantly melted. Los Angeles burned.

Beautiful hell of orange and crimson. A scorching apocalypse!

Then the flames stopped, and the fire vanished. Guy stood, mute and dazed on the sidewalk. Cars streamed by. A traffic light flashed 'Walk'. A car honked twice. A woman in a blue-gray suit stepped from the sidewalk. A typical L.A. autumn day.

Visions or sick hallucinations? Guy perused the surrounding cityscape. Whichever, it had been a beautiful, mad sight, magical and terrifying.

He wondered if snow and fire and Drunk Night had some mythic, eternal affinity.

He wondered if he was going insane.

*   *   *

Anna arrived at his apartment that evening at 7:30 p.m., believing that 7:30 was established in some immortal decree as the proper time to commence a special night. It had been so for time in perpetuum, or, at least, ever since she was a teenager: leaving for teen club, being picked up for the prom, piling into a car for a night of drunken partying. She entered Guy's apartment proudly bearing two bottles of Cabernet Sauvignon. Another was on reserve in her refrigerator in case events urged greater wantonness.

"Tonight, we are blessed," Anna announced displaying the gifts.

Her tone was spirited for that night Anna was Dionysus, the young Olympian god, bestower of wine and celebration and, as often sensationalized in Hollywood movies, orgies.

A most agreeable association, Guy thought.

His apartment's plethora of plants, green, lush and scented of nature, provided an appropriate ambiance of an earthy, bacchanalian festival. Guy was costumed as Guy—jeans, T-shirt, and a sport coat—but his consciousness was in revelry.

Anna Dionysus was wrapped in a beige cotton toga entwined with vines sprouting plastic purple-red grapes. Her wavy hair was parted in the middle, tousled loosely and flowing to her shoulders, characteristic of abandoned youth, and crowned with a laurel of colorful flowers symbolizing Dionysus's affinity with nature and its pleasures. Artful makeup diminished her feminine facial features transforming them into the androgynous look of a young man-woman.

Guy found that especially alluring. Confusing but delightful feelings and desires aroused that he had never before felt. Men, women, flesh, forbidden abandonment. He was not certain if he should express them to Anna, or how, so he just stood in his living room, his stare fixed upon her.

How I recognize that quiet look of desire in his eyes, Anna responded.

"I understand, Guy." She smiled and needed to say no more.

Guy gulped some wine, averting his gaze from the object of desire. "Excellent wine!"

He had cleaned and straightened his apartment for the night and thought it almost looked nice, possessing a rare casual orderliness. It was even forest scented by an air deodorant. Anna liked it. She flung herself on his couch.

"To my host!" She drank deeply from her glass.

"To my host!" She again proclaimed, laughed, and drank.

She is ready. But for what Guy was not sure.

Within an hour, both the Dionysian god and the urban poet were succumbing to alcoholic euphoria. Guy felt the dissipating of the self-conscious heaviness that often burdened him. The world danced in gentle flows. Seated beside each other on his worn but cushiony sofa, stories and drinking and reveries were shared into the night, always enlivened by Anna's excellent Dionysus. Guy found it intriguing to watch her surrender to deeper and deeper abandonment and alcoholic bliss, her expressions increasingly theatrical as she waved her arms grandly and transformed her face and voice into a charming ensemble of characters. He was especially entertained by her impersonation of Marlene Dietrich, Anna's favorite actress from the classic films she enjoyed watching and studying. The slurring of Anna's inebriated voice complemented the characteristic sultry timber of Dietrich's speech.

She reenacted a cabaret scene from the film *The Blue Angel.* Leaning back on the couch with one leg raised and her hand atop its knee, Anna sang in Dietrich's seductive voice a song about falling in love.

"Falling in love again,
Never wanted to,
What am I to do?
I can't help it."

It was an enchanting moment—Anna as Dionysus as Dietrich—art, wine, and seduction. *Such is the substance from which classics are born,* Guy mused with a grin.

Guy liked it when Anna laughed or felt something intensely, for he knew she was happy. Anna liked it when Guy became lost in the pleasures and creations of the moment, for she knew it was there that he was happy. Both experienced a delightful interweaving of their worlds and spirits. *Perhaps this is what we are always meant to create together,* each thought.

Suddenly Anna, the Dionysian god/goddess, leapt to her feet and swayed and swirled in an improvised dance to the rhythms of absent music. Guy felt no impulse to join in her free-form expression but was content to just sit and watch her move.

"Let's do goofy dances!" she boldly proposed with a giddy grin at the end of a wobbly spin. "Put some music on. Something fast and wild. Who do you have?"

Guy contemplated their choices, his face an absolute of intensity. "I've always liked Toby Dannon, one of the first truly *cool* rock-pop artists. Remember him?"

Anna, swaying, looked up astutely into space, her fingers drumming her chin.

"Toby Dannon, yeah, from the sixties. OK! He's cool. He's cool. Let's do Toby Dannon."

She giggled at her choice of words. Guy thought giggles coming from Anna seemed peculiar but cute.

He searched through a box of CDs beside his desk and found *The All-Time Favorite Hits of Toby Dannon.* The moment he inserted it into his stereo, the music charged the room.

"Hey there, it was quite a scare,
Strolling from my shower bathroom.

Bare as a babe, as disaster loomed,
All my friends were waiting there.
All my friends were waiting there."

To the pulsing rhythms of the song, which released a surge of childhood memories in Guy, Anna howled and punched and kicked in exaggerated martial art movements, her spoof of Bruce Lee and B Chinese action films, and then contorted her body and shook violently as if being electrocuted. She fell to the floor, squirming and rolling in tortuous death throes.

"I like dying to music," she deliriously moaned.

Few can die to, or for, art more masterfully than Anna, Guy thought. *It seems natural to her.*

Guy stomped and bounced across the floor, his limbs jerking in sharp, abrupt movements like a spastic robot. He held his arms straight and rigid at his side and jumped up and down, rapidly bobbing his head like a demented jack-in-the-box.

"A Guy-in-the-box," he shouted.

Anna, paused from her death throes on the floor, laughed. She bounded back to her feet to meet the challenge.

"Boogie bare, boogie bare,
All night until the naked dawn.
Boogie bare, boogie bare,
All night until the naked dawn."

With absolute passion and fevered commitment, they tried to out goofy dance each other. Guy was the more experienced at being foolishly goofy whereas Anna was more adept at being theatrically goofy. Guy, being naturally the less graceful and coordinated of the two, and in a rare instance when awkwardness was an asset, created the most insane expressions of nonsense.

He won.

A slow, romantic ballad next swooned from the stereo.

"Beyond, the stars of light,
Her vision dazed the night.
A mind dream, I thought dismayed,
But no, she flow-danced there,
Perfumed, with streaming hair."

Anna wrapped her arms around Guy, pressing tight against his body, and swayed in a sensual dance. She almost melded into him, and he felt her muscles rubbing against his. Guy was not an accomplished dancer. His movements at first were simple and timid; a step forward, then back, and a gentle swaying to the libidinous rhythms of the song. But he luxuriated in the warmth of Anna's body and the arousing massages by her thighs against his legs. Anna did not miss a movement or a moment, perfectly synchronized with her partner.

"The girl.

My heart, my life, my dream,

Dancing in that captured night,

Beyond, the stars of light.

A vision upon my shore.

Beyond, the stars of light.

My love in that awakened night!"

Guy experienced the rare and euphoric sensation of release. The boundaries of his body became fainter, moving without his effort, flowing with the music and Anna. At moments he felt he experienced what it was like to be Anna, how she actually *became* the music, and her feelings and passion. *How strange but marvelous!*

His steps grew broader and more graceful, and he circled the floor, carrying Anna with him.

"Beyond, the stars of light.

My love in that awakened night!"

Anna felt delighted, sensing Guy's joyful emancipation. "Now you dance!" she commented. She took a step back creating room for charged interplay, allowing them to more intensely experience both themselves and their partner, as in a tango, a dancer's choreography for passion.

Then she took command. Guy happily surrendered.

Anna was a masterful dancer. She positioned his left hand on her waist, extended his right arm outward and led him in a classic waltz, gracefully sweeping and circling the floor. Guy was amazed that he had absolutely no difficulty following her steps. He just glided with her as if on a cushion of air.

This is what it is to dance, he reflected and smiled unabashedly. *Never before have I truly danced.*

"My love in that awakened night!"

During a rotation, they looked into each other's eyes and smiled, both aware that they shared rare feelings. Anna never felt so gracious, Guy never so romantic.

Anna stopped moving and pulled tight against Guy, wrapped in his body. She hummed softly to the music and rested her head on his shoulder, then moaned deliriously. Guy looked at her dreamy, blissful face.

I could stay in this moment forever with Anna in my arms. And be happy!

As he pressed tightly against her, his mind and body lifted far above them. Guy floated.

Anna fell asleep in his arms, her smile serene.

Anna is a peaceful, sleeping angel, he thought. Guy was pleased that she trusted him enough to be so vulnerable—intoxicated, asleep, and pressed so close against him, her friend.

"I will not betray you," he whispered in her ear, feeling quite the gentleman.

"Why not, lover boy?" A hideous, witch's voice screeched in his head. "This is your big opportunity! The only one you'll probably ever get."

The protracted laugh of a second voice, higher and shriller, echoed in Guy's skull. "You'll never be her lover. She thinks you're pathetic!"

A chorus of demonic laughs ensued.

"She'd rather make love to sicko android man. Or herself." A childish, screechy voice heckled. "Android man rather than pathetic, no-man!"

Then the first voice again taunted.

"Loser Guy, to despair wed. Never his love to take in bed. No breasts, no loins, no trembling flesh. Only sad dreams until his death."

Guy's fists clenched tightly. He became confused. The veins on his neck gorged with anger.

"Look, Guy. Look how tender and sensual and so surrendered Anna is," a man's voice spoke, more rational. "Don't be afraid, Guy. Wouldn't you like to love her? She would enjoy it. A lovely Dionysus, she adores love. She wants you, Guy. Take her. Now!"

Guy looked at Anna in his arms, her body so soft and succumbed, her face so lovely. His anger became desire, deep from some empty but waiting, and wanting, place. Slowly he rubbed his hand down Anna's back and along the curve blending into her buttocks. He felt delirious.

Perhaps this saner voice is correct, a voice of truth, he reasoned. *Perhaps Anna wants me to love her fully as a man loves a woman. Yes! Of course! Every woman wants love. And tonight she is Dionysus, a god of pleasure, and she is with me. Anna waits.*

"Yes! Yes!" The voices chanted.

Guy nodded. *Yes! Anna, with her clever humor, would communicate her desires through such a persona, such a game. Of course! Anna's game of love. I've been such a fool.*

Guy remembered her delirious moan as she pressed tightly against him. Images of lovemaking excited his mind and flesh. *Maybe she would awaken to delightful pleasures.* He imagined Anna, thrilled, whispering one word: ecstasy. No, two words: ecstasy and Guy.

Guy gently placed his hand on her shoulder and slid it slowly down the swell of the bare top of her breast, which heaved beneath his touch. The warmth of her flesh felt so good. It reminded Guy of how deprived he had been of love and intimacy. *I am a man,* was his simple thought.

"Good, Stud Guy! Take her now. She wants it. Enjoy her. Finally! Take her! Take her!" The demon voices cajoled and applauded, rising in volume until they screamed in his mind like a demented Greek chorus.

"Take her!"

Then, an awful black feeling engulfed him. *No! This is not right. I will not betray Anna.* He removed his hand from her breast and whispered into her ear.

"Sorry, Anna."

Again he looked at her face, that intriguing, androgynous, goddess face, serene as a child. She appeared so alluring. A torment of conflicting desires and guilt wrenched him.

"It is all right, Guy." A woman's voice spoke in his head, one angelic and compassionate. "You will not harm her. Anna is safe with you. You love her. Trust yourself."

Almost mystically, the consoling voice assuaged his anguish. Behind it the other hideous voices, mad chatter in his mind, attempted to dominate the gentler one, but they gradually ebbed into a distant and quiet space.

Quickly, before conflict reasserted, Guy lifted Anna in his arms. Although she was a hearty woman, she felt surprisingly light. He carried her to the bed in the corner of the room and gently laid her down, placing a pillow under her head, and kissed her on the cheek.

"You are safe with me, Anna. I will not betray you. Ever! I love you." He stroked her hair softly. "I give you to Morpheus, god of dreams. May you sleep peacefully in his arms."

He pulled a blanket over her.

Guy walked to the adjacent corner of the room and sat on the floor, wrapping his arms around his knees. He rocked slowly. The leaves of a large plant brushed his arm like a friend. He looked at it and smiled. Above his left shoulder a window opened to a luminous night of silhouetted buildings and serene, glimmering stars.

Guy watched Anna sleeping—a child of life, safe in its womb. He felt proud that he had made the proper decision. He had not betrayed love. The insane voices had just disoriented him. He now wanted only to sleep, to share Anna's peace. His lids closed over eyes that had seen a night both joyous and treacherous. *Such is life,* Guy conceded. A heavy drowsiness pulled him down.

A rustling, scratching sound clawed his consciousness alert. He opened his eyes and jolted. A huge, dark insect form loomed over Anna, its thin, spiny legs caging her defenseless body. It resembled a monstrous ant creature as large as the length of the bed. But this was no ant from a kid's ant farm.

Guy gasped, unable to move or speak. The intruder slowly turned its giant, oval head and stared at him with protruding, dome eyes, black, glistening, and terrifying.

"I am the Counter Self," it communicated telepathically in a resonant and hollow voice. "All in you and her that counters the blood and flesh, life and joy. And love. I am your despair and her destruction. It is my time!"

Its hideous head turned back to Anna, staring down at her unsuspecting face. The three oval segments of its body arched up as when a creature is about to descend on its prey. Two gigantic pincers with jagged, razor edges, extending from its jaws, opened and lowered around Anna's skull, preparing to cut and crush it like a melon in a sharpened vise.

In a nightmarish way, the creature appeared to smile.

A thought raced through Guy's mind. *I kill love.*

He heard a cracking sound and saw gleaming spurts of blood splash from Anna's head.

"No!" he screamed about to leap to his feet.

The insect creature vanished. Anna stirred on the bed but was not harmed.

Guy, his eyes petrified with horror, sat still and silent, afraid to move as it might evoke another waiting demon. He wrapped his arms again around his legs and rocked, and rocked, staring into the empty space above Anna.

He wondered if he was doing things terribly wrong. A hallucination. First the voices and now this! *I am getting worse.* A feeling of cold dread assaulted, and he felt nauseous.

"Damn, it's happening," Guy mumbled. He experienced a potent impulse to run to the bathroom cabinet to get his medications but defied it.

Not yet. His face steeled with conviction. *I will not be intimidated to surrender by mad specters in my mind—things that do not even exist. There is spirit. There is love. And they can give strength. I will deal with this!*

Guy coiled into a fetal position on the floor and searched his mind for the kind and reassuring voice he had heard earlier, but now he only found silence and darkness, *the family I often return to.* He surrendered to that, in which there was a degree of welcomed solace.

"I have had enough," he groaned. "Just let this night end."

After shadowy and cutting passages of time, he fell asleep. He was slipping below the line.

Chapter 11

GUY AND ANNA visited Forest Garden Cemetery.

The antiquated green Toyota gracelessly drove through imposing iron gates and penetrated the cemetery in quest of its truths. Anna again borrowed her friend's car, that deathless soul in a car persona as she fondly perceived it. Guy had developed an affinity for the battered and clanky vehicle, it seeming a kindred spirit. In exchange for the loans, Anna assisted the owner, Jeffrey, on a performance piece he was creating about innocence corrupted by possessiveness. Her friend considered the more experienced artistic input of the older Anna extremely valuable, but Guy suspected he was also enamored of its source, Anna being creative, attractive, and more mature, but she revealed no interest in him other than as a friend and artistic colleague. Whatever the situation, as a friend, Guy tried to be impartial and unaffected, and yet was affected. So he tried accepting being affected and was more affected. Guy accepted that no matter what, he would be affected.

"And what do you call this persona?" Guy asked when he first viewed Anna that morning.

"The Elegant Death Persona," Anna replied proudly.

Elegant sexy death, Guy assessed. She wore a long sleeved black silk dress that sleekly contoured her body down to her ankles with one side provocatively slit up to her hip revealing a shapely leg in a black stocking. Her customary deep cleavage, even bolder than usual, revealed a healthy though paled bosom, more a celebration of lustful life than the morbid enervations of death. On her hands were thin, black gloves, on her feet black shoes. The costume reminded Guy of the

TV vamp Elvira, Mistress of the Dark, and it evoked the same enticed response.

All of the exposed flesh of Anna's body, her bosom, neck, and face, was cosmetically paled to the anemic pallor of a corpse. Her wavy hair and lips were black, and her eyes were framed in gray accenting the hollows of their sockets. Guy thought Ms. Elegant Death both alluring and morbid.

Sex and death, he mused. *That disturbing and intriguing association I have often seen in culture and have experienced in myself. The inevitable communion between Eros and Thanatos.*

Guy understood well the implication. If any human fully surrendered to his most powerful sexual longings, it must be accompanied by a death. To love deeply of the flesh and passions is to succumb to the beast and to, in some form, die. Guy suspected that with Anna it would be a beautiful death and a possible rebirth into something exciting but dangerous.

"Anna, your persona captures that powerful and eternal marriage of sex and death."

"As it should," she replied. "And one that I think you will find most appropriate for Forest Garden Cemetery."

Anna the death mistress, her mortal companion Guy, and the aged Toyota, overdue for its last rites, drove the peaceful, winding roads of the cemetery on a Sunday afternoon. The cemetery was an immense, lovely sprawl of grassy hills, trees, gardens, monuments and statuary, reminding Guy of a huge Hollywood fantasy movie set or a staged mock-up of heaven. It was so idealized and manicured as to make him uneasy, raising suspicions of an elaborate subterfuge.

What dark and dreadful secrets might it conceal?

They stopped and left the car to observe a hilly expanse of the cemetery park, the graveyard as Guy enjoyed referring to it. As far as his eyes could see was green grass and trees, half of their leaves hued with the orange and gold of fall and the remainder with the emerald green of perennials. Immediately he was surprised by the lack of any distinguishing gravestones that generally populated cemeteries and gave each interred resident an expression of individuality. Here all lay beneath the same ubiquitous rectangular brass plaques, flat on the ground, inscribing, but not defining, its tenant with identical, common words. Hundreds, thousands of them, tightly patterned in endless and eerie rows. *A burial hive. A metaphor,* Guy the poet thought. They announced to the universe, 'Here in death all are equal and nobody is anyone.'

And the cemetery's shadows seemed especially abysmal and black.

Guy and Anna traversed the grassy hills checkerboarded with the metallic plates. The air was bracing and fragrant. Birds flew lethargically overhead. It was a pastoral scene of serene escape. Guy selected at random from the sea of death one grave, one plaque, inscribed with the name 'Catherine Mathews', the number designation of her existence, '1934 to 1996', and a generic capitulation of her life, 'Beloved wife and mother'. His vision looked beyond his eyes.

The orator and ham, inspired by a flair of drama and memories of Hamlet, spoke. "Who be this woman, this Catherine, once so alive and beauteous, so of this world? Now a mute resident to dirt and cold plaques. How many eyes saw you when you walked among us? How many minds reflected you? How many hearts loved you?" Guy perused the cemetery. "Did you once stroll these hallowed grounds, musing on your awaiting home, and fate, and think, 'one day'?

"Catherine Mathews, where be now your passions and laughter, your kisses and prayers, your faith? Emptied into the earth, acknowledged by six words on a brass square."

Guy looked into the sky. "Let her be." His play-game oddly disturbed him.

Anna, observing, grinned. "Alas, poor Catherine!"

She shook her head despondently and then took Guy's hand, squeezed it and pulled him from the somber scene.

But it was not the presence and reminders of death that haunted Guy as they walked the lovely, groomed hills but rather their absence. All references or suggestions of dying were cloaked, hidden by an aesthetic, pastoral fantasy. A splendid denial.

"No terrifying yet wondrous mystery, no rebirth, no resurrection, no transcendent cycles of existence," he remarked. "Only metal plaques on invisible graves."

Anna applauded. "Profoundly spoken, but lighten up! Forgo your solemn demeanor, Guy, for there are delights that await you. Perhaps not profound, but fun." She paused, her vamp's face a jester's mask. "Yes, fun."

She broke into a lively dance-run, bounding across the grassy swells, pulling Guy to other truths.

They returned to their car and drove deeper into the rolling hills. Guy had the peculiar feeling they were lost.

"We drive into a world both divine and sinful," Anna teased with a glee incongruous with her persona's death pall.

The green Toyota belched a gaseous comment, and Guy whistled the music from the old Twilight Zone TV show.

Within minutes he discovered some of those delights, and sins, that Anna heralded. For everywhere, everywhere throughout the graveyard were splendid naked men and women, scores of them to delight his eyes and fantasies—reproductions of classical statues, most Greek or Roman, with perfect form and beauty, unabashedly bare, no doubt slyly chosen as much for their eroticism as their art.

Guy looked at Anna and smiled wryly. "Perfect! Naked maidens and men playing over mortals' graves in the Valley of Death."

Anna flapped her winged eyelashes in agreement, and they both laughed.

Guy had not seen so many naked men and women at one time since last he viewed a porno film.

They stopped and examined the treasures more intimately. Virile gods and sensual goddesses, most marble and life size. Perfect and immortal, not a wart or ripple of fat. Anna delighted in their immodest forms and was not the least timid about running her hands across the smooth buttocks and rippled muscles of the nude male idols.

"They feel nice, Guy. Touch them and fantasize."

Therapy for the body and soul, Guy reasoned. As his eyes indulged the curves and breasts and posteriors of the young goddesses, his hands touched their reality.

"Call it art or call it eroticism," he declared. "Truth is in the eye of the beholder."

"And I behold both!" Anna chuckled as she playfully kissed a male god's loin.

She tapped Guy's arm, directing his attention to an elderly white-haired couple standing nearby, observing them. Their complexions were pallid, disengaged from the blood and marred with brown age spots. The man was in a drab gray suit, the woman in a plain beige dress. Her eyes glared at Guy and Anna reproachfully. The aged gentleman smiled and nodded.

"We are immodest souls," Anna announced and did not cower.

When the woman looked away, the ageless gentleman ran his hand along the buttocks of a goddess sculpture and then smiled at Anna, fireflies in his eyes.

"So, Guy, do you like it? The cemetery?" Anna queried.

"Oh yes, indeed!" Guy smiled unabashedly. "Thank the gods for covert expressions of repressed eroticism. It redeems even the most sanctimonious."

They noticed a sculpture of a young maiden, fully and modestly clothed in her Grecian tunic, appearing virtuous and pristine. Although lovely, she seemed eternally lonely and sad standing in the midst of her lusty companions.

"Loser," Anna remarked.

Surveying the cemetery, Guy realized it was a rarity. He felt pleased that the park and works were there. The statues *were* splendid reproductions of classic artworks, much of which the public might otherwise never see, regardless of any covert intentions involved in their displaying. The critic in him momentarily tempered. *And we're having fun.*

Anna stood beside a statue of a handsome nude god with a sunray in his hand, who Guy believed to be Helios, the bringer by chariot of the sun to Earth each day.

"I feel like removing all my clothes, Guy, and being nude with this splendid god. I, the naked, sensual goddess! I don't care if we're in public." She looked down at her gown. "But I won't. I don't want to disarray my persona. Alas! Otherwise . . . ." She grinned.

Guy was not certain if he was disappointed or relieved. Anna assumed an erect and proud pose beside the deity, partially lifting each of her arms. Her right hand raised higher and extended out, as if welcoming an onlooker, or perhaps inviting him to a sublime encounter. It was a pose of sensual grace, an expression of integrity combined with inner beauty.

"One day I will be immortalized as an exquisite sculpture," she immodestly proclaimed. "Naked and splendid."

Guy believed her absolutely, but unease tightened his stomach muscles. *If women were sculptures,* he thought.

Anna's eyes brushed the cemetery. "Always I yearn," she whispered.

Guy and Anna returned to the car and drove further into the cemetery's enigmatic soul. Around a curve, rising from the rolling hills, appeared another wonder, a monumental god.

"Wow!" Guy exclaimed as they left the vehicle and approached the reproduction of Michelangelo's David, standing like the reigning deity of the cemetery.

"I didn't realize it was so large." he exclaimed. "Large and magnificent! Photographs fail to communicate its power."

"It is spectacular!" Anna concurred. "Oh David! Human god thy truly be."

They circled the perfect and noble representation of man, as tall as a giant, viewing it from all perspectives.

"And God created man in his image," Guy sermonized.

"We have such an exquisite and handsome God," Anna delighted.

The idol statue stood three times the size of a tall man in an enclave surrounded by brown walls with bronze plaques, each plaque engraved with a depiction of a portion of David's story. Surrounding plants and flowers contributed a garden ambiance.

David's nude form was masculine yet aesthetic, his musculature strong yet graceful, his face handsome and proud. The band of his lethal slingshot hung over his left shoulder and down his back.

Guy read an information tablet stating that the statue of David was perfectly balanced as he stood moments before confronting his giant foe, Goliath. His pose displayed strength and purpose, and an infinite faith and trust in God.

Guy saw that there was no intention to piously cloak anything. *This is the splendor of man—God's and Nature's creation.* Even his huge genitalia were a respectful and accurate expression of matured design, properly proportioned and shaped.

Anna's response to the sculpture was multifold. Anna the artist was enthralled by the ideal form and beauty of the magnificent work and the determined effort required by Michelangelo to create it. Anna the student of life analytically studied the ideal of human anatomy. Anna the woman was excited by viewing such a hunk of a man, huge and naked, with his handsome face, strong muscles, divine buttocks, and gargantuan male organ. She had a fantasy.

"I wonder if a woman, like me, of my size, could actually make love to a giant man, this enormous and perfect, three times normal size? Could that work?"

Anna tried to imagine the logistics, the positionings and pleasuring.

"I think you would find a way, Anna."

They laughed, sensing that David laughed, too.

Still enraptured, they pulled themselves away from the impressive icon and walked the hillside. They found a grassy spot where they could rest.

"Don't sit on one of the metal grave plaques," Guy cautioned. "We don't want to leave here cursed."

Beside them stood a majestic tree that reached toward the clouds, its branches twisted and its leaves viridian green. In a strong yet softest of voices, Guy heard the tree speak.

"As wondrous as man is, and as magnificent as is the mighty David, I, Nature, still tower over you. Be humble."

"But can you create a sculpture celebrating yourself?" Guy challenged.

The tree laughed. "I too, must be humble."

Guy was humble enough to listen to the wisdom of the tree.

Anna kept looking at the statue of David in the distance.

"I think I'll come here more often," she stated. "I confess it's giving me a thrill. It's been a while since I've even seen a naked man intimately, by my own choice, except for robot man. *That* was more confusion than intimacy."

Guy was surprised by her spontaneous confession although he had already known it.

"You know Anna, now that I think about it, it's been a while since I've seen a real, naked woman. By choice also. Or so I chose to believe."

Both laughed.

"We're a couple of true sexual libertines." Anna joked. "No wonder we're reacting to the statuary like post-adolescents. We're fixating."

"And desperate."

A moment of quiet.

"I think we're waiting," Guy spoke. "But that can certainly change at any moment."

"And I believe it will."

Guy detected a subtle but real promise in the smile that accompanied her statement and he smiled. Then his expression hardened, falling cold.

"Are we playing games, Anna?"

She looked at him compassionately, her eyes tender. A breeze rustled a few strands of hair across her blanched face.

"Probably. I tend to be seduced by games, like my personas. It's one way I work things through."

Guy did not respond, reflecting on her answer.

"Sometimes people have to be patient with me," she elaborated. "But I believe I've been honest with you."

Guy nodded. "Yes Anna, you have. And I am creating my situation. There are plenty of women in this world. Perhaps that waiting is also a game. But I do not want any more superficial or disappointing relationships." He paused, remembering. "Not that I've had that many. But I wait for truer love."

"Ah! The truer and purer love ideal." Anna's voice teased lightly. "But does this goddess, so true and pure, exist? Will she arrive, and if she does, will you know her?"

"Yes. She does, she will, and I will. I will know her, as well as I know you."

Anna smiled, her lips a black crescent. "You are a sweet soul, Guy."

Quiet followed. They enjoyed the beauty and tranquility of the park. *I prefer it as a park, rather than a graveyard,* Guy concluded.

Cawing cries pierced the sky. Guy and Anna looked up. Black streaks slashed the blue as several crows circled above the cemetery grounds.

"Crows are not a common sight in the Los Angeles area," Anna remarked, tracking their flight, pleased by their aerial show.

"Crows are considered by many to be mystical birds," Guy tutored. "Carriers of one's soul after death. So perhaps their appearance here is not surprising."

"I wonder whose souls they're carrying."

"*Our* souls," Guy replied. "Perhaps we are dead. This is how the dead are introduced to their fate. It's their awakening. They find themselves sitting in a cemetery watching crows carry off their souls."

"Eerie," Anna moaned.

One of the crows swept down and landed on the shoulder of David. Against the sculpture's massive form, it looked like a little dark demon slowly flapping expansive wings. Then it lifted off and flew back into the sky.

"Oh, oh!" Anna bewailed. "David lost his soul."

The crow circled over them. Guy watched its path. Suddenly the bird swooped down and dived toward Anna. Guy startled and tensed. Anna saw it coming and frightened. Then, as by some innate instinct, she extended her arm. The large black bird landed on it, appearing like an ominous shadow rising from her arm.

Shocked, motionless, Anna stared mutely at the bird. It cocked its head and its ebony eyes stared piercingly into hers. Then it cawed and expanded its wings like a black unfolding cape, lifted off and vanished into the sky.

Anna remained still and silent. Guy's expression astonished.

"What the hell was that?" She finally spoke.

"I don't know. It was strange. Are you all right, Anna?"

"Yeah, I'm fine. Just . . . startled."

A silent lapse.

"Anna."

"Yes?"

"Do you still have your soul?"

Anna looked down at her body and then stared straight ahead, sensing. "I think so."

"Good."

Their expressions perplexed.

Moments passed. Guy had a peculiar feeling, as if he was moving into a dimension of unreality. He examined his surroundings, verifying his location. Then he looked at the statue of David, standing so noble and proud in the center of its honorary enclave.

Why had Michelangelo made David so large? Guy pondered. *Were he a man of normal dimensions, would he not be just as noble?* Guy surmised it was a bold decision to create David so huge, for at the same moment that it deified man, it defied and challenged the gods. 'I am the true god,' it seemed to proclaim to the world.

"Anna, I wish I could discard both humility and self-negation and just tower over this world as a magnificent god giant, like David. I would have stature."

Anna displayed her mysterious Mona Lisa smile. An intriguing look possessed her as if a secret design was formulating in her mind.

"Perhaps you can."

In a peculiar move, she extended her arms forward and placed her hands on the ground, palms down. Suddenly a cloudy film obscured Guy's vision. He felt faint and closed his eyes. Something in a deep recess of his mind, a place of both enchantment and madness, opened. He heard a soft voice in his head, not one of the hideous, demonic voices that had recently taunted him, but the other voice, the gentle and sweet one he called the Angel's voice.

"So it shall be," she whispered.

Guy's consciousness grayed and he felt as though he was dropping and dropping into a gentle morass as if he was falling asleep, falling asleep . . . .

He opened his eyes. Anna was slowly raising her hands from the ground, and he was growing and growing.

He stiffened, astonished. As Anna continued lifting her arms upward as in the gesture of a tree growing toward the sky, Guy became larger and larger. Confused, he rose to his feet and took steps to the side to maintain his balance. It was as if the ground between his feet was shrinking. Anna kept dropping below him. In seconds he was larger than any of the trees surrounding him in the cemetery, and he grew bigger and bigger. The valleys and hills of the park became small ripples and bulges beneath him.

Finally, it ended. Guy was a half-mile tall, towering like an incredible mammoth man over the cemetery and all surrounding areas.

"My God!" He exclaimed aloud, dizzy from the extraordinary transformation. "I'm huge!"

His voice pounded across the landscape like rolling thunder. He looked down. Anna stood far below, appearing about one quarter of an inch high, waving her arms at him. From the distance he heard tiny voices.

"A giant! A giant man!"

He clearly heard them for as his dimensions grew his ears became monstrous receivers detecting the slightest of sounds.

"A giant naked man!" One small boy yelled.

Giant *naked* man? The words echoed in Guy's mind. Then he realized what was right before his vision, but he had not perceived in his disorientation. Between his feet were tiny cloths. As he had grown, his clothes had not. They had quickly torn and fell from his body. He was towering over the cemetery and surrounding city a half-mile tall . . . and naked!

Instinctively he placed both of his hands over his pubic area. He looked around. Everywhere—in the cemetery, in the streets, in the yards of the surrounding urban neighborhoods—people were standing and pointing at him. Some were motionless, in shock, others excited, or frantic.

"A giant man!" "Look at the naked giant!" He kept hearing them shout. Guy felt enormously self-conscious, standing so huge, larger than any physical object in the Los Angeles area. He could not believe or make sense of what had occurred. He stared down at his body and then at the people around him. They were like the tiniest of toys.

It is true. Everything else is small, and I am huge. Huger than huge!

Guy suddenly felt foolish, standing so exposed, so colossal, trying to hide his natural privates, like a naked character in a silly comedy struggling vainly to preserve his modesty, but more dramatically so! He looked at the statue of David, now the size of half his thumb, and remembered how nobly and proudly David bore his massive form.

What the hell! Guy moved his hands to his sides. Then he reached his arms toward the sky, as if beckoning the heavens.

"Behold the man before you!" He trumpeted boldly, his voice booming like the roar of a dozen jets. Buildings shook. Dogs placed their tails between their legs and ran. People scattered, some screaming. All heard.

Guy knew he was no David. He did not possess the perfection of David's form, *but what the hell! I still be a man, of flesh, and much, much huger than even the marble icon.*

Guy perused the surrounding terrain. In front of him, north, he viewed the cities of Glendale and Pasadena and their bordering mountain ranges, forested and lovely. A blue lake shimmered. To his left were the hills and woods of Griffith Park, a slither of the Hollywood sign and the narrow, congested streets of Hollywood. Beyond it, West Hollywood and a blurred strip he knew was Santa Monica. He even saw the hazy blue of the Pacific Ocean.

What an incredible vision! It reminded him of the view of the landscape as a jet descended for landing. Behind him was the city of Los Angeles, his home, profiled by its monolithic buildings and freeways and urban sprawl. With a boyish grin, he spotted the apartment building where he lived in the mid-Wilshire area. The sparser East L.A. communities faded into the distance to his right.

Look at me, L.A.! He felt like shouting but feared the resonance of his voice might fracture the nearer buildings if he had not done so already, so he merely delighted in the thought. But for some peculiar reason, he spoke a thought to the astonished spectators below.

"I am just a nobody."

Some of the people applauded. Others shook their heads in disagreement. Guy felt like he was a god to all the regions and people. The common man's god.

"It is a clear and lovely day in Southern California," he broadcast, mimicking a newscaster to his public. There was a chorus of cheers.

He noticed a Metro bus, a white and yellow capsule about the size of a Zippo lighter, driving on Beechwood Avenue, past the cemetery entrance. It was apparently unaware of him for most of the vehicles in the vicinity were halted, their passengers disembarked and gawking. He bent over and picked up the bus, being careful not to turn it from its upright position and injure the passengers. It was like a minuscule Tinker Toy in his fingers. He held it close to his face and through the bus windows saw the tiny, astonished faces of the passengers, each smaller than a mole on his arm, their expressions frozen in both terror and disbelief. An elderly woman with a wrinkled face and limp white hair stared back at him, her jaw dropped and her eyes as wide as full moons. Guy winked at her and smiled.

He remembered King Kong from the classic horror film lifting a train car off its track and glaring into its windows to the terror of the passengers. A sudden impulse of both power and cruelty swept Guy as he realized how easily he could crush the tiny bus in his hand. It surprised him, but in an unsettling way, it was also gratifying. A mere decision, over which he had absolute control, and the tensing of a few muscles of his hand, and the fate of the passengers and the lives of their families and friends would be forever altered. Never had he experienced such extraordinary power—the power of a killer, the power of a god! But the impulse was swiftly quelled and replaced by another, the desire to be gentle to the frail humans, his kindred. He was not a killer, nor a god.

Instead I give them an amazing experience, he thought, *one that they can recount to loved ones during holiday dinners and living room reunions for the rest of their lives. The day the giant godman held them helpless in his grasp. An incredible moment in their and L.A.'s, history!*

So it was a friendly smile that he presented to the astounded passengers, and a shrug of his shoulders, communicating 'who can explain it?' Very gently he placed the bus back on the road.

The passengers spilled out. Most ran frantically in a direction away from Guy, looking repeatedly over their shoulders, which they probably would continue doing for days afterward. The white-haired lady, more composed than the others, calmly walked to the sidewalk and then turned toward Guy, the giant naked man. She stared at him, all of him, for moments, and then her face appeared to express a peculiar thought. *Jesus! Now that's big! If I was in my younger days and was a lot taller, a lot taller . . . .*

She smiled at Guy and waved, and he returned the gesture.

A massive traffic jam congested the surrounding areas with people outside their vehicles staring at him. They were also out of their homes and office buildings, gazing in disbelief at the phenomena before them. Guy realized he had quickly become a communal event. Significant!

Their almost microcosmic mouths flapped and their arms waved. Some appeared terrified and fled from the scene, bumping people and tripping on curbs or over their own feet, panicking. But Guy suspected most knew they were in a Moment, a bizarre but incredible historical moment, like a major earthquake, or the assassination of J.F.K. If someone was filming it, they would be the people, the witnesses in a filmed footage that would be viewed with disbelief for ages.

He was giving them that special gift, and he, Guy, generally a nobody to this world, was the star! He had a feeling that was rare in his life, a feeling of great stature, of truly being somebody, an enormous and significant presence in the world.

Damn! That feels good! He now knew how it felt to be a celebrity or a superstar.

"I am Guy!" He announced to all onlookers. Many among the masses applauded. "Guy," he repeated, his voice thundering across the land. He was heard.

Guy then realized that many of the people were waiting, waiting to see his intentions, whether he be friend or foe. Slowly he turned in all directions and waved to the people. "Friend," he spoke. "Do not fear."

Some of the little, little people waved or applauded. "He's a friendly giant or god," he heard one teenage girl shout. Guy thought of the Jolly Green Giant in the frozen vegetable TV commercials he had so often seen as a child. It provoked a whimsical delight, and he could not resist. He placed his hands on his hips, stood tall, and spoke in his deepest voice, "Ho ho ho." His salutation bellowed across the terrain as if broadcast from a super-amplified speaker. Below, some of the children placed their hands over their ears.

"Shoot the big son of a bitch!" He heard one man yell. Guy considered squashing him but did nothing.

He became slightly unbalanced and took a stabilizing step. A small but distinct crushing sound rose from the ground as his left foot flattened a gold Mercedes Benz convertible.

A man in a gray suit standing nearby, the owner, Guy assumed, shouted curses. "Goddamn giant!"

"Ooops, sorry." Guy apologized but could not resist a smile.

A little dark blur, like a fly, moved in the air before his vision. Then it stilled, suspended, and when Guy focused more closely on it, he saw it was a tiny, tiny person with flapping dark wings.

"Wow! A little winged demon. How cute."

Guy extended his hand out, palm up, and the diminutive creature, a fraction of an inch tall, landed on it.

"Hello," Guy said, "and I apologize for being so large, for towering over you. Don't be intimidated."

He spoke very softly so his breath would not blow him, or her, off his hand. Then the being lifted from his palm, its wings flapping rapidly. Floating in the air in front of Guy, it grew, larger and larger, and then even larger, until it was half Guy's size. Astonished, Guy's jaw dropped.

"Better?" He, or she, Guy was not sure of its gender, asked.

"Yes, much."

"Welcome, Bro! Pretty cool, huh?" The dark being spoke. "I'm Mondi, Angel Protectorate of Forest Garden."

With immense curiosity, Guy examined the peculiar angel, whom he decided to refer to as a male for his voice was deep and resonant. He had a masculine face with a square jaw, a flat nose and rugged features. His complexion was ebony, his lips pronounced and full, his hair short and wiry, and his eyes dark coffee hued and exotic. The features indicated African descent. His body was definitely and proudly female with a lovely figure and lean, shapely legs, corseted in a tight, black leather garment laced up its front with a leather cord, resembling a kinky bathing suit, as might come from Frederick's of Hollywood. Its cleavage was deeply cut revealing a prodigious bosom, which its owner enjoyed expanding with each breath. Mondi wore black boots and black gloves, cut short, exposing the top half of his fingers. From his back rose huge black leather wings with chrome studs across their surface.

"Kinky, huh?" Mondi stated.

Guy nodded. "I'm Guy. Poet, painter, and now, giant. You're . . . an angel?"

The winged hermaphrodite scowled and then grinned. "It's OK, man. I understand. Yes, I'm an angel." His wings flapped slowly, keeping him afloat. "Every cemetery has one. The original angel here quit. Split! She got tired of all the theatrics and artsy stuff in the cemetery. She just wanted a prayer and serenity gig, you know." He laughed and his face softened, becoming radiant. "God needed an angel who wouldn't be hassled by anything, sooo he gave the cemetery to me! I'm weird anyway." He chuckled. "Pretty cool, huh?"

"Yes. That's wild."

"I'm buried here. Over there." Mondi pointed to a distant slope. "Plaque number 714,724."

"I'm sorry."

"Don't be, Bro. My last human life was a bummer."

Mondi looked down and shook his head. His dark wings kept slowly flapping like a billowing shadow behind him.

"Dig this. I was born of dual gender with features of both male and female. It sucked! If I concealed my body, my feminine figure, in loose clothes, people thought I was a man. If I hid my face behind a mask, as at Halloween, and raised my voice a little, they swore I was a woman. I felt like neither." He grinned. "Sometimes, though, like both. Most of the time, it was a bitch, I struggled all my life with identity problems. 'Lord, what the hell do you want me to be?' I would cry out." He glanced up with a tearful expression at the heavens. "I became a loser, a prostitute to confused Johns, err, clients, and a big time drug user. Real smart. I was in hell! Died from a speedball. You know, street jive for a death ball, cocaine and heroin." He laughed and shook his head. "Doesn't seem so tragic now."

"Sounds rough to me," Guy asserted.

"Well, yeah. When I breathed the last breath of my sad life, I said to God, please, next time, let me be good. I'm sick of all this! It'll kill you, man. Let me help someone." His plaintive eyes peered into the air above Guy. "Then, right after the death of my confused body, I saw two visions before me, like archways, one of darkness, the other of light. I chose the light one. And, to my great surprise, God made me an angel. Isn't that the bomb?"

"Bomb?"

"Yeah, like, pretty trippy, huh?"

Guy stared at him, startled, and more than a little confused. *It's certainly trippy!*

"But, your body form, and your attire. I mean . . . ."

Mondi grinned. "No, no. No matter what anyone may say or think, God's OK. He's cool. First he gave me the virgin lady form, dressed as the white angel. You know, like in paintings and movies. But man! It wasn't me. I couldn't get into it. I didn't say anything, but I frowned and sulked. God understood." Mondi looked again toward heaven. "He told me I could rag out, you know, manifest myself, however I chose, as long as I did my job. There was no required dress code." He laughed a very hearty, male laugh. "Sooo, I chose to maintain my dual sexual form. I thought it would be . . . amusing, and for once, accepted. What gender are angels, anyway? So I created this vibe and costume, dark and sexy." He waved his hand up his body. "It helps remind me of the human drama—life, death, sex, good, evil. Very rad, huh?"

Mondi's laughter carried a unique mixture of pathos and delight.

"At first God was tripped out, but he approved it. Believe me, he understands such things. He's experienced it all, either personally or vicariously. Besides, I can change at will, in an instant, if it's best for the people."

He passed his hand down his chest and, to Guy's surprise, Mondi changed into a beautiful, white virgin angel, pure as the dawn's air, like an archetype from a classical painting.

"It doesn't matter. It's the purpose that's important," the enchanting angel spoke.

He passed his hand up and transformed back into the dual sexed, black leather Mondi.

"But I like this one best."

He spun slowly, shimmying with his arms raised, displaying all sides of his darkly lovely form.

"I suspected you could handle it."

"Yes, I do like your appearance and attire," Guy replied. "It reminds me of one of Anna's personas."

"Yeah, your friend. She's cool! That sexy death trip. I like her."

Guy smiled and looked down at Anna, now sitting, below.

"But what do the people think? Like, now?" He glanced at the crowds.

"Oh, they can't see me. I chose who sees me. Then, if they agree, and want to see me, I appear to them. I can generally tell how they'll respond." His eyes scanned Guy. "Man, you're so big. God sent me a huge god angel."

"What?"

"I've been waiting for you, Bro. I asked God for help. Things have been rough here. Too many people dying, too much grief. Look at the people."

Guy perused the crowds. He could sense their pain.

"Feel it? I help the grieving hearts and souls who come to the cemetery to say farewell to loved ones. But perhaps even more, to confront mortality, that big, final trip, or so they think." Mondi chuckled. "And I help them to keep their faith and to see eternity, the eternal spirit. I give them a touch of God." He smiled proudly. "Sometimes I whisper Beethoven's *Ode to Joy* in their ear at the critical moment or, if they're kids, a rap song, like this: Death is bad, you know man, Baaad! Babes with wings and the Big, Man Rad." Mondi got down into his rap rendition. "Kickin', huh?"

He glanced across the beautiful rolling hills of the cemetery. Then he saddened.

"But of late, hearts and souls are graver, less receptive, more bummed out. Something about modern times. TV, computers, video games, Big Macs, hassles. They dull out the spirit, man! Look what happened to me." He chortled. "Well, God always helps. He sent me you. The biggest of big angels. A big *naked* angel! Don't you see the symbolism, man? Back to basics. Like an old Elvis song or a gospel hymn." Mondi swayed his head and sang. "Amazing grace, how sweet the sound, that saved a wretch like me!"

"But wait!" Guy interrupted. "I'm not an angel. I'm Guy. A poet and a painter, and not even a very successful one. I'm nobody." Guy swept his hand through the air, indicating 'nothing'.

Mondi laughed. "You're so humble. That's cool! I tend to be a bit arrogant myself."

"But, I'm *not* an angel! I'm not even a Christian."

"Neither am I," Mondi replied. "Nor God. It doesn't matter. You don't know that?" He peered curiously at Guy's face. "We serve all spirit and religions. God only cares that you love spirit and serve this world, as you do." He looked at Guy with knowing in his eyes. "You see, that's why God's so cool. He's like the ultimate best friend."

"Yes, I'm sure. But *still*, I'm not an angel, certainly not a god angel. I'm just a man and a very flawed one at that. Think imperfect, then think absolutely imperfect."

Mondi lowered his brow and cocked his head. "But that's often so. Look at who I was. You really don't know these things?"

"Well, no. I don't understand."

Mondi peered into the cloud-painted sky, as if questioning the heavens. He flapped his wings more rapidly, ascending higher, and then looked down at Guy, examining him from a different vantage point. Guy thought he resembled a haunting, shadow vision. Then Mondi descended. His face brightened and his eyes gleamed.

"Wow! You're a virgin, just beginning to awaken." Mondi smiled excitedly. "God sent me a virgin angel. The coolest!"

"A virgin angel?" Guy echoed back.

"Yeah, and so big! Humongous. A big, naked virgin. Even better than our statue of David. This is a day for rejoicing. Hallelujah! Hallelujah!"

Mondi glanced across Guy's nude body.

"God so adores the natural. And you do seem correct in *this* cemetery." Mondi laughed. "OK, you may remain so, naked, if you wish. I certainly don't mind. But trust me on this, Bro." He nodded assuredly. "You may have to dress for some of our subjects. A naked angel would freak them out. And they're already pretty freaked out. It may require white gowns and all. And you'll have to be smaller, no more than twice the size of a human, so they can hang with you . . . you know, relate. That's a good word. You must change your size as you saw me do. You will know how to soon. I hope." His cocoa-hued face skewered. "And we should get you wings. You don't need them, but people believe more if we have them. They expect it. I suggest," he drummed his fingers on his chin, "dove feathers. Yeah, peace and love. That's you, Bro! Very poetic. This is gonna be so kickin!"

Guy was silent as Mondi spoke. He began to wonder. *Could this be true? Me? A god angel? A virgin god angel? It does feel right, somewhat. My change was sudden and seemed . . . inspired. Guy, the angel?*

"It is so, Guy Angel," Mondi confirmed, detecting Guy's thoughts. "And don't worry, man, or bum out. I'll help you. Soon you'll be as exquisite and sane as me!" He chuckled like a Christmas Santa. "All you have to do is awaken. You will see all. You'll love it. Welcome to the coolest party!"

Mondi's eyes shined and his smile gleamed like heaven personified.

A thunderous pounding echoed from the distance.

"Yo, Bro! You have visitors, and I must return to my duties. Grieving but beautiful souls wait." Mondi eyed Guy fondly. "I'm so happy you're here. Awaken, god angel! God has blessed us!" His eyes glimmered radiantly.

Mondi's broad wings flapped gracefully, lifting him up and away. He simultaneously became smaller and smaller.

"Goodbye, Guy Angel. Check you out later. Remember, just keep awakening!" Mondi flew into the distance, reducing his scale until he was his original size, like a dark, angel fairy, and vanished.

Guy stood awed, staring into the sky and wondering. *A god angel?*

A throbbing, thrashing sound sliced the air. Three L.A.P.D. helicopters, looking to Guy like white dragonflies, appeared from the blue of the sky, approaching fast. He did not move as they neared, fearing they might misinterpret any movement or gesture as a threat. Terror seared his mind. He imagined the pilots radioing an Air Force jet squadron to take him down with vapor-streaming missiles.

The copters circled. Guy wondered what might be their protocol for encounters with half-mile tall giants.

Slowly, abrupt motions might be fatal, Guy fluttered his fingers in a playful greeting. "Hi. How are you guys today?"

One of the two inch long micro-toy copters swept closer and hovered in front of his face. Guy smiled. He could see the pilot's incredulous expression. The cool air current swooshing from the whirling propellers suddenly itched Guy's nose. His huge nostrils twitched.

Oh no! Guy pinched his nose tightly with two fingers, but it was hopeless. The sneeze was loud and ferocious, expelling a turbo-charged storm of wind and a violent spray of liquid, seizing the hapless copter and hurling it through the air, descending towards the ground.

"Oh no!" Guy foresaw disaster.

An instant before the copter smashed to earth, it stabilized just enough to abort its fate. It lifted upward and, after a wobbly maneuver, again approached Guy and resumed its orbiting flight around him although at a considerably farther distance.

"Sorry," Guy meekly spoke toward the terrified pilot.

A giant naked man. Big, really big! Guy imagined the pilots reporting on their headsets to the stations, hardly believing the words they spoke.

"This is wild, isn't it?"

A woman's voice spoke behind him. Guy turned, being most careful with his steps, and jolted. Standing behind him was Anna, a *giant* Anna, as tall as he was, and just as naked. The jaws of hundreds of spectators below dropped, as did his. The helicopters swiftly forsook him and fluttered nearer to her.

"Hi!" Her greeting was as immense as she. "How does it feel to have great stature and presence? Isn't this incredible?"

She looked at the surrounding landscape. "Fabulous view! I can even see the Pacific Ocean."

A chorus of excited yells ascended from the tiny Lilliputians below.

"Look! Another one!" "A giant naked lady!" "Wow! A sexy giant naked woman!" "I saw her grow, bigger and bigger!"

Guy perused Anna's bare body. The irony struck him of how, when he finally sees Anna totally nude for the first time, it was in this unquestionably bizarre scenario, and on such a monumental scale. *This is more than a memorable moment!* He could not take his eyes off her. She looked enormously, in more ways than one, sexy. Curvaceous, fleshy, and hugely erotic!

Stirrings excited him, quickly enlivening his body, *his pelvis.* A tribute to Anna began to rise, and Guy began to panic.

Oh please God, not now! Not before the entire city! He imagined his fantasized jet squadron perceiving it as a monstrous terrorist weapon and blasting it off.

Guy did not know that he was not the only male in the crowd to so honor Anna, but he did know his would be rather conspicuous. He was afraid to look down. He was indeed of ungodly size, more than he had ever dreamed of, *in my maddest, macho fantasy,* and becoming more so each arousing moment.

This is not the moment to proudly display my virility. Guy clenched his teeth and chose to believe, in an act of absolute faith and desperation, that there were in the universe gods bigger and more potent than him. He prayed to those gods.

"Please, not now! Spare me!"

With a new surge of strength and an act of will greater than he knew he possessed, he pried his attention off of Anna and onto the sprawling cityscapes surrounding him. He thought of serene days on mountaintops by placid lakes, he in a peaceful meditation. He thought of his body asleep and limp, snoring beneath an apple tree, *anesthetized, numb, rubberized.*

It worked. The uprising quelled. Repose returned to his world, calamity averted.

"Thank you. Thank you," Guy whispered to the heavens.

Apprehensively, he looked back at Anna, but only at her face, one lovely and excited and blissfully unaware of the crisis. He saw that she was not wearing the chalky, macabre persona mask. She stood as her natural self. Part of the mystery, none of it comprehensible.

"How Anna? How is this happening?"

She shrugged. "I don't know. Perhaps your wish and a little magic." She grinned. "Or maybe your Beautiful, Winged Madness."

That answer seemed the most plausible.

"Just enjoy."

So he did. It was not every day, in fact, never, that he could feel he towered over his fellow man. Be it ego or not, it felt good! A godman giant, perhaps even a god angel. He looked down at the masses. Everywhere people stared with awe at them, the gigantic couple, like a colossal Adam and Eve, especially at the gargantuan woman with the lovely face, erotic figure, and sleek legs longer than the height of the tallest high-rise building. Anna towered over the city, splendid and naked, like the perfect Los Angeles icon. *Yes! The true, monumental angel of the City of Angels.*

"You'll probably end up in Playboy from this," Guy remarked with a wry smile.

"On a huge centerfold." Anna laughed with her willingness to embrace all, profound or profane.

Several crows, like tiny black accents and apparently the same ones earlier seen, flew into the sky and orbited them.

Anna's vision tracked their flight. Then she turned to Guy and smiled. She raised her arms straight above her, holding them still for a moment. Guy's vision blurred and he felt dizzy. He closed his eyes and swayed. A deep and mysterious place in his mind seemed to be closing. When he reopened them, Anna was slowly, so slowly, lowering her arms as if mimicking the retracting of a tree into the earth.

Both of them grew smaller. Guy startled. He was shrinking as was Anna before his eyes. The trees below swelled as did the buildings and people and the statue of David, all growing bigger and bigger as he and Anna became smaller and smaller.

Guy kept stepping inward to maintain his balance. Then, instinctively, when he was the size of the neighboring trees, he sat on the grassy flat, as did Anna.

"Guy, wake up! Wake up!"

Anna's voice seeped into his consciousness. He felt his shoulder being shaken and his eyes drowsily opened. Guy looked around at the grassy expanse surrounding him. He and Anna were seated before each other, normal size. Far above them, the crows still circled, like a mysterious portent.

"You seem to have drifted off asleep," Anna stated.

"Asleep? Yes, of course, asleep." His eyes glinted. "I had this strange dream."

"What was the dream? Was it good?"

Was it good? Yes. It actually was. Rather delightful!

"Yes, Anna, it was. We were giants, you and I. Huge, naked gods over the city."

He recounted a summary of his dream, his hands and fingers waving and fluttering as he described Mondi and the helicopters. He omitted the part about his threatening arousal but did commend her on how astonishing she was as the giant goddess of Los Angeles.

Anna smiled affectionately. "It sounds like a wondrous dream. Guy, there's magic and spirit in the air today. Here, in the cemetery, in this home of death and transformation. Can you feel it?"

Guy could certainly sense it.

Then suddenly Guy felt small, so very small and vulnerable. He looked at the statue of David, so confident and strong, and then down at the grass, the tiny slithers of green. They seemed so fragile.

"We are so mortal and frail," he spoke as in a confession.

"But also giants!" Anna shouted and jumped to her feet. "Come. Let's explore more."

Do bigger events await? Guy wondered.

They returned to the humble Toyota, drove deeper into the memorial park, and then stopped and walked some hills. An observation engaged Guy. He noticed the cemetery was filled with a preponderance of Christian symbols and imagery, Christian iconology, especially crosses and Christian figurines in its gardens and around plots of plaques. No Buddhism or Taoism or Islamic or American Indian spirituality. Certainly no shamanism or Day of the Dead. Only classical mythology was offered as an alternative and a barren interpretation at that. Not eternal spirit, but the ephemeral delights of youthful flesh and amusing, metaphorical fables. Relatively innocuous.

The inference was clear and he spoke it.

"If you come bearing the Christian cross, the gates open to you. Bring your sunglasses and suntan oil. No Visa card required. Prepare to party, for you are headed for heavenly paradise. Hallelujah!"

"Right on! Right on!" Anna replied, looking up and swaying with her arms stretched toward that heaven.

"But if ye be a corpse of a different creed," Guy sermonized, "bring some blankets, for these will be cold grounds you lie in! And bring a good book or a boombox, for you'll have a long wait at those pearly gates."

Anna's arms dropped and she gloomily stared at the earth.

"Mondi, where are you?" Guy beckoned into the air. And a thought: *perhaps Forest Garden is truly the graveyard of the Western world.*

They walked to the top of a hill where Guy recited a Buddhist prayer over the cemetery.

"Whatever living beings there are, feeble or strong,

If great and long or medium, if short and small or large,
If seen or never seen, if far away or near,
If born or seeking birth,
May all be blessed with peace!"

Anna performed a sacred Navaho spirit dance, becoming a risen spirit of the earth dancing in the embrace of the sky.

"Anna, where did you learn a sacred Navaho dance?"

"From sacred Navaho Indians."

Of course.

Then. Thunder in the distance, pounding and ominous, rolling toward them. The sky over the cemetery swiftly became a cauldron of blackening clouds as if damnation manifested from nowhere.

"Oh oh! We're in trouble! Better move inside somewhere," Anna urged with a disconcerted glance. "And hide."

Quickly, very quickly, they found refuge in the cemetery gift shop adjacent to a mausoleum. It sold token offerings of the cemetery park's attractions, small, clever graces—statuettes, gift cards, books, knick knacks. No skeleton statues or elegant death masks. Only Anna provided that.

The storm outside hit, smashing the building, pounding its walls and ceiling. Guy and Anna trembled. Guy feared the ferocious winds and rains might kill cemetery visitors caught in its wrath or that demons and sinister spirits might be carried into the cemetery on turbulent airstreams from some hellish netherworld. He prayed.

Anna noticed a girl about ten-years-old, staring at her. She had a pallid complexion, ebony eyes and hair, and wore a black dress that hung loosely from her neck to her ankles. She reminded Anna of the daughter in the *Adams Family* TV show.

"Where can I get a costume like that? It's so cool and wild!" The girl excitedly asked.

"This is my Elegant Death Persona," Anna explained to her young fan. "I made it myself."

The girl's eyes brightened. "Elegant, *sexy* death." She revealed a surprisingly adult perception.

"Future performance artist," Anna remarked to Guy. "Or Death Mistress. I wish I could adopt her."

Anna kept smiling at the little incarnation of herself, and the girl smiled back as did Guy. He could easily see Anna with such a daughter.

"I'm Anna."

"I'm Sage. I'll see you again, somewhere. Bye!" the girl declared mysteriously and walked away.

Anna believed it was true.

Guy spoke with a saleslady seated on a stool behind a display counter. She was an attractive woman in her twenties, sensual with soft auburn hair and sparkling blue eyes. A short skirt fully displayed her shapely, crossed legs.

Rather sexy for a cemetery, Guy noted. *But then, not surprising.*

He was struck by how in this picturesque graveyard, his attention was again drawn to sex. As they spoke, the saleslady pulled at the edge of her skirt attempting to better conceal her legs. She knew.

Guy asked a couple questions about the statue of David in the park. She answered and then pointed to some large sculpture fragments in an adjoining room.

"They are from our original reproduction of David. It stood on the same site where our current one is," the alluring lady informed, her eyes lustrous. "An earthquake broke it, so they brought some of the pieces in here to display."

There was the colossal head of David and his two feet displayed on block stands.

"What happened to David's other parts, like his arms and," Guy paused, peering at the girl, and assessed that she could handle the question, "and his huge genitalia?"

The girl revealed a sly smile and an even brighter gleam in her eyes. She wagged a finger for him to come closer.

"Don't tell anyone I told you this," she whispered, "but the rumor is that one of the cemetery trustees brought David's giant penis home, it's the size of a large sweet potato, and displays it on the mantle over his fireplace. He uses it to help seduce women."

She stopped as if wanting to redeem herself for her indiscretion.

"But that . . . may not be true."

Guy grinned. *Probably is.* He suddenly felt a potent impulse to ask the young lady for a date, but didn't. She smiled at him, and Guy detected a slight tease in her expression. But then, it may have been her acknowledgment of the absurdity of the world they live in.

"The world's funny," she commented, seeming to confirm his thought. Then again, perhaps she was still thinking about the large sweet potato.

Anna purchased a block paperweight with a tiny reproduction of a resurrection of Christ painting beneath its glass. She liked tacky things.

"Guy, let's go to the Last Supper." She tugged at his arm.

They timidly peeked out the exit. The storm had passed, the menacing black clouds retreating. Radiant beams of sunlight penetrated the remaining ones, streaming on the cemetery grounds. One wide ray directly shined on Guy and Anna as they left the building, bathing them in a golden light.

"We and the world are forgiven," Guy announced.

They visited the cemetery's mausoleum, home of the Last Supper. The building's exterior was noble yet quaint, reminiscent of a European church with spires and arched windows. Inside, it impressed Guy the most of all the Forest Garden offerings with its reverential and elegant environment of tan marble walls, ornate Grecian columns, and colorful stained or painted glass windows depicting religious scenarios. A reproduction of Michelangelo's statue of a mighty Moses, bearded, standing tall and muscular, hailed visitors at its entrance.

Cone-shaped urns in rows along the walls interred the cremated ashes of the deceased, each designated by a bronze inscription plaque. That seemed to Guy more sanctified than mass graves in the ground beneath indistinguishable nameplates. Exquisite sculptures and luxurious paintings adorned the rooms and a subdued light graciously illuminated all.

Anna's Elegant Death Persona oddly seemed both an appropriate presence and a violating incongruity, a paradox. But then, Guy mused, is not life and death itself a paradox?

Anna enjoyed posing in her sexy, macabre costume beside the sculptures or before the burial walls.

"Meet your truth and your lie," she spoke and laughed.

The main chapel was dimly lit and silent, inviting souls to prayer and meditation. Light diffused through stained glass windows on the walls and its domed ceiling. Huge gold metal and glass lanterns hung from cables. The room had the poetics of a sacred monastery.

Along the walls were reproductions of some of Michelangelo's most celebrated sculptures including the Pieta, Day and Night, Twilight and Dawn, and the Medici Madonna. Guy felt joy at viewing the works all at one time, in one place. Theater seats faced a wall covered by an immense tan curtain. Guy and Anna took a seat. They were the only audience present, as if attending a private screening, and they waited quietly for the show to begin.

The curtain slowly rolled open, gliding as silently as a snake, and a booming voice resonated from the air. Guy startled and his knees shook. *God speaks!* It sounded like the voice of God echoing in the hollow of the chapel's dome. Guy and Anna apprehensively peeked up.

"Welcome to Forest Garden," the commanding voice greeted. "We are happy you could attend this presentation of our stained glass reproduction of Leonardo da Vinci's masterpiece, The Last Supper."

The opened curtain revealed the reproduction, the size of a wall and illuminated from behind. It was colorful, vivid, and intricate, an impressive feat of art and craftsmanship.

But it is not da Vinci's Last Supper, Guy thought as he beheld the dazzling spectacle. It seemed a crystallized and purified postcard interpretation. Missing was the depth and character of the original artist and artwork and the venerable quality of masterfully applied paint. *Missing was the masterpiece.*

It reminded Guy of a female acquaintance that one knew who was then seen as a model in a fashion magazine ad, airbrushed and idealized. She was lovely indeed in the ad but was not the beautiful woman one knew. Her soul was absent.

"Impressive, attractive, yes," Guy assessed to Anna. "A triumph of spirit and character, like da Vinci's, no! And here we have expressed the culture we, as artists, must create in and for."

Anna nodded. "More a work of pop art than classic fine art."

The narrator related the story of the sadness the Forest Garden founder felt when reading of the deteriorating condition of da Vinci's Last Supper painting. Then a brilliant idea spawned. He became determined to preserve the great masterpiece for future generations in the more permanent form of a stained glass reproduction.

Guy and Anna looked at each other and scowled. Guy was dumfounded by the statement and its naiveté. It seemed incomprehensible that people would believe that a painted masterpiece could be preserved as a glass clone. 'Oh, we may lose da Vinci's masterpiece but despair not! For we have its sparkling glass replacement.'

Then a moment of lucidity provided the answer. *They were confronting the thinking of popular culture.* That was it, encapsulated.

"Anna, we must commit suicide," Guy declared.

"Yes, we will. After the show. I don't want to miss the ending."

The narrator told of the more than five years of arduous work and dedication required by an Italian artisan to realize the glass treasure and related the intriguing and mysterious story of the figure of Judas.

Guy squirmed. "Judas. Whenever I hear a reference to Judas," he confessed, "I'm haunted by a feeling of guilt. I suspect that if I had been one of Christ's original disciples, I probably would have been Judas, the notorious betrayer."

Anna grinned. "That's the innate guilt every human being carries."

"It is the guilt of being removed from your God." A voice deeper and more resonant spoke from somewhere.

Guy startled and looked around. *An imagined thought in my mind.*

"If you do not accept and love me unconditionally, you will carry that guilt," the anonymous voice again spoke. "For you are of me, and I of you."

"What the hell?" Guy looked up and saw nothing but the luminous stained glass windows of the dome. *Voices,* he concluded. *I'm hearing voices again.*

"When the artist attempted to create the figure of Judas," the narration continued, "it broke four times as if it was not intended for the figure of the betrayer to be completed."

Guy shuffled uncomfortably as if it was not intended for him to be comfortable.

"The artist announced that he would make one final attempt to create the Judas figure. If it again broke, he would abandon the project. That attempt succeeded, and the stained glass reproduction was finally finished."

Charming music reminiscent of a TV show theme filled the chapel.

"Truth or myth, or a mixture of both?" Anna whispered.

Pop art. Anna had selected the correct term. In fact, much of the cemetery reminded Guy of an elaborate pop artwork—the recreation of popular symbols and illusions sanctified by a prestigious context: an art gallery *or a memorial park.* Here was David instead of Campbell's Soup Cans, a stained glass Last Supper instead of silk-screened Marilyn Monroes. In essence the same. Andy Warhol meets Jesus. Only in L.A. could such a cemetery exist.

"What an arrogant creature you are!" A deified voice in the air thundered. "Such presumption and disrespect! So critical and condemning!"

Guy trembled and the muscles of his stomach wrenched. Timidly, he looked up.

"You stand upon these sacred grounds where my children rest, like some mighty god, half-a-mile tall and naked, terrifying and awing my people. Judas! You think you are a god? You are a mere subject. A mortal. Like a fish or a worm. And only by my benevolence at that!"

"But, that was a dream," Guy meekly defended although not knowing to whom or what.

"That was *you*! *You* created it."

Guy kept looking up into the talking air, his eyes transfixed and his expression frozen. "Who speaks?" He asked with the voice of a mouse.

"You know who this is. And this time, you will listen! Andy Warhol meets Jesus? Listen, *Bro*," he mockingly borrowed the term, "are you acquainted with the concept of blasphemy?"

"No," Guy squeaked, his eyes now cast on the floor. "I mean, yes."

God roared, shaking the chapel like an earthquake.

"How should I perceive you?" He continued. "Arrogant, prideful, critical, condemning, egotistical, self-centered, hypocritical, despairing, suicidal, selfish, disrespectful, self-pitying. What have I left out? The offenses go on and on! Do you know this human?"

"Ah . . . no. I don't believe so," Guy mumbled.

"We both know him too well!" The Mighty One howled back. "I wish I did not, but I see him squirming before me like a lowly worm."

Suddenly a line of his poetry came into Guy's mind and the thought that sharing it might appease God. In desperation, he boldly looked up and spoke. "Worms beget angels, and angels our sons and daughters and poet warriors, as one." Guy grinned.

There was a long silence.

"Ohhhh!" God thundered. "What madness is that? Worms do not beget angels. *I* beget angels! What is the source of this insanity?"

Guy trembled. "I don't know. Inspiration?"

"No! Madness begets madness. You degrade my creation."

Guy had the proper answer. "I am an artist. I celebrate creation!"

Foolishly confident, he smiled. A minute thought assaulted his mind. *I am here, talking to God? Am I mad?*

"Who are you speaking to?" Anna asked.

Guy's eyes darted wildly. "Him!"

"Jesus!" Anna shook her head.

"Close."

"Worst of all is the offense that can damn you in an instant, faster than Eve eating the apple." God paused, apparently masterful at Anna's technique of employing silence to create drama. "Worst of all is your creative pretentiousness. You are not content with my Creation? You find it so flawed and incomplete that you must arrogantly correct and complete it?" He moaned. "It is not my Creation that is incomplete. It is your perception! It is not my Creation that is flawed. It is your vision!"

God followed with another tortuous quiet that spoke like a death sentence. Guy held his breath and closed his eyes, waiting for his fate. Then, suddenly and inexplicably, Guy became angry.

"I am me! And I am an artist! I'm proud of that! And I do not give a damn what you think!"

Guy could not believe what he had spoken. He waited mute in the most agonizing silence of his life.

Then God laughed, loud and boisterous and jolly. It reverberated through Guy's head like the laughter of a delirious, demented Santa Claus.

"I tease you, my son," God spoke. "You are such a good subject for that!" He again laughed. "You should not be so grave and profound about things. Listen to the laughter of the universe. It eternally sounds. The laughter of the spheres and the gods and all of life. And yes, even the artists. For I gave all laughter." God laughed more.

"So, God, you're not angry?" Guy asked cautiously, fearing this might be a supreme ploy. He was not even sure if what was happening was real, but figured he better assume it was.

"No, Guy, I am not angry. There is a method to your madness, that Beautiful, Winged Madness. But when you see and know all, that is when you will truly laugh."

And God did so again but with a human inflection.

Guy breathed more freely. "That's great, God. You have a sense of humor." He looked at one of the radiant glass windows with light filtering through it. "I've often wondered about that."

Anna nudged him in the side. "Shut up! Stop mumbling."

God laughed, this time more loudly. "You do not see an immense comedy in your life, your world?"

That comment did not particularly please Guy. "No, I see an immense comedy in *your* world!"

God chuckled. "Listen, son, you do not have much time."

Guy jolted. "What does *that* mean?"

"No human has much time." His response sounded evasive. "I will tell you simply. You are on Earth to live, to serve, and to be Spirit; to become your truth. And as an artist, to create, free and abandoned. Artists are among my favorite children. I gave them two of my finest gifts: creativity and inspiration. You are the ones who can reach all."

This sounds better. Guy smiled. "Can you show yourself, God? What do you look like?"

"I look exactly as you imagine me."

Clever, paradoxical answer, Guy thought.

"I look like you." God paused. "Do not put such import on all things that all things are lost, Guy. Life is a divine game."

"A game?"

"Yes, the Supreme Game—a game of being and creating our Being. If you do not see that now, you will. Be thee light, and thou shall have light. Be thee love, and thou shall have love. Be thee forgiving, and thou shall be forgiven, etc. etc."

"Now you really sound like God!" Guy laughed.

"Now you are understanding. Enjoy summer showers, sadness, rabbits, awareness, TV, and all people. But forgiveness is critical. To forgive is to be saved. I made it so. You must forgive others and yourself, Guy, and you must forgive Me. Do you understand that?"

Guy considered. "I'm not certain."

"Try. Forgive everyone and everything, for all is Me, and I am all. As are you. And most of all, listen to this carefully, my son, most of all, always be happy that you are alive, for you are always."

"Happy that I'm alive?" Guy echoed, both as statement and question.

"Yes." Then God was quiet.

"Well, God, thank you." Guy broke the silence. "I have listened. I was afraid not to."

God laughed. "I do love the works you create, as I do the works of all artists. And always remember, son. Be happy that you are alive . . . and as the evening light darkens, a gentle illumination infuses the face of Christ, creating a poetic tribute to the glory of the Savior."

The voice in the air was now again the narrator's, recounting the story of the stained glass masterwork.

"Damn!" Guy muttered. "What was that?"

Both overwhelmed and joyous, Guy thought about the advice given. *Always be happy that I am alive, for I am always.* He tapped Anna on the arm.

"Anna."

"Shhh. I want to hear this," she reproached, her attention on the narration.

"No. This is important!"

"OK. What?"

"Anna, are you happy that you are alive?"

She glared sternly and did not reply.

"Well, are you?" Guy stared at her as if probing truth.

"I guess so. Now, be quiet, and stop mumbling!"

Guy kept repeating the commandment in his mind. *Be happy that I am alive.* He smiled, for he did understand. So simple, yet so profound! *Finally, I have found the purpose of my existence!*

Guy sat in the light of grace. Thousands of angels sang *The Ode to Joy* in their most glorious voices, in perfect German. All of the birds of the planet flocked over him in a beautiful aerial display. Soft feathers from their wings fell on his head, tickling his nose.

The gateway to the Garden of Eden opened. His compulsion to watch TV and eat donuts evaporated.

"I am happy that I'm alive! Hallelujah!" Guy shouted in a voice so loud it reverberated through the chapel and, he believed, the entire universe!

Anna smacked him. "Next time, I'm leaving you home!"

"And Jesus continued his sacred journey onto the Mount of Olives to fulfill a prophecy and into the souls of man."

The narration completed, and the curtain closed.

*   *   *

Guy and Anna drove the contorting roads through the remaining portion of the cemetery, the budget backlot as Anna referred to it, where those of modest means, and the poor if they could afford it, were laid to eternal rest. Grass, trees, humble plaques, and little more. No fantasy naked virgins or virile gods to tempt the dead back to mortal pleasures and madness.

"As is probably appropriate, they most rest in peace," Anna commented with a smile.

Afterward, they drove back through the central portion of the cemetery and then toward the cemetery exit. The cooling early evening air still carried the aromatic scent of flowers. The park ambiance was serene. Guy looked over the rolling, sylvan hills and the proud trees swabbed in a potpourri of colors from golden orange to emerald green, reminding him of Grant Wood's stylized rural paintings. A gentle breeze blew, and a chorus of birds sang.

Yet Guy again felt disturbed. The question kept haunting: Why do they try so desperately to cloak death? What horrendous truth may lie beneath those lovely hills and innocuous plaques?

"As a cemetery, I don't think this place works," he confided as they circumvented a lily pond. "I've never felt so terrified of death in my life!"

His facetious comment yet held an edge of truth.

Anna looked at him disconcerted. Then they both laughed.

"Alas, poor Guy! I knew him." Anna entreated their Bard friend. "For in that sleep of death what dreams may come when we have shuffled off this mortal coil must give us pause. The undiscovered country from whose bourn no traveler returns."

Guy perused the park's idyllic, fantasy landscape and thought of its attractions. *This is our culture, and that is what this day has really been about.*

"Such exquisite deceptions," he spoke. "A nice place to visit, but I would never want to be buried here."

"Never? It's an action you only have to take once."

Guy grinned. "Yes, and give me a humble but charming cemetery, solemn as death yet beautiful as life. Not a grand production Hollywood fantasy, but a gentle and reverential prayer of continuance. A death and transformation."

"Amen," Anna concurred. "Well spoken, and let it be soundtracked not by music from *Gone With The Wind,* nor even Wagner, but by a small string quartet playing a lovely Mozart sonata."

"Yes, perfect, Anna! A quartet performing over my grave."

"Over our graves," Anna corrected.

Her statement, with its hint of permanence, absolute permanence together, pleased Guy deeply.

They drove through the cemetery's exit gate, the same gate as its entrance gate, iron and ironic, not pearly. One leaves the way one enters.

"What did you enjoy most about the day?" Anna asked as they turned onto Beechwood Avenue.

"Why, the naked women, of course!" He paused, a moment of caution seizing. "And God."

Anna flashed her dark eyes. "Yes, never leave out God!" She stated both joking and profoundly sincere. The old Toyota hummed and rattled gently.

As they drove away from the graveyard and back into the city of the living, two thoughts floated through Guy's mind, pacifying all and filling him with a wonderful sense of grace. *Be happy that I am alive and just keep awakening.*

He felt behind him the wind of flapping wings. *Mondi?*

Guy and Anna's Sunday in the graveyard came to a peaceful close. All was well in the City of Angels.

Chapter 12

EXCITEMENT AND APPREHENSION, like a man's first date with the woman of his fantasies, Guy reflected as the Metro bus maneuvered the grayed, congested streets of downtown L.A. *One does not know whether to celebrate or moan.* Guy celebrated with a moan.

It was the Friday night premiere of Anna's performance play to be presented in the Paul Dubois Theater, an annex to the venerable and historic Inner City Cultural Center. Anna had arrived there hours earlier to prepare the staging and rush through a final rehearsal with the actors.

This was Anna's night.

A white sign in the lobby of the center billed the event as 'The Three Odd Graces'. Idiosyncratic art and visions were particularly enticing to Angelinos who prided themselves on being individualistic and progressive. 'Odd balls' was often the term applied by outsiders encountering this phenomenon, and the label was considered complimentary to its recipients.

The Paul Dubois Theater was small but distinguished with plush seating and the professional equipment required to stage any needed theatrical effect. Its regal aesthetics and the efficiency of its operation while on a budget Guy assumed to be modest impressed him each time he visited.

Something done right. It is a good home for Anna's premier, he critiqued perusing the facility. *But where are the celebrities?* He suspected some might be present, incognito, or would arrive later. Celebrities are always there, Angelinos, including Guy, chose to believe.

It was thirty minutes before curtain time, and Guy took the seat he calculated to be the precise center of the theater providing him the fullest experience of the event. That small detail was critical.

"Perfect!" he proclaimed borrowing Anna's expression.

His stomach fluttered and occasional beads of sweat streaked his forehead. He wanted Anna to have a success and ignored a gnawing, self-conscious feeling induced by attending a social event alone. What might people think? He didn't care. He said a silent prayer for Anna and for himself, that he would not be assaulted that night by the worsening voices and hallucinations plaguing him. The possibility that he might not be able to distinguish between the plays and his own delusions distressed him profoundly.

Please, not tonight.

Amber light dimly but warmly lit the theater. Show time approached, and the room thickened with people. Admission was free and the attendees eclectic, some formally attired in fine evening wear—suits and elegant gowns. Others could have been cloned from a rock concert—jeans, T-shirts, purple hair, and body piercings. Guy was dressed in black Levi's, a black shirt, a wide blue tie printed with alternating smiling and frowning masks, that classic symbol for the world of the theater, and a blue-gray sport coat. He was Guy being Guy. Beautifully, wildly mundane.

Two minutes before show time. A dreaded vision. A portly, Guy was too considerate to even think the term 'colossally fat', woman in a green dress splattered with images of brashly hued bouquets of flowers squirmed between the row of seats, her thick-mascara eyes targeting the empty seats on each side of Guy.

"Oh no," Guy moaned.

She was accompanied by her antithesis, her husband, Guy assumed, a man as frail and thin as his probable male self-image. When she reached Guy, looming like a freakish assault from a nightmare dream, she flashed a grin that terrified.

"Would you mind moving down one seat so my hubby and I may sit together?" she asked in a saliva-drenched hippopotamus voice.

Damn right I would! Guy thought. "Of course not, ma'am," he replied politely and moved one seat to the right. The zeppelin lady plopped into the seat to his left, her corporal excess spilling over into his and pinning him tightly against the opposite arm rest. The pencil man easily slid by to occupy the far seat, which he only half filled. He and his charming wife looked at each other and grinned.

The brutally cosmeticized woman's face, reminiscent of a German Expressionist painting portraying the horrors of human existence, turned to Guy and presented a smile that courted lunacy. He meekly smiled back.

"Damn!" he mumbled.

A spotlight burned down on front center stage, and the audience silenced. In the beam stood an impeccably groomed man with slicked black hair, a chiseled face and a suave mustache, wearing a black tuxedo with tails and a top hat. He tapped on the stage three times with a cane—tap, tap, tap.

"Welcome! The Paul Dubois Theater is pleased to present The Three Odd Graces, performance plays by three of L.A.'s gifted artists." He explained the contest the artists had won.

"Each is what it is, a reflection of itself, and perhaps of us. Or, maybe something vitally different. If you find yourself in one of the plays, rejoice or despair." He voiced an ascending, cosmic laugh. "And now, our first presentation, The Amazing Mathew Mathew."

He waved an arm toward the curtain, and the spotlight extinguished. The luxurious red with gold trim curtain slowly rose on a dark stage. To the right a precise spotlight beamed on the bodiless head of a man that appeared to float in dark space. His face looked mature, kind and wise, as that of a spiritual master possessed of enlightenment beyond his years. The performer stood inside a black cabinet, his head protruding from a hole, to create the decapitation illusion. Some in the audience sighed with awe, some laughed softly. The woman beside Guy snorted.

On the left of the stage, a second spotlight shined on the body of a headless actor, his head covered by a black skin-like mask contributing to its invisibility. The body was sinewy and muscular, a superb expression of the male form, and wore a tight crimson leotard.

A bodiless head and a headless body shared the stage. Then the head sang, engaging and resonant.

Surprisingly voluminous for a voice without the power of billowing lungs, at least within the logic of the presentation, Guy reflected with a grin.

"Come on, let's get happy!" It was a jaunty tune from the 1940's, its cheerful lyrics so upbeat as to sound ironically cynical as if mocking the very lyrics being sung. A recorded dance orchestra sounding through stage speakers accompanied the singer.

The decapitated body broke into an energetic, superbly executed dance, a mixture of modern jazz and bebop. It moved with the power and grace of a primal animal, strong, sexy, and dangerously threatening. Guy found the performance by the bisected duo both jubilant and eerie. When the song and dance ended in a joyous vocal crescendo and a passionate dance abandon, the head and body stilled and quieted like two spotlighted estranged forms, floating in a disturbing tension.

"Hello. I'm Mathew," the head spoke. "And this, or he, is Mathew."

He glanced toward the body which bent forward performing a bow made bizarre by the absence of a head.

"Together, we were Mathew Mathew. Apart, we are Mathew and Mathew. This is our story, as real and as unreal as any."

The head told their amazing tale. As a young and then integrated man, Mathew Mathew had been torn by severe conflicts of mind versus body, spirit versus flesh, the agonizing dichotomy of the human self. On the eve of his twenty-fifth birthday, he said an almost incidental prayer.

"Dear God, separate my battling parts and grant me some peace. Amen.

"When I awoke the next morning, I leapt out of bed, or at least, my body did. My head remained on the pillow, very alive." He grinned. "Be careful what you pray for."

And thus he, they, have existed since. As the head spoke, the body moved expressively, often with exaggerated gestures, and employed a simple form of mime, easy to decipher to add emphasis to the relayed events of the drama.

The bisected performers told of a career created from their unique and, some proclaimed, freakish condition by performing as a song and dance team, like a Twilight Zone twist on Broadway, and sharing their insights, hence the performance being witnessed.

Guy realized the entire play employed a cinema verite style where reality is presented as art. The audience was participating in the story being presented by playing the audience in a tale of life and the theater.

"Two to be or not two to be," the head jokingly stated and recounted the joys and anguishes of being a mere head/mind or body/flesh—a head of sublime thoughts and visions, a body of sexual ecstasies and animal pleasures. And the times when the parts lamented for the whole.

The head related an amusing anecdote of their experience with a prostitute.

"We responded to a tabloid ad by a woman named Anastasia. 'Eager to please. A woman of exceptional mind and body.' We called her and arranged a rendezvous for her services at our home.

"When she arrived, I was attached to my body by a securing collar I had made for that purpose, temporarily creating the illusion that we are joined; one. I told her how delighted we were that we had found a woman of both exceptional head and body, a perfect partner for our pleasure. When I said we, she appeared confused and surveyed the room for a second client." He paused. "Well, she at least did have an exceptional body!"

Mathew the body bounced excitedly.

"Perhaps you can satisfy us both, I stated as my body gently removed my head and held it before his chest. The dear lady stood shocked and then screamed. 'Oh my God!' She fled from our house in terror. Later I phoned her and explained our condition. I did not want her to be plagued for the rest of her career by nightmares of headless client lovers and talking decapitated heads. But when she called us weirdos, I suspected she doubted my story. Weirdos! Can you imagine that?" He laughed unabashedly.

"Matty the body, I call him that sometimes, does have a girlfriend. She considers a headless man the perfect boyfriend and lover." The narrator scowled and rolled his eyes. "No ego or mind games or head trips. A woman's fantasy.

"I, too, have a female companion. She's trying to evolve her mind and spirit and finds a bodiless man an ideal companion. Our minds make sublime love together with immaculate thought and mystical vision. It is, in its way, euphoric.

"Each day without my body, my intellect and spirit evolves, becoming more transcendent. Each day without a head, my body counterpart becomes more of nature and the bestial. I have found a god of purer thought and divine vision. He has found a god of the primordial and elemental. Both are worthy gods! But the question I'm often asked is which is preferable, a life of unbounded separateness, each part whole within itself, or a life of conflicted integration, experiencing both realities, but neither fully?"

The head was silent for a moment, expressionless.

"That I must leave to you, dear audience, to contemplate and explore with mind and body. I have no definitive answer. The body awakens to passions of the blood and flesh and then sleeps, lover to dreams of spirit and transcendent death. The head awakens to visions sublime and purified ideals and then sleeps, lover to dreams of flesh and orgasmic deaths. Connected and estranged, together or separate, as sun and moon, life and death, reality and wish. Perhaps there can be an armistice.

"This is Mathew and Mathew, thanking you for participating in our amazing journey."

The theatrical duality closed their performance with a song and dance interpretation of *Heart and Soul* with a slight alteration of lyrics. The head sang with purity and beauty. The body danced with savage elegance.

The curtain dropped and darkness descended. The applause from the audience was generous and, Guy believed, sincere. He thought the play amusing and relevant. Guy understood well the conflicts of mind and body. Guy and Guy. The human mastodon beside him clapped loudly and chortled and snorted like a woman deliriously tortured by tickled feet. She obviously connected to the play's themes. Her husband clapped politely and wheezed.

The spotlight and the announcer returned.

"And now . . . ." The curtain rose. Twenty minutes of sound, movement, and bewilderment. Voices, motions, fast, mad. The ending: seven people stepped to the front of the stage and simultaneously recited the truths of their lives; an incomprehensible verbal confusion. The curtain fell and the stage darkened. Ten seconds of applause.

"What the hell was that supposed to be?" The elephantine woman blurted rudely loud to her fidgeting husband.

Guy rather enjoyed the play, thinking its erratic confusion a valid metaphor. He glanced at the woman beside him. *So true.*

Next. A silent wait for the final performance—Anna's. Leaden minutes dragged a burden of hours. Guy felt apprehensive, worried for Anna. She had not told him anything about the play, not even a meager hint about its concept.

"You must experience it as the audience does," she instructed resolutely. "As a mystery and surprise, be it for better or worse. Until you see it, you, dear Guy, will know nothing."

"As usual," Guy responded, resigned.

What he expected to see was perhaps an empty stage, vaguely lit, expressing a nothing purity. Or maybe Anna just standing alone and still, beneath a spotlight, totally naked and silent, for the entire performance. Or something amazingly exotic and flamboyant, carrying the audience into a wild or forbidden fantasy. He had no idea. It could be anything or nothing, for it was Anna.

He even had a clawing fear that she might kill herself on stage. *The ultimate performance piece.*

The tuxedoed announcer returned to front stage. "And now, ladies and gentlemen, our final presentation!"

Then he stood motionless and quiet, like an ominous, black presence. *Oh no!* Guy dreaded. *A bad omen?*

"Do not expect anything. Expect anything. It is The Shadow World by the artist Anna, Anna Spirit Persona."

The curtain slowly, slowly rose. For moments the stage remained black and silent, then on the back of the stage gradually appeared shadow images: people and objects, oddly shaped objects suggesting machines and technology. They were behind a panoramic screen with lights shining from behind transforming them into silhouettes. The forms moved and intermingled with what appeared as both repetitive, mundane motions and an expressive, abstract dance. Music gradually sounded, a mixture of dissonant electronic tones and Eastern meditative rhythms.

Anna has created a demented dance of life, Guy surmised, pleased with the concept. The staging reminded him of a life-sized Japanese shadow play. Then a dim light illuminated the stage and Anna appeared, dressed in a white gown. She stood in front of the screen, being the only figure that seemed real and not a shadow form, and paced back and forth before the softly illuminant, ghostly wall, like a desperate animal planning an attack strategy. Occasionally she stopped and stared into the animated shadow scene. Periodically the music silenced, and the dissonant shadow motions froze turning the stage, and Anna, into a taut, haunting tableaux of loneliness in a world of alienation. Guy felt the audience vicariously experiencing Anna's estrangement.

Then action and music resumed. Anna erratically moved and danced before the screen, mimicking the Shadow People and their world. She imitated the pose of a tree chair and became a whirling blending device. Sometimes she laughed joyously as if she had achieved a moment of wondrous connection and then stopped, still and mute, and stared again into the silhouetted world. She could not get in.

After repeating those cycles several times, she turned toward the audience and sat in the center of the stage, quiet and despondent, with shoulders slumped and head down, and remained in that state for a period of time that Guy experienced as disturbingly tense.

A man, young and lean, dressed in beige slacks and shirt, walked onto the stage. Anna did not notice him at first, being absorbed in her lamentation. Then, as if directed by an inner sense, she turned toward him and watched as he performed an identical ritual to hers before the screen. Eventually he too gave up and sat on the stage beside her. He stared down as though not aware of her.

After a comical period of Anna looking at him, and then at the audience, and then at him, she addressed him.

"Hi!"

He looked at her but did not respond.

"Hi!" She loudly repeated, again vainly.

"We have nothing, and are nothing," he finally spoke, looking at her apathetically.

Anna glanced around the empty stage. "Yes, that appears true. There is nothing."

She looked at the audience and grimaced in exaggerated despondency. They laughed.

"We are nothing because we are out here, and I see you," the young man moaned, his head hung in resignation. "We are not Shadows. We are doomed!"

Anna nodded. "'Tis true. So, so true. To not be, or to be not. That is the only question."

A resigned silence followed. Anna placed her finger to her chin as in a deep contemplation.

"I know what!" Her face excited. "I will look at you without seeing you, and you look at me without seeing me. Then we will be as Shadows, doing Shadow things."

The man stared into space. "Maybe. OK! Let's do it."

His voice was more animated. Anna and the man observed each other intensely, looking up and down the others' form.

"I don't see you. I don't see you," they repeated convincingly.

"No," the man said.

"No," Anna said. "It doesn't work. I still see you."

"And I you."

"Bummer!" They both exclaimed in unison and again sat silent, staring into the audience.

"Maybe we can do things together but not actually do or experience anything. So it wouldn't be real, like the Shadows do." Anna's voice conveyed a faint hope.

"Yeah. That might work. Let's try it. What the hell!"

Anna and the man stood up, joined hands and danced around the stage, skipping and hopping in a spoofy country dance. Then Anna pretended to dig a hole, and the man pretended to fill the hole. Falling to his knees, the man looked up and howled like a wolf wailing at the moon. Anna duplicated his actions, their howls filling the auditorium. The audience laughed.

They moved closer to each other and allowed their hands to flow over their bodies. They joined, intertwining, and moved in exaggerated spasms, moaning and breathing deep and raspy, as in lovemaking. The audience again laughed.

Suddenly they stopped.

"Nope. Isn't working." Anna's expression exasperated. "I'm enjoying it too much. Not only do I still see and identify you, I'm feeling and experiencing you, and myself. No joy in that."

"Or freedom," he added. "You're right, it's worse. I think it's hopeless."

Again they moved to the center of the stage and sat, facing the audience. A long silence ensued. The audience, including Guy, fidgeted.

"There must be a way." Anna boldly broke the silence. "There must be a way in. To be a Shadow. Look at them." She pointed to the frenetic dark shapes in the abstract pageant. "They do it."

"Yes, there must be a way," the man droned as in a trance. "To be among the Shadow People is my only dream. As the

Shadow of the great Bard wrote, 'All the world's a stage, and we but Shadows upon it."

Anna peered at him puzzled. "Is that what he wrote?"

"It is. Beyond the shadow of a doubt."

The audience moaned.

Anna nodded. "It is also my highest vision. To have not substance and color and life and meaning. To be the beautiful gray. I'm sick of being somebody—that cursed me!—of doing things and knowing things. What is there to know? I still know nothing, yet must be something. We are damned!"

"Yes, damned!"

They sat mute, staring at the floor as the otherworldly Shadow dance played behind them.

"You know, or rather, I don't know, but I think there is a way," he declared. "The dark way." The man slowly looked into Anna's distraught face.

"What way?"

"The ultimate way. The Shadow way." His voice edged into excitement. "The counter life—death."

Anna did not respond immediately, staring at the audience.

"Death, yes," she finally remarked. "The eternal door to the Shadows. Is that what they did? Perhaps that is our only way in." Then her form sank. "But wait! What of the danger of dreams? Dreams of *this* world. You know, the Hamlet thing. To sleep, perchance to dream. Ah, there is the rub." Anna recited the quote with a theatrical, masculine voice.

The man peered into empty space. "No, I don't believe there is a danger. If there are dreams in death, they would be Shadow dreams. What else could they be? They would have no substance or reality. Right? That would actually be wonderful!"

"Yes, wonderful!" Anna's voice again buoyed. "Thank God!"

They abruptly looked at each other, perplexed.

"God. Yes. And what of God?" he asked. "Do you think God is a Shadow?"

Anna considered, her chin upon her hand. "Well, sure! He's not a person, or a tree, or a car. He's unsubstantial, without physical form. He's basically nothing, right? He's a Shadow God." She paused. "He must be, for He is truth." She smiled delighted.

"Yes, you're right. He would have to be the God of the Shadow World."

"He certainly wouldn't be the God of *this*!" Anna pointed toward the audience. She and the man laughed heartily. The audience laughed modestly. The human mass beside Guy grunted.

"And He made the real people in His image." Anna gestured to the Shadow People.

"Well then, it's decided. We can join the Shadow World and God. The answer is death, right?" His brow cocked, his expression dubious.

"Yes, it is decided. Death it is. Death to life, rebirth in Shadow."

Anna nodded. Then they sat silent for moments.

"But how? How do we do it?" Anna questioned.

The man revealed a child's smile and then reached into his pocket and withdrew a gray vial. "With this."

"What is it?"

"Poison. A narcotic poison. Fast and pleasant."

"Poison? You just happen to be carrying poison on you today?"

The man shrugged. "This morning I woke up and the little dark voice, the whispering inner Shadow, said 'carry poison today. It may be needed.' So I did. I always listen to my little dark voice. I knew someday it would free me and guide me to the true world."

Anna cocked a brow and grinned. "You are wise to ignore common wisdom, seeking instead a truer voice. I admire that."

"Yes. The Shadows know." The man tilted his head, appearing perplexed by his own statement. The audience laughed.

"That other so-called wisdom," he said, "traps one alone, in the terrible, blinding light."

"Please, don't even mention it." Anna held up a stopping hand. "Those days will be over."

The man pulled the plug from the vial. "So, ready to die? Then to live? I'll go first." He moved the vial close to his lips.

"Wait! Wait!" Anna placed a hand on his shoulder. "One more thing. You know, I rather like you." She smiled sweetly. "In a non-substantial kind of way."

"I like you too." The man smiled warmly and then cringed. "Although, I think we must not, or, really . . . don't."

"Perhaps when we enter the Shadow World," Anna suggested, "you and I might stay together and, well, create something more lasting." Her face contorted. "Something more of nothing. Not meaningful. It can be . . . an infinite illusion."

"Yes, I think that would be nice," he responded. "We could have a Shadow marriage. It wouldn't really be anything. We wouldn't have to do anything. It would just be. Perfect!"

"Yes, perfect!" Anna's face lit. "And we could have children, little nonsubstantial Shadow children. Thin as air, vague as illusion. Every parent's dream."

The audience laughed.

"And they could be ours because they wouldn't be." The man added fondly. "We could have them while not having them."

"Perfectly imperfect." they both decreed in unison.

The man again brought the vial to his lips. This time, he stopped himself. "But there is one more thing. I don't even know your name."

"I'm Anna."

"Good name! I'm Guy."

Guy stirred. A smile graced his face and being.

"To us, Anna."

The man held the vial toward Anna and then brought it to his lips. He quickly swallowed and passed the vial to her.

"And to the Shadow World," she proclaimed and drank the remainder of the toxin.

They both lay on their back on the stage floor, looking blankly into the air. They took each other's hand.

"Don't feel too much," he advised.

"I won't."

The lights dimmed gradually, submerging the stage and the screen into darkness. Then the screen appeared again illuminated with its Shadow Beings and constructs like animated black paper forms. The dark figures divided into two groups, opening a space between. They stopped their movements and stared at the floor of the gap.

Anna and the man had moved and were lying limp on the floor behind the screen. Slowly they rose like specter beings lifting from a grave. Standing, Anna stretched her arms and looked around.

"The Shadow World!" She shouted through the screen, thrilled, and then quickly suppressed her expression.

The man stood and repeated her exclamation, also aborting it.

They embraced. For a moment.

"I feel nothing."

"I feel nothing," they both stated matter-of-factly and looked at each other.

The Shadow People resumed their dissonant, Cubist dance of nonexistent existence. Anna and Guy quickly merged into it with angular motions, slicing and mechanizing, undifferentiated from the flat silhouette forms consuming them. Three small Shadow Beings, childlike without being children, emerged from behind them, mimicking their movements in the dark Shadow Dance.

All continued without distinguishable variation. A placid and monotone man's voice sounded from the stage.

"And so they remained, a Shadow family in the Shadow World, being non-being joyously without joy. They looked for and occasionally glimpsed their Shadow God, who satisfied them with His comforting message of no truths—everything as nothing and nothing as everything. It was all perfect without perfection. The Shadow World."

The light aura behind the shadow screen faded into black. All forms vanished, and the curtain fell. A still silence hung in the theater, an edgy moment of nothing. Then waves of applause rolled through the room and persisted.

The curtain rose to a fully lit stage. Anna, standing front center, bowed graciously to the audience. A small figure on the stage, she seemed to Guy immense and beautiful, her presence engulfing the entire theater. The other cast members, former shadows now fleshed and visible, acknowledged the audience's enthused applause with a number of bows.

Guy exhaled and mentally imprinted the scene in his mind. He was happy for Anna, and relieved. Her play was a success!

The woman times the mass of three applauded and snorted, applauded and snorted.

*   *   *

As the theater cleared, Guy gained permission to go backstage and see Anna. Still in her white gown, she stood with several of the cast, all talking feverishly. As if sensing his arrival, she suddenly turned and greeted him. She seemed pleased but not excited.

"Equilibrium?" he asked.

She immediately comprehended his question. "Yes. I've found it necessary for artists."

"Or Shadow People," he drolly asserted.

She grinned. "No, I'm very pleased. I think the play went well, and it was fun. I'm happy!"

She now smiled effusively, her cocoa eyes glimmering.

"And I'm very glad you came, Guy, and saw it. That's important to me."

"I know. I'm glad I came, too. I wouldn't have missed it. And thank you for naming one of the characters after me. It was a nice surprise."

Anna nodded and smiled more.

"And on this night, a star is born!" Guy declared.

Anna moved closer and embraced him tightly. He kissed her on the forehead, and she looked into his eyes. He thought the galactic space in her eyes seemed infinite and alive, vibrating. Anna was glowing. Then she kissed him on the lips.

Guy experienced one of those perfect moments, feeling like an adolescent boy who had received his first kiss. He floated, free and light, and actually saw himself and Anna in their embrace below him as if viewing from the ceiling.

"Some of the cast and I are going to the Encore Café to celebrate. I promised I would go. Why don't you come along?"

Anna stepped back and took his hand, tugging several times.

Guy shuffled. He was not comfortable in gatherings with strangers.

"No. This is your night. You go ahead and enjoy it. I'll take the bus home."

"Are you sure?"

"Yes. You go ahead."

They embraced again, Anna hugging him especially tight. Then she walked away.

*   *   *

Metro Line 888, downtown to all other worlds. The bus ride home seemed quiet, as in an emptiness. The city had darkened and stilled, preparing for a comatose sleep. The night lights outside the bus window streaked by Guy's vision like harsh, glaring knives. *This can be a cold city,* was the thought that seized his mind and that surprised him. The excitement and intensity, and the pleasure—the glow, he phrased it—of the evening were but moments past, and yet his spirit had turned cold.

He felt alone.

He thought of Anna and was so pleased her presentation had been a success. He knew she was happy when being the artist and happiness was what he wished for her. It was not difficult to remember the days and months and years of loneliness, like a bleak and cruel suffocation, that had afflicted him before meeting her. Since their first encounter on that mysterious night of The Event with the enigmatic ghost of beauty, he had not felt that pervasive, cold loneliness. It was simple. He loved her. Only Anna.

And yet, he felt alone. It seemed a cruel paradox, like something spawned in Anna's Shadow World. Life can suck while being wonderful.

Guy looked out the window at the blackened cityscape, which appeared attenuated and removed from him. *The City of Angels offers little comfort to one plagued by a lonely soul,* he reflected. *Concrete angels with wings of steel. A black night raped by glaring lights.*

He tried to feel gratitude that the demented voices and visions, those intruders from an even more ominous terrain of his mind, had spared him that night. They were worsening, but he had been given a reprieve. He said a simple prayer for a resolution to that plight and for the realization of more intimate and exquisite thoughts he harbored in his mind and heart, thoughts of Anna and him.

"Make it so."

He tried to envision Anna's face, the face that had given him so much pleasure so many times, but it appeared filmy and distorted, like a perplexing mask in an eerie dream. He plunged, as if descending into the earth. The temperature in the bus grew colder, and he shivered. Something frightening was happening.

He looked at the interior of the bus, attempting to anchor himself to things near and solid. The bus ceiling was nondescript and gray, that gray of nothing, ribboned by two rows of white lights in yellowed plastic casings. It did not help. An ad illustrated a shiny Metro bus merrily rolling through an idealized postcard city of glistening streets and vibrant palm trees, beneath it the word 'Rest'. An anti-drug message showed a lean female athlete in a skimpy blue track uniform displaying a victorious smile, beside her the caption: 'Drugs destroy dreams. Be your dreams.' A dozen passengers sat quietly in their seats staring toward the front of the bus as if gazing through a vacancy for a vision waiting at its eventual end. Or they were just waiting, for there was nothing else to do.

Waiting, waiting, in dreams of mating, Guy's mind silently sing-songed. *Fate-ing. Do you know where the dreams end, my friends, and reality begins? Where do your flowers grow? In endless, skewered rows.*

He heard the giggle of a woman seated across the aisle. She was Mexican, attractive, with night-black hair and eyes and skin the hue of fertile earth, at that provocative age between a girl and a woman, innocent yet maturely erotic. It could drive an older man to reckless desperation. Beside her was a young Hispanic man, muscular and cocky, with the air of a conqueror. His shiny black hair was pulled back tightly and descended in a narrow ponytail down his neck. His torso was sheathed in a fitted beige T-shirt beneath a smooth black leather jacket.

A player of the night streets and the flesh, seductive and dangerous, Guy suspected. Observing both, the word 'raw' came to mind.

Although they occupied two seats they were wrapped together almost in the space of one. She wore a short violet skirt and her bare leg, which Guy noticed was trembling, intertwined with his.

"Para! Stop it! Stop touching me," she reproached her suitor, slapped him teasingly on the cheek and giggled. Guy saw his hand was reached under her skirt and moved in a stroking motion. The girl alternated between laughs and short gasps.

"That feels goood," she sighed and then scolded him again as if defending her virtue. "You're bad!"

His other hand discreetly slipped under her blouse. "That's because you're a bad girl," he rebutted.

"Nooo! I'm a good girl. Muy bueno. *Very* good." She flashed a seductress smile and laughed.

"No, you're a *bad* girl, Muy mal. I like bad girls who are good."

She laughed and pulled his hand more firmly against her breast.

Guy wriggled, and his face tensed. *There should not be such a display on a public bus. They should be thrown off!* But he could not remove his sight from the couple. They noticed him watching. Guy squirmed with embarrassment but still did not look away. The girl smiled and giggled, and Guy realized they enjoyed having a spectator.

"We're exciting the guy," he heard the young stud whisper.

They both laughed and the girl pulled her violator's hand up her leg higher.

"Mmm," she purred loud enough for Guy to hear and then trembled and moaned with exaggerated delirium. She and her partner laughed.

Guy thought of Anna, beautiful Anna, and what she might be like in such a scenario, so sexy and forbidden. He became excited, his heart pulsing faster.

Then deep razor resentment sliced him. His stomach tightened and his hand clasped into a fist. A terrible pressure welled inside his body and mind. And sounds—sounds growing louder and louder. Confused. The Hispanic girl, so young, so sexy, her sighs and moans amplified. A frightening roaring in his head thundered like the cry of a tortured elephant.

Guy's vision bleached white as if a powerful spotlight shined in his eyes.

A thought: *You are plunging into psychosis.*

He stiffened, terrified. A little voice in his mind kept speaking until he was able to hear one word: rage.

Rage! He realized he felt rage toward Anna, mad and burning. Something he had not permitted to surface or be seen. He felt tremendously strong, and frightfully weak.

I should kill her! Kill love! The thought smashed into his mind. *I kill love.*

He struggled to change his focus. *I love Anna. It's not her. She's innocent!* He kept silently repeating.

A new target was found.

Damn you, artistic spirit! That turns all into ephemeral bullshit! Flesh and fire, beastly power and passion become delicate gardens of flowers and illusions. You create gods of worms and deflesh all, turning me into a pale and anemic ghost—some idiotic ideal. You kill life. I denounce thee!

Thee. His choice of words angered him. *You are a trap! I cannot escape you.*

The hiss of vacuum brakes and the swoosh of the bus door broke his distraction. The young couple rose from their seats and walked toward the exit. The man had his arm around her waist and reached down and rubbed her thigh. The sultry girl-woman wrapped her arm around his neck, pulling his face closer to hers. They were still joined like Siamese twins. The woman turned her head and presented Guy a temptress smile, a smile that ridiculed him to the core of his quixotic being. "Fool!" it said, and Guy knew she was right.

As they descended the steps to leave the bus, Guy glimpsed the expression on their faces. It was excited anticipation. Images flooded his mind of what he knew awaited them. His anger reignited.

He heard the voices, the demented Greek chorus in his head. None were angelic and comforting, and they spoke no words. They just laughed, increasingly louder and more hideous, a laughter of ridicule and madness, sounding from far beyond his mind as if originating from the entire cosmos.

Damn you, madness! Damn you, artistic sensibility! Damn you, Anna! Guy retaliated. *A world of illusions and dreams. Illusions collapse and one awakens from dreams.*

Guy knew he was in dire trouble.

Damn!

*　　*　　*

In the late hours of that night, gravely alone in his apartment, Guy thought about his life, the city, love and hate, madness and violence, and Anna, be the thoughts real or illusion. Through his window he looked at the gray and anemic moon. *All the world seems sick.* Attempting to purge his demons, he wrote some of his darkest verses.

'Amongst quivering thighs and blood,
By bronzed entrails of lurid wars,
State jesters die,
As Giorgio girls peddle their fluids,
And famined, dark wings compass the sky . . . .'

Madness and death, Guy thought. *Not love.*

Chapter 13

STREAMING PINK CLOUDS dyed the dimming azure sky—complementary colors, warm against cool. At dusk on the following evening, Guy and Anna sat on an outside bench observing the descent of another day. The sun bled red as it hovered in its final moments before dropping behind the cloak of the earth.

"Adieu, sweet, bloody sun," Guy remarked.

Anna had been surprised earlier when Guy approached the bench. The left half of his face and neck was painted white with strange configurations, like coded symbols, in black around his eye and mouth. Other bizarre black shapes imprinted his white flesh, and the tiny word 'DIE' was in red on his cheek. It looked like half of a mask of madness. The other side of his face was normal. When he sat beside her, she did not react or comment. She enjoyed playing the game.

Anna was covered in dust, but Guy made no remark.

"I should have been a lifeless vacuum," Guy spoke placidly. "A hole in static space."

"Having a bad day?" Anna smiled facetiously. Guy responded with the same. Moments of silence.

"Anna."

"Yes."

"Anna, I love you, and I hate you."

She turned, her eyes widened with surprise. "You love me, and you hate me?"

"Yes, it is true, it is true as love and hate are two sides of the same phenomena, each often accompanying the other. If one did not know love, he would not know hate and vice versa. Like yin and yang. Perhaps one cannot have one without the other.

Thus I've decided whenever I tell a woman I love her, I also will tell her I hate her."

He looked at her with fallible, sincere eyes.

Never before have I received such a proclamation of love. Anna looked up and examined a streak of clouds above the bleeding horizon. It seemed more comprehensible.

"I see," she finally replied.

Guy knew there was more to his statement than the innocuous philosophical concept, but he did not express it. That refusal made him feel cowardly.

"Guy."

"Yes?"

"Guy, I love you, and I hate you," Anna proclaimed matter-of-factly.

He smiled. *Good.* Anna's umber eyes glistened within her ashen face. Suddenly Guy had a strange thought.

"Anna, remember the guy, the Cupid Killer, who shoots arrows through people's hearts to kill love?"

"Yes, the news stories. He just took his sixth victim." She peered at him curiously.

"What could be more tragic? Yet, I understand it. In its way, it's disturbingly beautiful."

Anna considered his remark. *How odd. Guy is in a peculiar mood.* She peered into the darkening sky and watched a flock of pigeons, a sight native to Los Angeles. The birds resembled gray slashes streaking the air.

They watch me also, she sensed. *What might they think of the peculiar creatures seated on the bench below?*

"If you were a pigeon, what do you think you would think of humans?" she queried.

"I don't know."

Guy became again silent. Monastic. Anna kept observing the birds and wondering.

"You know, Anna, sometimes when I realize that *today* is my life, not tomorrow or next year, I feel panic, even terror. For I can't decide what I could possibly do now, today, that would be meaningful and fulfilling enough."

Anna looked at him sympathetically but also laughed, thinking there was an essential humor in his despair.

"Decide that you're going to kill yourself," she advised, "then decide that you've changed your mind, and that your life will continue, and you may feel, at least for a moment, relief and joy because you are still living."

She smiled, gray-lipped yet brightly as if presenting a resolution to all things.

"Sounds good. I will try that." And he did and, for a moment, he felt relief and joy.

More silence. The evening—the people, the cars, the motions of the city—played around them like the backdrop of an urban movie drama, a movie they were in.

"Anna."

"Yes?"

"Why are you covered in dust?"

"I am one of the Dust People."

Makes sense. "Yes, I understand. Of course."

Anna was literally covered by a layer of dust. Wearing a gray leotard, she had coated her entire body, including her face, with a thin layer of oil. Over that she sprinkled a solid layer of dust, actual dust she collected over a period of time and kept in jars. Her hair was colored gray as were her lips and nails. Only her galactic, glistening eyes varied from the monochromatic light gray design. She looked like a gray ashen specter with two dark pits staring out at the world. When Guy saw her, his first impulse was to sneeze from all the dust. It was the only persona that he had ever seen her in that he did not respond well to; he thought it looked too eerie and deathly. It disturbed him, and the word 'sick' entered his thoughts, and he had profound difficulty perceiving Anna, so alive and vibrant, as a woman of dust, a Dust Person, even in fantasy.

But as he observed her seated on the bench gazing dreamily into the sky, she became increasingly mysterious and intriguing. The persona suggested nothingness, a recurring theme in their lives and appropriate for so many people in the world. Or the absence of true identity or a genuine self. Or the biblical passage.

"From dust we came, to dust we return," he spoke aloud.

Anna looked at him and smiled, her lips a gray crescent.

Guy felt an impulse to touch her because she appeared so fragile, turned to dust and provoking anxiety as if he was losing her. He touched her arm with one finger and then looked at it. Its tip was gray, and on Anna's arm was his flesh fingerprint. She looked at the small imprint and then at him but did not reproach him. She smiled gently. "Branded," she said.

Then her gray, negated form recalled in his mind the brutal eradication of human lives throughout history, like the ashen corpses of the Hiroshima victims. Or perhaps vanished or abandoned dreams. It also seemed existential and both sad and strangely dignified. So many associations came to him so fast that he finally concluded, and had to concede, that Anna's conception of the Dust People was powerful, basic, and even ingenious.

"I like it."

"What?"

"Your persona. The Dust People. It's like the Shadow People in your play. It's simple and disturbing, but powerful."

"Yes, I know." She grinned.

"But it makes me want to sneeze."

Anna laughed. It did not disturb Guy that no one, including himself, could touch her or the persona would be marred as it had been by his slight violation. That, too, seemed disturbingly appropriate and truthful. It alienated her.

The Dust People—untouchable. Alone. Perhaps cursed. Is that so rare?

"Guy."

"Yes?"

"Why is half your face painted like a mask of madness?"

Guy cocked a brow. "Because I am a duality, half sane and half insane, half reality and half illusion, half alive and half dead, half creator and half destroyer."

Anna nodded. "Yes, I understand. We all are. I like it." She rubbed his arm. "Welcome to humanity."

A time of quiet.

"Anna."

"Yes?"

"I think you and I live under a curse."

"Wouldn't surprise me."

She shrugged her dusty shoulder as a passerby stopped, stared at her, sneezed, and continued on.

"It's a curse we've created," Guy elaborated. "I've been thinking about it. It's the curse of not totally fulfilling our purposes. There is something in this life, perhaps in spirit, that is very harsh, very unforgiving of that offense."

"But many people do not fulfill their purposes. Are they all cursed?"

"Many people do not even know or care to know their purpose."

"Like a Dust Person," she interjected.

"Precisely. Perhaps there is an exemption for those people. They are not considered as responsible or guilty. But it's very different for those who do. We both do know and care and cannot deny or rationalize it. I am a poet and an artist. You are a performance artist and an actress. It is in our very being, so we must be and do and live it fully. It is who we are. It's as simple, truthful, and real as the dawning of the sun each morning or the impulse of life to survive. It *is*. And if we are not realizing those purposes *fully*, and I believe we are not, then we are cursed. Cursed with relentless discontent and unhappiness, even a form of death. Never at peace. A simple but brutal reality."

"Perhaps that's as it should be, like a . . . dustice." She giggled. "Guy, that's a severe viewpoint. Almost cruel." Her expression was now mildly reproachful, her eyes tight slithers.

"Yes, it is harsh, but I believe true. A blessing like a talent can be a curse if one isn't fully responsible to it. I see and feel it every day. Don't you?"

Anna shifted. "Yes, I do. But then again, perhaps nobody or nothing even cares." *I prefer to look at lethargic pigeons,* she thought.

Guy had to concede her point. Again they sat silent. Anna considered his concept more fully. It made her ill at ease. She looked for more pigeons.

Guy mused aloud. "After times pass and passing times, after life is born and life dies, after creations destroy creations to create creations, all remains the same. This world is conceived from economics and work schedules. Clock radios, Internet sites, cups of coffee, TV, and amusement parks. One measures his life by mundane wonders."

Anna nodded mutely.

"We must help this world more, Anna, with our gifts and mad inspirations. We must measure our lives by created inspirations and visions. It is our job as artists. Or we are doomed."

Anna smiled feebly. "Yes, doomed."

An extended, but peaceful, silence followed. The lyrics of a 1970's song drifted through Guy's head, and he silently sang along to them. *Love is the need we seek, love is the want we need. Only love, love is all.*

"Anna."

"Yes?"

"Only love, love is all." He looked at her with a barely discernible smile. "Is that true?"

She examined his face before responding, thinking he seemed unusually distant and disconnected. "No."

That was the entire discussion. Issue closed.

Anna watched some kids skateboarding on the sidewalk, attempting to perform leaps and spins in defiance of gravity and earthly reality, often falling. She smiled.

"I don't know if I like life," Guy confessed. "I certainly doubt that I love it."

Anna started to raise a hand to stop him but didn't.

"I only love the illusions of it, the creating or recreating or fantasies of it in my mind and work, or the work of others. I enjoy a poem or a painting of life more than life itself."

"Yes!" Anna's face animated. "With that I can totally agree! We may well be doomed because we love more what does not actually exist than what does. We love a painting or an idealized sunset more than any sunset we've seen. We love a play about love more than love."

"Yes, it is so." Guy nodded. "We are doomed."

"Two doomed souls. How exquisitely despairing!" Anna feigned a melodramatic anguish, arching backwards, a hand placed before her eyes as one blocking the sun's glare, a pose that seemed especially potent in her dust persona.

"Alas!" She spoke. "Two doomed souls, sitting on a bench, one an anguished poet, the other an ashen wench."

They looked at each other, shrugged, and laughed.

"Delighting in discussing their doom." Guy added.

"How like the artist!" Anna was pleased his humor was returning.

"I love the struggle to love life despite all its obstacles and offenses," Anna divulged, her face now a dreamy wonderland. Of dust. "Even though it often all seems irrational. Life, the Exquisite Irrational! And I love you, Guy, for anguishing with such issues. It gives sensitivity and depth to your soul."

She kissed him on the cheek leaving a gray imprint of her lips. Guy smiled, despair temporarily dissipated.

Again, silence. Guy observed several people walking on the sidewalk and wondered if any of them was out of their body, observing their self, their body, meandering merrily below them. Perhaps they could even watch their spirit observing their body. He examined that possibility but could not conclude if that could be.

"Are you all right, Guy?"

"Yes, I'm fine. I'm sorry."

"You seem so severe, like you're haunted."

"No, I've just been working things out in my mind." He spoke without looking at her.

"Let me know if I can help."

"Yes, I will. Thank you."

They watched a girl, about seven, on the sidewalk attempting to learn to use a pair of inline skates. She stood straight with her arms extended from her sides, occasionally waving them through the air to help maintain her balance. She kept stroking the sidewalk with the skates but remaining stationary. Guy thought it a humorous sight, worthy of a scene in a Charlie Chaplin movie—the little girl in her blue jeans and pigtail hair scissoring her legs repeatedly as she moved nowhere. He realized she was failing to angle the skates outward so the rollers could push off against the resistance of the sidewalk. But Guy and Anna did not laugh at her; they sympathized and admired her persistence.

Guy thought it was an excellent metaphor for so many people in the world, he probably included, treading desperately but going nowhere. He wondered if resistance, like the sidewalk against the rollers, was always necessary for any progress or movement in life to occur.

If so, I am fortunate, Guy surmised. *For I certainly encounter enough resistance in my world.* He grinned.

Anna disrupted his ruminations. "I would like to buy a car," she said.

"I would like to be a car," he heard.

"You would like to be a car?" Confusion and worry marred his face. He recalled their talk that day at lunch when Anna said she believed she could be anything, and he had come to accept that premise even if it seemed outrageous. *If she can be a Dust Person, she can be a car.*

She looked at him puzzled. *He's teasing me.* She would play along.

"Yes, it would be rather nice to be a car. Sculpted and shiny, powerful and fast. Perhaps a sports car!"

"Why would you want to be a car?"

Anna eyed him concerned but continued. "If I were a car, you could drive me around, and gun my engine, and . . . fine tune me, pump me with gas, and waaash me!"

She spoke the last two words slowly and provocatively as she mimicked with her arm the sensual motions of washing a car.

She realized she was crossing the line into seductive allusion but decided to permit it. "It might be fun!"

Guy frowned. "Please, Anna, don't become a car. I like you as a woman, so we can be friends. Together, like this, and talk."

As soon as he spoke the statement, he felt ridiculous having said it, but he had to. *I cannot take a chance.*

He looked at Anna, and she startled, for in his eyes was desperation.

"I won't. Don't worry. I'm teasing. I won't become a car."

She felt ridiculous reassuring him of such a thing but thought she should. She placed her hand on his arm, creating a gray ghostly imprint on his sleeve.

"Are you sure you're all right? Is something disturbing you?"

"No, no, I'm fine, sorry. I'm just in a strange space." *But I am not fine.* "Just please, don't become a car."

Anna did not answer but smiled and nodded. Then she laughed, trying to lighten the exchange. Guy felt better from her assurance, and his rational mind told him he was being absurd. *A woman does not become a car. And yet . . . .*

Anna kissed him on the cheek and then his forehead. Two gray stamps of her lips were left behind. *His face softens.*

*   *   *

Strange days. Peculiar nights. For Guy, within and without. Strange as blights, blighted desert storms and ferocious terrorist attacks. Sights without sight. Like silent, invisible bombings. Blinding.

Slights of night in strange deranged flights, he ruminated. *No, it wasn't so. But yes! It was! My god! Madness. Sadness.*

A car, unfamiliar, parked in front of the apartment building one morning. Unique, beautiful. *Oh god! An old classic. '51 Ford,* Guy believed. *Deep purple. Anna? Her character and charm. Her unique, inimitable style. Possibly, Anna.*

Worse! Now a red Audi TT coupe sports car, one of Anna's favorites.

"A car designed for artists." "A piece of sculpture on wheels." "I want to get one," she commented whenever she saw a TT on the road.

The Audi seemed to call to Guy, and he walked to it. He thought the car beautiful, unique, and funky. *Like Anna.* He ran his hand softly across the car's descending rooftop. It was so smooth it felt sensual. The car's artistically sculpted body with its crafted accents and curves blending into one alluring and strangely intimate form appeared to invite him to indulge in its pleasures. He immediately wanted to slip inside it.

Yes, Anna, definitely!

He struggled against an awful despair that threatened to engulf him. He stared at the Audi, that beautiful and terrible car and then retreated to his apartment and sat silent in his favorite chair as the room darkened. He had no thoughts or feelings.

Madness.

Then there was a knock on his door.

Who could that be? The thought did not occur to him that it might be Anna. But when he opened the door, it was her.

"Anna, you're back!" he spoke both startled and delighted, smiling broadly.

She stared. "Back from where?"

Guy suddenly had a moment of clarity and trembled. *Am I going mad? No! I will not let it happen!*

"I've been worried about you, Guy. You've been acting different. Is everything all right?"

"Yes, Anna, everything is wonderful." He took her in his arms and held her tight.

He was slipping below the line.

Chapter 14

"LISTEN, GUY! CAN you hear it? Do you feel it? The Day of the Dead calls us. It dances and screams."

Like spirits called to source, Guy and Anna rode the metallic tubular Metro subway that needled through concrete tunnels beneath the fevered skin of Los Angeles. They disembarked at Union Station, left behind modernity and its soulless technology and walked a couple blocks to historic Olvera Street.

Enter now a world of deathless spirits and sacred and profane rituals.

A living dead man in black with a skeleton imprint across his form greeted them with the slyest of smiles. Macabre death characters, their faces painted in interpretations of that dreaded, awaiting foe, swept past or danced jubilantly, beckoning and challenging. Youthful men in Mexican shirts silkscreened with Hispanic gods and suns and women in festive dresses, ruffled and mottled with colors, paraded the streets, asserting life. A six feet tall skeleton lifted on a pole shook and rattled. The air vibrated with music and life, scented by tantalizing Mexican food: burritos, enchiladas, and tacos.

The grave underworld of the spirit dead rose to celebrate with the living left behind. Dia de Los Muertos!

A banner draping a wall read: 'Don't fear dying. Fear not having lived.'

The Day of the Dead was a Mexican holiday honoring the spirits of the deceased. Homes and public sites displayed extravagant, decorative altars with mementos of the life of the departed, complete with snacks and gift offerings for their spirits who were believed to visit that day. It was an expression of love and remembrance from the living to the immortal dead.

Participants dressed as skeletons and death figures playfully paid tribute to the Dark Master. Processions paraded down streets traveling toward a central location of festivity offering music, food, art exhibits, poetry readings, and candlelight celebrations. Religious, mainly Catholic, symbolism mated with primitive myth and icons. Life and death partied together, and spirits were the guests of honor.

It was a perfect domain for Guy and Anna. They loved the colorful and bizarre fusion of festival, creativity, religion, and spirit that characterized the annual event. It was as their world where one could live and die and resurrect with mystery and joy. A place of both light and dark.

Like a story of love and death and the reality of illusion, Guy characterized it.

Dia de Los Muertos.

Anna wore body tights with the image of a white skeleton painted on it. The tights were scarlet, rather than the customary black, communicating an erotic partnership between passion and death—the Scarlet D.

Anna teases mortality, Guy mused observing her persona. *The Master of Death dances with the seductive and lusty mistress of life.*

Her face was painted scarlet in the image of a skull with dark eye sockets, hollow cheeks, black lips, and a mouth of yellowed teeth.

Guy wore black pants and a T-shirt bearing Day of the Dead dancing skeletons, a black tuxedo bought from a thrift store and a black top hat Anna loaned him. Her makeup mastery transformed his face into a jeering skull, and he carried a black cane with a white skull on its top that he repeatedly tapped against the pavement as he walked. *A dapper death figure,* both he, and Anna, appraised.

They strolled past an outdoor pavilion; a round, white, open stage with a wooden roof where Mexican musicians with guitars, horns, and drums played jubilant ethnic music. Young women in flowing native dresses as colorful as the fancies of their hearts, flowers in their hair—girls as seductive women, women as frivolous girls—danced jubilantly with handsome male partners. A rhythmic, pulsing excitement charged the air.

It was a late October afternoon, and the temperature was brisk on Olvera Street, one of the oldest streets in Los Angeles, now a commercial tourist area closed to traffic and lined with gift stores, bars, a museum, Mexican food stands, and racks of festival T-shirts, posters, and souvenirs. Open-air shops occupied its center strip.

Colors, symbols, scents, shapes, motion, music, and laughter crushed into one dizzying reality of macabre festivity.

Guy and Anna threaded the thick crowds and entered a small neighborhood museum exhibiting the more lavish altars and finer artworks. Most of the paintings were in a folk, primitive style, colorful and brimming with death and spirit and Catholic icon imagery.

"Death mocks and baits while life grieves and worships," Guy commented to Anna who, enthralled, studied the presentations.

"As we do every day," she replied.

They both laughed, but softly, knowing that one must be cautious about mocking such realities.

The dazzling altars were immense and extravagant, often constructed around a central photo of the honored deceased engulfed by an intricate display of figurines, candles, photos, flowers, personal symbols, food, and religious tokens.

"The ghost of Uncle Fernando will be delighted by this!" Anna remarked standing before a particularly elaborate shrine. She threw Fernando a kiss.

The altars were not elegantly or precisely designed. They were expressions of the people, their emotions and aesthetics, raw, commonplace, and clustered. Yet, both Guy and Anna agreed that they possessed a beautiful and primal power, like the force of the earth, or family.

Anna felt an intrusive presence. She perused the museum and noticed a man standing in the room's corner. He was tall, about six-feet-five, and muscular, dressed in tight, body contouring black shirt and slacks, and his face was black with white eye sockets and lips that framed black teeth, a reversal of the usual skull hues, as in a photo negative. He wore a flamboyant black fedora hat with a sweeping brim. His dark piercing eyes stared.

Anna trembled. *He is waiting for me,* she immediately and puzzlingly surmised. He was dauntingly attractive, sexy and alluring in a mysterious yet frightening way.

"That man is watching me," she whispered to Guy.

When he looked at the stranger, a shadow presence boldly standing before a colorful altar, Guy detected a slight smile on the intruder's ashen lips. The man's size and apparent strength shivered Guy's being.

"Yes, you're right. He probably finds you attractive. Ignore him."

Anna redirected her attention, examining another monumental, gaudy altarpiece. She observed the interesting relationship between the domestic symbols of home and family and those of greater, potent religion and fates. There was a crucifixion figure of Christ, Cristo Reyes, splattered with blood and a lovely, three feet tall figurine of La Virgen de Guadalupe, Madre de Dios, Mother of God.

Compelling and conflicting images of a sacred violence, Anna critiqued. *A sacred violence* echoed in her mind.

"It is time to meet." A solemn man's voice whispered over her shoulder. When she turned, the masculine figure of death that had been intently observing her was walking away toward a door. He looked back for an instant. Anna, glaring, watched him leave.

"Beautiful, but also bizarre," Guy commented on the altarpiece.

"Yes . . . yes," Anna replied.

Returned to the street, they perused the gift items of an outdoor stand. Guy sorted through a rack of Day of the Dead T-shirts searching for one particularly unique or artistic. He collected such shirts. Anna examined a display of small skeleton tableaux, a popular item at the festival. Each was a half-foot or less square, like small, open boxes, and inhabited by skeleton figures, a few inches tall, often costumed. They were miniature rooms, *miniature worlds,* she reflected—a living room, a doctor's office, a chapel-like tiny, inhabited stage sets. Death playing in and mimicking the world of the living. Anna thought they had a funny yet haunting quality. She especially liked the tiny artist studio mockup. A skeleton in a painter's smock and artist beret, holding a brush and palette, painted a lovely nude woman clay figure, posing reclined on a dollhouse bed. But on the easel's small canvas, she was depicted as a skeleton. The painter's bony skull smiled gleefully. Miniature Day of the Dead paintings decorated the three-sided and roofless studio's walls.

A gift for Guy, Anna thought. *He would love it.*

"Guy!"

He halted his search and looked.

"Could you please step around the corner of the stand for a few minutes? I'm getting you a nice gift, but I want it to be a surprise."

Guy nodded and walked around the stand. Anna waited for the saleslady to finish with a customer purchasing a poster of a handsome Aztec god carrying a lovely, dead princess in his arms. She felt a hand on her shoulder.

She turned. The death costumed man stood before her, looking at her, silent. Anna stared into his darkly terrifying yet hypnotic eyes. She felt both fear and intrigue. He kept his hand on her shoulder. She swayed, becoming dizzy.

"What . . . who?" she whispered. Her vision blurred, and her legs weakened. Everything plunged black.

Guy walked back around the stand. Anna was not at the counter. He looked through the crowd. Shock froze him. Between shoppers, he saw the shadowy death man carrying Anna away.

For an instant, Guy stood motionless. His artist's mind became captivated. *What a strangely poetic image. The beautiful, unconscious Anna, as in a swoon, carried away in the arms of Death.*

"I am taking her." He could almost hear the Death Master's words. "She is mine. I will possess and love her!"

Alertness returned. Guy yelled. "Stop! You! Hold it!'

The man and his captive edged deeper into the crowd. Guy ran after them in a panicked desperation, his heart pistoning loudly. He glimpsed traces of the man's black form and Anna's scarlet suit between costumed pedestrians. He pushed and shoved past the people, trying to keep them in his sight.

They vanished. Guy fought through the crowd, looking in all directions, but they were gone. The sounds of the crowd—voices, singing, screams, *screams*—amplified louder and louder.

He comprehended. The impossibility. They could have gone in any direction to escape and hide. Anna could have been taken anywhere. He might not find her. He thought he heard her scream, distant and plaintive, and then realized he probably had not. Then he heard it again and again, from somewhere in his mind. And the other voice. *She is mine. I will possess and love her!*

Guy searched for a police officer.

*   *   *

A hazy light crept from a crack in a gray space somewhere beyond, and the frankincense of candles beckoned her senses. Consciousness slowly returned, and Anna felt peaceful as when one awakens in the morning after a tranquil night's sleep. Then she remembered and jolted.

She was seated in a chair. She looked around. Scores of burning candles hauntingly lit a room filled with altarpieces even more extravagant and decorous than those in the museum. Colorful, ritualistic, trembling candlelight slicing across them. Two eerie figures, the size of humans, sculptured of wood, cloth, paint, and knickknacks, stood near the center of the space. One figure was draped in black and hooded, carrying a scepter. The other wore a flowing white gown, pure and angelic with a crude makeshift gold halo above a cascading blonde wig.

A stunning, nightmare prison.

She looked down. She was not bound. Seated yards in front of her was her captor, dark, face black, eyes glistening in the candlelight, staring at her with a fixed gaze and a duplicitous smile.

"What is it you value in this life, this world?" he asked in a resonant, underworld voice. "Wealth, power, beauty, family . . . children? Love, sex?" He grinned broadly. "Ah yes, love and sex, fathomless and passionate. The truths of a woman."

Anna wanted to rise and run but felt seized by a strange passivity.

"Well, you should have it."

His ebony eyes gleamed frightfully. He breathed slowly and deeply, his chest expanding beneath the tight black shirt that delineated his powerful musculature.

Anna tensed. She felt again the disturbing confusion of fear and intrigue.

"Who are you?"

He did not answer. Candlelight danced across his macabre yet handsome face.

"You are a creator," he remarked. "I can see by the attention given to your costume."

"I'm an artist."

"Yes, art, that is good! This world needs art. Beauty."

He nodded, smiling. Then he rose slowly from his chair, lifting like a phoenix ascending. He took a couple steps toward Anna and stood before her. His form was powerful and masculine, possessing the force of the earth. She felt his strength.

"If I ravish your flesh and tear your body, if I take your dreams and your future, if I expel your soul and wed you to dust, if I force you to surrender all, could you still love me?"

His question startled Anna. Her vision voyaged slowly up and down the muscular stranger. Oddly entranced, she did not feel resistance. She looked into his question, and herself. She wanted to answer.

What she said surprised her, and yet did not. "Yes. I could still love you."

The Death Man smiled and then took a few steps back. He sat down and kept staring gently at her. "Are you ready?"

Images sprinted through Anna's mind, wildly delirious and terrifying. Forms stolen and possessed, seduced and ravaged, slack and floating. She peered at him now with piercing eyes and forced composure.

"Ready for what? Who are you?"

The dark questioner's brows lowered, and his expression puzzled. "You really don't know who and what I am?"

"Some . . . ." She did not say what she thought. "Some lunatic in a death costume."

Her inquisitor laughed, his voice as an echo in a well. "I am why this celebration exists."

He waved his arm and then remained silent. Anna glared defiantly into his eyes.

"You are not ready. It is not your time." He shook his head slowly.

"Time for what? What are you talking about?"

"We will meet again." He paused, his eyes captive as in a vision. "Beautiful woman, you should find love. But be cautious. The same love that can grace you can threaten you. It can give and take all. Be warned!"

Anna stared back but did not respond.

"Look." He pointed to a painting on the wall.

Anna looked and then slowly stood and walked to it. The painting depicted, in a space of browns, the spirit of an attractive woman, a ghost, floating before a young man, whom Anna assumed to be her husband or lover. The image was lovely, sad, and haunting.

She turned around. Her death persona host was gone. The room was eerily quiet, broken only by the chaotic sounds from the outside world. The room's door was open.

She walked out. Anna saw that she was still on Olvera Street, still among .the shops and stands and crowds. The building where she had been taken was on the lower level of a dual row of stores, a gift shop with costumes, figurines, and posters above it. She watched a young couple enter her now reopened captivity room. Apparently, it was another festival attraction.

She felt confused and disturbed, yet also oddly excited. Beguiling visions visited her mind as if placed there by another source. Erotic death images. Beautiful lovers entwined with dark, handsome death masters. Flesh dissolving into spirit, and spirits possessed by flesh. She shook her head, trying to dispel it.

She surveyed the crowds but could not find Guy. She walked a distance down the street searching and then saw him speaking to a police officer as he gestured emphatically with his hands. She approached them.

"Guy."

He turned and saw her. An immense expression of relief softened his face.

"Anna, are you all right? Were you hurt?"

"No, no. I'm all right. He just talked to me. I . . . must have fainted. It was strange."

Guy placed both his hands on her arms. "Who was he? Where did he take you?"

"I don't know who he was. Some bizarre guy. He took me to one of the altar buildings." She pointed down the street toward the site.

"Do you want to fill out a report, miss? We can investigate it," the officer in a L.A.P.D. blue uniform, curiously examining Anna, asked.

Anna considered. "No, that's all right. I wasn't hurt."

"Are you certain?"

"Yes, yes, it's all right. Thank you."

Anna made an effort to smile at the cop.

"All right, miss." The officer nodded. "But be careful. There are some weird characters here."

"Yes. Yes there are." Anna fully agreed.

Guy and Anna walked away from the crowds and commotion to the end of Olvera Street. They sat on a bench near the pavilion that was now empty. She told him the mysterious story of her abduction, omitting some of her reactions. When she looked at Guy, she saw he was worried. His face was tight and strained, a painted, anguished skull.

"Are you sure you weren't hurt?"

"Yes, I'm certain. He didn't even touch me. He may have had a plan in mind, but he didn't do it. He just told me some things."

Guy hugged her tightly and then pulled back. "Wait, I know what it may have been!" His expression agitated, but his eyes excited. "It may have been part of the festival. I've heard of it. People costumed as death will choose someone and take them somewhere alone and speak to them of death and spirit, whatever they believe the person needs to hear. This man may have chosen you because he found you interesting, or attractive. That would be why he acted mysteriously. It's part of the game. Yes, that may have been it."

"Perhaps," Anna replied. "I don't know. It was all strange."

She saw that Guy seemed relieved and that helped comfort her. Whatever had occurred, she knew it was a Day of the Dead that would not be soon forgotten. She remembered the macabre man's words: *we will meet again.*

Anna suddenly felt cold.

Chapter 15

THE DAY OF *the Living,* Guy mused, relaxing in his apartment, enjoying his own humble moment of celebration, two days after the dead. He wanted to sit quietly for a few moments without everything being metaphors, without life being so meaningful and significant. Just being.

He fidgeted. He squirmed. Boredom gnawed. He went to visit Anna.

*　　*　　*

"Immortalized to exist forever, yet forever existing in its own immortal, petrified form."

Anna, in her apartment, tutored Guy on her newest persona. A return to significance. "Its ecstasy is to inhabit the eyes of its beholders, forever perceiving and idolizing itself. Its despair is to forever perceive the reality of that self."

After their visit to Forest Garden Cemetery, Anna kept thinking about the statues, their proud beauty and sensuality, and the unease a viewer might feel when confronting the form of living beings, like themselves, fossilized into lifeless stone. *A dead illusion of life, yet so true and beautiful,* she assessed. *One of those wondrous paradoxes!* It inspired her to create a new persona: the Beauty of the Everywoman Statue Persona.

"This is one of my truest personas. It is both alive and dead." Anna's eyes dug into a mysterious and nonexistent space. "Spirit as matter and matter as spirit. A woman as a symbol and a symbol as a woman. I am all of that, and that is all of me."

Guy smiled and nodded, uncertain if she was totally serious or if her dramatic opus was part of the persona. *I like it when Anna is in her meaning game.* She maintained a motionless standing pose as she spoke with both arms partially raised, the right higher than the left as in an invitation or offering. It was the identical pose she had assumed in the cemetery when mimicking a statue.

"A ghost trapped inside its own shell," Guy contributed.

Anna did not nod agreement because she was being a statue.

She was dressed in an evening robe descending to her knees, its light fabric draped loosely around her body, laying on and delineating every curve and contour, thus subtly defining her feminine form. The cloth was silkscreened into the hues of marble. All of her exposed flesh—limbs, neck, face—were cosmetically painted in the same marbleized effect as were her lips and hair, the hair glistening white with cream streaks. Only her eyes remained human, their whites melded into the surrounding marble color. In contrast, her pupils appeared black, like dark portals opening into an enigmatic inner space.

She even painted flaws onto her marble skin surface, cracks, a few deeper and more pronounced, most fine fissures like delicate spider webs. Some, painted with the smallest of brushes, gave the immortal beauty of her face the frailty of mortality.

Guy observed her posed absolutely silent and still with the afternoon light filtering through the windows to play delicately on her stone features. She appeared to be an additional piece of furniture, albeit it a lovely one, and he believed he was, indeed, perceiving a statue.

Then, in a gesture he knew was reserved for his eyes alone, Anna dropped the robe off her left shoulder exposing a bare breast, as often presented in classical art. The elegant, sensual breast was painted marble with a large crack on it, revealing her display to be premeditated. Anna did not speak or smile, but simply stood motionless in the provocative pose.

That little presentation, that consideration from Anna, pleased him immensely.

Guy thought the persona was a beautiful yet disturbing illusion. It was Anna with all her sensuality and grace and yet, it was also a dead manifestation, a cold symbol of her.

A terrible chill penetrated him. His breath seized as he looked at Anna's static, marble face. A plaintive absence consumed its beauty. He felt a powerful impulse to take her in his arms and hold her close, but he did not.

"One day," she decreed without the slightest alteration in her statuesque pose, "I will be as this precious yet flawed statue of myself. I do not know how many people will behold me, but I do know that at least one person will look upon the statue of me and his or her soul, and fate, will be altered forever."

For the slightest moment, she gave an elusive smile and then her face returned to a mask. Guy wanted to smile back but couldn't.

For over an hour he remained in her living room, observing her, saying little. It was the most difficult persona for him to be around, but that was part of its intended effect. Anna arrested all movement and speech, staring at that nonexistent point in space. She became the statue, a living and dead soul. Whatever pose she was in, she periodically changed them, standing, sitting, or gesturing, was held for long, and at times excruciating, minutes. Guy could only speak to her, not with her. He thought it would be the perfect persona for a wife driving her husband mad with her incessant chattering and nagging.

He also realized something profoundly. *If women were sculptures, he could enjoy just sitting and watching this one be, her sensual curves a play of yearning, her essence of intrigue, a question.*

Although the persona's passive state conflicted with much of what he embraced about life—life as animated being, as motion and expression—and it unsettled him, he did not care. He loved looking at Anna whether she was a woman or a statue, flesh or stone. And he could do so forever. For it was simple. He loved her.

Guy smiled and wondered why he had placed his thoughts in the third person.

"So sad and yet so beautiful," Anna, her head now tilted as in puzzlement, uncannily remarked although Guy did not know to what she referred.

Anna knew it was correct to wear that persona at that time before Guy although she did not know why. She trusted.

Then the statue told its story. Anna took a seat on top of a stool. She found a comfortable position, back straight, hands on her lap, and petrified. The room was quiet in its gentle ambiance of afternoon light. Guy smelled the scent of roses that were in a vase on the coffee table beside him. He realized that for the first time since he met Anna, she did not have her musky yet sweet fragrance, the scent of a woman. She had no scent. She was stone. Only her lips moved as she spoke her tale.

"Five centuries ago, in Milan, Italy, a young countess, about thirty with black hair, olive skin, and cocoa eyes, named Geneva de Florenzi, visited an artist, in his mid-thirties, named Francesco. She offered herself as a model for a sculpture.

"'Although I do not wish to sound vain,' she explained, 'I know that I possess a beauty and perfection that is rare in this world. I have been blessed by God with a face and body that is a woman's ideal. I would like you, dear artist, to preserve that beauty, that ideal, the perfection of a woman, for eternity. It would be my gift for all the people of this Earth, for all time to come.' She then removed her garments and displayed herself to the young sculptor.

"'Behold!' she proudly summoned, 'and sculpt me like this so all my glory is portrayed.'

"Francesco walked slowly around her, studying her nude form from all perspectives. What he saw surprised him, for she possessed many flaws, many imperfections—wrinkles, ripples of celluloid on her thighs, a trunk of disproportionate features, and a face no finer than plain. And yet, for his purpose, she was perfect.

"'Every man who looks upon me worships me and flatters me with proclamations of love. It becomes rather tiresome.' The Countess sighed. 'But such is the price of perfection! If you create this work, then it can be shared with all the men of the world.' She looked down shyly. 'Never have I lain with any man, for beauty such as mine should not be violated by such coarse intrusions. You, dear artist, will sculpt a virgin beauty.'

"Francesco's body and mind were suddenly inflamed by an excited design, but he pushed it aside. He was committed to his work.

"'Every woman is a virgin, and is beautiful,' the artist responded with a smile. 'That is one of the many truths this work will express.' The Countess did not quite understand but was pleased by his words.

"Francesco realized that the woman lived a delusion. She had never truly perceived herself.

"'But you must promise me this, dear artist,' she beseeched him, 'you will not fall in love with me. It will be the work that is important.'

"Well, the sculptor knew that he needed to be most tactful. 'I do not know if I can make such a promise, my Lady, for I too am overwhelmed by the sight of you. Love could, like a demon of passion, possess me at any moment.'

"'Oh yes! I understand. But please, do try your best. Be strong.'

"'I will, my Lady. I promise.' He bowed before the Countess. He thought she did possess a handsomeness of the most common type and, for the new sculpture he envisioned, for which he needed a model, that was ideal. He wished to sculpt the eternal Everywoman, with all her imperfections and aberrations and all her hidden beauty and truths. But he wanted her in an open robe, suggesting both the erotic and the modest domestic. He had to be clever.

"'It is true, my Lady, such beauty and perfection as yours has never before, and will never again, walk this Earth,' he spoke with convincing, feigned sincerity. 'Aphrodite herself would stand in awe. It can be seen, but never captured, by mortal eyes. For if any were to truly perceive such beauty, in its totality, all the world, in contrast, would appear so coarse and crude, so ugly, that one could not bear to look upon it, or to live in it again. If one could not be before you exclusively at every moment, he would conclude he must take his life. Your beauty makes all else sadly repulsive, and thus, can be mortally dangerous.'

"The Countess was pleased and flattered, and she knew the words he spoke were truth. 'Oh my!' she replied, distraught. 'I do not wish to send the world to its grave.'

"'Allow me to make a suggestion,' the artist shrewdly responded. 'I will sculpt you in an opened robe that will reveal but half of your exquisite form, its front, and evoke the other half. Perhaps that will be less lethal.'

"The Countess smiled. 'Your words speak wisdom. It will be so. We will give them a provocative yet constrained vision. Agreed. Proceed, dear artist.'

"He dressed her in an opened, beige evening robe. The artist also knew he must sculpt her in all her imperfection and commonness. He feared that if she viewed the work as it was created, she would be devastated by what she saw and might flee, abandoning the project.

"'And you must not look upon the work until it is completed,' he instructed. 'Anything but your beauty's wondrous totality would be a profanity to your perfect vision.'

"'Again, you are wise and correct, master artist,' she quickly concurred. He placed a blindfold over her eyes.

"'And you should be graciously holding a mirror,' he prompted, 'turned toward the world, so all people know that the beauty that shines in you is a reflection of the beauty that is in everything, and everyone.'

"'Excellent!' the Countess applauded. 'An act of benevolent humility. That properly communicates me.' She took the hand mirror and held it, turned outward, before her body.

"Every day that followed for weeks the artist chipped and chiseled at the marble block, gradually bringing forth the Countess de Florenzi's flawed, yet perfectly human form, and the sculptor's vision. The Countess stood before him, partially robed and blindfolded, and distracted herself with endless vain ruminations about her beauty and perfection, and the extraordinary treasure it was to the world. Francesco found her self-adulation annoying and boring but remained committed to his project, his vision, and appeased her with agreement.

"'Yes, my Lady, 'tis true,' he said a thousand times over.

"Finally, the sculpture was completed. The Countess, overwhelmed with the most euphoric expectations, removed her blindfold to behold what she knew would be the most divine expression of beauty and perfection ever created; to behold herself!

"The lady was horrified. For many minutes she could not speak. She was as paralyzed and mute as the statue before her.

"'It is an abomination!' she finally screamed.

"'No, my Lady. It is beautiful. It is you,' the artist countered.

"'It's ugly!' she ranted.

"'No, not at all.' The artist walked to the sculpture. 'It possesses a beauty and truth beyond any ideal. It, and she, is indeed perfect!'

"'The Countess's face went pale, her eyes turned to ice. 'This is not me! She is hideous! You are a worthless artist!' Her voice rose to a scream. 'You turn my beauty into horror! This . . . monstrosity must be destroyed!'

"Francesco glared at her angrily. 'This is a masterpiece, my greatest work! Such beauty as this cannot be seen by your vain and deluded eyes!'

"The Countess mumbled incoherently as a creature succumbing to madness. 'It is a lie! Destroy it!' she fanatically repeated.

"The artist smiled slyly. 'You are so perfect? I will show you.' He took her hand and pulled her before a full-length mirror. 'Remove your robe!'

At first she refused, unaccustomed to being ordered to do anything, from anyone, least of all to disrobe. Then she grinned and accepted his challenge. She dropped her garment and slowly turned toward the mirror, knowing the vision it reflected would validate her argument.

"'Look!' Francesco demanded. 'Look honestly and see!' He proceeded to point out every flaw, every coarse defect, every aesthetic aberration on her body and face, and they were numerous. He turned her around, so all was exposed to the mirror's unprejudiced scrutiny.

"At first the Countess de Florenzi refused to listen, and her eyes did not look to see the designated flaws. Then, slowly and excruciatingly, she began to hear and to see.

"She was horrified. Her hands covered her mouth, concealing repeated gasps. For the first time in her life, she saw her reality, her truth. She was but a woman, another flawed and common human being. And each flaw magnified a thousandfold in her distraught mind. She was ugly, she concluded. She was nothing!

"She grabbed the robe from the floor and fled the studio. The sculptor watched her leave, shaking his head. He felt a sudden and deep compassion for the tragic woman.

"Francesco never saw her again. That night, alone in her bedchamber, she had no family and few acquaintances, devastated and terrified, the Countess drank a vial of poison. She took her life.

"The artist was extremely pleased with his creation. He knew it was his finest work, and the city agreed. Immediately the sculpture was purchased for a generous sum and displayed among honored artworks in a garden pavilion in the center of Milan. All who beheld it were moved, some even transformed. They saw in the sculpture a deeper beauty and character, a perfection and truth that celebrated the essence of every woman.

"'This is what a truly beautiful woman is!' the people unanimously proclaimed. They had their new goddess, their new ideal. And it was especially celebrated by women who saw in its common, yet profound beauty liberation from the oppression of the superficial. The Countess helped free them.

"And in all the centuries since, millions have honored the statue of the Countess Geneva de Florenzi. All saw its infinite beauty and perfection, except the woman who inspired it.

"And this persona," Anna swept her hand along her body, "celebrates that beauty and truth. The Beauty of the Everywoman Statue Persona. And it speaks of me. For I am both that beauty and that vanity of the Countess, that imperfection and perfection, that truth and that delusion. The persona is universal. Both the sculpture and the Countess live in me. I am them, and they are me."

Anna the statue bowed her head and sat for a long moment in solemn contemplation. Then she heard the cry of spirit, one spirit, and all spirits.

In an odd moment of confusion between reality and fiction, she felt a compulsion to pray for the soul of the Countess, so tragic and yet so human, and for all the deluded spirits of the world who choose vanity over their inherent beauty. And for herself.

"Time to go to church," she announced.

Anna knew the story she had told was a fabrication, spontaneously spun from her vivid imagination—it was just a tale, for fun—and yet, to her, the Countess seemed real, as real as the warm flesh that resided beneath her persona's marble facade. Envisioning the Countess as a Catholic, it was to that church that she made her pilgrimage.

*　　*　　*

In the chilly autumn dusk with a smoggy haze graying the vanishing light and colors of the descending sun, Anna the statue and Guy the man visited Lady of the Angels Cathedral on Wilshire Boulevard where the soul, humbled and surrendered, can seek salvation. Anna began feeling very strange.

They walked through towering wooden doors that evoked a medieval castle, across a front reception chamber embellished with life-sized, beige statues including a welcoming Christ, a compassionate John, and a reflective Paul, and into the main chapel. *How odd,* Anna thought. *Like my persona, the entire cathedral appears carved from one monumental block of stone. Perhaps the statue of the Countess has finally arrived home!*

The splendid stone cathedral infused her with both a comforting grace and a penetrating cold. Too cold. Her spirit lifted as her body trembled. The church was spacious and gray, a hollow within ornately carved walls. *Like a forfeited soul within a lovely body,* she thought.

The dimming evening light transformed stained glass windows into subdued kaleidoscopes of colors. Guy examined each as they passed. Catholic mythology. Iconic symbols. Hushed and lovely. The air felt heavy with a reverential silence. The thump of their footsteps on the wooden floor self-consciously echoed in the space of the immense chapel room.

They sat in the center of the long rows of wood pews and quickly surrendered, as one should in church, to a devout meditation, especially the statuesque Anna who barely moved or twitched or even breathed. She was a cold stillness.

Such a peculiar sight, Guy reflected. *The human marble statue in quiet reverence within a millenniums old tradition.*

Guy perused the people seated around them. They were a diversity of ages and ethnicities. *The people,* he thought. Many were Hispanics, humbly dressed in modest yet lovely fashions, ornate white blouses and dark skirts or trousers. Most wore silver crosses. A couple of young women with black lustrous hair and eyes possessed an earthy beauty like the heroines of tragic romantic Mexican films. Guy felt a compulsion to ask one if she would walk with him along a flowing river beneath rolling hills where they could discuss their futures, and matrimony, and children. Fantasies.

Others were Koreans, more formally attired in dark suits and evening gowns. *The business community.* A small child with disheveled hair and scanning eyes climbed around a pew, ignoring her mother's admonitions to be still and then stared at Anna. *The children.* An elderly, frail woman in her seventies bent forward in prayer. Guy thought he saw the pale mask of death on her face. *The aged.* And a huge, ten-feet-high wooden crucifixion at the front of the church watched over them all.

The community, Guy summarized his observations.

And then there was Anna, an iconoclastic presence; the woman of stone, so pristine and cold in her pose of reverence, sitting in the House of the Lord. Throughout the chapel, fingers pointed and heads turned and stared.

Bless the people, Guy thought, and then he prayed. The marbleized Anna, head bowed and hands in lap, said a blessing for the spirit of the Countess, wherever, and whatever, she might be.

She kept feeling strange, and her body became heavier. *Why? Because I'm a persona in this world of personas?*

The priest, a black silhouette with a human head, stood behind a shellacked oak pulpit and sermonized.

"And man must be humble before the awesome power and benevolence of God, his only and final salvation. It is vital that we honor God's creation."

Anna squirmed. She wanted to slip to her knees, not to pray, but to hide behind the pew's back. To be a human statue, a bizarre alteration of man and art seemed a mockery in that holy place and not a gesture that would invite the grace of God.

A disturbing thought assaulted. Perhaps in a previous lifetime, she actually was that vain and deluded Countess and that was why she now felt the impulse to create this persona. Perhaps that was why the story came to her so effortlessly. It was her story, and now she sat in the statue of herself.

More. Even worse, perhaps her current body, as Anna, was another flesh incarnation of that sculpture, imprisoning her for another lifetime within a shell of herself, dooming her life and hopes for love. She looked up at the ornate chapel ceiling. *And I, as the incarnation of vanity and egotism, cannot, as a woman and spirit, truly love, as with Guy. I am screwed!*

She viewed the tall, painted, wooden figure of Christ crucified on the cross, so sad and yet so serene, that hung over the altar. In a way, his life and mission seemed so simple.

I should become a librarian, Anna concluded as she nodded to Jesus. *Marry and have a family. Simple and normal and blessed by all. No dead Countess sculpture personas. Just me, books, service, my family, and the Lord. And die an old lady and be buried and grieved and saved. Simple!*

Surprisingly, she actually liked the concept. She smiled at the facsimile Christ and then looked at Guy who was praying and appeared so serene.

He is a good man. She prayed for all the world's librarians, families, countesses, and simple lives and loves.

But Anna knew she was not of that serenity. She glanced around. The stone cathedral had changed, now seeming as thin as air, the people like cardboard cutouts propped on pews. It was all so much, so much there, and yet it barely existed, barely existed. She felt certain that all of the heads of the worshippers were about to turn to her, their eyes condemning. Indeed, perhaps all the eyes of the world!

"Why do you violate our world, and the sacredness of life, with your madness?"

Pressure inflated inside her. The muscles of her stomach tightened, and her vision blurred. She squirmed.

I think I am insane! An insane and desperate woman and artist. How many women walk around this world dressed as the statue of a dead virgin countess? Might one consider that a little peculiar?

The air in the cathedral became suffocating. The dark countenance of the priest moved in slow motion; his voice grew louder and louder. He seemed to be looking at her, and Anna knew he directed his closing message to the mad human sculpture.

"And God wants all of his children to be truthful. Falsity and pretense is condemned. Surrender yourself to His truth. Surrender yourself to be saved!"

Anna cringed. People stood and solemnly queued before the altar to take communion. She looked at the poignant figure of Christ.

Cut out my mind and heart, Lord, and serve them to a feast of lunatics! Change me!

Anna felt an intense, probing stare upon her. She looked at the person who had sat to her left. It was a handsome though oddly vague woman with a regal continence, black hair, pale olive skin, and cocoa-gray eyes. She was dressed in a beige evening robe, similar to the one Anna wore. *Most inappropriate for church,* Anna noted.

"I am the ugliest and most imperfect woman ever on this Earth," the ghostly Countess spoke in a voice saddened by ages of pain. "You must help me!"

Anna's muscles petrified. Horror engraved her face. She struggled to look away from the spectral woman.

Anna rose and walked to the front of the church, fighting an impulse to look back at the haunted Countess. She stood beneath the figure of Christ that towered over her like a surreal dying god. With a finger she touched her body four times in the gesture of a cross.

"Bless me, Lord," she pleaded.

Although not Catholic, she stood in line, nervous and fidgeting, to take communion. Moments scratched. Then her turn. The priest looked up and down her bizarre, marbleized presence and then smiled.

"This is the flesh of Christ," he spoke and placed a wafer in her mouth.

"This is the blood of Christ," he said and handed her a cup. She drank.

More than ever, Anna needed the blood and flesh of Christ.

Guy remained seated in the pew, curiously observing Anna performing the ritual. *How amusing,* he thought and smiled. Then she quickly walked to him, took his hand and virtually dragged him out of the cathedral.

*　　*　　*

The darkened city streets. Anna walked in a frail state of detachment. *I am a ghost,* she thought. *A nonexistent presence.*

Enveloping fright. Voices of pedestrians, slowed and amplified, floated past. Motions, leaden and ponderous. Buildings stood as hulking props on a theatrical stage. The illuminate beams of car headlights slashed like violent, glowing swords through black space. The city's soul seemed terrified into an alert consciousness.

Guy watched her, worry etching his face.

"What is it, Anna? What's wrong?" He several times asked, but Anna did not reply. She kept anxiously looking deep into the dark of evening, into the inky pit, as if a ravenous beast waited.

Fifteen minutes later, they walked down Alexandria Avenue toward their apartment building. Few people were on the street. The city seemed paused and still. Phantom shadows invaded the diffused light of street lamps.

A sonorous pounding. Hammers of the gods drummed the ground. Red blinking lights appeared in the night. A police helicopter swept into the blackness above them and circled—a monstrous, silhouette bird searching for a threat.

Suddenly they were enveloped in a brilliant white light. The copter's searchlight beam locked onto Guy and Anna and tracked them down the street. They walked inside its near-blinding luminance.

"Wow!" they both exclaimed, their bodies blanched white like ghostly specters.

Guy looked up. His poet and artist mind beheld a spectacular vision! Magnificent angels in flowing white gowns, their feathered wings flapping, circled in the rapturous light. Like a chorus from heaven, they sang a sweet hymn, their voices creating intricate yet perfectly woven harmonies.

"Rise, light souls, of beauty and grace.

Rejoice in Him who brings you peace!"

Bathed in a baptism of light! Anna thought as a pressure, the terrible pressure, lifted from her. She looked upward, and her vision was erased by whiteness. With the eye that sees when sight is blinded, she saw the figure of the Countess, awakened at last to that beauty that may not be seen or touched, but always is.

The Countess lifted upwards, both captive and willing, into the source of the light and disappeared, Anna knew, forever.

"I feel oddly saved," she shouted to Guy, her marble face glistening in the light's radiance. "Although I'm not certain from what. Time to discard the statue shell and return to life."

"I rather like you as a statue," Guy shouted in her ear. "Will you continue to be silent and still?"

"No. Only in my soul and death," Anna replied, her voice barely heard over the thunderous pounding of the helicopter, which seemed to negate her. She puzzled for a moment over her words.

Light, then gray, then dark and silence. Peace.

*   *   *

Back in her apartment, still in her statue persona, Anna stood before a bedroom mirror. She looked at herself, a reflection of the sculpture of a common woman.

"Every woman is beautiful and perfect!" she affirmed aloud, once, with conviction.

She removed the persona, showered, and then returned to the bedroom and stood again, naked, before that large mirror of truth. She stared at her reflection, examining its face, its body, its demeanor. The image looking back seemed estranged and distant.

Who, and what the hell, am I?

Chapter 16

It was simple and unexpected. One evening, in Guy's apartment, he and Anna drank Morellino di Scansano Italian wine and dined on French bread and Brie cheese while listening to the impressionist music of Ravel. Anna was in her Vestal Virgin Persona wearing a white gown that wrapped from her neck to her feet, a suffibuluma, or white veil, and a long pala, or shawl, and demure cosmetics. Suddenly Guy decided to communicate some of his truth, his truth about Anna, to her. *It was time.*

But he could not just speak it. That was too commonplace. So he abruptly stood and performed a complex, impromptu mime.

He waved his arms, bloated his eyes, and moved like a ghost. Then he exploded his hands through the air.

Anna deciphered it, excitedly bouncing in her chair. "A ghost! Me! The Woman Inside the Ghost of Herself. The Event. The first night we met."

Guy then patted his chest above his heart rapidly, simulating palpitations.

"Intense feeling. Love!" Anna shouted and laughed.

Guy then swept through fast scenarios: swimming in the ocean, running a long distance, playing a game in the desert, assisting a depressed person, frolicking among statues in a cemetery. Between each enactment he pounded his heart harder and faster until he finally swooned dramatically and dropped helpless onto the floor.

Anna grinned. "I believe you are trying to tell me something. Mmm, what might that be?" She drummed her finger on her chin. "I think I can interpret it."

Guy sat beside her.

"OK. The moment demands words." He spoke. "Here goes. Anna, since I first met you, I've wanted to be with you. And from the second day, when you were Nature's Rapture, I've wanted to be with you, totally." He looked into her eyes. "I wanted *you*."

Anna startled, flinching. "Repeat that last statement, Guy. Please."

Guy peered at her curiously. "I wanted *you*."

"Can you put it in present tense? Would that be correct?"

Guy had no difficulty saying it. "I want *you*."

Anna leaned forward and kissed him long on the lips. *That* surprised her.

"Guy, I'm very happy to hear that. It feels good. I think. Although, I'm a little . . . astonished! Yet, not really. Yet I am. Not. Am." She paused and grinned. "Something in me has been asleep. Dormant. A long, long time." She stared into significance. "Waiting. Maybe hiding. But now, it is awakening!"

His eyes brightened. "Awaken, Anna!"

"Ever since the night of my dark depression," Anna trembled at the memory, "my thoughts and feelings have been changing. You were so kind and loving to me. It seemed critical to you that I recovered, as if *your* life and being depended upon it. I've never experienced that from another person. It affected me." She smiled luminescent. "So whatever you do, do not leave. Do not leave my life."

"I don't think I could."

"I think I've been foolish and unfair to you."

"No, Anna, no." He took both of her hands and squeezed them gently. "That's not how it's been. Every moment I've been with you has been special. It hasn't really mattered what we've been doing. Just think of everything we've already experienced together."

She did think. "Yes. It's been fabulous! And that's part of what I've feared. Losing that. Love is so splendid but treacherous. Its kiss can carry the serpent's bite. And I'm afraid I've become cowardly in that area." She took a large gulp of the sublime but potent wine. "But listen Guy, listen now."

She straightened and looked with piercing intensity into his eyes. Guy sat attentive.

"On this night, I make a vow to you. I will confront our relationship, fully, and my fears. For I know it's time for change. And now, I want that change." Her expression animated. "Yes! I speak the truth. I want . . . the life beyond the shell. This is a turning, and I like turnings."

She smiled, surrendering into his caressing eyes.

"You know it's already changed," she augmented. "It's changed over recent weeks. I do feel different. Do you feel it?"

"Yes, I do," Guy replied. "It feels like growing up. Like we've been kids in some wonderland, some enchanted and strange place of visions and creations. And now we're walking into the world, the world of streets and families and . . . real life. 'Look Anna! There's a broken street light on the corner.'" Guy pointed dramatically toward nothing. "It's darker and mysterious, but exciting. Does it scare you?"

Anna stared. "Yes, it does scare me, but let's walk through it anyway."

Guy nodded. "Dear Anna, I think it's about fear. That paralyzing nothing! Painted demons in the air. Threats that do not even exist. And even if they do, they are much weaker than love. We have to deal with our fears better. I do not want to lose you to fear."

"You're right, and you won't. Don't worry!" Her tone was convincing although her expression tensed. "We won't lose our relationship to a broken street lamp." She laughed and then sipped her wine. "More wine, Guy?"

"Yes, please. We can always just get drunk."

For a long moment, Guy and Anna sat quiet, reflecting on their talk and their relationship, each in their own world and yet sharing it with the other.

"I feel strange, Anna. Do you?" Guy interrupted their meditations. "I think we've come into reality more, whatever that is. A bigger reality. And it demands we confront it more boldly."

Anna lifted her wine glass in a toast. "To reality, our greatest challenge!"

Guy tapped his glass against hers. "To reality!"

They drank. Guy suddenly felt a powerful impulse. "Anna, I need to tell you something."

He was about to explain his worsening lunacy, his relapse into the hallucinations and voices, an immensely dark but present reality. A cold intruder stepped in front.

"Yes?"

"No, nothing. Nothing important. I'll tell you another time."

"Well, OK." Anna stared at him curiously and then stretched her graceful arms. "Weariness befalls me. I must sleep." She feigned an exaggerated yawn.

"Anna, I enjoyed this night. It was memorable. And critical, I think."

"Yes. A turning."

When they stood, she embraced him warmly and kissed him on his lips.

"That was nice. Things are turning well," Guy said, and Anna smiled.

She pulled him tighter against her and held him close for a prolonged, precious moment. Guy felt she was communicating something but he wasn't certain what. He wanted to present an affecting gesture so he borrowed from Juliet.

"Goodnight, goodnight. Parting is such sweet sorrow, that I shall say goodnight till it be 'morrow."

Anna completed the sentiment. "A thousand times goodnight."

They released their embrace, and Guy walked toward the door.

"Guy, wait!"

He turned.

Anna shrugged and smiled. "Artists and lovers," she said.

Guy did not understand. And then he did.

Chapter 17

LATER THAT NIGHT. Guy, resting on his bed, stared at a delicate dance of light on the wall cast by the outside moonlight filtering through the leaves of a palm tree rustled by the wind. Its mirage patterns appeared both real and illusion.

As my life and romances, he, amused, reflected. Although he felt unusually happy, he could not prevent a profound sadness from encroaching.

Duality, he thought.

Later. Floating in the absolving womb of sleep. A loud knocking, a violent intrusion, echoed through his somnolent consciousness. Guy awoke. The knocking was at his apartment door. A glance at the green illuminated numbers on his clock radio indicated it was 3:21 a.m. He noticed an unusual stale scent.

"What the hell?"

Guy pulled his drowsy, leaden body off the bed, stumbled to a lamp and switched it on. The light's sudden glare seared his eyes. More knocks.

He walked to the door, opened it and startled. A woman stood in the hall's stark fluorescent light.

"Mother?"

"Hi, Guy! I came over to play. Is it OK?" The woman-child asked.

She posed with her hands on her hips in a stance of impatient waiting. Her hair and facial features were that of his mother—rounded cheeks, soft nose, full lips—but she was attired as a little girl, wearing a pink blouse and a red plaid skirt with cream ruffle trim, falling to just above her scuffed knees. Her socks were white, her shoes red sneakers, and her hair curled like his mother's with a pink bow clipped to its top. Doll patches of red rouge brightened her cheeks.

Guy looked through the woman into a black space. A terrible memory haunted his mind: his mother, regressed into the six-year-old girl, eerily playful. He pried his attention off the image and investigated the face of the woman before him. It was her, but her eyes were Anna's.

"Anna, is that you?"

She smiled and shuffled past him into his living room. Then she skipped around the floor, occasionally spinning, her arms floating through the air like a dancer's.

"This is the night of nights," she sang in a little girl singsong, her head rolling as her eyes scoured the room. "Light and dark. Good and bad. So, so happy and sad. Hi Guy!"

Her dance stilled, and she stared at him with electrified eyes.

Guy did not respond. He stood motionless in his tan pajama pants and white undershirt and stared back. Quickly his logic scrambled to comprehend. Anna had created a persona of his mother from a photograph on his wall and then improvised the look of the six-year-old girl from the story he had told of his mother's regression. But why?

"What . . . are you doing?" His words were paced.

"I wanna play! I wanna play!"

Her rhythm was again singsong, and her head rocked. She raised her arms and skipped in one rotation.

"There's nobody on the beach. Mom and Dad's asleep. I'm tired of counting sheep! I wanna play and love!" She shook her finger at Guy. "Don't be such a creep!"

She seated her hands on her hips, cocked her head, and waited.

"You're not gonna play?" Her voice was a plaintive whine. She sighed and plopped onto a chair, her legs sprawled out, and twirled a finger through the ribbon on her hair.

Guy glared sternly. "What is this, Anna? You are Anna, right?"

The girl-mother looked down, her brow lowered.

"Anna? Yes, I think I am, and I am not!" She giggled. "I am her, and I am more. I'm a little girl and a mommy." She examined a point in space. "Yes! I'm Little Girl Mommy Anna! I'm here to play and love. You like?"

Her smile broadened and her eyes gleamed eager.

Guy stood mute. She sunk lower in the chair and frowned, her lips puffed and her eyes sorrowful.

"You keep leaving me in my room all by myself. It's so lonely there." She sounded an exaggerated sigh. "It's lonely and quiet. It's cold and dark." She wrapped her arms around her chest and shivered. "Like a grave. You keep me in a cold, dark grave!" Her eyes emptied. "You didn't really love me, your Mommy, or your Little Girl Mommy. You didn't love either. You put us in a cold dark grave. Alone with worms and death. A cold dark grave. Cold dark grave. Cold dark grave!"

Her eyes gazed wildly around the room. Her repeated incantations twisted at Guy's mind. His face hardened into a mask.

The girl's voice deepened and she looked at Guy with lost-soul eyes.

"I loved you, Guy." The mother spoke. "I loved you as best I could since the moment you were born. But you didn't help me. You watched me go mad. You buried me." She paused and sniffed. "Why does it smell so stale in here? Like being buried alive."

"Oh, Mommy! You can be such a dreadful bore!" The little girl spoke.

Then a seductive smile. Slowly, teasingly, she rubbed her left breast. "I've come to be with you tonight, Guy." The voice was Anna's. "I know you've been waiting, and *now* is the time!"

She rubbed her thighs together and giggled. She leapt from the chair and skipped in a circle around Guy.

"Let's play skip and sit! Skip and sit, skip and sit!"

She continued skipping and then plopped onto the floor and frowned. "Ooops!" She giggled, sprang to her feet, and resumed skipping.

"Stop it, Anna! Stop it!" Guy shouted. "Why are you doing this?"

The little girl Anna halted her skipping. Her face drooped. "You don't want to play no more?" Her lower lip trembled. Then she straightened and her expression sobered.

The mother. "But we always played games, Guy. Everything was a game—the mother-son game, the love and madness game. Don't you remember?"

The little girl. "Mommy and son. Flesh and breasts and other things!"

Anna. "Everything is a game, my dearest Guy. Like personas, and love, and tragic mothers, and sons and lovers and friends."

"Same game, same game!" The little girl swayed. "Mommy's insane, Guy. And I'm insane and you're insane. We're all insane! Same. Insame." She grinned. "Sanity. Samity. Sane. Insame. We're all insane same!" She laughed with the abandon of a lunatic.

Then the girl-woman calmed. Gleaming eyes probed Guy's. "Love, death, and madness." She spoke hushed. "Oh! I like the madness game! Let's play madness and death! Madness and death. Madness and death."

Guy's muscles tightened. He felt queasy. "Stop it! Stop it!" he screamed, anger tautly rimming his eyes. He raised his arm about to strike her.

The girl-woman stilled. A thick silence suffocated the room. She suddenly seemed to Guy an artifact, motionless in the dimly lit space, like a sculpture or a painting. He observed her curiously, and she stared back, her eyes beseeching. They stood staring at each other. The girl-mommy took a few steps back until she was leaning against the wall-sized Edenic Garden painting. She glanced over her shoulder, looked at Guy compassionately, and breathed deeply.

"You have waited a long time for me, Guy, and I have waited for you. Too long!" She unfastened the top button of her blouse. "Make love to me. Now. Tonight."

She removed her blouse and dropped it to the floor. A black lace bra with deep cleavage lifted her breasts, which heaved with her breathing. The Anna woman reached behind her, unfastened the clip, slowly peeled the bra off and dropped it.

"When you were a little baby," the mother spoke, her eyes tender, "I used to love being naked and holding you close against my chest as you nursed. I loved your sweet baby body, so warm and soft."

She rubbed her left breast and then rolled the nipple in her fingers.

"Can you still feel my nipple in your mouth, Guy? Can you taste my milk?" She looked at her breast. "You were my love, Guy, and I yours. Remember?" She smiled lasciviously.

"I know you like my breasts, Guy." Anna laughed softly. "You *always* look at them. I like that. I tease you with my cleavage. Look! The breasts of a woman!" She pushed a breast up. "The breasts of the woman you love. *Your* woman, tonight, Guy." Her eyes reached, teasing. "Tonight, these breasts are yours. Touch them. Taste them. Go ahead. Enjoy them!"

The little girl giggled. "Nice, big boobs!"

Guy looked at her rounded breasts, flushed with pink, their nipples erect. The hard anger in his face softened, and he felt a molten desire. His hand reached toward them and then halted.

"Stop it, Anna, please! What the hell . . . ."

She cut off his protest with a finger before her lips. "Shsssh." She unfastened her skirt and shimmied, the skirt dropping to the floor. Her hips gyrated.

"Nice, yes? It's all yours, Guy. Everything you desire. No Anna Spirit Persona tonight, babe! It's Anna Sex Persona!" She laughed and rubbed her inner thigh. "Love me, Guy. Tonight. For I love thee."

Her thumb hooked the top of her black lace panties and, wiggling gently, she pulled them down, past her pelvis and then her knees. She stepped out of the panties and stood naked.

"You never really loved me, Guy." The mother spoke. "Love me now, son. Hard and deep. Love your Mommy. I need it!"

She rubbed her breast with one hand as the other gently massaged her pubic area. Her legs trembled.

"Let's make love, hot and nice! It'll be all flesh and spice!"

The little girl sang and giggled. Her head rolled back and her eyes closed as she massaged her breast and pubis. Her body swayed, rubbing against the painting, as in a sensual seduction of the garden paradise. The seductress moaned, and her eyes opened and stared at Guy.

"Let's play fun, bad games!" The little girl laughed. "Flesh and breasts and incest. Can you make love to this little girl? Yes, oh yes!" She wiggled her body. "Love me, Guy, your Little Girl Mommy Anna. Your Little Girl Mommy Anna." Her fingers stroked deeper, and she moaned. "Love me, your Little Girl Mommy Anna!"

Guy's stomach wrenched and his fist clenched. His face and eyes hardened, stabbing coldly at the woman-child before him. His arm rose aggressively. Then a paralysis froze him.

"Love and madness. Madness and death. Love and death," his naked lady chanted. The erotic pleasuring of her body became more rapid and her sighs deepened.

"Your Little Girl Mommy Anna!"

She laughed, a laughter increasing in volume, at moments abandoned and hideous, and then provocative and taunting, like a mad, seductive demon. For a frozen moment Guy believed he was hearing all the tortured passion of human life, of his life. She glared invitingly, and condemningly, deep into his eyes, laughing that terrible, deranged laughter.

"Stop it! Stop it!" Guy shouted, his eyes piercing and enraged. He reached toward her shoulders. His fingers touched her flesh.

She vanished.

An empty space and the garden painting confronted him. He stared at a painted emerald plant with violet blossoms.

Trembling. Several steps back. The room silent. So silent it reverberated in his ears like a grieving song in an empty tomb. His hands tousled his hair. His eyes turned down and fixed on the rug. He could not see anything. A blur and a crushing feeling.

Everything betrays me!

He felt heavy, his body numb. With movements dragged, pulling a deadened weight, Guy retreated to a small space in the corner of the room and sat on the floor. His arms wrapped around his legs, pulling them tightly against his chest, and he rocked. He rocked and rocked, his eyes closed, mumbling words. Broken words.

"I can't, no I won't, oh god, I have to, no, yes.

He dropped on his side and curled into a fetal position.

Guy prayed for sleep to bring him unconsciousness, kind and redeeming unconsciousness. He waited, trying to think only of that nothingness and sleep. Time, unkind, clawing, passed. He stared into his mind. *Madness.* A descending darkness. *Madness.* An absence. *To sleep. To nothing.* A numbing void consumed him.

He was slipping below the line.

*　　*　　*

Guy awoke the next morning, curled on the floor, lying in a gentle light, the resurrected sunlight that washed through the expansive living room window. He felt a blissful moment, a peaceful sense. *I awaken and move into a new day, fresh and pure.*

Then a terrible dread descended; he sank. He would not, and then he did, open his eyes. "Oh God!"

The memory of the previous night's visitation assaulted his mind. He rolled onto his back and stared at the ceiling. A stained vacancy. He did not move, feeling afraid to rise, afraid to walk into another tormented day.

The communication with Anna, the expressions of hope and change, only an evening earlier, now seemed attenuated, drifting away.

Guy thought of praying, praying to some greater power to relieve his plight. *No!* he resolved. *What rational mind accepts the illusion of divine assistance, or the expectation of any help at all from a glorified abstraction?*

The words of a poem he once penned seized his thoughts. 'To deaden the weight, a prayer for gods and white winged things, and dreams in the ether of soul of an essence atoned and whole.'

"White winged things, ether of the soul," he spoke, accented by a cruel laugh. "As my life, as dreams and hallucinations and nightmares, it's all madness!"

Guy suddenly knew what he must do. He believed that a return to his medications would quell his worsening symptoms, his hallucinations and voices, his terror, within a week.

I have failed. I cannot bear this. There is no other recourse but the drugs. So be it!

His resolution was quick and determined, and yet he felt as small and helpless as a child, reluctantly receiving a punishment he had desperately hoped to avert. He stood.

Then. Suddenly. A surprising sensation! Gentle, ascending from within, appearing to emanate from his heart, or perhaps his spirit. A feeling light and warm. He suspended all movement and focused on the sensation. He thought it was like the touch of a reassuring love, as he had only experienced at rare times in his life. And it embraced his being.

Where does this come from?

An answer floated into his consciousness. He had encountered it before. It was higher spirit, or the Spiritual Universe, communicating to him, *to help.* He smiled excitedly and looked around the room. The space of his world no longer appeared so grave, so gray, but purer. The colors on his wall garden painting glimmered. His plants appeared vital and alive. Even the air seemed charged with a peculiar, vibrant energy. He felt immensely relieved.

"Prayer or not, spirit responds!" he whispered in a voice as gentle as the breath that carried it.

And as a soft yet pervasive light, that wonder lifted the darkness.

A most remarkable phenomenon! I am in a Moment, he realized. *Rare and transforming. Something helps me!*

Again he recalled the previous night and its taunting assault, but now it did not seem so menacing.

What is it that so terrifies and threatens me? Hallucinations? Conjured voices and visions? Are they not like illusionary demons in a nightmarish painting? Of no substance or power? Guy smiled and looked at a painting on the wall. *Only a child is terrified by painted devils. I am a man!*

Those last words fortified him with confidence. *Yes, a man! A man who does not need cushioning drugs to face his world. A man who obviously has more sublime help. Yes!*

Guy walked to the window and looked out at the world. The morning light was white and pristine, serenely painting the city in pale colors.

"Every day the world is renewed, as I must be, too," he spoke to the day. "I am not the lunacy that haunts me. There will be no return to medications. Let love and spirit redeem me. So be it!"

Guy looked into the hazy, cerulean sky and smiled.

"I will visit Anna before she goes to work. And she will be Anna, not some mad confusion of ghosts. Perhaps we will take a stroll or have breakfast. We may speak of a stirring philosophical concept or a captivating movie. Then I will go through the remainder of my day, hour by hour, with strength and faith, and without medications. And I will be fine. Amen!"

Chapter 18

"I HAVE TO go to the hospital, Anna. The psych ward."

Anna's apartment, days later. Guy, a paragon of patience, sat on the sofa observing Anna, domestic queen, vacuuming; she casual and floppy in baggy knock-about clothes. *Funky,* Guy thought.

A polka dot scarf wrapped her hair, like Lucille Ball. Guy felt charmed. *I Love Lucy;* nostalgia. Lucy devotedly attending to household chores. Ricky Ricardo, hubby, bursts through the door. An urgent crisis. A madcap lunacy.

Never lunacy with Anna! Guy did not know whether Anna was merely dressed for housewifery or was in a persona—the American Housewife Persona; he could never be certain of the truth behind Anna's veils. Either way, she looked cute, like a domestic fantasy. I Love Anna.

"Honey, can we slip in a quick romp before the baby's bottle?" He, the devoted and passionate husband, asks.

"Trying is half the fun, dear!" She, the loyal yet playful wife, replies.

A persistent mystery was resolved. Anna's apartment was always ordered and clean, in contrast to the slovenly disarray of his own, even though he never witnessed her cleaning. He had come to believe that some mystical power, perhaps from Anna's own spirit or from higher gods, maintained a clean order and grace in her home, for no other reason than it was correct, for it was Anna's space.

Alas! Another fantasy crushed, Guy bemoaned. *Truths of domesticity in the American household.*

"What is it? What's wrong?"

Anna now sat beside him on the sofa, her chores completed and her eyes fraught with dismay. Psych ward? A gray streak of dust marred her cheek. Guy rubbed it off with his finger.

"Tell me what's happening."

"It's nothing, Anna. Routine. Once a year I have to spend a week in the hospital for group therapy and psychiatric evaluation. It's a requirement to maintain my disability benefits and part of my ongoing therapy. They do believe I'm quite sick, you know."

He contorted his face, a lunatic.

Anna no smile. "But what happens there?"

"Just group sessions and some private talks with knowing doctors. And medication reviews. Then they declare you still insane, but improving, and everything continues; status quo!"

He looked past her through a window at the sky. A clear day. Pigeons in their aerial dance. *A constant in this world,* he thought.

"People try to understand their pain. Why they have trouble loving. Why the world is insane."

Anna stared down at the rug. She stared at rugs when perturbed. She knew rugs well.

"And whether they're better because they're insaner or worse because they're saner, or something like that," Guy added.

"You're improving your life, all the time. I see that. Don't they?"

"I don't know if I want them to see that fully. I could lose the disability, and the benefits are good. It helps."

Anna inverted happy face. "Disability? You're not disabled! You're a wonderful, gifted man, a good person. You're no more mad or disabled than any human."

"Then I still qualify." He paused. "There are things that plague me."

"Things plague all of us!" Anna glanced at her Cadillac model with the smashed front end. *Crash!* she thought.

Is this the time to tell her more? Instead, Guy grinned.

"My lunacy, it's a little more than I've told you, but nothing to worry about. It may actually be a blessing. You know, helping me as an artist, or it may be just par for the human condition, helping me maintain my humanity. Although, do you know what I've been thinking, Anna?"

"What?"

"I've been thinking of giving it all up, my disability benefits and therapies and medications and doctors, all of it. Even though it's been granted to me interminably. That was decided over a decade ago, by psychiatrists, when they labeled me borderline schizophrenic." He looked away. "But I never agreed with that. I'm considering letting go of it. All the crutches. Like starting over."

Anna happy face. "Starting over. I like that! Or at least a major change. I believe in you, Guy."

"But it's hard to give up financial support. To try to survive."

"Bullshit! You could. I know you could! You could live off your work, your paintings and writings. It might be a struggle at first. We all struggle. But you can do it. In fact, you're meant to do it."

Guy happy face. "Yes, I think so."

"I know so. Drop all this lunacy business, no matter what you're going through. Who cares if we're mad anyway? Artists are supposed to be insane because the world's insane. Do it, Guy! I'll help you. And forget the hospital visit. That frightens me."

"Why?"

Like some devastating horror in a movie. She curbed it. "I don't know. Something's wrong there. Like something final. Like you may not be able to return."

He took her hand, shook it gently, and chuckled. "No, no. I've gone many times. I actually enjoy it. All the drama and insights. And I'm such a loner, except for the time I'm with you. It's good for me to be around the people there. It helps keep me connected and gives me perspective. And I do learn about myself, my most compelling subject."

"But you're not alone. I'm with you."

"I know. Listen. I tell you what. I'll seriously consider making this hospital stay my last, and leaving the entire program. But give me a little time. It's a big change. It does worry me, and there's something I think I would need."

"What? What would you need?" Anna leaned closer.

Guy looked at a small painting on the wall across the room. The image was of a man and a woman on a desert plain, a black sun hanging above them.

"I need some of my dreams to become more real. Something deeply fine and lasting. I see it poetically. Like a more fertile earth to walk on, or my blood again joined with nature, a union weakened long ago. Or a death and rebirth into art. To live it." Guy searched. "Or perhaps a new family. Something deeper like that." His eyes roamed uneasily.

"I think I understand," Anna replied. "You want something more real and . . . sublime, to make it worth the risk." She glanced at that elusive nirvana. "That's good! There'd be something wrong with you if you didn't. I don't see why you couldn't have it. In fact, you do have it."

Guy's expression grew intense. "Yes, you're right. I do have it."

Instant enlightenment. Guy was not certain what he had but felt in his core that he had it.

"OK! For now I'll go to the hospital. I'll look at it more there. That's part of what we do there."

Anna not nirvana. "You have me in a trap. There's nothing I can say."

"Sorry, but I promise, Anna, things are changing. A turning, and I want you to be a part of it. Like we talked about. I need that."

She smiled and squeezed his hand. "I am, we are, it is." She took him in her arms and drew him close. "I will help, whatever you do. I want you to do well."

"As I do you, Anna."

She squeezed him tightly and kissed him. She wanted to kiss him again, but something pulled her away.

"I think I should go to the program, too. I don't make any sense."

"You make non-sense." Guy grinned. "There's something wondrous about a shared madness."

Anna laughed, but reservedly. "I will ride to the hospital with you."

She glimpsed an idea.

*   *   *

The morning of Guy's departure for the hospital, a surprise waited.

He knocked on Anna's door. "Enter!" bellowed from inside. He walked in. A haze of sunlight filtering through the room's gold curtains created that dawn-on-the-first-day-of-creation aura Guy always loved in Anna's apartment. Anna stood in the center of the living room. *Yes!* She looked more beautiful than he had ever seen her before. She stood straight and dignified, as a goddess possessing her domain, her hands at her side with their palms turned outward as in a receiving.

It was the Anna he knew and yet an illusive beauty redefined her. Guy struggled to comprehend the effect. *It was transcendence.*

She waved her hand down the front of her body.

"I call this the Aesthetic Being Persona. I create it about once a year to acknowledge the importance and power of aesthetics, the pursuit of ideal form and beauty, or on special occasions. And since this is a day we share before a parting, I thought it such an occasion."

Anna had devoted hours that morning to her creation. Aesthetics involves discriminating subtleties but potent transformation. Hers was the masterful application of cosmetics and fashion to create the most beautiful and ideal expression of herself, a pursuit of every woman elevated to the stature of art.

"Although aesthetic perfection may be impossible to achieve, except by God in nature," she elaborated, assured but humble, "every person can approximate it, can pursue the illusion, for every person is innately beautiful, especially me!" Anna grinned. "I truly believe that. That is what this persona expresses."

"You've come damn close!" Guy commended, his eyes a rapturous meditation.

Every detail of Anna's appearance, every color, shape, texture, and item of clothing, was meticulously chosen or created to achieve, as near as possible, aesthetic perfection. Gorgeous hues of sienna and auburn browns, accented with soft gold, were blended through her hair to suggest the natural loveliness of an earthen landscape in the sun, as during the glorious moments between afternoon and dusk. Several wayward strands danced across her forehead in a ballet of colors. Delicate cosmetic tinctures ideally reshaped her face, cheekbones higher, chin rounded, and nose redefined to be precisely proportional to surrounding contours. Her complexion had a radiant, translucent quality. Her already full lips were painted with rose hues into an alluring bloom with precisely the correct color and chroma to complement her eyes, balancing her face and keeping its plane perpendicular. Her lips edges were darker fuchsia, evoking a seductive mystery.

The woman of common beauty becomes the woman of extraordinary beauty, Guy thought and drifted into a reflection. Often when he and Anna were in public, he wondered why every man who beheld her did not immediately fall in love with her. So, as inquisitive artists often do, he placed himself into their viewpoints and perceived her through their eyes. It was in those moments that he realized that others probably viewed Anna as a woman of pleasant, although common, attractiveness. He saw that it was love that painted a woman into such absolute beauty as he perceived Anna. She was always beautiful to him, and whether spoken and reciprocated or not, he always loved her.

But that morning Guy believed that if any man viewed Anna, as she now stood before him, he would think it was truly a goddess he beheld.

Her eyes! An artful blend of flesh, turquoise, and pale green eye shadow framed them in a mystical aura. They were the most alluring colors on her, properly drawing one's attention to her captivating eyes, that gateway to the soul, that portal to infinite mystery. Employing mascara and eyelash extensions she created, but did not overstate, the illusion of her eyes sweeping up and outward in the classic exotic expression.

"According to students of the cosmos and science fiction," Anna tutored, "the upward and outward sweeping eye, as in many Orientals, is the dominant eye shape among beings in the universe. Thus in our consciousness it is associated with a universal and classic ideal, which we then interpret as a perfect aesthetic, the eye's most beautiful form.

"It is not coincidental that Martians and other extraterrestrials from 1950's films on have graceful, upward contoured eyes."

Anna smiled, proud of her esoteric presentation, and blinked those celebrated archetypal eyes. A glint of the infinite looked upon the world.

Her persona's attire consisted of a European gown suitable, meaning aesthetically ideal, for either evening dining or afternoon strolls through the park. Sleeveless with thin straps over her shoulders, it was lovely and comfortable for all occasions. Its cut and lines complemented her body's form creating smoother curves and more graceful rounds. A precise degree of cleavage offered a sensual and feminine, although not exploitative or fixating, revelation of her sultry breasts, and a sublime expression of Nature.

Noticing Guy's momentary and pleased attention on them, Anna looked down and examined the edge of the dress cleavage. The tone of her face hardened. With two fingers she adjusted the gown's edge over her left breast, pulling it a fraction of an inch inward.

"Perfect!" she proclaimed, grace repossessing her demeanor.

The sleek but comfortable silk dress was black; the absence of color sometimes being the ideal color, the simplest of aesthetics, always elegant on a woman. Her earrings were gold rods, adding an accent of class, and a precious gold chain encircled her sleek neck. Her stockings were black with a delicate semi-transparent design.

Guy took a step back and viewed the totality of the persona. He thought most impressive of all was Anna's achievement in creating an expression of herself that was simultaneously physical and ethereal, as if her material form had evolved into an illusive spiritual presence. That mirage ideal of herself achieved the true triumph of aesthetics: the transformation of the physical into the spiritual, as when a masterful painting transcends the solidity of paint and canvas to become a mystical vision. It was her most subtle yet powerful persona.

"Anna's ideal form and beauty!" Guy heralded. "Now, how do you assess me, scruffy in my old jeans, faded T-shirt, and thrift shop sport coat?"

Anna grinned. "Perfect!"

"We must share your presentation with the world," Guy declared. "Art is for all the people."

"Yes, as are we. We offer our aesthetic ideals to this flawed but wondrous world. And I know where we should dine."

Anna presented her enigmatic, Mona Lisa smile.

*   *   *

The Forty-Fourth Floor. The most dangerous restaurant in Los Angeles, and the most spectacular. Guy and Anna stopped there for breakfast in route to the hospital. They read a warning sign at the door and signed legal waivers.

Guy looked down and jolted. Below a glass floor was absolutely realistic imagery of the city streets and sidewalks far below. Cars and pedestrians scuttled like toys. Guy felt like he was walking on air hundreds of feet above the city.

And there were no walls.

Men at their tables stared at Anna the aesthetic ideal as she walked her runway. She and Guy sat at a rectangular glass table one yard from the glass floor's edge. No guard railings. No perimeter chain. Nothing but a half-inch blue line at the floor's edge whispering caution; beyond it a forty-four story drop to the streets below. In what Guy thought a humorous touch, seat belts hung from the sides of the chairs.

Anna pointed up. An extraordinary vision! Above the glass ceiling appeared a majestic, fantasy sky, lucid blue with explosions of white clouds and gorgeous gold and orange sunrays. Angels, appearing alive, flew or floated through the splendor. A couple were archetypal white angels of classical art. Another was ethereal semi-transparent—spirit. Others were in a variety of styles. Expressionistic in vibrant colors. Black leathered, including wings—a punk angel. *Mondi!* Guy thought with Mondi glee. Two, a male and a female, were naked with flesh wings. Another Guy designated pop art, painted in brash Andy Warhol hues. An L.A. Lakers angel, in Lakers gold and purple uniform, tossed and caught a basketball. An otherworldly futuristic angel wore a chrome suit and glimmering metallic wings.

Using rear projection technology from the movie industry, the three dimensional vision of the glorious, angelic sky and the imagery of the city streets below were projected onto the ceiling and the floor. The sky angels, a homage to the City of Angels, were a mixture of filmed costumed stunt people and realistic computer simulations.

And around the diners an open-air panoramic view evoked the experience of dining in the clouds over Los Angeles. And always the fateful edge beckoned, creating the type of voltaged thrill Angelinos loved.

"So, Anna, why did you choose this restaurant?" Guy, looking over the top of his menu, queried, although he suspected he knew the answer.

Anna glanced at the ominous edge and then at the dazzling vistas beyond. "We are in a change, Guy. I think we both feel it. And with change is danger, and spectacular rewards. Hence the Forty-Fourth Floor Restaurant!" She grinned.

Guy understood. No more needed to be said.

He perused the stunning panoramic view. To the west were the contours of a distant Santa Monica and the blue-gray of the

Pacific Ocean, to the south the congested urbanscape of West Los Angeles, and far to the East loomed the hazy metropolis of downtown L.A., the city within the city.

A woman, a svelte blonde about twenty-five, seated with a female companion at a neighboring table, kept looking at Anna and then at Guy. Her smile sent discreet, seductive invitations. *It must be a fine man who would be the escort of such an exquisite woman,* Guy supposed she was thinking. He smiled pleasantly back at his admirer but offered no overt encouragement. He needed to be nowhere else. *I am already there.*

"Guy, the hospital visit. I . . . ."

Guy aborted Anna's statement with a raised finger. "Do not worry. I'll be fine."

Both fell silent. The odors of coffee and eggs tantalized Guy's senses. He looked beyond the floor's edge. The drop. Suddenly he felt terrified. Then he felt a powerful urge to stand and walk off it. Then he felt exhilarated, as if he could ascend to the heavens.

"To be or not to be. This restaurant works," he stated succinctly.

"Yes."

They studied their menus, made of transparent sheets of plastic with offerings in blue or gray print.

"I recognize you." A woman, standing before their table, declared with a high-octane smile to Anna. She had been seated at a table across the restaurant. "You're the shadow woman."

"Shadow woman?"

"I saw your play, *The Shadow World,* at the Paul Dubois Theater. It changed my life."

Anna leaned back and looked with intensified interest at the woman.

"I realized watching it that I was one of those shadow people," the becoming woman, dressed in a peach gown with a slit up a leg, explained. She was petite, about thirty, with stylishly short red hair and eyes as blue as the illusion sky above her. "Allow me to explain." She looked at Anna for agreement and Anna nodded.

The woman delayed a moment, staring into space. "My life seemed unreal. I always believed my world, the true world, waited elsewhere. I lived in the hope that one day, somehow, it would arrive." The woman shook her head. "Then, watching your play, near the end, it was like I just got it! I understood. It was *me* who had become a shadow. My world *was* real and true. It always had been! But it was as if I was not really in it." She peered at Anna intensely, as if seeking her understanding. "Something opened in me. I began to feel and experience everything: my work, my pain, my pleasures, my son. He's nine." She smiled. "And I took more command. I made new decisions. It was wonderful! I'm not a shadow anymore." The woman's grin sparkled.

Anna raised a brow. "I'm very happy to hear that. I know now at least one person got something from the play."

"And I'm so glad to see you again, to be able to thank you."

The admirer extended her hand and they shook.

"This is Guy, my friend," Anna announced.

"I'm very pleased to meet you, Guy." She turned again to Anna. "I'm Camille. Perhaps we could meet again and talk. I would like to buy you a dinner."

She removed a card from her pocket and handed it to Anna. It read, 'Awakened Fashion Boutique'.

"It's my new business, a fashion store. One of my changes. It's doing well, and it's fun."

"That's wonderful, Camille." Anna wrote her phone number on a napkin and handed it to Camille. "I'll call you."

"Very good. I'm so pleased I was able to thank you."

Camille suddenly silenced, her face grim. Her glance swept the room.

"I have a peculiar feeling. There's something dark in the air. Do you feel it? It's strange." She looked at Anna. "Be careful." Then she smiled again, shifting back into her salvation space. "Well, don't mind me. Probably just the restaurant. Enjoy your meals. I'll talk with you again. Bye, Anna. Bye, Guy."

Camille returned to her table. Anna looked at Guy, her face awakened as if touched by a wizard's wand.

"Wow! Often we don't realize what effect we may create on others."

"Yes. I think you have a new friend." Guy paused. "Something dark in the air," he spoke softly.

"What?"

"Nothing, Anna. Let's enjoy this morning."

For a couple minutes Anna sat silent, savoring her experience. Guy granted her those moments.

"This is a special occasion." She broke the silence. "It's my treat. Order your favorite." Her eyes reached at Guy. "I'll miss you. I'll . . . ." She halted her statement.

Guy ordered Eggs Benediction to the Gods and a Stratospheric Cappuccino. It was delicious. He did not want to think about missing Anna.

Meals completed. Tip left. The Aesthetic Being Lady and the painter/poet destined for the psych ward stood to leave. A voice spoke in Guy's head. *I kill love.*

"No!" He shouted. A force pushed. He took two steps and looked down. The tips of his shoes were on the blue line. The streets were so, so far below.

"Guy! Be careful!"

Anna grasped his arm and pulled him back, perplexity straining her face.

"Sorry. It's . . . oddly alluring." His smile was razor taut.

Guy trembled.

*   *   *

It seemed like Guy had entered a freshly scrubbed bathroom. He and Anna were in a Los Angeles Memorial Hospital hallway leading to the intake area. It had the pungent scent of ammonia disinfectant. *It challenges its foe,* he mused. Amiable graphic artworks broke the white purity of the walls with accents of colors and shapes and strategically located plants contributed a green reference to nature. A chrome wheelchair with an elderly male patient, ghostly in a white gown and pale, ailing flesh, quietly rolled by, navigated by a solemn pastel blue uniformed attendant. For a moment life sparked in the old man's eyes as he beheld the vision of Anna sweep by.

It was a hospital.

They passed through a swinging door with a sign above it announcing 'Psychiatric Ward'.

"Psychiatric ward," Anna moaned, her demeanor perturbed in contrast to the grace of her persona. She looked down at the tiled floor. "I hate that term."

"I'll have them change it to Department of Lunacy," Guy replied.

"Better, but not much."

Behind the intake counter sat a slender woman in a stolid gray suit and black frame Buddy Holly glasses. A gold charm of a baboon hung around her neck. Her mouth flapped urgently into a phone as her fingers sprinted across a computer keyboard. She held a hand up toward Guy commanding him to wait.

"I'll visit you here tomorrow," Anna said, taking Guy's hand in hers.

"Name please!" the receptionist barked as she slammed down the phone.

"Guy. Guy Noname."

Scowling eyes impaled him. "No name?"

"Yes ma'am."

Bony fingers stabbed at her keyboard. Her expression surprised when Guy Noname appeared on her screen. She mumbled incoherent words.

"Yes. You're scheduled for the annual psychiatric evaluation." She slowly looked at Guy with a devilish smile. "It's on Ward Eight."

"Ward Eight. That sounds humane." Anna rolled her eyes.

"But the lady," the receptionist scrutinized Anna, "the woman is not permitted there. She'll have to leave. Now!" She grinned combatively.

Anna's glare counterattacked. "Time is irrelevant to the insane. Surely, *you* must know that."

The receptionist's smile hardened into a grimace. Her compressed face reminded Anna of the Grinch from Dr. Seuss.

"I'll visit you tomorrow, Guy," Anna repeated.

"I think not, lady!" the Grinch interrupted. "This year no visitors are allowed during the week's program unless it's an extreme family emergency." She grinned smugly. "And that means *no one!*"

"But in the past visitors were always allowed," Guy rebutted.

"Yes, but it's a whole new game now. Isolation is critical to success. The world will totally disappear for you this week."

The Grinch emitted a ghoulish laugh, paused in thought, and then laughed louder, suggesting the caw of a crow.

You're a mean one, Ms. Grinch! Anna stared at her and then pulled Guy to a quieter corner of the lobby. Anna's voice sank.

"Why don't we just leave now? You don't need this." She looked at Ms. Grinch and then around the room. "I don't like it. Something's terribly wrong here."

"No, no. It's OK," Guy reassured. "It'll be fine here."

Anna grimaced. "It's a theater of insanity. Look at that witch!" She pointed to the Grinch.

Guy laughed. "I'm afraid it won't be that intriguing. Talk, tears, some drama, and an occasional witch. I'm melting! I'm melting!" Guy mimicked dissolving as his eyebrows flapped. "I've been through it many times."

Anna probed his eyes deeply, as she had when they first met on his rooftop.

"'Tis now the very witching time, when doctors' plot and patients weep! Please Guy, take care of yourself here."

They exchanged a few more expressions of concern and reassurance. Guy felt confident his stay would be an experience of benefit. Anna felt certain the gates to Bedlam had opened. Before departing, she hugged him tightly.

Anna felt warm and comforting in Guy's arms, and he again had his thought: *happiness could be found in an eternity of such moments.*

Anna kept him pressed tightly to her, as a mother protecting a child. She ran her fingers through his hair, kissed him on the forehead and then the cheek. *Must I send him into the jaws of psychiatry? Of madness?*

Very slowly she released him. Holding his hand, she struggled to leave. Guy accompanied her past the swing doors. Their hands remained touching until separation demanded their parting.

Guy watched Anna walk away down the hall, like a lovely, fading spirit returning to another domain. The Grinch receptionist observed, shaking her head and laughing slyly.

Chapter 19

"WE MAY NOT say it, man, but I know it. Like a mask, we wear the pallor of the loss of our humanity."

Raphael was in his mid-thirties, a sturdy man of six-feet-five. His complexion did not display the pallor of which he spoke, and his life attested differently.

"Our blood is with the people, and we have forsaken them. Look at me!" He gestured toward his face. "That is why I have this pallor, this damn cadaver face. It's the mask we all must wear."

Raphael was one of the nine members of Guy's therapy group and was his roommate. They sat in metal chairs in a circle, confronting themselves and each other. The room was medical pale green with two windows veiled by beige curtains. There was a stuffy odor, as if the room had not been aired for weeks. Guy could see that Raphael was extremely self-critical and conflicted, but he liked him.

"My soul hears you," Guy replied in support. "And your face does not bear that pallor."

Raphael grinned broadly, his intense umber eyes now fixed on Guy.

"I welcome my demons," he declared. "I love and hate them. They give me life—mad perhaps, but oh so passionate! So cruel and beautiful."

He laughed heartily, the resonant laugh of a man who had grown from the earth. His fingers rustled through his unkempt hair. Despite grooming standards for patients, he sported a stubby shadow beard.

"Like the people I've tried to help, I, too, am homeless in this world."

Guy felt sympathy for Raphael's plight and believed an injustice had been done him. He knew his story. Raphael was a self-proclaimed architect. Although unschooled, he built apparently livable structures of fiberboard and junk materials for homeless people throughout Los Angeles, wherever zoning laws were lax. But baffled, influential citizens were worried by his presence and creations. Shelters or trash? They questioned. And Raphael did display eccentric behavior.

He also possessed a passion for making love to women and had acquired a notable reputation in that arena. He seemed to infuse women with a sublime madness. After the wife of a city district attorney unabashedly abandoned herself to him fully, having enticed him with every seductive offering she could devise, he acquired new enemies. One day he was arrested for walking through the streets in his underwear after giving his clothes to an ailing, aged homeless man who had nothing. The city declared Raphael insane.

"Seems like you're just nice to people," Matty, short for Matilda, a name she detested, said in a timid voice, as a nun in prayer. "I don't know nothing about demons and stuff, but if I talk with people for more than three minutes, I become terrified."

She was a short, frail, middle-aged woman with hair beginning to gray and eyes carrying the fear of a child alone in the dark. She looked at her watch.

"Why three minutes?" Waldo, a tripolar shoe salesman, queried.

"Cause that's the time I can talk and not be terrified."

"Makes sense, kind of," Joseph replied with group member compassion.

Matty spoke rapidly, relating events of her daily life. "And I sit in Benny's with a friend, drinking coffee, you know, their coffee's good, talking 'bout time I spend in my garden, just weeding and watering my plants and stuff, or in my living room, taking care of my tropical fish, they're so pretty, or almost anything, you know . . . He tells me 'bout his wife, and I'm liking the talk. I really am! I'm not afraid. Nothing seems wrong. The waitress comes over, friendly girl, asks for our order. I tell."

Matty abruptly stopped, her face rigid.

"Go on, please, complete your story," Dr. Minfield, the group therapist, encouraged. But Matty sat mute, solid as stone.

"Why doesn't she continue?" Angela, an elderly lady recovering from a suicide attempt, questioned.

"Because her three minutes are up," Raphael replied. "It's OK, Matty. You don't need to speak."

"But try to speak just one minute more, or a few words, Matty, and see what happens," the doctor coached, leaning forward, his eyes prodding.

But Matty remained a mute wall, looking back at him with confused vacancy.

The group dropped into silence. Seconds wrenched by, elevating the patients anxiety.

"Sometimes I feel like a mad palm tree, screaming its truth into the night. No one listens, and even fewer care," Waldo confessed.

He bore the rare diagnosis of being tripolar. His emotional state alternated between extremes of being up, down, and in some other direction no one could identify. A couple patients nodded and presented consoling smiles. Guy attempted to comprehend his metaphor.

"I often feel like the spirit of my dead self," Thanos contributed. "And I think I like that. I'm an artisan. I carve caskets. It's an ancient and dying art. I think I've been driven insane by my obsession with death. Death. Death. Death!"

"We all think about death a lot," Waldo replied. "I have three reactions to it."

Thanos laughed eerily. His appearance evoked a corpse, with white skin, dark eye sockets and dry, gray hair. He wore a black suit.

"I sleep in a coffin. My home is filled with images of death, morbid paintings and sculptures. Funeral requiems continually play on my stereo. Every day, indeed, almost every moment, I ponder the question, why do I die?" His expression was grave.

"I decided years ago that I could prevail over my terror of death by embracing it. I even legally changed my name to Thanos. I try to be death."

"Are you on medications?" The doctor asked.

"Yeah. I like strong medications because they make me feel dead. Can you give me more, doctor?"

The doctor smiled supportively. "We have plenty of excellent medications."

Silence followed. The group returned to fidgeting in their chairs and gazing into nothing space. Nada, a chubby but cute Peruvian girl in her early twenties, twitched anxiously as she stared vacantly. "The space is looking back at me," she whispered.

Guy thought about Anna.

"Do you know where . . . my self is? I can't find it. I feel . . . so alone."

The woman spoke in a hollow voice, her words labored and wooden, and her eyes fixed down at the floor. She called herself Julie Not Julie because she believed she could not be just Julie until she found her missing self that she said vanished when she was a small child.

"Maybe . . . it was never there," she continued, slow as a setting moon. "I remember thinking my self was . . . my mother, then it was . . . my room. Then it was . . . nothing."

"Why do you believe your self is gone?" Dr. Minfield quizzed.

A fly flew in front of Rebecca, a dark Rumanian male, and his eyes tracked it around the room. "Buzzz," he spoke.

"Because . . . there's nothing there. It's empty . . . Inside of me is hollow." Julie Not Julie's voice was like a monotone recording. "I'm an empty hole . . . and the whole is empty."

"An empty hole and a whole that's empty," a portly woman with fiery red hair echoed back, singsong. "I like that!" She laughed heartily.

Julie Not Julie was about forty and wore a drab tan dress that fell like a sack from her neck to her knees. Her brown hair, dry and streaked with gray, was loosely brushed but not styled. She wore no makeup and sat erect as she spoke, moving little, her hands in her lap. The small finger of her right hand twitched repeatedly.

"But do you feel anything?" Nada asked, examining Julie Not Julie with a curious gaze.

Seconds passed before she was answered.

"Sometimes, I have felt some things . . . but even they did not seem real. Like I was feeling . . . someone else's feelings . . . It's because my self is lost, gone away, far, far away." Her anemic eyes stared at nothing. "Always, every person I meet . . . on the streets, in stores . . . I ask, do you know where my self is? I can't find it. I feel so alone." The rhythm of her speech increased slightly, and her eyes widened. "But they just look at me like I'm crazy . . . I'm not crazy. I just lost my self."

She pouted, and her left leg jerked as if someone tapped her knee with a mallet.

"I lost my last job . . . I worked on a computer. I kept searching the websites . . . the ones about spirit, psychology, anything . . . there's actually one called Self.com . . . My boss, I think he was upset, asked me what I was doing. I told him the truth, 'I'm searching for my self.' He fired me."

She looked again at the floor, silent.

"You're experiencing a type of depersonalization," the doctor explained. "A self-disassociation because there's too much pain inside of you. Pain you cannot, or will not, feel."

"No, doctor, I would welcome pain." She mimicked slashing her breast with a knife. "That would be real . . . My self is lost. It went away. Far, far away." She stared unfocused into a distant nothing, far away.

"But your self is inside of you." Meow, a pretty, early-thirties former assistant at the Art Heritage Museum, purred. She had a lithe, feline figure, short red hair and animated green cat eyes. *Fantasy woman!* Guy thought observing her allure. She was committed to the hospital after she, one night, replaced the museum's landscape paintings with erotic, nude photos of herself. She claimed she now wished only to be a trashy sex kitten. She spoke with a purr. The men in the room repeatedly stared at her with notable interest.

Julie Not Julie replied. "I've looked inside, many, many times . . . thousands, and found nothing . . . All I see is me looking for myself, and I've looked everywhere." She glanced up at the group, her expression static. "I've looked in . . . thoughts, books, nature, trees, art, dogs. In rocks . . . in dreams for some clue to where my self has gone . . . For a while, I thought it might be in my TV, showing me my life . . . my self, on the screen, but that too, was a lie. It's lost . . . Gone." She looked up. "I think maybe it's somewhere in the sky, far, far away, with God."

"Why would God take your self?" Dr. Minfield logically queried.

Julie Not Julie responded with an iota of a smile. "He that giveth, taketh away."

"You might try doing what I've done," Nada suggested. Nada believed she embodied a 'perfect, textbook neurosis', which she was reluctant to relinquish because it was the only thing about her she felt was perfect, even though it was destroying her life.

"I saw the movie *Being John Malkovich*, where the actor John Malkovich like plays himself in the fictitious story. I wondered if it would be hard, you know, to play yourself in a movie—like, confusing. So I tried it. I pretended I was like in a movie playing myself, but I found it disturbing. The person I was being—you know, I was observing myself, as you would a performance—the person I was being was like so boring and obnoxious. It was terrible! Like I wanted to kill myself. So I decided instead to be the actor who was playing myself, instead of being myself that I was playing. That was like months ago, and you know since then I've continued just being the actor. It's much better!"

Julie Not Julie looked at her vacuously. "Won't work," was all she said.

Guy suspected Julie Not Julie was mad, or at least desperately lost. He noticed her eyes seemed distant as if they did not focus on anything they saw. She looked but did not see. And yet, he could not avoid perceiving her as a sad, poetic symbol for much of mankind, endlessly searching for their selves. And he sensed something sublime, deep inside her, where her lost self hid.

"I think you are a wonderful person, lost self or not. Always remember that," he told her.

A struggling smile amended her empty face. "But do you know where my self is? I can't find it . . . I feel so alone."

For one instant, her eyes connected with Guy's, as if she saw something. Her expression turned curious. He noticed it. Then she peered down at the floor, mute, and became mummified.

"I have myself," Jonah asserted boldly. "I experience it all the time. It's just crazy as hell!"

Several members of the group, including Guy, laughed.

"I may be the maddest of all," a woman who had sat through the session almost silent, observing, proclaimed.

"And why is that, miss?" The doctor asked with an intrigued grin.

"Ms. Bouchet. Because I believe I am a spirit, a goddess, a Muse to be precise, and one of the three graces—Brilliance, Joy, and Bloom. I am Bloom, a manifestation of exuberance and life and, most of all, inspiration." She bowed to the group. "Immortal, essential to humans, and absolutely beautiful!" She leaned back confidently, her jovial, pumpkin face smiling. "In fact, I know I am!"

Ms. Bouchet was an extremely rotund woman, as one whom the world, if permitted, would torture with endless and futile diets. Her flaming red hair exploded from a soft, round face and her eyes were an intense, supernatural green. Blazing colors splashed her flowing gown. Guy thought she resembled a Matisse painting. The doctor stared at her as one would a most peculiar specimen.

Meow purred. "I think you are grandly lovely, Ms. Bullshit."

"Ms. Bouchet," the woman corrected.

"As you are here, I assume you are experiencing difficulties," Dr. Minfield interviewed her. "Have you received a diagnosis, Ms. Bouchet?"

"Indeed I have, good doctor. I have been declared a delusional megalomaniacal schizophrenic disassociative. In brief, a basket case." She smiled and flapped her eyelids frivolously.

The doctor's quick nods suggested that he concurred with the diagnosis.

"Well, there is always hope," he assured. "Our new therapies and medications are extremely powerful."

Ms. Bouchet clapped. "Oh wonderful! Free me, please! For I insanely inspire people." She peered intensely into the doctor's eyes.

The doctor jolted and then began rapidly writing words on his notepad, as if the words were writing themselves. 'Little boy. Hugh, monstrous dark figures. Chanting. "Crazy boy! Crazy boy!" Weapon. Military, gigantic! Boy blows away tormentors. Blood. Yes!' The doctor's hand stilled. He shook his head and looked shocked at Ms. Bouchet.

Ms. Bouchet grinned. "And I am a woman of extraordinary beauty!"

Startling the group, she leapt to her feet, threw her arms over her head and spun. She danced around the room, waltzing and spinning, her dress streaks of color whirling around her corporeal form.

Her movements were awkward and clunky, like a comical ballerina. Guy smiled, recalling the drunken, dancing hippopotamus in the Disney animated film *Fantasia*.

Doctor Minfield removed his glasses and stared at the ludicrous sight. He began to raise his arm and speak, and then stopped. His hands clenched tight into fists and shook. Then they softened and his arms appeared to reach out, gently, toward Ms. Bouchet, and then were quickly withdrawn. His face blushed crimson and his expression bewildered.

Raphael sprang to his feet and danced around Ms. Bouchet. His movements were a playful mixture of a gliding sailor and an Irish jig. Then Meow leapt forward, joining the two with a sensual dance of slinky, feline movements. Within moments, half the group were on their feet, leaping and spinning and waltzing across the floor. There was bursting, staccato laughter.

Guy remained seated, grinning and observing the madcap abandonment that consumed the room. He thought it delightful. His attention fixed most on Ms. Bouchet. As he watched her swaying and twirling like a dancing blimp, he suddenly felt inspired to write a poem, a poem about an eccentric woman, clumsy and awkward, a fool to many, who yet possessed a grace and beauty beyond anything of the world; an inner goddess.

A muse? He wondered. *Could that . . . .* Ms. Bouchet looked at him and smiled.

"Stop it! Stop it!" Dr. Minfield was on his feet, his face rigid. "Sit down, now! We have important work here to do!"

The room immediately stilled. Heads hung down. The patients scuttled back to their chairs. Ms. Bouchet plopped into her seat, placed her hands in her lap and stared at the floor like a chastised child.

The doctor glared fiercely at her and then scribbled notes on his pad: 'Bouchet. Muse delusions. No doubt sickest of all! Perhaps dangerous.'

The room became as silent as a crypt and as heavy as the earth. Time ticked, ticked, ticked.

"Much better. Now, who is next?" The doctor, recomposed, asked. For a time, no one spoke.

"Seven billion people are experiencing both pleasure and pain today around the world," Raphael announced, fracturing the silence.

"I . . . thought it was fun, the dancing," Nada professed meekly.

"We are not here to have fun, Nada," the good doctor clarified as he wiped the lenses of his glasses with a handkerchief. "We are here to get well."

*   *   *

In a hospital of madness, I do not escape madness.

Hideous voices spoke, several times taunting his mind, during the first days of Guy's hospital stay. The angelic, kind voice offered the only redemption. Mocking faces appeared in his dreams. Twice hallucinations visited, neither identified by him as such until they ended. He told the doctors he had stopped his medications, but not about his delusions. They encouraged him to take them.

"Medications are a salvation," he was told.

Sitting in the cafeteria at the long dining table with fellow patients one evening, Guy was convinced it was lunchtime. He could not comprehend why the food being served was from the dinner menu. When he looked at the clock he saw it *was* dinner time. He could not recall anything that had happened that afternoon.

Later that night, during their free time, he lay on his bed in his room, reading. He looked at Raphael, stretched out, staring at the vacant white ceiling, smiling. Suddenly Raphael sprang up.

"I'm gonna visit Meow. She's a hot little thing! She said she'd be alone tonight, and I think she could use my . . . guidance."

Raphael laughed. A flame of adventure flickered in his eyes.

Guy nodded and smiled. He knew the psychiatric ward had prohibitions against intimate rendezvous between patients, but he also knew that Raphael did not give a damn about rules, nor did Meow.

"Enjoy!" he advised his friend who quickly brushed his hair, spied out the doorway, and departed. Guy was alone. He returned to his novel, *Great Expectations*, by Dickens.

Suddenly he shook. "Who are you?"

There was another presence in the room, a shadow figure seated in a corner chair. Guy slid, slowly and apprehensively, to the end of the bed where he could see the figure more closely. It was not a woman, as he had suspected, but a young boy, cloaked in a black funeral gown, a dark veil obscuring his face. He sat mannequin still, staring at Guy.

Guy became frightened. "Who are you?" he repeated, but the boy did not respond. Hesitantly Guy stood and walked nearer to the visitor. He leaned closer to his face and struggled to see past the veil. The boy had a cherub face and wavy, brown hair. There was great pain and loss etched into his child features. His eyes were cobalt blue, although grayed by the veil. They looked at Guy sadly and oddly, almost apologetically. The boy seemed familiar and his enigmatic eyes reminded Guy of his, as a child.

The boy whispered.

"What? What did you say?" Guy asked.

"I kill love."

Shock petrified Guy's face. Slowly he reached toward the boy's shoulder. His hand passed through the grave form. The dark visitor vanished.

Guy stumbled backwards and fell onto his bed. His stomach hurt and a terrible dread consumed his mind. He stared coldly at the ceiling, afraid.

He was slipping below the line.

*   *   *

By day four, patients were disappearing.

"Where's Jonas and Rebecca?" Nada asked as she perused the group during their morning therapy.

"Room B," Julie Not Julie answered, her voice haunted. "Room B."

"What's in Room B?" Waldo implored the doctor. "I keep hearing rumors about it."

"Well, first of all, good morning, everybody," the doctor replied with a perfected fatherly expression.

"Good morning, Dr. Minfield," the group, except Raphael, responded in unison. Raphael's attention was on Meow, who glanced at him and purred.

"Room B is a passage," the doctor explained, his smile and eyes euphoric. "In there you are re-evaluated. If you are deemed well, cured, you are released, and you may leave, returning to *that* world." He grimaced and pointed to the world beyond a window. "But if you are found still sick, then you are fortunate." The doctor laughed, but not too assertively. "For then you are moved deeper into the system."

The patients looked somberly at one another.

"But, man, no one ever comes out of Room B," Nada stated. "They check in and like never check out. Is anyone ever found well and sane?"

The good doctor chuckled, then laughed more heartily, then stopped abruptly.

"No, not yet. Why would any sane person be here? But they might, one day. It's actually a wonderful thing!" His vision ray-beamed each patient. "The program that waits in Room B has powerful new technologies and drugs. It's very exciting. If you are so cursed, and blessed," he laughed again, a peculiar sight to the patients since the doctor rarely laughed at all, "as to receive it, kiss your present life goodbye, for you will never be the same again. But that's a positive thing."

His effusive grin distilled the pride of all the saviors of humankind.

"Sounds like oppressive bullshit to me," Raphael countered.

Doctor Minfield flung butcher knives for an unguarded instant and then smiled cordially. "Well, with that hostility, I'm sure you'll find out soon."

"Right, Doc."

The group was hesitant that morning to open up and share, to trust. Finally Angela, a delicate nervous woman in her sixties, spoke of enslavement, sexual abuse, and torture by her parents.

"But I know they always loved me." She looked down with a quivering, tightrope smile. "My parents, they had some problems, but they were good people. When they abused and tortured me, with all those beatings and burns and days locked in a closet, it was just their way of expressing love."

Matty spoke lovingly of her cat, Spiro, aborting her story after precisely three minutes. Finally, Guy decided to speak.

But first he looked into his soul, *my disturbed, mysterious, and beautiful soul.* He found a surprising lucidity and the words he sought.

"My truth is simple. I create and I love. That is all I can do, all I'm supposed to do. I am a man, a spirit, and an artist. Know that, and you know me. Spirit decreed it so.

"I am sick when I do not do my purposes, when I do not create and love. I am well when I do. Simple!"

Guy glanced around the group. Their attention was absolute.

"And I believe that is a part, my part, of a greater spiritual design and purpose." He paused, looking down. "But this world often seems indifferent to me, and to my purposes. It doesn't seem to care. *I* must chose and do it. The world simply provides the stage and people and materials with which I can love and create. To be or not to be. That is its beauty. It is perfect." He peered into thought-space. "A beach of sand sweeps up from the sea, intended or not. It lies there in its perfect, pale golden beauty. It is not interested in me, who walks upon its sand.

"But if I love it and create from it a magnificent sandcastle—for that is my job, to create visions that inspire and help people—all who behold it are joyed, or at least challenged, and I am happy and move closer to God.

"But if I abhor that beach, or am indifferent to it, and create nothing, giving no gift to the world, then I am unhappy and move further from God. It's as simple as that. And if I live and be that simple truth, I can connect with incredible forces beyond my comprehension. And if I don't, if I chose instead a lie, I can be extraordinarily sick. A madman."

Guy looked at his fellow patients. Their faces were rapt and bright. Doctor Minfield stared at him with a focused but skeptical eye.

"But there is a complexity," Guy continued. "A mystery, which I confess is difficult to fathom. My spirit tells me that I am also the beach, and the sand, and the sandcastle, and even the onlookers who adore my creation. Now the little becomes the all.

"And if I do not remember these simple truths, one day I will feel a horrible betrayal, for I will have betrayed my life and spirit. I will die in sorrow. But I hope that will not be so.

"I am a sick man or a well man, whichever I chose. And that is the treatise of Guy, spirit and man and artist, who loves and creates."

For a period the room remained reverentially silent as if a nurturing grace had filled it.

"Wow, that was like heavy, but beautiful!" Nada, not seeming so like Nada, spoke.

"You really sound like an artist," Meow purred, swaying sensually in her chair. "I want to pose naked for you, for one of your paintings."

"I want . . . to be your friend," Julie Not Julie declared, looking curiously at Guy, her eyes unusually focused. "If I find my self."

Raphael applauded, his claps syncopating the room. "Well spoken, roomy! And I believe your words."

"Yes, yes, well, Guy, that was good," Dr. Minfield interjected. "I liked your sandcastle metaphor, and rest assured we have powerful therapies and drugs to help you. We will make you the well man."

The doctor's eyes brightened, and his brow shrewdly lifted. He grinned.

Guy stared at the good doctor but did not respond. He felt nauseous.

"Trust your spirit, Guy," Ms. Bouchet, having sat quietly through the session, spoke. A radiance in her eyes reached out and touched him, sending a tingling through his being. "You have everything you need, and more."

"Yes, Guy," Meow concurred. "Listen to Ms. Bullshit. She is wise."

The doctor glared at Ms. Bouchet. "Yes, Ms. Bullshit." He scribbled notes. 'Lunatic! Can't wait 'till we work on her!'

Guy received the spirited woman's words and knew there was truth in them. He realized how much he liked and admired

Ms. Bouchet, this mysterious woman of strength and rare beauty, and how she inspired him.

"I think you *are* a goddess and a Muse, Ms. Bouchet," he confided. "I can see it."

She laughed like a child with tickled feet. "It is so! It is so!"

Every patient nodded. The good doctor rose to leave the room, then groaned and sat.

Chapter 20

MUSIC—VIBRATIONS OF THE soul. Anna, in her apartment, listened to Richard Strauss's *Death and Transformation*. The first half of the composition, plaintive and mournful, reminded her of her past. *Passed.* The second segment, the transformation, sublime and inspired, expressed the present, and her newly awakened emotions. *Vibrations of my soul.*

She wore jeans and a white T-shirt that descended to her thighs. It was not a persona.

It feels good to be myself, she reflected. *Whatever myself be.* She realized in recent weeks that she liked that self more than ever before. Surprising and wonderful things were happening inside her, reborn yearnings and passions.

Let there be life! She smiled and then raised her arms and performed a curtsy to the universe. She sensed the universe bowed back.

During the first days of Guy's hospital stay, Anna missed him immensely, pushing her into her heart and soul where she was, and was not surprised to find him residing. She sat or walked with him there, whispering quiet things. *Do you know? Yes.* She experienced something she had not felt in years, a feeling of connection and childlike innocence, and of being loved.

She sat in an old and comfortable chair in the middle of her living room where she often located when reflecting. She felt it placed her in the center of her universe. A playful fantasy entered her thoughts. She was Eve in the Garden of Eden, its imagery drawn from the wall painting in Guy's apartment. He was Adam, and they were as innocent children, graced by a love for one another but strangers to that love's intrigues. They were in the light of God.

What might cause these two innocents to fall? Perhaps falling was part of the delight. She amused herself with a scenario.

She took not an apple from a tree but a forbidden book of poetry from atop a rock, written by rebellious angels somewhere at some time and left to tempt, or perhaps to enlighten. Seated on the ground, beautiful in her natural nakedness, she read the poems that ranged from the profound to the profane and erotic to Guy as Adam, her love and partner.

Guy found beneath a tree a pencil and a pad and began drawing her, lovely and sensuous. As she recited the exquisite and provocative poems and he drew, for the first time on Earth, representations of a woman, their minds and bodies awakened.

"Who are we?" they wondered aloud, "and why are we here? And what are these peculiar, urgent stirrings deep in our bodies?"

Soon spiritual innocence was not all that defined them. They fell together into the flesh, into self-will and the Great Drama—into a death and transformation.

Anna exited her fantasy and grinned. *I want to fall with Guy,* she thought. *We should fall and rise.* Suddenly her face brightened.

A gift! I will get Guy a gift to welcome him home from the hospital. She examined possibilities. A plant? An artwork? Perhaps a Pre-Raphael print, a style I know he enjoys? A book of poems? Perhaps . . . myself?

The perfect idea came, an inspiration. It was both something he would treasure and a lovely expression of the transformation occurring in her feelings. But she had only several days to obtain it.

How? She walked to the living room window and looked out. A fog had drifted in from the ocean, graying the morning city into a ghostly shell of itself. It breathed in slight and hushed breaths, as one who was comatose.

Marko. He is the only option, she concluded. *I will have to visit Marko.*

Anna looked down at the alley below. She felt a descent into its narrow, shadowy space. It seemed isolated and dangerous. She became queasy.

Marko was Anna's former lover and boyfriend. Her relationship with him had been her most passionate and most destructive, ending over two years ago, and she had not seen him since. It had been a drama of intense emotions and surrender, of betrayals and suicidal despair; a crossroads in her life. *Or perhaps a toxic X.* She had not been in a committed relationship with a man since.

Anna remembered the nights, long and lost in flesh and heat. Her left arm began to ache. An inflicted injury.

Can I do this? The first of a series of rapid questions. *Am I strong enough? Have I matured?*

A dread in her body answered no, and her mind tried to close its blinds to the idea. But her spirit answered yes. *I have changed, and I want this gift for Guy.* Her emotions and resolve lifted.

It was decided.

*   *   *

Marko's studio was in a white, wood paneled house with a blue shingle roof in the Silverlake District, almost hidden within a street corner jungle of palm trees, plants, and vines. It was a former store that he converted into a workplace home, a larger studio with smaller living quarters at the rear. Anna had spent many days and nights in both, days and nights both delirious and tainted. As she walked the stone pathway to the studio door, she looked at the side patio with its cement floor, thatched, wooden overhang and aged, oak benches and chairs. The afternoon was hazy, and the patio appeared desolate and forsaken.

Memories. Innumerable nights seated in that secluded haven beneath a patio light with Marko and fellow artists. Fertile discussions of the arts and philosophy and love, and the madness and beauty of the world. Marko quite amiable and interesting. The good times. But a small portion of what she had left with.

Present. The studio door was partially opened, and Anna entered without knocking. She walked into a space populated by pale, petrified human forms, sculptures, each eerily estranged in its own space like a community of lone individuals who never make contact, nor wish to. Most were women, naked and erotic, ranging in height from two feet, his specialty, to life-size. She recognized Vanessa, a dancer and friend of hers and Marko's, now frozen in a paralysis of resin, holding in her outstretched left hand the head of Medusa with her hair of tangled snakes. Vanessa's expression was elation, or madness.

A grim fantasy. Vanessa as both figures—the elated woman who Marko seduced with sexual pleasures and the Medusa after he then took her head in conquest, her betrayed passion turned to ravenous snakes. Anna trembled.

Marko was at the far end of the studio. His hulking form knelt over a life-size sculpture of a reclined nude woman with her head rested on her forearm. The pose suggested both a woman swooning and a woman dead. He was polishing the surface of her thigh.

"Anna," he announced in his resonant voice, without turning to see her. "I recognize your footsteps. You walk like a dancer."

"Hello Marko."

"It's good to see you again, Anna." Still he had not turned toward her. "What do you think of my newest work?"

Anna stepped nearer. "It's stunning, although ambiguous. It looks alive and dead."

Marko laughed, his voice like a throaty carburetor, gunned. "As we all are! I call it The Death of Beauty." He turned his head slowly and looked at Anna. "I envisioned her as a mistress who brought great pleasures to many men. But, alas, life and the world, intolerant of such women, killed her." He stood and smiled.

Anna examined the sculpture. "It's coldly beautiful."

Marko nodded. "All beauty is cold, for it is easily lost."

Anna perused the studio. It was congested and disheveled in a customary artist fashion. Tables were cluttered with boxes and jars. Sheets of paper revealed sketches and sculpture designs. Soft light filtered through expansive windows. The air smelled dusty and stale, a combination, Anna assessed, of odors from his materials and the stagnate spirit of its occupant. She felt she should not breathe too deeply.

"So, how have you been, Marko?" Her eyes reached and withdrew.

He inhaled, expanding his chest. "I've been well. Much better. Business is good, and I'm almost sane." He smiled, cragged. "It's been a long time, Anna."

"Yes." Anna rubbed her fingers on her left forearm in a repeated circle.

"I'm glad you're here. I hoped you would visit again." His eyes journeyed over her. "You're not in one of your infamous personas."

Anna was dressed in jeans, a mauve T-shirt, and a brown leather jacket. She had not wished to wear a persona knowing that Marko would give it his own provocative interpretation, even if she appeared as a nun. 'A nun,' he would think. 'How kinky!'

"No. I came as myself. This is business. I need a statue."

Marko often reminded Anna of a lumberjack. He was tall and hearty with a rugged face, brunette shoulder length hair and a full, though trimmed beard; Paul Bunyan. In response, when with her, he often wore Levi jeans and a red plaid flannel shirt. He practiced flashing a wide, country grin. Anna used to think it was cute.

Marko flashed that broad, country grin at her now. This day he was dressed in worn jeans and a loose, untucked gray shirt, half unbuttoned, revealing his brawny chest. *Like an animal, or a handsome beast,* Anna thought and then suppressed the thought.

He looked into her eyes. "I have missed you, Anna."

"I need a statue of myself, about two feet high."

"I was never able to apologize and explain things."

"It's a gift for a friend, but I need it quickly."

"I think about you often."

"Do you think you could do it?"

"I've changed. I'm a different man now, I'm pleased to say. You should get to know me again."

"Marko, can you do it for me?"

"What?"

"A statue. I need a statue of myself!" Anna placed her hands on her hips and glared.

A counter-glare. Marko's facial features hardened, resembling the demeanor of one of his sculptures.

"Business! Yes, of course. Why else would you have come?"

Anna tensed. An inference in his tone evoked memories and an aching in her upper right arm where she had been violently struck. She felt a black hollow and wondered what the hell she was doing.

"Perhaps I made a mistake, Marko. I apologize." She turned to leave.

"No, no. Please stay." He took her arm and gently pulled. "I am happy to see you, Anna. Let's forget old wounds. Come, join me on the patio. I want to know how you've been and what you've been doing. Stay awhile."

For an unguarded moment Anna was tempted. Then her stomach constricted. "Thank you, Marko, but I really came to see if you can do this project for me. It's important."

Marko shook his bearish head and sighed. "OK. OK. What is it you need, exactly?"

"I need a statue of myself, about two feet high," she paused and looked at the floor, "nude, and finished to look like marble."

She looked up. Marko raised a brow and smiled.

"Do you still have the photos you took of me, when we were considering creating a sculpture of me?"

"The photos? Well, no. I'm afraid I destroyed them." His eyes softened. "You see, Anna, after you left, it was . . . difficult. Postpartum trauma. I destroyed or threw out everything that reminded me of you: the clothes you left behind, the photos, your fake vampire teeth, that picture of you looking like a kinky, erotic Shirley Temple." He grinned. "Remember? Even the sheets and the pillow case you laid your head on. They carried your scent."

Damn! Anna thought. Marko had taken pictures of her nude to help him create a sculpture of her to mass produce and sell. Then she changed her mind, deciding she did not want a replica of her body sold to the public; but even more, she was having disconcerting feelings about Marko's intentions in everything. She realized he was an exploiter. So she appeased him by declaring that her body was for him alone, not to be seen or touched by any other man. His flattered male ego, which was sizable, agreed. The statue was never created.

"So I would need to take some new pictures of you. Is that agreeable?"

Marko walked part way around Anna, examining her form.

Anna's expression tightened, her flesh quivering. She clenched her teeth and steeled her jaw. *Resolve!*

"Yes, that's fine. I need the statue by the end of the week. Is that workable?"

Marko's eyes scoured the air as if scrutinizing floating data. Then they cruised across Anna, slowly.

"That's possible, if I set aside my other projects. But tell me, Anna, what might I expect in exchange for this favor?" His smile was subtly seductive.

Anna suspected trumpets sounded in his mind. "I haven't much money, and I know what you charge for a statue. But I'll make you a deal."

"Yeah?" He nodded once, grinning.

"If you do the statue for me, I'll sign an agreement."

"Agreement?" Marko's brow lifted. "Wait, Anna, I have a better idea."

More trumpets. An entire orchestra. His eyes impaled hers. For a moment he did not say more. Neither did Anna.

"Do you know what my idea is, Anna?" He stared into her.

Anna shuffled. She wanted to be angry, but she did not quite feel it. She saw something black, and then blinding white. Cold snaked through her.

"Remember our nights together, Anna? All those nights?" Marko grinned devilishly. "I've never been able to forget them."

Anna did indeed remember. She had not had such nights since. Something reckless and desperate awakened in her, like the craving of an addict for a forsaken drug. To experience that wild euphoria again might negate any consequence.

Thoughts consumed her: *Marko—selfish, savage. Still, the best lover I've ever had. Dangerous, wanting to possess me totally, in life and in love. I wanting that. Being hurt and torn by a controlling lover. The only way a man could love me, and I could love!*

Anna tried to block the thoughts, but they pressed forward. *Perhaps I am mad.* She gazed around as if in a distraction.

"You do remember. I see it in your face."

His old tone of conquest. Anna suddenly felt an abysmal self-disgust.

"The answer is no, Marko, simple and clear! Forget your little fantasy."

She wanted to leave, but didn't. She placed a hand on her hip and stood straighter. "The deal is this. You do the sculpture of me, give me one, keep the mold. I'll sign an agreement. You can reproduce it, as many as you wish, and sell them. That should bring you more than what you would charge me for the statue."

She challenged him with the assured expression of an entrepreneur, her eyes confronting and her lips resolved.

Marko's eyes brightened and he looked into thought-space, a finger scratching at his beard.

"I've always believed a statue of you nude would be a very profitable commodity. You possess a body and bearing rare among women, classic, as that of a goddess or a warrior princess. Xena, warrior princess meets Aphrodite, love goddess."

Anna suspected there was more. She saw the thought in his eyes. *Big money! All right, sweet Anna. Besides, I can get the contract and you, too.*

"All right, it's a deal, Anna. When do we start?"

"Now. Take the pictures now. Then I must go."

The broad, country grin. Marko directed her to a corner of the studio where there were some photo lights on stands. He turned them on and took a camera out of a cabinet.

Anna stood in the center of the space. Marko stepped in front of her and waited.

"Well, undress!" He grinned slyly. "My camera doesn't see through clothes." *Although I do!* his eyes spoke.

A deflation sank Anna. She could not move. She pushed. *The purpose! For Guy!* She removed her clothes; first her shoes, then her jacket and T-shirt.

"Slowly!" Marko commanded in the intonation of a man to a mistress.

Anna glared. *Screw you, Marko!* But she did not stop. She removed her bra and jeans and then hesitated, awkward before him.

"Well, don't be modest. I've seen you scores of times. I'm not going to sculpt you with your panties on. It's all or nothing, love."

Anna regressed to a young girl forced to undress before an older man. *This is ridiculous!* She took a reinforcing breath and removed her final garment. As she stood before him in her total nakedness, she felt her spirit retreat from her body. She felt humiliated.

This may have been a mistake. She noticed the air against her bare flesh was chilly. She felt disturbingly vulnerable. A confusion of feelings possessed her.

"Take the pictures!"

Marko's eyes looked up and down her, leisurely cruising each curve and round of her form. He smiled and nodded. "Yes, love. The pictures."

Anna assumed a pose with her arms reaching partially out, one more than the other, as in a welcoming or invitation. It was the same pose she had taken at Forest Garden Cemetery when posing beside one of its statues and also over two years ago when Marko took the previous pictures. It was her favorite pose, one of both assuredness and vulnerability.

"The beseeching goddess lover," Marko critiqued with his confident grin. "You haven't changed, Anna."

He took several steps to each side, examining her, continually smiling, without raising his camera. She felt his heavy eyes slithering across her flesh, with or without consent.

He raised the camera. Its lens glistened in the photo lights. He took several pictures of her from the front and then slowly, cunningly slow, moved around her, photographing her from all angles. He spoke softly.

"I have changed, Anna. I'm not the man you knew. I'm more, and less. I've stopped drinking. I'm rarely with women. After you left, there were few women I wanted to be with."

He took a shot of her strong and statuesque legs.

"Good." Anna replied succinctly.

"I'm sorry if things were . . . rough between us. I didn't intend that. I failed to respect you enough."

He snapped a shot of her perfectly rounded buttocks.

"I know you may think I'm just saying this, and I question it myself."

He took another picture of her buttocks, closer, and then lowered the camera and just looked at them.

He whispered into her ear. "If I'm completely honest, I have to say, I still love you." His hand moved toward the mounds of her posterior and then stopped.

What bullshit! Anna thought. Yet, to her annoyance, some part of her liked hearing the words.

"I admit some of it is just sexual."

Marko walked in front of Anna and took a picture of her breasts, looking at them for a moment before aiming the camera. His demeanor spoke. *So ripe and firm. Breasts, feed me!*

Anna tried to prevent it, but her breasts heaved gently up.

"Nice! Very nice." He continued staring at her breasts. "You were the best lover I ever had, Anna. Both savage and sweet. You possess an eroticism that is vulnerable and dangerous. It excites me! And I know you remember our passionate nights. They are not some fantasy."

He paused, waiting while Anna remained silent, statuesquely staring into the air. Then she smiled slightly.

"You do remember." He walked behind her and sang in a whisper near her ear. "Did you ever see a dream walking? Well I did. Did you ever hear a poem talking? Well I did." It was a 1930's song they sometimes listened to while making love.

It was true, Anna had to admit. Marko knew how to excite and please a woman, in his savage way. She had loved being explored and violated and torn by him. She had needed that. But now, confusion. Emotions fomented.

This is crazy! she thought, and she had to wonder why she was really there. A desperate excitation seized her. In an urgent moment, she wanted to be seductive. There, naked before Marko, so seductive as to torture him, torture him by inflaming in him painful and desperate desires. He deserved to be tortured, and she to be the dominating temptress. She would control him, making him satisfy her every wild desire.

Yet, she did not make any moves.

Perhaps one night with Marko, or even just a few hours, might be good for both of us, she reasoned. *What the hell! He would be satisfied, maybe even helped, and the statue easily and quickly obtained. And I—it's been years since I've enjoyed passionate lovemaking. Perhaps it would reawaken me as a woman.*

Marko squatted in front of her, taking closeups of her pelvis and vulva, much closer than necessary for the project. "So tender and beautiful," he whispered, just loud enough for her to hear. Anna's leg twitched, and Marko noticed. He looked up and into her eyes, making certain her attention was on him. With a finger, he traced the contours of her vagina in the air.

"So sweet, Anna, sweet and waiting," he spoke softly. With the finger, he went inside the illusion. "And it has been waiting. Hasn't it, Anna? For so, so long."

Anna knew there was a certain vulgar truth in his words. She closed her eyes. *Waiting,* she kept thinking as urgings intensified in her pelvis. All of the defiance and assurance just minutes earlier evaporated. Images of their heated nights of lovemaking returned. *Waiting!*

She looked at Marko, who had lowered his camera and was staring at her. There was anticipation in his smile and the old fierceness in his eyes.

Then she felt the blackness. She saw the bruises and swelled eye and felt the soreness around her neck from his assaulting grips. Anna suffered again the terrible scourge of humiliation, the self-loathing, and most of all, the searing pain of betrayal that had been their love. She remembered the other women he had slept with and her disturbed, suicidal descent.

Am I insane? she questioned as if suddenly awakened. She looked into the air as in a plea for higher guidance. *What am I thinking? Passionate lovemaking? It was control and violence!*

An image seized her mind of a brutal, primitive man, a beast, viciously screwing a woman who pleaded for more until she cried, and then screamed, and he screwed her to death. Anna trembled.

She looked into Marko's eyes. His stare possessed the same fierce cold, like a rage pressed down hard and pushing for release. He had not changed, but she, despite her lapses into weakness, had.

Anna suddenly realized something with a clarity that had previously eluded her. *Marko, my best lover? That is a delusion. I've needed to hold on to it for over two years because only with self-abasement did I believe I could feel any passion, or semblance of love.*

What we had, all those heated nights, was not love. Not even passion. We had shared a sickness.

"This is sick," she spoke aloud to him.

Marko smiled, shrugged his shoulders and lifted his camera for another picture.

All a lie. Anna saw that she had raped herself, like a self-flagellation. She had not needed it then, and she certainly did not need it now.

In an odd moment of imagery, she saw her entire nude and vulnerable body reflected in the lens of the camera.

Where is my spirit? She questioned. *Where are my grace and values and ideals? Where is Anna?*

She knew. She had grown up and in that reflection was a beautiful, mature woman. She inhaled deeply, freely, and her posture straightened, almost lifting her off the floor. Anna knew that now, for the first time, she could truly love a man. She felt like a virgin.

"You are wrong, Marko," she spoke with a true woman's voice. "I am not the same. I've changed." She smiled.

Marko lowered his camera and stared, perplexed, and then with a warring resolution. He grinned and his hand reached toward her breast.

Anna believed it would have been proper to smash him in the face, and it would have pleased her, but it was not what she felt. With one delicate finger she stopped his reach.

"No, no, no," she chided in the voice of a teacher reproaching a problem student, a juvenile, and then wagged the finger and smiled. "No way!"

In an unmasked moment, Marko frowned. She actually thought it looked cute. The macho man fallen to the boy.

"You will never touch me again! What you call passionate lovemaking is more like rape, your passion manipulation, your love betrayal. I will not be raped and manipulated and betrayed. I was a fool then, but not now."

Marko took a step back as if wanting to leave.

"No, no! Please stay. We're having quality time together." Anna smirked. "My days of being controlled and hurt are over. I have a real man in my life now, and you will never touch me again." She paused. "Actually, you never have. Got it?"

Marko's eyes grew beastly hot. His face hardened, and he raised a hand to strike her.

Cold clenched Anna. Then she again raised a finger.

"No, no! You touch me with even one finger," she wagged the finger, "and I will bring assault charges against you. Comprende?"

Marko stopped as if seized by paralysis. He looked like a stuffed bear in a museum; an arm reached out to attack. Then he lowered his hand and laughed. Anna detected the ridicule in that laughter.

"Cocky bitch! No wonder I still desire you." He laughed again. "But tell me this, miss mature woman sweet whore—this new man, this boyfriend, has he loved you as I did?" His brow lifted in confident challenge.

Anna maintained her pose, and poise. Silently she had to admit it was true. She and Guy had not lived at that depth of the flesh. *And yet, we have loved, a thousand, a million times more than I ever had with Marko.*

And at that moment, Anna knew with certainty what she had recently been feeling. *With Guy, there was now to be all. And it would be wonderful!* She felt a soaring joy. *It was him, and it was done.*

"Yes, Marko, we have loved. Deeply," she answered with confidence. "But you would not understand." Anna grinned. "It's a Beautiful, Winged Madness. And in an ironic way that is common in our mad lives, you have helped. So I thank you."

Marko's face whirled into confusion. Then an insane glint entered his eyes. He straightened his posture and swelled his chest.

"But know this, dear Anna. We will be together again. Call it love or call it rape, you will want it. This year or ten years from now, you'll come back. I know you."

He crossed his arms over his chest and smiled. Anna smiled back, undaunted. Then in an instant she perceived how pathetic and desperate was this man before her. *Poor little Marko,* she thought but did not speak.

In contrast, she felt more confidence and strength of integrity than she had ever before experienced. *Welcome home, Anna!* she thought.

"Finish taking the pictures, Marko. I have a life to return to."

Marko looked at her with his mask of forced intensity and then shook his head and grinned. "As you wish, love."

He finished taking the photos, shooting several more than Anna suspected was needed. His victorious smirk explained it. *To get off on later.*

Anna dressed.

"I will call you in a few days to see how the work is going," she informed him in a businesswoman manner, properly clothed and efficient.

"Fine."

She walked toward the door.

"Anna, you know I still do love you."

His words chased behind her. She looked back over her shoulder.

"Have a drink, Marko, and get a hooker."

Anna walked out into the day.

*   *   *

Marko stood staring at the door. "Stupid bitch! I have a hooker whenever I want her." Then a broad grin animated his face.

He opened a tall, white, wood cabinet. In the left lower corner were items Anna had left behind: some clothing, the Shirley Temple picture, a wig, her vampire teeth. He sometimes displayed or used them at parties. From a shelf, he took down a statue.

It was a two feet high sculpture of Anna nude. She was in the same pose she had presented that day. Marko examined it.

Perfect! He concluded. *You have not changed, Anna.*

He created the statue from the photographs, which he kept after Anna left, over two years earlier. To continue possessing her, he had asserted. He still had the mold but had never replicated and sold the sculptures fearing that Anna, wrathful in her belief that she had been betrayed, might sue him.

He laughed. It would take him but a couple hours to cast another statue from the mold. Then he would tell Anna that he worked on it slavishly day and night, to the brink of exhaustion. She would sign the agreement, and he would make money from his sweet whore. *And I still might seduce her yet. I know Anna.*

"Perfect!" He spoke aloud, borrowing Anna's phrase.

He considered her accusation of rape. Perhaps it was so, he concluded, but he knew that many women, whether they admit it or not, like to be raped.

"My little bitch," he whispered and then went to the refrigerator for a beer.

*   *   *

Three days passed. Anna called Marko to check on the progress of the project.

"It's finished, Anna." His voice was labored. "I worked on it day and night just for you. I've hardly slept. It's beautiful. I think you'll like it."

"Good. Thank you. I'll be over to pick it up." Anna smiled and shrugged.

Marko, in his studio, hung up the phone. "You gotta leave, Dedra. I have business. Come back tomorrow, love, and we'll continue." He patted her bare rear.

Dedra pouted. She was a curvaceous blonde in her twenties, Marko's latest model and conquest, posing for a statue of a nude lady rising like a wounded and abandoned woman from a shallow pit in the statue's base. Dedra dressed and flittered out the door.

An hour later, Anna arrived. She wore a conservative beige outfit that hung straight along her body, concealing her curves. Again, no confounding persona.

Marko was seated in a chair with sculpture's dust and paint on his clothing, hair and beard. He slumped as if fatigued, and his eyes were bloodshot. He had rubbed them before Anna arrived. He presented the sculpture to her.

Anna examined it—a lovely two feet tall representation of herself, created in a smooth, plastic resin with an enamel marble finish. It was naked and provocative, yet feminine and tender.

"Perfect! It's beautiful, Marko. Good job."

The artist nodded and smiled. "Always for you, Anna."

She thought he seemed unusually amiable. He walked to a desk and then returned with a paper. He handed the agreement and a pen to Anna.

She read it quickly. It was a consent permitting him to use her likeness for a marketed statue.

"As we agreed," Anna said and signed the paper. Then she looked at him and smiled kindly.

"I do appreciate this, Marko, thank you. And I wish you well. Take care." She pivoted to leave when he took her hand.

"Anna," he spoke softly.

She freed her hand. "No. There's nothing more to be said, except goodbye. Goodbye."

Anna walked across the studio toward the door. A life-sized sculpture lured her attention, and she paused, examining it. The piece was an alluring nude woman, standing, who appeared to be singing, her hair blowing in an illusionary wind. Her hand reached outward, fingers relaxed, as if calling to someone. The figure's body was more petite and less busty than Anna's, but it possessed her face.

Anna smiled. It did not bother her. She did not care.

"That's my siren," Marko explained, noticing her attention on the work. "With her beauty and voice she lures sailors to their death. I call her Anna."

Perhaps at times in my past I've been siren-like, Anna thought. *But all that is over. Now I can love.*

"You would be a good siren, Anna," Marko remarked with his bearish grin as he stroked his fingers through his dust-speckled beard. His eyes flared. "Beauty and death!"

"I think not," Anna responded. "Goodbye."

"I'll see you again, Anna," he replied.

Anna left the studio, closing the door behind her.

Marko stared into the space where Anna had stood. "Sexy bitch!" he mumbled. "She'll be back." He grinned.

Then an empty feeling suddenly and surprisingly taunted. For a moment, Marko felt alone. He shrugged it off and went to the refrigerator for a beer.

*   *   *

On the way home Anna stopped at Sweet Sentiments Gift Store to pick up a card to include with Guy's gift. She searched carefully through the racks for the ideal choice. Bingo! Her selection had the painting, *The Kiss* by Klimpt, a gorgeous, seductive image, on its front.

Back in her apartment, Anna wrote in her personal journal a summary of the events of the past several days and of her newly awakened feelings and decisions.

'The universe seems a vast and dazzling place, and new life is emerging everywhere. The gods rejoice and the goddesses love!'

She kept the journal open on her desk for she knew there would be more beautiful entries to come. Then she had a provocative thought. When Guy arrived home from the hospital, she would be waiting for him in her apartment dressed in the same persona she wore when they first met, the one he called the Woman Inside the Ghost of Herself. But this time, she would not wear the flesh leotard. It would be only herself inside, nude, and for him. Anna became excited. It would be beautiful and poetic! As he removed the ghostly veils, it would be as if he was removing the ghost of the former Anna, and waiting inside would be the new Anna, naked and real and fully for him. And they would love in a symbolic death of their old relationship and a rebirth into their new truth of intimacy and completeness.

Death and transformation. Perfect!

She paused, examining her thought. *No, it would not be perfect. Perfection was of the old Anna. It will be right and beautiful. It will be . . . love! Yes. It will be a perfectly real and flawed love and life, together. And that is all the perfection I now desire.*

Perfect! she thought and smiled.

Chapter 21

THAT EVENING, GUY sat alone in his hospital room. He felt sad. Only two of the patients in the program remained: he and Julie Not Julie. All the others had vanished into the mystery and fate of Room B, and he feared they might never be seen again. Even the feisty and flamboyant Ms. Bouchet, the self-proclaimed goddess Muse, appeared to have mysteriously vanished.

It is insane! he thought and felt a cutting anger. *What right have they? These doctors, administrators, oppressive lunatics?*

Then he smiled remembering that Raphael had escaped. He had been scheduled for the dreaded appointment that morning. Guy walked with him, solemn as two inmates on death row, down the hall to Room B. As they stood before the ominous door, Raphael suddenly grinned.

"To hell with this damn place! To beyond hell! I'll not be condemned. Manipulated and drugged into oblivion. I still have shelters to build and women to love. I'm leaving!"

Guy was surprised, but yet not, and felt his own spirit lift with Raphael's words.

"But how will you get out? The security here is so tight."

Guy knew a patient could not just leave the program, short of committing suicide. They were considered potentially dangerous by the psychiatric staff. If a patient requested to leave, it was deemed a symptom of his illness, a resistance to help, or paranoia, and would be grounds to move him deeper into treatment, more drugs or therapy, or an immediate visit to Room B. When you entered this new, revised program, this hospital stay, you were there until the end and then could leave only if the doctors agreed to release you. They could keep you longer. Guy knew it was lunacy and, as Anna feared, threatening.

They were inmates of the system, subjects in a devastating experiment. He wondered who were the mad and dangerous ones. The only certain way out was to escape, and Guy believed that if someone did escape, the hospital would not send the police to retrieve him. The new psychiatric hospital program, being potentially controversial and a liability for administrating officials, would not want to draw such attention to itself.

For a gratifying moment, he considered burning the hospital down, watching the doctors and administrators and their damnable asylum vanish in flames, as if scorched in hell. But Guy knew there were many in the hospital who were innocent—patients, staff, and visitors—and such a plan would be reprehensible.

He repeated his question to Raphael. "How will you get out?"

"Well, the same berserk way I got in, by being me."

Raphael laughed bearishly, his eyes again ignited with an inspired madness. Then he stared fiercely at Guy.

"Listen up, Guy. You're an artist, man, and, I suspect, a lover." Raphael flashed his embracing grin. "Walk through those doors with me, not this damn one." He pointed to Room B.

Guy's first impulse was to agree and just flee free with Raphael. But something deeper inside himself told him to stay. His business there was not completed.

"I would like to, but I believe I have more to do here."

Raphael eyed him puzzled. "OK. I believe you, man. Trust your spirit, as our feisty Ms. Bouchet would say."

He grinned and held his hand out. They shook.

"We're friends forever, roomy. Bonded! When you get the hell out of here, and I'm betting you will, come visit me. Just ask any homeless Joe or Jane, or lost soul on the street, where's Raphael? They'll point the way. Farewell, ol' friend."

He shook Guy's hand vigorously and then gave him a firm bear hug.

"Farewell, my friend," Guy replied.

Raphael walked down the hallway and then turned toward Guy.

"While you're here, whatever the hell you do, don't act too sane. Then you're doomed!" He laughed gleefully and continued down the hall.

Guy watched him stop before the nurses' station. Raphael spoke for a few moments with the nurse and then suddenly threw himself onto the floor. He writhed, squirmed, and trembled like a man in the fit of a tortuous seizure. The shocked nurse bent over the counter and yelled some words at him. Then she turned and picked up the phone. That was his opportunity. Raphael stood up and walked quietly down the hall and around the corner.

Guy, reminiscing on his bed, smiled. He did not know how Raphael got past the other security posts, but he knew he had made it. His friend was free.

That thought assuaged Guy's sadness. He thought of the night to come. Perhaps some splendid dream, with all the charm and wonder of that nether world, awaited him. He stretched back on his bed, content yet restless, closed his eyes, and anticipated.

Excitement in his spirit withheld him from that consuming mistress. For hours he drifted in and out of her arms, floating in the narcotic domain between wakefulness and sleep. Visions, real as the world yet fanciful as dreams, teased his mind. He witnessed vivid landscapes: lovely paradises and shadowy cities. And living artworks, sculptures that seduced and paintings that invited him into their worlds. He entered the golden wheat fields with fluttering crows of a van Gogh landscape. And he greeted women, exotic, sensual, and waiting.

In a hazy vision he saw a nurse enter his room. She swept across the floor and attended to some items on a table. Soft in the illumination of the room's night light, like a floating white ghost, very slowly she strolled along the side of his bed. As in an enchanting dream, he felt a warm kiss on his forehead. He looked up, struggling to focus his bleary eyes, and beheld a surprising sight.

"Anna?" Guy was uncertain whether he was communicating to a dream, a hallucination, a woman, or all.

"Shhh," she whispered, a finger before her lips. "I have come to you, Guy. Like a dream." She smiled and then laughed.

"Anna?" He repeated, rising onto his elbow. "Are you really here?"

She peered at him curiously and then with gentle reproach. "Trust your vision, artist! I am here."

"But how?"

Again she smiled. "Intrigue and subterfuge. To put it simply, I snuck in." Her voice sounded as blissful as that soft kiss. "I put on my Nurse Persona, with a few modifications." She pointed to a blue line on her nurse's cap. "I remembered their uniforms and duplicated a name badge. See." Anna tapped the badge on her uniform. It bore the fictitious name Eroica. "Then, with a smile to the guards and attendants, I walked past. It was actually disturbingly easy."

"Anna!" Guy blurted for a third time, although now in a happy declaration. He sat up and took her in his arms, hugging her tightly. "I'm so happy to see you!"

"And I'm happy to see you! I was worried." She glanced over her shoulder. "Wait."

She rushed across the room, looked into the hallway and then shut the door. She shimmied back to his bedside, her expression delighted. Then it fell solemn.

"Are you all right?" she asked.

"Yes, I'm well. They haven't erased me yet."

Anna pouted. "Erased you. That's what I feared."

"No, I'm fine. Still here and so glad you came!"

"I couldn't wait for your return." She placed a hand on his arm. "I kept thinking about you." Staring, her eyes melded into his. "Guy." She stopped and sat on the bed.

"What? What is it?"

"Oh, nothing. We'll talk later. Let's just . . . be together."

She drew him into her arms and held him tightly. Guy was surprised but pleased by the unusual desperation he detected in her. It was generally he who was the desperate soul while she maintained a gracious poise that he found admirable but frustrating.

He rubbed his hand up and down her back in consoling strokes. For a period of time they remained quiet. Then Anna spoke subdued.

"I've been in my apartment, thinking and feeling some things. I wrote in my journal and worked on a new performance play, about a reverse creation, the devil creates the universe. And I listened to music. I looked at the sky a lot. The sky . . . so deep and pure and empty. At night the stars so wondrously bright!"

She looked above his head at the gray ceiling.

"I kept worrying about you, but felt excited too. I would suddenly spontaneously dance in my apartment." She chuckled. "Either very sexy or goofy, like that night we got drunk. I even cried, but not really because I was sad. I wasn't sad at all . . . I don't know why I cried."

Anna looked down, pensive.

Guy thought her communication unusually disjointed. "What is it, Anna? What are you trying to say? Are you all right?"

"I'm fine, yes." She pulled back from him and glanced around the room. Her face displayed a tenderness touching on vulnerability. "I just . . . ." She stopped and looked at Guy and then back into the air.

Suddenly Anna became composed with a glinting certainty in her eyes and the smile of an excited debutante. "Yes!" she declared so loudly that Guy jolted. "What I'm trying to say is, I have a nice gift for you, my love."

Anna stood. She removed her nurse's cap and tossed it to the floor and then ran her fingers through her hair, appearing like a scene Guy had enjoyed many times in movies.

Teasing? He wondered. Then, to his immense surprise, Anna unzipped the back of her nurse's uniform and with shimmies allowed it to drop to the floor. She stepped out of the dress, hooked it with her foot and flung it into the air.

"Do you understand?" She asked provocatively.

Time suspended in a wondrous moment of clarity. Guy smiled and nodded.

"'Tis the time! I want to be with you tonight, Guy," she whispered. "I was going to wait until you returned home, but I couldn't. So I've come to you, like a mistress to her lover." She looked into the air, dreamy. "No. I want to say this perfectly. Like a lover in a dream." She paused. "No, like a virgin to her first seducer." She paused again, reflecting. "No, like flesh to a fantasy!" She giggled. "No, like a woman to a man. Better!" She smiled. "I feel excited, but somewhat foolish." She paused. "Yes, I know! Like me to you. I've come to you, Guy!"

Guy stared. "Anna, are you sure you're all right?"

"Yes." She touched him on the cheek. "Yes, I feel wonderful, and very right." Then she looked towards the door. "The nurses, will they come in tonight?"

"No. After 11 p.m., they only come in if I buzz them."

"Great!"

Anna stood tall and assured before him in her black lace bra and panties. She waited before proceeding, encouraging seductive drama and pleasuring Guy's vision with the sight, and promise, of her partially undressed body. She knew with her woman's, and lover's, intuition that he would enjoy that, a sweet enticement!

And he did, with transfixed eyes. Guy had trouble believing that the moment he had so long yearned for was finally arriving, and in such a surprising and clandestine fashion.

"And the night opened to precious delights," Anna pronounced as she reached behind her and unfastened her bra. Very slowly, she peeled it off presenting a gradual exposure of her breasts and then tossed the bra over his head onto the bed. Her breasts were voluptuous, their swells traced by the illumination of the dim night light. To Guy, they appeared perfect and virginal, as if never touched by anything coarser than a man's fantasy vision; strangers to a lover's touch.

Anna rubbed her left breast in a slow, circular motion and then with a middle finger massaged its nipple. She looked down at it, then up at Guy and smiled.

"Dear poet, do you have a verse for my sweet breasts?"

Guy understood and was willing to play. "Indeed! The poet does."

"Speak it to me."

He spoke the words of a poem he had penned.

"A grace and beauty to flesh,
As earth risen to sensuous form.
The veil and fear is dropped,
And love is sure.
Just flesh, yet the fullest truth.
That dream of joined being.
Its beauty in desire, its grace in need.
In woman to breast and breast to man,
Surrender and love,
A manchild, a womanman."

"Good!" Anna commended. "It's erotic and lovely."

"As are you, my love," the poet replied, and they laughed.

Anna ran her thumbs inside the top edge of her lace panties. Ever so slowly, she drew it down, unveiling a smooth, maturely fleshed pelvis and her dark, mysterious portal. She dropped the garment to her feet, playfully lifted it with a foot and flung it onto Guy's lap. He smelled its pungent, woman's scent.

Anna stood fully naked and vulnerable. Guy thought her more beautiful and sexy, more tender and sensual, than any woman of dream or fantasy. She leaned forward and kissed him on the lips. His arms reached for her, but she gently blocked them from touching.

"Not yet, my love," she whispered and then kissed him again, passionately, only their mouths touching. Her tongue circled the edge of his lips and then moved inside to play with his.

She drew back, stood tall and elegant and slowly turned, exposing her backside to Guy. It was as sleek as the contour of a swan's neck. She ran a hand slowly across her rounded buttocks.

"Dear poet, do you have a poem for my awaiting buttocks?"

"Oh yes. The poet does, my love."

"Please, recite it for me."

Guy grinned and then evoked his favorite derriere verse, a fleshy play of puns.

"Oh divine, vulgar buttocks! That could arouse a saint to sin! To hee-haw and play the ass, leaving the virtuous behind, nun reared, to rear. Persuading him to resign, for a twitch of fated flesh, serene spirit design."

Anna applauded delicately. "Bravo! 'Tis clever and racy."

"As are you, my love."

Anna smiled and turned around. With one finger she touched her pubis. To Guy it looked excitingly primitive.

"And most of all, had my sweet poet words for my garden of unearthly delights?"

Guy nodded. "In truth, my love! The poet hath."

"Speak them to me."

Anna displayed a coquettish grin. Guy spoke with mock drama a memorized verse.

"Oh sweet portal! So exquisite and raw! Of spasms and quakes, of blood and foam. Whore and angel, slave and free; in rapture and in pain, I am born and love and die in thee, again and again.

"A passion play is told of a man who loves a woman, where from love he was born, in velvet folds and volcanic depths, and returns to love and die. For love always carries death, and death life reborn.

"A virgin flesh with spirit, perfect and torn."

"Oooh, beautiful and a little scary," Anna responded.

"As are you, my love," Guy replied and they laughed.

"Undress," she gently commanded.

Guy rose and removed his pajamas and underwear. True to the game, he hooked each item with his foot and tossed it across the room. Anna giggled.

For a long, quiet time, Anna had him look at her, and she at him.

"Behold, my Lover Persona!" She announced proudly, sweeping her hand down the front of her naked form.

Anna thought Guy's naked body grandly handsome. It appeared strong and yet softly cushioned as to be invitingly cuddly, and had sufficient tone and musculature to excite her with its masculine sculpture. Cute curls of dark hair shadowed his chest. Her eyes looked down.

Knowing Guy was shy, Anna appreciated his unhesitant willingness to be so exposed before her. She thought what she saw, that personification of the male, was properly proportioned and finely shaped to please any of her fantasies, which were arriving rapidly. It had not yet risen to its full glory but was proceeding nobly.

She grinned. "What was it you once said? Preciously elated, not monstrously inflated?"

"Preciously stated, not monstrously baited."

She nodded. "Indeed. Divinely so!"

He was pleased.

Guy delighted in just looking at Anna's body, so naked and lovely, her flesh speaking of pleasures deep and mysterious, and could have for the entire night had not even greater promises awaited.

There is something noble in her bearing as she stands before me, so exposed and vulnerable, he mused silently. *As if she carries the treasures of all women. And indeed, she does!*

Guy had never before seen Anna totally nude, except in a hallucination and dreams.

Hallucination, or dream? The thought disturbed him, but he forced his attention back on Anna. *No! Yes!* His eyes voyaged around her, adoring each precious part.

Anna waved her fingers in beckoning. "Come to me, my love," she spoke in the alluring voice of every woman throughout time calling to her lover.

Guy took her in his arms and pulled her close, feeling the warmth and tenderness of her naked body pressed against his.

I feel her heart beating, he thought. *Her beautiful, little heart.* He kissed her on the forehead, and she looked deep into his eyes.

"It has been so long, Anna, that I have wanted to be with you as at this moment, and I think my patience has been admirable.

I now wish to feel and enjoy every inch of you, every wondrous surface of your flesh."

Anna nodded and smiled gently.

His hands caressed down each of her arms and then up. He kissed their tender underside. Her hands—with a simple touch they can fill a man's soul with joy! Kissed. Each slender finger in his mouth.

"Mmmm," Anna purred.

Guy and Anna

Made love.

Anna's smooth shoulders and the graceful curve of her neck. Massaged and kissed.

Her elegant back.

Goose bumps.

Buttocks. Creations of erotic perfection!

Anna's eyes closed.

Her legs as those of a dancer; possessed of a lovely grace. Luxuriated and kissed. *What a calm assurance I feel,* Guy noted, *as if joined with the strength of the earth.*

The hush of sighs.

Feet massaged and kissed. *There is a wondrous childlike play in Guy's lovemaking,* Anna thought.

Her legs spread. Guy in between. With one hand he gently massaged her belly, kissed it several times, and then laid his cheek against its soft cushion.

For minutes, he remained in that peaceful retreat. Anna stroked her hand gently through his hair and kissed the top of his head. She enjoyed being able to offer him that nurturing in those moments of affectionate connection. It touched her tenderness as a woman.

Whispers.

Breasts men dreamed of. Nipples and mouth. A lovely rose flush.

Time nonexistent. *Suckling. Infantile?* Guy did not in the least care.

How profoundly satisfying to give myself to Guy as both a lover and a nurturing mother, Anna thought. Soft streamings flowed through her body.

"Thank you," she whispered. "Now, to source!"

"Both exquisite and raw," Guy spoke. "The perfect marriage of the goddess and the beast."

Guy approached it gently, orally. He wanted to be tender to that most sublime gift she offered. Silky, moist, warm. Anna heaved and trembled and spoke words that were a colorful fusion of poetry and vulgarity.

Seated in velvety folds, an exquisite tuning fork. Guy played upon it. A lover's song of rapture.

"Suns are burning white!" She said in a raspy breath.

Anna convulsed violently, her body arching high. Her head flew back and her eyes rolled. Fluids streamed, some entering his mouth.

Then limp, almost meditative. Lost to some delirious depth. "Thank you, thank you," she whispered. "Your turn!"

Little girl mischief. Anna knew her craft. A loving mouth. Guy off in some euphoric place.

"Like a pleasure palace of opiates and whores," he murmured.

An opiate and a whore. Anna delighted in perceiving herself as such. Streams flowed deep within.

Stopped.

"No! No!" Guy pleaded. "Don't stop!"

"It's OK, my love. Just breathe and relax."

With a wave of her hand, Anna directed him to move more onto the bed. Then with slinky, sensuous movements, the alluring catwoman in seduction, she climbed beside him on the bed and growled and purred.

She gently pulled Guy over her. Nails scratched his chest. Her legs spread. Guy entered from above, *as I always enjoy a man first moving into me.*

Anna below, vibrating, her skin flushed with color. To his amusement, Guy recalled articles about erotic lovemaking.

His clever, erect beast played at the lady's doorway. Circling, entering, withdrawing, entering. Probing, teasing.

"Good!" Anna whispered. A dance of arousal.

Then Anna begged.

"Not yet, my love," Guy replied.

The moment Guy entered Anna fully was one of the best of his life. For her to surrender so, begging him to be inside of her, and the feeling that he possessed her, fulfilled a desire in him even more profound than he had suspected. Although there was a sense of conquest, at that moment he loved Anna more than ever.

"My sweet," he whispered. "My love!" And he proceeded to love her with passionate eagerness.

"Slow down, Lothario, slow down!"

Anna wrapped her legs around him and with a tightening and releasing of her strong thigh muscles, or with her hands gripping his chest, or with a few whispered words, regulated his motions, choreographing their erotic dance.

Then stopped, completely, Guy surprised at how wonderful it felt just being inside of Anna, inside a woman. *A warm and intimate union. A fusion of flesh and spirit,* he thought.

Guy had never felt totally comfortable in his own skin, but at that moment, he felt completely comfortable in hers.

Then proceeding. Stroking and stroking. Maintaining a balance of passion and restraint.

"Long," she whispered. "Long and delirious is what we want, my love."

And feelings, so sublime.

Anna's body moved in smooth waves with his. He rotating his pelvis. Touching sensitive areas. Stroking high and shallow, sometimes slowly, sometimes rapidly. Anna almost lost all boundaries. An ecstatic frenzy.

Guy: like a man becoming the joy of a child, a child growing, through the most intense sensations, into the fully experiential, mature man. Not philosophy, not dream or fantasy, not even hope, but intensely experienced life!

Not yet. Wait! Anna restrained. She clasped the end of his aching warrior in her fingers and squeezed. "It's OK, my love. Relax."

His aching excitation diminished, the charged sensations dispersing more evenly through his body.

"Yes, Anna, thank you."

She kissed him all over his face and then lustfully on the lips.

"Now, Guy. Continue!"

Reentered. Stroking slowly and rhythmically, gradually increasing the pace.

Two lovers as one. Partnered twice as beastly, raw and sweet! Guy's poet mind improvised. Sensations of heat and electricity. Guy lost inside his, and Anna's, flesh.

Even my toes come to life—little, electrified toes.

"Divine whore." He whispered.

"Yes!" She replied.

Rapid assaults of sensations—ecstatic, edging on painful, like thousands of electric charges, blinding Guy's vision and flinging him into a delirious confusion. *Stop! Flee!* His mind urged. Guy was unaccustomed to such intensity of sensation flooding his body and pushing against the walls of his skin. He feared he might not be able to contain them. They threatened a disturbing disintegration.

He realized he was holding his breath and released it. As his breathing deepened, the electric excitation smoothed and then flowed like living rivers, less dangerous and more blissful. His fear vanished, and he surrendered.

It is happening! he thought joyfully.

He looked at Anna and frightened. She appeared lost in a secret possession, one of delirious torments, as if a demon occupied her body, ravishing it. Words flashed through his mind: *The Rape of the Goddess.* She was Anna and yet, not. Her unfocused eyes rolled wildly, and he knew they saw nothing except inner fires. He expected she would cry into the night like a warring animal. Her mouth gasped, her breathing fast and staccato, and her face contorted. Guy thought her both beautiful and terrible, like some divine erotic demon, a mad image from a Bosch painting. She grabbed his arms tightly and tugged him forward as if trying to pull him deeper inside of her.

"Tear me!" she implored coarsely.

Thinking Anna might be in pain and out of an instinctive impulse to protect her, Guy slowed his thrusts. "My love," he spoke, but it was too late. Anna's body arched severely, her head thrown back. She convulsed, trembling, as if lifted by a mighty force and shook. Then the depths of her sexual core erupted. Fluids flowed from her loins, making her quivering passageway even warmer and more silken, and Guy was pulled into her convulsions, wanting to join in her consuming euphoria. To be lost in Anna! His sensations escalated.

Then Anna suddenly softened, melting and limp. Her breathing slowed. But Guy the impassioned lover kept pumping and pumping.

"Wait! Stop!" With a hand against his chest she gently pushed him out of her. "There can be more, much more, if you stop now." Her eyes were loving. "I can orgasm many times, but it might be different with you, my sweet."

"Orgasm . . . yes . . . different." He complied, sitting still between her legs. It was agonizing; his body ached.

"Now, close your eyes," she instructed, "and breathe deeply. Relax your body fully and allow everything to just flow through you."

Although it was difficult for him to act against the urgent pressures in his body, he complied. Gradually the excitations softened, dispersing evenly, filling him with a sublime vibrancy.

"Oh, I see!"

Anna also performed the ritual, breathing and relaxing, transporting herself to an even more vibrant plane. They remained in that state for minutes, occasionally touching each other.

With each touch, the energy of my lover's flesh tingles through my hands, each thought.

"Now, more play," Anna decreed.

She rolled him onto his back, grinned devilishly, and positioned herself over top of him.

"The goddess mounts the god," she whispered teasingly.

Very slowly, she lowered herself onto his erect member. She rolled her pelvis in a circular motion once and then lifted off it. Then she lowered back onto it, allowing it slightly more inside of her. She repeated her pelvic rotation, a joy of both sight and sensation to Guy, and then several times moved slowly up and down.

An erotic pelvic dance. *How deliriously aching to feel Guy inside of me so gradually, each time deeper, more throbbing and intense.* Anna adored the sensation of a man's erect penis inside her flesh. *A blessing for being a woman!*

She leaned down and whispered to Guy. "I love you."

Moments later. Fully penetrated. Pelvis rolling and rocking, as a little girl riding a rocking horse. Alternated motions and tempos.

How erotically Anna plays above me! Guy reached up and cupped her breasts. Sometimes he caressed the smooth curve of her neck or softly touched her face.

Periodically Anna lifted her arms and performed a cute shimmy dance. Those were the moments Guy thought she looked most adorable. The erotic girl-woman, dancing and playing, giving love and pleasure, with her lover inside of her.

Guy kept his breathing open and deep allowing the excitations and pulsations to increasingly grow. He moved with Anna's motions, synchronizing his pelvis to hers; two lovers becoming one.

And Anna's sequence of orgasms began. Her body kept arching deeply, like a contortionist, and her head flew back, swinging, her hair flailing across her face. She gasped and sounded low screams. Then she sat more erect on him, her movements slower. But very quickly they accelerated, and her back again arched. A sublime violence. Streams of fluids flowed.

Watching her above him mesmerized Guy. He had never before seen a woman orgasm so many times so fast for so long. He had heard about such feats in sexual lore but had not known if it was true. It was true.

I definitely chose the right woman! And during those moments, not glimpsed by him, his poet's mind, which sometimes operated independent of conscious thought, composed a poem—a poem about Anna, and lovers, and rapture.

Guy felt pleased that he was able to delay his own eruption. His lovemaking was now more gentle and tender. The delights provoked, deep in his flesh and spirit, were wonderful.

"Good, my sweet," Anna spoke and kissed him. Then she took him in her arms and pulled him up, seating him upright, and she sat in his lap, his legs beneath hers and hers wrapped around his waist. They embraced and pressed their bodies tightly together, breast-to-breast.

Guy relished that position, so close and intimate. All of Anna's flesh felt soft, hot, and moist. *A perfect caress,* he thought, *made even more perfect by my deep penetration inside her. Two lovers sublimely entwined as one.*

Anna repeatedly kissed his face. Both lovers vibrated. Then she laid her cheek against his.

"Do not move. Be still," she spoke softly. "Be as still as the truth in your heart."

And for long yet timeless moments, they remained wrapped together, sharing a loving intimacy.

"The embrace of love," Anna purred with a dreamy smile. "Our perfect union. I love you, Guy."

"I love you too, Anna."

Then Anna rocked, slowly, like a mother tenderly rocking with a child. She hummed a soft song of pleasure.

A sea of excited sensation rose in Guy. Their rocking became more rapid, and Anna added her pelvic rotations. After minutes of consuming union, Guy heard Anna moan. He looked into her eyes and saw that she was lost—lost in yet another orgasm, one more gentle and tender yet, as he knew by the trembling of her body in his arms, even more sublime.

A powerful excitation flowed from her body into his and in an intriguing moment, he felt her orgasm within himself.

Anna kept gushing, soft and silent. Her fluids spilled across him and sweat glistened her skin. She breathed in rapid sighs as she vibrated in an ecstatic frequency, and Guy followed, deeper and deeper.

Guy and Anna went subterranean, far beneath the earth's crust, beyond all crevices and fissures, beyond boulders and steamy rivers. It was a place Guy had never before visited, beyond heat and friction and desperate passions, beyond flesh and foam and blood. They passed through some mysterious and vague world where delirious shapes were like thin, trembling illusions, and the illusions kept vanishing as they, absolute lovers, swept toward something more immense and allusive. Guy's head felt like an egg cracked in it and its yoke flowed through his entire being. Transparent, wondrous energy streamed through his body, dissolving all coarseness and structure. Walls melted and passages expanded, becoming vast spaces, each like the nebulous center of the earth. All physicality was disappearing.

"Drown with me," Anna whispered, and they entered a sea. Guy transformed into a vibrant ocean—an ocean of fine sensations. He could no longer feel his arms around Anna. Then his legs and trunk melted. His face could hold no expression. Moments later, he did not even feel Anna entwined with him at all. Instead they seemed blended together in that rapturous sea.

It was euphoric . . . and terrifying! Guy realized there was something profoundly frightening in that total loss of form, of the comfortable identity of his body. It warred against a powerful and persistent need in him, the need for integrity and defining borders. A terrifying word entered his consciousness: *dying.*

"No, no!" Anna countered, struggling to speak between deep breaths as she felt his fear. She rocked more rapidly in a display of confidence.

"It's wonderful! Trust it, Guy. Surrender." She drew a breath. "It's love!"

Immediately, Guy felt comforted. He trusted Anna. She knew. In a brave moment, he surrendered all and sank deeper into the sea, from which all life is born.

And it *was* euphoric, the most splendorous of deaths! He relaxed and breathed, embracing his escalating delirium. Charges and vibrations tingled in an unbounded space. All felt alive.

"Close your eyes, Guy. Drown with me," Anna urged softly.

And he did. There was nothing but the vibrant and illuminant pool. Even though Guy was still aware of his own being, he melded into that pool and experienced with tenfold a usual intensity all of its pleasures and energy.

"The Beautiful, Winged Madness," he whispered.

Guy had a redeeming feeling, one he had so long yearned for: all struggle was gone, all need to struggle ended.

And without a separate identity, all of that dreadful self-consciousness that made him feel so awkward in the world, and so alone, vanished. There was no time or space, no individuating form, no fears or regrets. There was only one thing: ecstatic being.

Guy became nothing and loved it. Nothing in the midst of a rapturous everything. They were that ocean, and that ocean was them, and that ocean was truth, and that ocean was beauty and love and a mystical vision, formless and vibrantly alive! They touched the edges of the universe and found there were no edges.

This is it! Guy thought.

And then there was more. Though he could no longer feel his bounded body, he detected that he had orgasmed. It felt as if the form that had been him flowed uncontained into both Anna and that immense, euphoric sea, for they were one, exciting all to an even greater love.

Anna moaned, and then she too released new streams of life into that vibrating ocean. And Guy saw a brilliant luminance, first beyond him, then all around him. Then there was just that radiant light and energy, and Guy knew it was what infused all things. Anna was somewhere in that luminescent field, selfless, surrendered and consumed. Both knew they *were* that radiance, that grace, now even beyond the great sea of sensations.

He heard Anna speak, but her voice was distant, as in another universe. "Guy." And then another word, in a floating whisper. "Sublime."

He repeated the word back to her, and it floated in the sea of light.

Guy sensed their little bodies, somewhere far away, locked in their exquisite embrace of love. It pleased and amused him, two such loving and desperate beings. And he sensed Anna looking at those same intertwined lovers, and smiling. He too smiled, a smile of his entire self, and he realized it was his first smile of total happiness in ages beyond recall.

And he felt a communion with Anna, simple and yet profound, as a tree to the earth and air, or a single spirit to all spirits. And in that communion, Guy felt more love for her than ever before, more than he could ever have imagined.

Words came, and he spoke them into the universe of light. "A truer and purer love."

Somewhere in that expanse of radiance, Anna heard his words and whispered back. "Yes. Truer and purer love."

Guy felt something warm and soft, unidentifiable in that vastness. He held his attention on it, and it intensified, becoming more material, something of the flesh. It was his lips. Anna was kissing him.

"Come back, Guy." She spoke hushed. "Open your eyes and come back."

He opened them and saw Anna's face close to his as she kissed him again. Her expression was excited, and her eyes glimmered.

They were still entwined, sitting up, he inside of her. His erection was almost as firm as before.

Anna smiled. "Welcome back, lover."

"Anna!" was all he could say.

"Once more, my love," she said with a playful voice. "But a little more of *this* world."

She laughed and rocked. The sensations and boundaries of his body, and hers, returned. Guy repossessed the flesh. The flows and streaming and vibrations assumed more physicality.

As Anna rolled and rocked and her pelvis rotated and danced upon his savage, magic wand, their excitations grew coarser. Anna kept kissing him, delighting him with her playful tongue, as he caressed her breasts.

Their passion, now more raw and bestial, fevered quickly until Guy and Anna convulsed together, their heads flung back at the same moment, sending an explosive thrill, hot and white, through their bodies. Love fluids flowed and intermingled. They held each other tight and gasped, then yelped, then laughed.

After vibrating and trembling and vibrating and trembling, they became limp, collapsed in each other's arms. Anna cried.

"I sometimes cry after lusty orgasm." She sniffled. "And after sublime raptures. Tonight I've enjoyed both!"

Guy kissed her tenderly on the forehead and the cheek. With his finger he wiped some tears from her face. She released her tight embrace of him and fell on her back on the mattress. Guy plopped beside her, and they lay silent, euphoric in their bodies and minds, staring into the vacancy of the ceiling. The room seemed especially peaceful and yet vibrant, and both were immensely aware of being there, and being alive, and being together.

"Wow!" Anna finally spoke.

"Wow!" Guy echoed.

"What was all that?" She stared into space as if searching for insight into a splendid mystery.

"That was . . . great!" Guy proclaimed. "The paragon of great! I don't have words for it."

They looked at each other, their eyes like gleaming galaxies, laughed, and then kissed.

Anna became reflective. "I made love for the first time tonight. I am no longer a virgin."

Guy looked at her bemused. "You mean, I helped corrupt you?"

"No. You helped free me to be a woman, and to love."

Guy's chest inflated. "Yes, of course! But you'll always be a virgin in my eyes."

Anna smiled and then pointed to herself. "*I* became as vast and fluid as the ocean."

"And *I* became as radiant and pure as a sea of light," Guy countered.

"So did I! And also wonderfully bestial and blood-like. And I surrendered completely."

Guy grinned. "Yes, I noticed."

Anna kissed him and laid her head on his bare chest that was heaving gently. "I should have known," she confessed. "I've been a fool."

"Yes."

"Hey!" She lifted her head and glared.

"But I've been a fool, too. I should have expressed to you my desires, long ago."

"Two delirious fools." Anna paused. "You were very good tonight, Guy. An excellent lover!"

"I followed you, and you were an excellent teacher, and lover." He took her hand in his, lifted it graciously, as one does a lady's, and then shook it playfully. "Thank you."

"Thank *you!*" She kissed the top of his hand, as one does a king's.

Anna looked softer and lovelier than Guy had ever seen her. She glowed, and her eyes were fathomless, peacefully Zen-like.

"Welcome to nirvana," he joked. *God, am I in love with this woman!* He almost spoke, but didn't.

"Our lovemaking," Anna interjected, "it was not just hot and raunchy, it was beautiful, Guy, metaphysical." Her hand floated through the air.

"Yes, definitely metaphysical," Guy concurred.

They both laughed and then were silent, and then laughed again. Guy glanced around the room. In the dim light, its colors were wispy and rarefied and its shadows like intriguing illusions. *Love changes all*, he noted.

Anna drew his hand to her lips and kissed it. "My prince, you know that ideal I've spoken about, that perfect union of being and action and purpose?"

"Yes, I remember. Like being a tree."

"Well, I think for some moments tonight, I achieved that." She looked into his eyes. "It was like being in perfect love."

She paused, considering. Light from a passing car on a ramp outside the room window streamed across her face, illuminating her reflective pose. Then it swept across the wall like an abstract dancing form. She danced with it.

"Yes, pure love," she added. "Do you know what I'm saying?"

"I do." Guy smiled. "The truer and purer love. That's *my* ideal."

"Yes, and now it's mine, too."

She rested her head back on his chest, and they lay again silent. Anna noticed that the air around them seemed enchanted.

"Perhaps tonight we both got to experience our highest ideals," she critiqued. "The only thing that was missing was art."

Suddenly Guy saw it. "Wait! I have art! In the midst of our lovemaking, my mind composed a poem. It's complete and waiting." He looked excitedly at Anna.

"Your mind composes poetry while your body makes love to me?"

"Well, yes! Isn't it wonderful?"

"And odd. Poet lovers." She winced in mock exasperation.

"Listen! I'll recite it." Guy paused. "I'll call it the Goddess and the Beast."

"You're the beast?"

"No, you are. As am I. We're both. You know, just like your," he pointed to her pubis. "So exquisite and raw, like the perfect marriage of the goddess and the beast."

Anna's playful look of reproach.

"Well, it is."

"OK, recite the poem."

Guy went into his poet's bearing, his expression focused and his eyes feeling.

"She seduces his longing to rejoin . . . splendorous, primordial forms. Elegant, symmetrical. Like her fierce leopard loins, sleek tight cords, black jungle eyes. And deep within, luxuriating velvet folds seat an exquisite harp—a tuning fork. Plucked, it resonates her being, as a thousand suns burn white.

"The beautiful, naked beast, now partnered twice as beastly, raw, and sweet, in a dissolution of time and architectural shapes, melds and dies, incandescent red in a molten sea—a warm, blood fluidity."

"Oooh, nice," Anna responded. "It's sexy and eloquent."

Guy smiled. At that moment he felt appreciative of all things. *Life can be good.*

"Thank you body," he ruminated aloud. "Thank you spirit. Thank you poetic mind. Thank you artistic sensibility."

He looked at Anna's sleek, naked body stretched across the bed like a sensual cat at rest.

"Thank you, Anna."

"Thank you, Guy. We are blessed to be both human beings and artists."

"Yes," was the only reply Guy felt was needed. He kissed her.

Anna achieved the delightful experience of smiling with a kiss. The flesh of her bosom flushed pinker.

"Guy, when we're back home, we need to talk about our plans. New plans. Long-term plans. I think you'll like my suggestions."

He cocked an intrigued brow. "Yes, I think I will."

Anna pushed back some wayward strands of hair from her face. "Some things have profoundly changed in me, Guy. And not just from tonight." She laughed. The strands of hair fell back over her face. "Although that *is* part of it. But it goes back farther. This I want to tell you now. I love thee."

"I know. I love thee too."

"No, I mean I *really* love thee! Different than before. Do you understand?"

To Guy, lying naked on the bed with the only woman he loved, those words were the most welcomed of all.

"Yes, Anna, I understand, and I *really* love thee too."

She smiled and then laid her head back on his chest. Her smile persisted. Out of curiosity, she tried to see if she could stop smiling. She couldn't.

They lay quiet, just enjoying being in each other's presence. They did not speak again. Guy fell into a drowsy lightness, undaunted by the approaching dark of sleep, and then into that dark. Anna just fell and was elated that she could finally do so. With closed eyes, she hummed a melody. "Here comes the bride, here comes the bride." But Guy, lost in a dream, did not hear.

She opened her eyes and looked at Guy one final time, he sleeping so peacefully beside her. She thought he looked beautiful. In her mind she heard the night calling her and knew it was time to leave. A sentiment entered her thoughts, and she whispered it to Guy.

"Sleep well, my love, come what may, until we join again in awakened sleep. Parting is such sweet sorrow."

She kissed him.

Chapter 22

ANNA WALKED BACK to her apartment late that night after a most memorable evening out. *Guy,* she thought. *He is probably sleeping peacefully in the hospital, frolicking in a fanciful dream.* Anna smiled. She now knew. Somewhere in the deep of night was love.

The Wilshire District streets were empty, in a serene anesthesia of sleep. Even her footsteps seemed a violate intrusion, like the thumping of a giant through a slumbering land. Anna looked into the night sky. It was black and pristine, speckled with glimmering, pin-light stars. *How infinitely immense and lovely,* she appraised.

She felt deep stirrings in her body and spirit, new affinities that had grown in recent weeks. She knew they were for Guy, *dearest Guy,* and for all creation. Anna was in a rare experience of contentment and appreciation for all things.

"And 'tis a time for love!" She whispered to the infinite heavens.

She stopped, startled. A small boy stood on the sidewalk in the amber light of a street lamp. His presence was surprising for that late hour, and he appeared to be alone. She approached and saw that he was about nine-years old; a cute child with a soft, round cherub face, luxurious wavy auburn hair that tumbled gently over his forehead, and immense cobalt eyes. He wore a white cotton bathrobe, as one might don after showering.

How sweet and sad, Anna thought. *Like a little, lost angel.*

"Hello, are you all right? Can I help you?" Anna offered her warmest smile.

The boy did not respond but just looked at her, an intimation of a smile on his face. Anna glanced around the area but saw no one else.

"Are you lost? Where is your mother?"

Still the boy was mute. The night light glistened in his eyes, eyes that Anna thought appeared strangely vacant, like eyes that had forsaken hope of seeing, or concluded there was nothing to see.

Then the boy spoke. "Do you . . . believe in love?" His speech was slow and intent.

What an odd question, Anna thought, examining his small form in the quasi-mystical light, *but then a fair one, for the boy was probably separated from his family, or perhaps had run away, feeling forlorn of love. Alone, and so adorable!*

"Yes, I do," she answered. "Ultimately, it is the most important thing."

"I don't," the boy stated stoically. "I kill love."

Anna flinched. The angelic child took a long, slender object from beneath his robe. Anna thought it was some type of stick. Then in his other hand appeared another long, thin shape. Before she comprehended, he swiftly and assuredly drew back the string of the bow and released the arrow.

A hissing sound. Then a tear, like a knife into a cushion. Anna felt a sharp, piercing pain in her chest.

Flashes of glaring white light. Weightlessness. The space around her appeared to tumble.

Anna realized she was on the ground, her vision alternating between a blur and exceptional clarity. She saw the black sky above her, its stars so brilliantly radiant she though they would explode. All was silent, only the coo of a pigeon in the distance, a lone pigeon in the night.

A terrible, sharp pain lacerated her chest, but only for a moment. It quickly became soft and numb.

Anna was a little girl walking to kindergarten that was in a fenced schoolyard at the end of her street. It had recently rained, and the morning was moist and gray. She slipped and fell into the mud, coating large portions of her newly purchased pants and jacket in a thick layer of brown. She stood, her expression upset, and then ran back home.

Her mother, standing in the living room, turned and looked surprised at her daughter. Anna, crying, told her the traumatic tale.

"I fell in the mud. I'm . . . dirty! All dirty!"

Her mother smiled. "Everything's OK, sweetie."

She cleaned Anna up and redressed her, speaking gentle, reassuring words. Anna remembered she was late to school that day, but it had been OK, just as her mother said. She smiled.

She now felt not only her own distress on that muddy morning, but all of the emotions of her mother—her sympathy and concern, her amusement, and her heartfelt desire to comfort her daughter.

"Mother," Anna whispered without a voice.

Moments from her life swept by: birthday parties, childhood loneliness, teenage dates, lovers, friendships, performance pieces. She again wore all of her personas. She thought the Elegant Death Persona especially beautiful on her and, in a peculiar way that she did not comprehend, correct.

How do I ever know who I am? she wondered bemused as she examined her costume menagerie. She performed a part of the Shadow People play, but now she was both the audience and the performers.

And the night felt colder.

Anna experienced her own feelings and those of all the people she had affected as she cruised through seemingly endless incidents. She felt the pain and love, the anguish and joy she had brought to each. She heard them laugh and cry and was saddened by those who had suffered by her. *Please forgive me,* she asked, and she was elated for all whom she had brought happiness and grateful that she had been able to do so.

Before her appeared a tall, muscular man in a body contouring black shirt and slacks. His face was black with white eye sockets and lips that framed black teeth. The brim of a flamboyant black fedora hat swept above his brow. Anna recognized him as the man who abducted her at the Day of the Dead festival.

"I told you we would meet again. But do not be afraid. I am gentle."

He smiled warmly, and Anna did not feel afraid. Then he faded and vanished.

Anna stood in a desert, the night around her a gray of shapes and shadows. She looked up. The night dome offered a dazzling operatic display of millions of exquisite glistening stars. She gasped, realizing that she was beholding the extraordinary beauty of the universe.

And Anna realized that time did not now exist. *What an amusing thought! I have all the time in the world. In fact, it never did exist.* She did not know how she knew that, she just did. The entirety of her life was in one moment and that moment was forever. She recalled the words of a beloved Chinese verse.

'One instant is eternity; eternity is the now. When you see through this one instant, you see through the one who sees.'

And what the one who sees now saw most vividly were images of Guy and their times together. How she loved him! And she felt how much he loved and longed for her. His words came back: *a truer and purer love.* It was a wondrous gift she had been given.

Anna saw his face as close as if he were holding her in his arms. He smiled and she kissed him. "I love thee," she heard herself whisper and he whispered back.

Then Anna saw in the lucid, ebony night sky an image of herself, pretty but graven, pointing toward the ground. She looked down and saw a form beneath her. A body, a woman, still and silent. *Her* body, lying on the sidewalk in the hazy light of a street lamp. She thought it looked lovely and peaceful, and it pleased her. Then she became confused. She saw glistening red liquid on her chest and the wooden shaft of the protruding arrow.

What is this? What has happened?

Then she remembered. The cherub boy. The arrow. *I kill love.*

In a moment both terrifying and oddly exhilarating, Anna realized that she was dead.

But how can this be, since I am still here? Her thoughts were like abstractions in the air. *I am dead, and yet I am not.*

Then in an epiphany moment Anna realized that all she had suspected and had chosen to believe in her life, those wonderful faiths of spirit, were true! Her vision of herself, which she knew was not herself—her body below her—blurred. With both a profound grief and an ascending euphoria, Anna understood.

Then her world went black.

Then her world went white and light.

Chapter 23

GUY AWOKE TO blackness. He opened his eyes and the flooding illuminance of the morning light blinded him, erasing the world and creating the peculiar phenomenon of being simultaneously in both light and dark. No forms or colors or substance. There was nothing.

Then a remembrance. *Anna's warm body beneath mine.* He heard again her voice and words of love, and it lifted him into joy. A flurry of exuberant birds flew beyond all ceilings and skies into a dazzling heaven!

"Anna," he spoke as he looked to his side, but she was not there. His eyes scanned the hospital room.

Anna must have left last night after he fell asleep, he surmised. Of course, she had to. He smiled, envisioning her, still moist and flushed, quietly escaping through the hallways, pleased by her clandestine mission. He imagined her hair disheveled and her eyes sparkling and the front of her nurse's uniform unzipped low offering her provocative trademark cleavage, now a symbolic tribute to the night's event and part of her ticket of escape past the admiring guards.

"Sweet, dear Anna," he whispered. "My love!"

It all seemed like a wondrous dream.

A dream? His chest sunk. *Perhaps a hallucination?* He examined the bed beside him and ran his hand along its surface. It was smooth and cool. He searched for a trace of her presence, perhaps moisture or a strand of her hair, but found nothing.

Guy looked at a table for a note or some clever and sweet token, as Anna might leave. None. He perused the room. There was not anything out of the ordinary, no item of clothing inadvertently or intentionally left behind. No black lace bra or panty lay on the cushion of a chair, concealed by a newspaper, with a strap dangling to the floor.

A hallucination? He tormented. Mystical birds darkened into mangy scavengers, hovering, waiting to feed. A kind yet cruel delusion? Those of recent weeks had been so vivid as to trap him in their reality. He remembered the nighttime visit of the Little Girl Mommy Anna, and the human dolphins at Santa Monica Beach. Both had fully possessed his mind, body, and emotions. Was this another?

Or perhaps a splendid dream, woven by the enchantress of sleep from the threads of his desires and passions? Dreams can be masterful illusions, pleasing and haunting, especially in lunacy.

In madness.

His body felt alive yet rested. Would he feel so rested?

Guy closed his eyes and interrogated his memory. He remembered the lovemaking with lucid clarity—his feelings, her words and body movements, her scents. They seemed real beyond reality, and that worried him.

He wanted to call Anna and ascertain the truth but he had no phone, and calls were prohibited unless one was a thread away from death. He felt a powerful impulse to escape the hospital and find her. Anna would tell him, and even if she did not, and played it as a teasing game, he would be able to tell by her responses to him. If it had occurred, she would not be the same. *I would know.*

Then the truth of his situation seized him. The pale hospital walls and innocuous hygienic decor folded in on him. This was the final day of his scheduled hospital stay. He had a 2:30 p.m. appointment in Room B.

Guy rolled over and buried his head in the pillow. *Room B.* The thought filled him with dread and confusion. What to do? It was time to confront it.

"This is bullshit!" he muttered. "If I am mad, let me be insane in the world with Anna."

Guy struggled out of bed and showered. Its warm, soothing water and soap seemed a baptism, washing conflict from his being, and he kept thinking of Anna, on her bed, waiting for his return.

He dressed and then left the room and walked to the cafeteria. He had arrived late for breakfast, and the kitchen attendant, a burly African-American in a white uniform, grinned at him from behind a metal-framed open window, his eyes like glistening white pearls with ebony centers. He was removing the trays of food from the counter.

"Few minutes more and the food would be gone," he informed Guy and then halted his labors until Guy filled his plate.

Guy took a large serving of scrambled eggs, bacon, cereal, toast, and coffee. Despite his uneasiness at what might follow that day, he felt exceptionally hungry. *From the vigorous workout the night before,* he thought and hoped. He drank two cups of coffee and prepared a third to bring with him. He wanted to be very alert on this day. D-Day, he designated it—Destiny Day.

Or perhaps Death Day. He suppressed that thought.

There were no meetings or activities scheduled that day, only his appointment. Guy returned to his room and lay on his bed. He thought of his friend Raphael, the escaped humanitarian lover madman, and grinned imagining his friend's feisty presence back on the most destitute streets of L.A. helping the dispossessed, a true angel in the City of Angels, and free.

Conflict tormented. What to do?

Escape! As Raphael had. But Guy knew all his disability income and benefits, on which he had depended for so long, would be lost. *What a clever trap. What madness!* Guy felt imprisoned and a disturbing question taunted. *Who has sentenced me?*

He packed his possessions in his suitcase to be prepared. Whatever happens, he would not be remaining in his room. Guy felt a scary yet oddly exhilarating sense of fate.

He waited for his hour. He tried to read but was too distracted. The words floated through his mind like meaningless symbols.

He walked to the recreation room. Julie Not Julie, the other remaining patient, was not there. He watched television, a panel discussion of a fomenting war somewhere in some nowhere place. He returned to his room and waited, and waited.

Guy skipped lunch. No appetite. He thought of Julie Not Julie. At 1:30 p.m., he decided to check the hallway near Room B. Perhaps she had an appointment before his and would provide company.

She was there, sitting quiet and slumped, her arms on her knees, in a chair opposite the door to Room B. She was dressed in her customary nondescript attire: a tan dress, her hair brushed but not styled. She stared at the floor, resigned. Guy sat beside her.

"Hello, Julie Not Julie. How are you?"

She lifted her head and turned it slowly toward him. The moment she looked into his eyes, they locked onto his. Guy flinched, feeling caught in a vise. The small, magenta triangle on his left cheek twitched.

"Do you know . . . where my self is? I can't find it . . . I feel so alone." In a dragged, monotone voice, she spoke her plaintive refrain as if pleading to his soul.

Guy placed his hand on her shoulder. He felt an immense sympathy for this sad and desperate woman, possessed by such a peculiar madness, perennially searching for what was there all the time. He stared back into the infinite space of her eyes, gateways framed by her pale face and scruffy crop of hair. Julie Not Julie had the plainest of faces, yet Guy thought it was still lovely. Her eyes seemed now partially awakened. *Awaken, fair vision!*

Guy knew that he, and most people, were not that different from the woman who stared curiously into him. He continually searched for his true self and never believed he had fully found it. And he often felt alone. Guy Not Guy.

Julie Not Julie kept staring into his eyes as she seemed to probe the space inside his being. He was affected.

When did the human race go mad? Guy pondered. *At what point in our troubled history?* He wondered if it happened all at one moment, the entire species suddenly waking up to the overwhelming realization that they did not know who they were, or why, or where, discovering they were lonely souls lost in some incomprehensible void, some mad irrationality.

"When did we all go mad, Julie Not Julie?"

She did not answer and the small finger of her left hand twitched. She kept staring into Guy as if searching for some key to a mystery. He noticed a tiny spark of excitement in the infinitely plaintive orbs of her eyes.

Guy did not understand what she was doing but intuitively knew he should participate. Occasionally she tilted her head in an expression of curiosity, as a cat observing a compelling object.

She stared and stared. Looking for so long into Julie Not Julie's eyes became for Guy an enjoyable meditation, a quiet floating in a vast space of life. It was a pleasant and unexpected retreat, and he decided she could stare into him for as long as she wished. *We are sharing a precious madness—a Beautiful, Winged Madness.*

Minutes passed. Julie Not Julie's eyes opened more widely, and Guy detected new animation in them. The corners of her mouth lifted in a slight smile.

Curiosity finally overtook him. "What do you see, Julie Not Julie? What are you looking at?"

At first she did not respond but kept staring with a visible curiosity. Then she answered.

"I'm looking . . . at you. I can see you . . . and feel you."

Guy cocked a brow. "What? Explain."

Again she did not reply immediately, but her slight smile became slightly less slight.

"Inside of me . . . I can feel you . . . and I can feel myself feeling you. It's . . . strange, and wonderful."

Guy smiled and kept looking into her. For the first time, he thought he saw her, the unique and special person before him.

"Good, Julie Not Julie. Good."

Then she appeared to dive into a peculiar trance, her eyes troubled. She spoke mysteriously.

"I stopped feeling myself feeling thousands of years ago, when I woke up, and all the world was dead."

Strange, but fascinating! Guy thought. "What was it? What happened?"

Her eyes now seemed infused with terror, peering into a nightmare.

"I . . . don't know. We did . . . a terrible thing. I was part of it . . . everything went black. My self died."

"Can you see it? What was it?" Guy leaned forward and stared even deeper into her eyes.

She searched. "I'm not sure." She squinted, her stare penetrating. "It's like . . . we killed God. And at that moment, we killed ourselves . . . we were lost. I was lost . . . and it's continued, until now. Over and over and over . . . to this world we're in."

She kept peering into the terror, her eyes frozen. Then, suddenly, her demeanor gentled, and her eyes softened.

"But now, it's over." Tenderness infused her expression.

Guy sensed that her being, her spirit, that lost self, had lifted outside and above her body, assuming a position of dominance, a state he was acquainted with. He perceived it as a very subtle radiance and thought it was beautiful; her beauty released!

They continued staring into each other. Minutes passed graciously.

"I can feel you, Guy. I can feel me. This is it!" Julie Not Julie's speech was more fluid and connected, and her eyes brightened.

"It's over. I understand now." Her voice assumed a reverential tone, as one in prayer. "I can feel now. The terror, that terrible, black terror, is gone." She breathed deeply and smiled vaguely. "I found my self."

Yes! So simple! Guy thought. *It's all absurd. This world is so mad, and beautiful!*

Her eyes unlocked from his, and her vision moved to his forehead, then down past his nose to his mouth. She leaned forward and kissed him on the cheek.

"Thank you," she whispered. "After decades of searching, and twenty-two years of therapy, I'm free."

Her voice had more resonance and a minor variation in its tone. It was no longer the drone of a zombie. The corners of her mouth again lifted in a partial smile. She was slowly resurrecting into life.

Julie Not Julie looked again into his eyes. "I . . . love you, Guy," she spoke shyly. "You are my truest friend."

Her declaration surprised, and pleased, Guy, and he understood. He placed his hand on hers.

"I love you too, Julie Not Julie. You are a wonderful person. I knew that when I first saw you. And we are friends."

Guy realized at that moment that he had a true friend for life and it delighted him. He remembered the incident the previous week in the restaurant when he and Anna met the lady affected by her Shadow World play. Anna made a new friend. Now he had also. Perhaps they would all be friends. Things were improving.

Julie Not Julie stood and looked into the air. "I'm free now. I feel so much . . . passion."

Her voice expressed half of what would be designated human excitement, but it was half more than Guy had ever before heard from her. She lifted her arms and slowly, awkwardly spun once, taking small, consecutive steps.

"I have myself. I'm free," she proclaimed to the universe with the enthusiasm one might announce "the mail is here", but for her it was a significant breakthrough.

She glanced at the clock on the wall. The second hand advanced one notch. It was 2:00. She looked at the door.

"Two o'clock. It's . . . my time," she stated with calm resignation.

Dread impinged on Guy, like a sinking blackness in his chest. He looked at the face of his new friend, so plain and nondescript, so real and lovely. She did not appear frightened, but he was.

"Are you going in there, Julie Not Julie?"

She looked again at the door.

"Yes. I'm not worried." She smiled.

Anxiety clawed Guy's face. "No! Don't go inside! People get lost in there." He looked at the door's Room B designation. "There's something terribly wrong in there. We know that. Leave! I'll go with you." He smiled. "Yes. I'll go with you. We can leave together. Free!"

Julie Not Julie gazed at him kindly but remained silent, as if examining a critical question.

"You can stay with me, or with my friend Anna, until you know what to do. She would like you. You'll be all right."

She responded quickly. "That's very kind. Thank you. But I must do this. It's my life." She surveyed the rigid anxiety on Guy's face. "It's all right. I'll be fine. They can't hurt me now. I have my self."

Guy lowered his head, shook it, and then looked up.

"Are you certain? Is this what you want to do?"

"Yes. I have to see this through." She looked at the door. "I think . . . I may be able to help things in there. Something is waiting for me there."

Guy did not reply. He did not know what more to say.

"Goodbye, my friend." Her voice caressed and her smile was the fullest yet. "Thank you, and I will see you again, Guy. I am certain."

"Goodbye, Julie Not Julie. Be careful."

She turned and stepped to the door. She grasped the doorknob, opened the door and started walking through. Then she stopped and looked over her shoulder.

"I have a new name now. It's just Julie."

She smiled and went into the room, closing the door behind her.

Guy sat mute and still. The hallway suddenly seemed painfully vacant, its white fluorescent lights sterile, its antiseptic odor ominous. He felt a confusion of joy and anger.

He did not fully comprehend what had happened, but he knew it was important. Julie, he smiled at the thought of her new name, had truly changed, in one of those rare breakthroughs, and he was gratified to have participated. And he had a new friend.

But he feared. In her rebirth, she might yet be naive and foolish and could make severe mistakes. *This world may not be as good as your soul, Julie.* He looked up. *The damaged human struggling for healing and transformation is a beautiful thing.*

Guy considered walking into that room and pulling her out. As her new friend, perhaps it was his responsibility to rescue her, and yet that seemed futile. Julie made her own decision, as she must.

Conflict and indecision. Guy sat immobile in his chair. His stomach hurt.

He looked at the clock. His time was next. He clung to a thought. Maybe there was not anything so terrible behind that door. Just more doctors and therapies. More of the same. More madness in a world of madness, and all the mysteries and fears about Room B were just the paranoid suspicions of disturbed patients.

But a profound assault of dread betrayed that hope. Something malevolent waited behind that door. It was the curse of all mental patients throughout history. Room B. Bedlam—its new incarnation.

He squirmed in his chair. His body tightened. The minutes passed excruciatingly slow. The clock, its face staring indifferently, ticked the seconds like drops of water falling on a bound, tortured prisoner's forehead—plop, plop, plopping toward the dreaded moment. He kept watching the door, but it did not open. Julie did not come out. It cannot open, Guy knew, or the structure, the illusions and lies, would collapse. A vise closed, compressing the space in his mind.

My time has arrived. Room B. My time has arrived. Room B. I must make a decision. A decision!

Guy stared at the door and its metal letters. The air in the hallway seemed thick and suffocating. He feared he would not be able to breathe.

He knew if he did not enter that room, within minutes, all the disability benefits that he had depended on for so long to survive, would be lost. The program requirements were strict.

What do I need? he challenged. *My fear is as a child's who was about to lose his parents.*

A child? A child? Anger contorted his face.

Then Guy saw. All became lucid. In an instant he knew what he must do, what was right. He was in a Moment, one of those critical life-transformative moments, as Julie had just experienced. Now it was his turn, and just as profound. *Every person gets his chance.*

Guy smiled as he realized that Julie had helped him as much as he had helped her. She gave him strength.

"Thank you, Julie, my friend," he whispered.

This was the moment he had spoken of with Anna when he would relinquish it all: his past, doctors, therapies, drugs, the concept of disability, illusions and lies born of fear and confusion. He would let go of it all, no matter the consequence.

It was a moment of freedom. And it was so simple! He just stood and walked away from the door. *The wrong door,* he thought with a smile.

It was done.

*   *   *

Guy returned to his room and added a few unpacked items to his suitcase. He looked at his bed and delightful memories of the night before, real or illusion, pleasured his mind. He would always remember them.

He knew he had made the correct decision. *And I am not afraid.*

He needed an escape plan. Most difficult would be getting past the guard station at the psychiatric ward perimeter, then the receptionist station in the lobby, where he might be recognized, and then the guard at the hospital exit. Like a secret agent devising a vital mission, he mulled over clandestine options.

A mad idea came. This was a bold act of personal freedom, a rebirth, and one should experience freedom and rebirth naked and wild. It would also inject the element of surprise and confusion and would be a fabulous story to tell Anna. An escape wild and symbolically correct. Courageous and poetic. That felt right to his heart and spirit, and heart and spirit was what it was all about. So be it!

He removed all his clothes, everything, including shoes and socks, and placed them in his suitcase. In an odd touch, he took out his brush and tidied his hair. He wanted to look good.

Then a thought halted him. *Children.* There would be children in the hospital. How would the sight of a mad naked man impact them? Might it haunt them for . . . God knows how long?

A concession. He put his underpants back on. The *near*-naked mad patient!

Guy went to the door and peeked out. Two nurses were walking down the hall chatting about the 'crazy patients'. They passed, and the coast was clear. He inhaled a slow, reinforcing breath and prayed to the gods.

"Gods, help this mad, near-naked man reach his freedom and love. Amen."

He stepped into the hall. It was brightly lit and pristine with its white hospital walls. A pure stage for the performance of a bare lunatic. With suitcase in hand, he ran, fast!

He raced down the hallway and turned the corner. A young brunette nurse. Her mouth dropped and her eyes bloated. Suspended in her steps. Guy streaked by, smiling.

She would call security. It would take her some moments to recover from her shock and reach a phone. He had time.

Running at maximum speed. He passed an orderly pushing a patient in a wheelchair. The orderly, a young Hispanic male, startled and then smiled.

"Fue por ello! Go for it, man!" he shouted behind Guy.

He bounded around a corner. Faster! Run! Targeted the main security station at the ward's exit. The brown uniformed guard looked up from his desk. Saw Guy, a mass of flesh, charging down the hall, fast. Astounded, the guard sprang to his feet. His hand reached toward a phone. He hesitated. Confused. Looked at the phone. Looked at Guy. His expression spoke. *No way!* He stepped out from behind the station. An obstructing positioning, in front of Guy's path.

Faster! Guy charged, holding on tight to the suitcase. The guard extended both arms out. Guy leapt into the air, his arms lifted. Upon landing he spun, his arms waving and the suitcase swinging, and he yelled.

"Yaaaa! A di a di da! Yaaaaa!" Like a lunatic ballerina.

The guard startled, and his jaw dropped. He stumbled back and his hand slapped Guy's chest as he darted past.

"Yaaaaa!" Guy screamed. *Another down!*

Guy flew through the swinging exit doors and raced down the hall toward the elevator. The elevator's door was open, about to be boarded by three hospital visitors, two middle-aged women and an elderly man. One of the women saw the almost naked man hurtling toward them and gasped. The others turned and stared shocked at Guy. They stepped away from the elevator.

"Hello!" Guy greeted them. He alone leapt inside.

Elevator door closed. Safe! For the moment. Guy released a captive breath. He looked at his bare flesh. Sweating, but exhilarated. And strong. He pressed the lobby button and jogged in place to maintain momentum. He knew time was critical.

"Come on! Come on!"

The elevator stopped its languorous descent, and its door began opening. Guy frantically envisioned uniformed guards, strong, stern, waiting outside. None were there. He sprang into the crowded hospital lobby.

A wave of astonished faces throughout the room. A couple women saw him and screamed. Most of the people, startled and mute, moved aside to allow him passage. He darted between them. An African-American man in braids laughed as Guy swept by in a blur of flesh. An obese woman in her mid-thirties in a frumpy blue dress viewed Guy, startled, screamed, and hurled a bouquet of flowers into the air that landed on the rug. Guy noticed the gorgeous colors against the beige rug and smiled.

Confusion in the lobby. The Grinch! The hideous woman who had registered Guy into the hospital glimpsed the fleeing escapee. "What the hell!" Her face a clownish expression of shock. Her features harden and her eyes are like Scud missiles.

"Him!" she shrieked in her witch's voice. She grabbed the phone and poked at buttons.

Guy dashed out of the lobby and into the hallway leading to the hospital exit. *This is it, the final stretch. All or nothing!* His energy bounded; his heart jackhammered in his chest.

The station at the end of the hall. A huge, burly, brown-uniformed guard spoke on the phone. The guard turned his head toward the hallway. He saw Guy charging toward him, nodded, and slammed down the phone. His expression became fierce. He muttered and took a step out from his station.

Guy's breath seized. He only had time to imagine one hope. *Spiritual Universe, help me!*

Guy saw the mountainous man standing like an impenetrable barrier in the center of the hall. Waiting.

"Oh my god! It's over!" he spoke through raspy breaths and then ran faster and again prayed. *Help!*

Then a stunning woman walked by the guard. She was one of the most gorgeous and esthetically perfect women Guy had ever seen. Her cascading hair was raven black, her skin earthen-brown, and her eyes glimmering ebony. She wore a body-contouring black dressed that sensually delineated her prodigious curves. Guy assessed her to be South American, probably Brazilian, and his mind swiftly envisioned her in a scanty, sparkling costume dazzling celebrants at the Carnaval de Rio. She smiled at the guard.

The guard's attention shifted to the temptress and he displayed a simpleton grin. That was all Guy needed. He flew by the guard and by the time the guard reoriented, Guy was safely past.

"Thank you, Spirit. Thank you, lovely goddess," Guy whispered and smiled.

The glass exit door ahead. *Just a door.* A roll into it. Through it. A cool gush of air swept his flesh.

He was out!

"I'm going to make it!" Guy spoke aloud and ran even faster. *Running to my freedom!* He galloped across the parking lot, dodging cars. A couple pedestrians stood aghast, stilled by the sight bolting by. Guy left the parking lot pavement and ran to a grassy sidewalk isle bordered by large bushes. He scrambled behind one of them. His body glistened with sweat and his breathing was staccato and raspy. But he felt great. Free!

Discarding one's clothes is wondrous and liberating! he mused. *The entire world should do so. Humankind would be saner.*

Guy opened his suitcase and removed a pair of jeans and a burgundy T-shirt and slipped them on. He looked around the protection of the bush toward the hospital entrance. Several guards ran out and began combing the parking lot searching for the escaped lunatic.

Guy put on shoes and socks, took a towel from the suitcase and patted the sweat from his skin. He stood, inhaled a slow breath and casually strolled from the bush and down the sidewalk. One of the security guards reached the perimeter of the parking lot. As Guy walked past, the guard glanced at him without expression and continued on, his eyes scouring the area.

Guy walked a block away from the hospital, tension seeping from his body with each step. He dropped onto a bus bench. His body vibrated with energy and excitement, and he breathed deeply. He looked back toward the hospital. No one was in pursuit. He smiled victoriously.

Guy felt a sense of triumph he had not experienced in years. "I made it!"

He looked at the sky. It was vivid blue and glassy, spotted with cushions of white clouds. A perfect, glorious sky! It felt as if his being expanded into its entire immense space.

Rapid thoughts deluged his mind. He would return home. He was hungry. He would stop on the way to eat. He would now earn his living as an artist and a poet, as it should be. He would probably struggle, but that was fine, part of the experience. Anna. *Anna, Anna. Living Persona.* He grinned. He would ask Anna to live with him. They could share a place. They would play and love and create and have fun. Yes, have fun! He would somehow handle his hallucinations and voices. He had faith and would pray. All would be fine.

Some pangs of anxiety needled, and the thought: *what if I cannot survive?* To be expected, he quickly reasoned and pushed aside the fears.

Guy stood and brushed a hand through his sweat-dampened hair. He was energized and alive and decided to walk a while before finding a restaurant.

I am free! Now to Anna.

Chapter 24

HOME.

Although Guy's five-story apartment building would not be characterized by any as luxurious, or even quaint, with its sullied, pale green walls, cracked window frames, and rusting railings, as he stood before it at that moment of arrival and delighted anticipation, it was aesthetically, and spiritually, wondrous.

No, better. It was home! And the residence of Anna.

Carried by an energized athleticism, Guy bounded up the five flights of stairs to his apartment. He sensed a surprise, fumbled with his keys, opened his apartment door and, behold! Anna's statue gift, sensual and lovely, stood on his living room floor like a little vision from a dream, cast in a mellow sea of afternoon light, beckoning with an outreached arm. Using a key she had to his apartment, Guy surmised, Anna had placed it there.

He walked slowly toward the sculpture, wanting to extend that moment of encounter. An exquisite gift from Anna! He knelt before the statue as one would before a religious icon and looked at but did not touch it, examining its tiny face and erotic curves and the confident bearing of its pose.

Yes, Anna. Naked and lovely.

Excitement charged his body. Gently Guy ran his fingers along the statue's hair, across its shoulders and down an arm. He touched one breast.

"The Kiss," he whispered viewing the cover painting of a card on its base. He opened the card and read it.

'I love thee.' The words were so simple, yet perfect.

"I love thee too," he spoke to the statue, and to Anna.

Guy remained kneeled, Zen-like, before the sculpture in the quiet of the room. Its smooth, elegant curves seduced his longings. There seemed a mystery about it, this little Anna that was, and was not, her, and its offered invitation. He sensed that in some curious way, it was prophetic.

Guy wanted to visit Anna immediately, but didn't. He rushed to the bathroom and commenced the fastest shower of his life, his clothes barely stripped off as he jumped into the tepid stream of water and lathered fiercely, soap stinging his eyes.

No! Slower! On this day the flesh should be pampered. So he did, massaging his body gently with a loofah sponge and spice-scented soap.

Guy thought of Anna waiting in her apartment, perhaps also showering, nude, preparing. *It was for days like this that God blessed us with love of both the heart and the flesh,* he reflected with delight.

He stepped out of the shower and felt a powerful impulse to run, naked and wet and glistening, to Anna's apartment and when she opened the door and stood in surprise, sweep her up in his arms and carry her to the bedroom. Guy was not bold enough to execute that theatrical act, although he almost did anyway.

Like a movie fast-forwarded. He threw on clean jeans and a white shirt with a colorful archaic map of the world on its back, brushed his hair and then brushed it again, and splashed on cologne, Trompe l'oeil, 'illusion as reality'.

Guy headed for Anna's apartment. His attention was lured by a severe crack bordered by a brown stain on the hallway wall. It looked . . . decrepit. No, another term. Dead. *Odd,* he thought and shrugged.

Guy used their code knock, three knocks then two then two. He waited. The door did not open. He knocked again. Still the door did not move, remaining a solid barrier before him.

"Damn!" His shoulders slumped, and his eyes dragged down. He believed that Anna knew he was returning that afternoon, he having given her the date before he left for the hospital.

I will wait.

In his apartment, the minutes scratched like jagged claws across his mind. No diversion eased the plodding time. So he just sat, listening to a Beethoven symphony, the Third, the *Eroica*, trying to rest, occasionally looking at the little sensuous statue, Anna's gift, and smiling.

Every half hour he returned to Anna's door and knocked. A couple hours passed. Guy became worried and confused. *Where is she?*

The light in the room subdued as evening descended on the city; becoming darker. Guy noticed it was growing colder, and he shivered, but it did not seem without, but rather within, within his own flesh. He watched television, occasionally dozing off. A story, on the evening news. A sentence, words, pierced his consciousness.

"The Cupid Killer has struck again."

Guy startled alert and focused on the screen. Foreboding crept over him.

"Taking his eight victim in the Mid-Wilshire District. She was a woman in her late twenties identified by police as . . . ."

Stopped. All time and reality and feeling. Stopped. His body petrified. *I am asleep, in a nightmare.* He looked around the room. It appeared real and present. Cold, but solid.

"Relatives have been notified. The woman was apparently walking alone late last night. No other details have been released at this time."

I must have misheard the victim's name, Guy concluded, *or my mind is playing a cruel joke. Yes. That is it! The voices in my mind spoke her name. Damn voices!*

"Police Chief Thomas in a press statement this morning expressed sympathy for the relatives and friends of the victim," the reporter stated. "He vowed the killer would be apprehended, and asked the community for any possible assistance in solving the case."

A struggle against inertia. Guy went to the phone and called the local police. A voice like a rake through gravel answered. "Wilshire Police Station."

"I'm a relative of the woman announced on the news as the latest Cupid Killer victim." Guy had difficulty speaking the words, but persisted. "I would like to . . . verify her identity."

The officer transferred the call, putting Guy on hold. He stood with the phone in his hand, barely breathing. A horrible, empty quiet. Guy's face cemented into a mask, his eyes fixed, staring into nothing.

Words, vague. "Anna," he heard, and her address.

"I am sorry," the police sergeant said.

Guy hung up. Reality collapsed.

He had not heard the news story no news story or made the call no there was no day when he returned from the hospital he had taken a shower yes he remembered the soap burning his eyes that was real a shower so he could visit Anna.

She was in her apartment perhaps putting on a new persona what might it be? An angel, she somehow creating the illusion that she was lifting off the ground, ascending to heaven.

No, not an angel! Not an angel! Something earthly a wench yes a lusty nineteenth century wench with provocative cleavage on a scarlet dress Anna was preparing her Wench Persona lusty and witty.

It would be fun! Everything was fine.

Guy did some things in his apartment. Moved objects. Opened a window. The air was bracing but fresh. He breathed deeply, twice.

He looked at his paintings on the walls. *I will do a painting of Anna,* he vowed. It surprised him that he had not already done so since she was his favorite subject.

He felt he was going to cry and forced his attention back onto the painting concept, as an artist should do. He considered possible ways of painting her as he stared at a blank space on the wall where her painting could hang.

Of course he would like to paint her nude. The prospect excited him, and he grinned. But that might actually not express her best. How do I really see her? What is Anna's primary truth?

Dead! The word thundered in his mind. Suddenly he thought a terrible avalanche was about to fall on him, burying him. Then it fell. Guy could barely breathe. He thought he was going to die.

*　　*　　*

Night. Long, hollow hours. Guy lay on his bed in the dark, staring into nothing. He did not want to see any light or shapes or colors, nor hear any sounds. He did not want to see or feel anything.

Images and memories of Anna. Pushed away. He wanted only stillness, complete stillness, and darkness and silence. Nothing.

Then the voices, the witches and demons.

"Dead, dead. Anna's dead!"

"Did we forget to tell you, Guy, that Anna was soon to die?" A shrill woman's voice shrieked and laughed.

"Anna's dead, in morbid mirth. She'll make love to worms in the earth!" A demon heckled.

"Well, loverboy, can you love a cold, white corpse? Of course! A curse! A corpse!"

"Anna's dead. Skull and bones. Asleep in the grave while you're alone."

Guy put his hands over his ears, but the voices persisted, louder.

"Dead, dead. Anna's dead!"

And there was no consoling angel voice, no escape, and Guy screamed. The voices silenced. Nothing.

Alone.

Comatose. The room black, empty, horribly empty. Breathe, slowly. Comprehend. He could not. It seemed as if it was happening to someone else.

Anna cannot be gone.

One vision he could not erase from his mind. He was seated on the floor in an empty room. There was no furniture or doors. Anna sat opposite him bathed in a gentle, morning light that flooded through the room's one window. She looked beautiful, her eyes radiant and loving. She smiled.

It was only he and she, alone. There was not even a world outside. Nothing.

"We will always be together, my love," she spoke. "This time, next time, and the next."

He reached out and touched her on the cheek. At that same moment, as he lay on his bed, Guy reached into space, but he could not feel her. He could not feel anything. The darkness around him went inside and became him.

Guy did not know if he slept that night. There was little difference between being awake and being asleep.

Morning, pristine and cold. Guy rose and stood, dressed in his undershorts, in the sunlight that streamed through his living room window. He could not feel its warmth. He thought a tear rolled out of his eye and streaked down his chest, but it was not felt. He wanted to feel something, but couldn't.

I, too, am dead. I am a ghost.

He felt a comfort in that realization. Peculiar, confused thoughts floated in his mind.

Through what eyes does a ghost see? Through the eyes of death? Does Anna see death now? Does she see me? Are you with this ghost, Anna, standing in this light that I cannot feel?

His ghost eyes looked at the city outside the window. The world had died. Yes, it could not possibly still exist! There were no longer any forests—they had dried and withered. The oceans had evaporated—only their parched and cracked desert floors remained. The cities were destroyed—crumbled, smoldering ruins, and shadows. All the people of Earth—gone, lost. Only he remained—a ghost, floating across a barren planet, searching for his love, Anna, in the desperate belief that somehow, somewhere, he would meet her ghost and they would join.

And he floated and searched and floated and searched forever.

Suddenly Guy wanted to be in Anna's space, to feel again her presence. He took a key from the drawer of his desk, a spare Anna had left with him in case she got locked out of her apartment, and walked from his apartment down the hall and stairs to her door. He did not worry that he was undressed. Who can see a ghost?

He stood before her door. A thought tortured. *I should have protected her. I should not have gone to the hospital. She asked me not to. If I had not gone, I probably would have been with her that night. Anna would be alive.*

The door was partially open. With a limp hand he pushed it and entered.

Anna's living room was precisely as she had always maintained it, clean and ordered and delightfully eccentric, its colors and shapes gentle in the ambiance of the morning light. Sounds came from the kitchen, but Guy did not hear them.

The room felt terribly vacant and lonely. Anna would never again stand in its space, nor would it ever again hear her voice or laughter. How could the room exist without her presence? He thought it should be destroyed. Yes! Smashed and burned!

A woman walked out of the kitchen, out of the flames. She saw Guy in his undershorts and halted, her jaw dropped. "What the . . . ?" Then she recognized him. She was one of the building's maintenance crew and was inspecting Anna's apartment.

Guy did not recognize her and looked at her vacantly.

"Could I be alone here? She was my friend." His voice was so subdued it could barely be heard.

"Yes, of course."

She walked to the door and then looked back over her shoulder.

"When you leave, please close the door."

Alone. Guy surveyed the artworks on the walls. They were as images of Anna's spirit. He was pulled to one that he had not put much attention on before, an original painting of a ghost, ethereal and beautiful, resembling Anna. On the bottom right of the canvas was her name, 'Anna'. She once explained to him that the artist was a friend of her sister. The painting pleased and deeply disturbed him. He took it off the wall to keep in his apartment. He believed Anna would have agreed.

Guy looked at the couch where they sat when they first met, talking of their lives and listening to opera. *So long ago.* Something welled inside of him, black and thick and terrible. He could not sit on the couch.

Guy remembered their long, probing conversations; the insights they had shared. *How will I live without our talks?* And he remembered her touch.

He noticed a journal opened on her desk. Believing she would consent, he read some of the pages. Anna's voice spoke the words, words about changes and new, exciting feelings and passions, and plans, and of Guy. A passage slashed his heart.

'And surprising thoughts of marriage keep entering my mind and heart. The more I have them, the more they please me. They are the most beautiful of thoughts.

'I believe that Guy and I will marry, perhaps soon. It frightens me a little, but excites me more. A whole new world and life is opening up for me, and I know now that we will be together, almost every moment, for a very long time. Forever! And that is what I want. I can feel and say it now. I love him. I love him.'

Guy's ghostly pretense dissipated. Floodgates cracked. He collapsed onto the floor on his side and cried, deep into his belly. Through his entire being. His body became tears, and the tears drowned his soul, and the ghost became a man dying.

"Anna," he kept speaking as he cried.

*   *   *

That evening, alone, in the dimmest of light, Guy sat comatose in his favorite, comfortable chair that seemed now a sorrowful friend. His apartment had become a black sea pressing down on him. It required an immense effort to stand and walk from one point to another. He felt as heavy as the earth, and wished he was in that earth, and it was over, it was over.

Guy prayed for numbness. He did not want to feel again, ever. Each time an image or thought of Anna entered his mind, an empty hole deepened in his chest.

How many times can a spirit and heart die? he tormented.

Robotically he picked up the remote and turned on his television. *Perhaps the evil monster who took Anna's life would be on the evening news, apprehended and damned for eternity.* He was trying to comprehend.

It was the lead story. A young blonde news anchor named Petrina Jones—yet a girl, Guy thought—her face solemn, spoke.

"Los Angeles was both relieved and shocked today by the news that the Los Angeles Police have a Cupid Killer suspect in custody. He is a nine-year-old boy turned in to authorities by his mother. A police spokesperson said the mother became worried when she noticed that hunting arrows in her son's room resembled those of photos of the killer's weapon released in the press. When she questioned her son, the mother reported his only reply was, 'I kill love.' The shocked mother then notified authorities.

"The boy's identity has not been officially released because he is a minor. But it is known that the he was proficient at archery and possessed sufficient strength to have used a bow in the manner required for the murders. KWBC News has learned that the boy's family resides in the Mid-Wilshire District, and we have a live report from correspondent Suzanne Beechem."

Guy leaned forward in his chair. The newscast shifted to a brunette reporter standing before an apartment complex on a city street.

"Residents in this Los Angeles neighborhood are shocked and grieved tonight by the news that the Cupid Killer suspect is one of their own children. An only child, age nine, he lived with his parents in this apartment dwelling on South Normandie Avenue. Although the parents are in seclusion, KWBC news has learned that the father is a computer systems analyst and the mother a secondary school teacher. The parents are reported to be in shock.

"Police have presented a probable scenario for the murders. They believe the boy suspect snuck out of his home at night wearing perhaps a long coat with the bow and sheath of arrows concealed beneath it. He hid in the shadows and darkness until a lone person, either a man or a woman, happened by and the boy appeared to the potential victim. The adult, not suspecting any danger from a child, and probably concerned for the boy's welfare, offered help. Then at some moment the boy removed his bow and an arrow from beneath his coat and sent the arrow through the victim's chest around the sternum. It probably occurred so fast that the victim did not have time to comprehend and respond. The boy was known to be a competent archer for his age.

"It is quiet on the streets of this neighborhood tonight. Few people are outside, as you can see." The camera panned presenting a virtually empty urban street. "But earlier neighbors and relatives of the suspect spoke with the media."

The broadcast presented a man about forty dressed in a white shirt and jeans. "I've known the family for years. We're close friends. I was shocked, shocked and horrified when I heard this news. I still don't believe it. The parents are good people, hardworking. But they weren't at home much. Maybe that had something to do with it." The man looked at the ground and sighed. "The boy seemed like a good kid. Kinda quiet and shy, and I think he was lonely. But he was always friendly to me when I spoke to him, and he was very bright. Nothing like . . . this nightmare."

The newscast then presented a pretty woman, about thirty, who was identified as one of the boy's teachers. She looked into the air and shook her head.

"I'm devastated by this news, if it's true. It's terrible, terrible! He's a good student, keeps to himself, but never causes any problems. He always has high grades and is bright. I think he's a bit of a dreamer. For a writing exercise, he wrote a strange but enchanting story, something about a deformed man living alone in the woods with animals. It was like the boy could go off into another world.

"I like him, and I cannot imagine how this could happen. I just pray there may be a mistake."

The report next presented an interview with an uncle who commended the virtues of the parents and the promise the boy showed. He said he found it hard to believe and was very worried about what the boy's parents must be going through. He had not yet spoken with the boy's father, his brother.

"And so all the testimonials go," the reporter picked up the story. "A good, promising boy, hardworking parents, and what appears to be a normal American family. Police this evening released the results of a preliminary psychiatric evaluation of the suspect. The doctors found that he did not display indications of abnormal mental health. He was not schizophrenic, as the police had suspected the killer was. Nor was there any evidence of suspicious physical, sexual, or emotional abuse of the child. The report stated the boy seemed a normal, though quiet, child." The reporter stared intensely into the camera. "A normal, quiet child who for some unknown reason may have chosen to kill love, and to murder. The Cupid Killer took eight lives, the last a woman, an artist, two nights ago. Ironically, the number eight is considered to symbolize God and eternity. But these murders were not an act of God. They were an act suspected to have been committed by a child of America."

The reporter paused, her eyes downcast, apparently disturbed by her own editorializing. "How could this have happened? Tonight it still remains a mystery. This is Suzanne Beechem reporting from a shocked Mid-Wilshire District."

Guy clicked off the TV and sat still, staring at the blackened screen, his face chiseled in ice.

How could parents and a community and a school not know a killer was growing in their midst? Is everyone blind or insane in this world? Did anyone ever talk to the kid? When will we wake up?

Guy saw an image. He was holding a gun to the boy killer's head. Anna stood nearby. At the last instant, he turned the gun and shot Anna.

Guy jolted. Cold wrenched his stomach, and his spirit numbed. Yet, he understood.

"I, too, am responsible. The murders. Anna." Guy mumbled aloud. "I know what it is to be in this world and yet be totally alone. I know the pain and the darkness and the hate." He quieted. *I know the monster who wants to kill love.*

Anna was lost. And in some way, he was not innocent.

Guy struggled to imagine what was left for him, what might be in his life. His work: poetry and painting. Perhaps some friends. Walks in the city. Cool, quiet nights. Enchanting dreams in sleep. *Loneliness, pain, and nothing.* All cold and vacant.

Only one thought held any meaning. *All I want is to be with Anna.* The thought kept playing in his mind, like a mantra. *All I want is to be with Anna.*

In those few words he saw a truth, the only truth he could now embrace. It was so simple and clear.

All I want is to be with Anna.

Guy experienced a slight, fine light enveloping him. He recalled his conversation with Anna about finding one's truer and purer love and her challenging question: What would be the test of such a love? He spoke again his answer.

"If one died, the other would take his or her life so they could be together, in spirit, or perhaps in their next lifetime."

Were those just romanticized words or were they my truth? The question seemed so correct. *Do I believe what I speak?*

It did not take Guy long to know the answer. His vision suddenly extended beyond his pain and encompassed the room, and then the world. *The way out!* He felt an oppressive darkness lifting.

All I want is to be with Anna! He knew what to do. And he would do it.

Guy looked out the window at the gray silhouette of the city buildings with their tiny square eyes of lit windows. Night was falling. There was one factor left to consider. He assumed Anna's funeral would be in the next day or two, and he wanted to attend, wherever it would be. It seemed the correct and dear way to say goodbye to his love from this world, a proper completion. And he believed she would want that. *I must attend.*

He looked at the statue on the floor, standing gracious in the evening half-light, and then kneeled before it. Guy had not moved it from the spot where Anna had placed it. It was such a beautiful and heartfelt gift. He wanted to give Anna such a gift and tribute before he left this realm. Examining the statue's serene face, Anna's face, he remembered the passage he had read in her journal and he knew what the gift would be.

All was decided—the funeral, the gift, and his reunion with Anna.

Chapter 25

GUY SPENT MOST of the two days before Anna's funeral in strange absorptions, both sublime and mad. Minutes passed in hours, and yet, there was no time. It was often both light and dark. A precious scent from his plants, chlorophyll, suggested life. There was silence, sometimes comforting, sometimes unbearable.

A Dark Yet Gentle Beast entered his mind. Guy wanted pain but welcomed nothingness. The Beast promised both.

Existing, and not.

He did not bathe or shave a shadow crept up his face his eyes were sometimes emptied sometimes radiant and manic absorbed by peculiar sights he rarely slept and ate once a day in the evening but could not taste the food afterward he did not remember what he had eaten occasionally he felt like drinking beer or wine a lot but didn't fearing the specters alcohol might deliver he knew he felt his mind hung from an edge his mind hung from an edge.

It was like that.

Disorientation. *Night? Or perhaps it is day, and the days are dark. Perhaps the sun no longer rises.* He concluded it did not matter. The world must be and not be. *I must live but touch no life. A sublime stasis. I wait.*

Soon I will be with Anna.

On noon of the day of Anna's funeral—a day of endings and beginnings, he thought—a mechanism took over. He prepared properly, showering, shaving, and brushing his hair, twice. He splashed on Trompe l'oeil cologne, a scent Anna liked, and breathed its musky yet floral fragrance.

"You smell nice," she whispered from somewhere.

He put on a white shirt and a blue tie decorated with abstract designs of burgundy birds. The motif of flying and ascension felt correct. Dress slacks and a black sport jacket, he did not own a suit, completed his attire. Around his neck he wore a nineteenth century Russian monk cross, slipped beneath his shirt. Both he and Anna liked its ornate design.

Guy stood before a full-length mirror. He made an adjustment to his tie so it was evenly placed in the white space of his shirt between his jacket's lapels. He wanted to look his best. This was the day of Anna's gift.

Perfect! He concluded.

"Perfect!" He heard her whisper.

Guy left his apartment for the first time in days, except for once when he went to the Seven Eleven for canned foods and bread, and the brilliance of the afternoon sun had seared his vapid eyes. Walking now down Wilshire Boulevard he experienced the peculiar sense that the entire city was moving in a cautious slow motion, as if terrified or trapped in a morass of loss.

The blood of all the citizens should spill from their bodies and stream through the streets, he thought. *Everyone should be anemic and drained of life. The City of Angels should be the City of Ghosts.*

He remembered when, as a three-year-old child, for the first time he saw his mother frightened. He knew not by what—a thought, a threat, a demon. As her eyes turned cold with fear, he, the boy, realized the world was imperfect and threatening and no one, not even a superwoman mother, was immune.

*   *   *

The Dark Yet Gentle Beast crept over the cemetery as Guy entered, over the rolling, grassy slopes, over the dry autumnal trees and bushes and the solemn, pallid gravestones. The Beast was shadowy and massive with dim amber cat eyes that tracked Guy's moves. It paused, slouching, and Guy passed beneath the swell of its belly and felt its presence—black, hovering, and waiting.

Welcome, my friend, both thought.

It was a lucid and sunny day, the temperature cool yet comfortable. That annoyed Guy. *This day should be mournful, gray, and frigid.* He looked at the sky. In its pure azure blue were some filmy streaks of gray clouds, like grieving accents. *Better.*

Good Heavens Cemetery was a small but pleasant sanctuary with grassy hills sparsely gardened with twisting trees and, at that late autumn date, mostly flowerless bushes. It was solemn yet lovely, mournful yet charming, as Anna had wished. She, perhaps with her uncanny, prophetic insight, had recently rewritten her will requesting to be buried in that cemetery. Anna wanted to remain in Los Angeles, the city of her awakening, she stated, rather than on the East Coast of her past. Her modest savings were bequeathed to Guy, 'to be used for pursuits of art and the soul.' Personal possessions were distributed to family members, she having carefully chosen what should go to each. They were gifts from her spirit to theirs. The Cadillac model with the smashed front she left to Guy as she did her CDs of opera and, prophetically, the painting of the ghost.

I will place the Cadillac and the painting around the statue of Anna, Guy quickly decided when phoned with the details of the will. *The money I will donate to proper organizations. I will not require it.*

Her extraordinary wardrobe of persona costumes was donated to a theater company she had worked with except for the Woman Inside the Ghost apparel that she left to Guy. When he was told, he cried. She had left him the memory of their first meeting.

Anna the woman, Anna the artist, Anna the ghost, Guy reflected as he approached her gravesite. Twelve people were present, all adults except for one child, a girl. Dressed in the black of mourning, they stood like shadow specters surrounding the rectangular hole of Anna's grave.

Shadows to shadows, Guy thought. *The opera of life?*

Her dark, stained oak casket lay on the hole's bottom, waiting to be consumed by the earth. It was not to be covered by soil until that night, an odd, possibly metaphorical condition Anna had requested. When Guy saw the casket he plunged into a black place behind his soul. He wanted to flee, to just walk away, and pretend none of it was happening.

I will escape to a beautiful lake, he ruminated, *somewhere far, far from the city and the cemetery, where the air is fresh and birds are singing. I will lie on the grass and gaze into the blue sky. I will feel peace and a love of nature. All will be well.*

Then I will drown myself.

But he stayed. Behind the grave pit was a two-by-three-feet rectangular stone inscribed with some words, undecipherable from where Guy stood. The previous day there had been a memorial service for Anna in a cemetery chapel. Guy had not attended. His last rites to Anna would come later and be more intimate. He also had not wished to view Anna, his vital and sensual love, lying lifeless in an open casket, but his imagination kept conjuring that image as in a sadistic torment.

The image: Anna lay still, white, naked, and cold, a morbid persona of herself, in a black casket, the Corpse of Anna Persona. She appeared both alive and dead, real and illusion. The life and spirit, the vitality and sensuality that continually attracted Guy to her were abandoned. Only a mocking shell of it remained. And yet, she was still so lovely, even with her glacial flesh and death-mask face. Anna possessed a beauty that not even death could steal.

The words of his poem entered his mind: denoting a robust design and determined force, now emptied, yet uncannily willed perfect in being still.

Such was Anna in death.

Guy stood in the group of mourners queued before her grave, the pit, he kept thinking of it. On the opposite side stood a minister. He seemed a peculiar man, a small, about five-feet-six, frail being in a cloak of black, in his fifties with graying hair and silver framed glasses and dressed in a black suit and a shirt with a clergy collar. Guy thought he looked lost and dazed, as might a missionary estranged and alone in some inhospitable land, struggling to bring a foreign god to earthy, primitive souls. Sorrow emanated from his eyes, but Guy suspected it was more of futility than mourning. His fingers nervously rubbed a black Bible held in front of his waist.

Not a figure of comfort, Guy concluded and shivered. He smelled an unpleasant odor, stale and musty, as of a long-enclosed basement. The Dark Yet Gentle Beast shifted above them, and Guy felt its frigid breath.

The minister looked at the group, then at Guy and smiled. Guy suddenly felt nauseous and dizzy. The minister glanced at his watch. He waited a few minutes, minutes that scratched through Guy's consciousness. He looked away from the minister. The cemetery seemed a green and brown landscape painting dotted with dark little souls, all more illusion than real. The mourners near him stood like silent, grave witnesses, gazes transfixed on the ground, waiting. He heard soft crying and a few louder sobs. He saw, or imagined, he could not determine which, his vision had become hazy, an umber shape pass before the sun, as in an eclipse. The cemetery fell gray and shadowy and the rectangular pit housing Anna's casket black and endlessly deep.

The minister spoke. "We are gathered here to both honor and bid farewell to dear Anna, family member and friend, who ends her journey through this perplexing and mortal life."

His voice was solemn, possessed of a haunting echo as if he spoke inside a hollow chamber.

"She walked bravely through this world, loving and creating, as a woman and an artist, and a child of God." The minister looked into the sky. Guy noticed his expression hardened and his eyes steeled. "We shared that journey with her. We shared her dreams and triumphs and defeats. She was one of us. Anna loved and pained, as we all do. She searched and found wondrous and terrible things. She questioned and was offered many answers. But some questions were never answered."

The minister gazed into the pit of Anna's grave. Anguish engraved his face.

"But from the light comes a darkness. A frightening and terrible darkness from which no man or woman ever escapes." He looked up at the group, his stare scanning slowly from person to person. "Then death took her, just took her!" He snapped a finger in the air. "Just like that. Gone! Gone away! Somewhere, or into nothing."

The mourners shuffled. Several looked at each other.

The minister's speech slowed, and his eyes peered hypnotically into space. "It cared not how beautiful she was, and she was. Nor that we loved her, and we did. Death took Anna as if it owned her, and she was his. And it did, and she was." He nodded repeatedly. "It's true. It's true." He stared into the grave.

The minister's words startled Guy, and he looked into his strange, transfixed eyes. *This one is mad,* Guy concluded.

"Death—sweet, terrifying death." The minister spoke into the hole. "With every step I hear you walking behind me." He stomped his feet. "Thump, thump, thump. I turn. Mr. Death, I say, you follow me. Yes, he says, always!" He kept stomping his feet like a kid stepping on ants.

Definitely mad!

"You woo me with your seductions: sleep, peace, perhaps nothing. Beautiful nothing!" The minister perused the group. "Isn't that what we all really want? Beautiful nothing? It's what I want. Not prayers or salvation. Not even God. Just beautiful nothing." The minister laughed, a laughter suggesting an odd, torn, and yet welcomed resolution.

"To let myself go. To lose myself totally. To be nothing!" The minister reached his arms out over the grave. "Come to me Death, my lover, my God. You are the final, the greatest power." His voice grew zealous. "I fear your terror no more! I no longer fight. I surrender!" He stared again into the hole. "You are my fate, my truth, my God. I must love you! Sweet and terrible Death, master and mistress of all, I love you. Take me!"

The minister reached into his coat and removed a metal object. It glistened in the sun. Guy saw it was a gun, a pistol. The minister placed its barrel against his temple.

A loud, sharp explosion echoed through the cemetery and smashed against Guy's mind. He saw a splash of bright red spurt from the side of the minister's head.

Then, for an instant, time froze and Guy looked curiously at the glistening red globules suspended in the air. He thought they looked oddly but wonderfully beautiful against the brown and green tapestry of trees and bushes. In a peculiar moment, Guy realized that he was seeing the beauty that is in all things, at all times. It is innate, even in violence and death. For that moment, it lifted him from pain.

The black shadow form of the minister fell forward into the dark pit. Guy heard the thud of a heavy object against wood. He took a few steps forward and looked into the rectangular hole. There was a curious human shaped shadow across the top of Anna's casket.

Then he noticed a silence, anxiously suspended, like the quiet of a crowd watching a man on a ledge about to leap to his death. Guy looked up and saw the gaunt minister staring at him with an expression of perplexity. Guy glanced over his shoulder. The eyes of all the mourners were fixed on him as he stood on the very edge of Anna's grave, as if he were about to jump in.

A hallucination, he realized. *Damn!*

Then Guy saw that he was still standing in the line of mourners. He had not moved from that spot. No one was staring at him. He had been looking toward the ground, for minutes, listening to the minister speak in his plaintive, hollow voice, but had heard little of what was spoken.

"We were blessed to have shared our lives with Anna," the minister continued. "This lovely and courageous spirit and her memory will be carried forever in our hearts. This world is a better place for Anna having been in it. May she rest in peace in God's love."

Guy struggled to remain in the reality of the moment, to recover his bearing. *Only a short time more.*

The minister opened his Bible and read a passage about ascension to God and heaven and then led the group in a minute of silent prayer. Guy closed his eyes and silently recited to Anna a poem he wrote that they both liked.

You are in the ebb and flow. A tide recedes, another grows. A design from beauty and grace—that knowing illuminance, that I, that will remain and be when the sea, and all, is dry, and nothing their domain.

Guy prayed for a death and rebirth, and that all this be gone, and that again, soon, he and Anna are together, not in any transitory world but in each other's eternal being. Let all the stars be gone. Let all else be dried and done.

Several mourners stepped forward and dropped flowers into Anna's grave. They fell like tiny splashes of color from the hands of shadows. From a black shoulder bag Guy removed a sunflower, Anna's favorite, but not one of the giant size. It was smaller and more delicate yet lovely with its bright yellow petals and black eye center and the best that he could find. He tossed it into the pit, and it appeared to fall in slow motion like a bright, visual poem of farewell and passing. That moment seemed to Guy so, so sad, and he cried. He wanted to fall into the grave, into its depth and dark, and lie on top of the hard, wooden casket and be closer to Anna, to comfort her and share her fate. But he did not. He had a grander plan.

The ceremony concluded. The mourners remained, talking among themselves, consoling and reminiscing. The afternoon sun casts lengthy, coal-black shadows from each as if coupling them with dark, waiting partners. Guy had difficulty distinguishing the mourners from the shadows.

In the end, all are but shadows upon the Earth—shadow people, he reflected. *This seemed a day of shadows.*

In their voices Guy heard both frowns and smiles. A summation.

He saw the performance artist, Jeffrey, who had loaned Anna his Toyota, standing alone; a short, portly man in his mid-twenties dressed in a black suit. Guy approached him and shook his hand.

"Man, this is a bummer. It's painful! I always liked Anna, and admired her," the boyish man said in a lamenting voice.

"She was a unique woman and artist, and a friend. A beautiful person. She helped me. I'll miss her." He looked down and then smiled. "And I'll miss her provocative personas. They were wild!"

The presence of Jeffrey, a fellow artist, was one of the few reminders at the funeral of Anna's life in Los Angeles, as Guy knew of it, and he was pleased that he was there. The rest seemed like visitations from a foreign past. A time gone.

"She'll be back," Guy replied, although uncertain of the meaning of his statement. He just knew it was so.

Jeffrey eyed him curiously and then smiled and nodded. "I'm gonna sit under a tree." He glanced across the cemetery and pointed to an aged tree with anguished, contorted branches and molding bark. "That one. I'm gonna sit under it and remember Anna. She told me once she wanted to live like a tree, natural and integrated. Maybe she now is. So for a moment, I'm gonna feel happy."

"Yes, she would like that," Guy agreed.

Jeffrey walked solemnly to the tree and sat on the grass beneath its shelter. He became still, appearing more as a priest in meditation, or a tree, than a mourner.

Guy surveyed the remaining group and spotted two women and a man whom he believed were Anna's family. The mother was looking down as the sister spoke. Dressed in funeral black they reminded Guy of the Shadow People behind the illusion screen in Anna's play. *Are they wondering if they might be in the wrong world?*

Guy decided to meet them but was uncertain what he would say. There was no possible way he could express the reality he shared with Anna, and they probably would not understand anyway. How could they?

He did not know if Anna had told them about him, but to an extent, they seemed like family. He walked to the mother. Beneath the gray of her mourner's veil he saw that she resembled Anna, only more aged, having the same face that communicated a common woman and yet was lovely and proud.

Anna would have aged well, as I suspected, Guy surmised. *And would always have been beautiful.*

But the mother did not possess Anna's dark and mysterious eyes. Those were Anna's alone. Guy sensed that he would look into those enigmatic eyes again, soon, and perhaps become forever lost in them, surrendered with Anna to a Beautiful, Winged Madness.

He offered his hand to the mother. A corsage of white carnations was pinned to her dress. On one of the petals was a black plastic ant.

"I'm Guy, a close friend of Anna's."

The mother looked at him with silent interest as one would examine a peculiar visitor from a foreign world. Then she smiled and shook his hand.

"Anna spoke of you, the poet painter with the odd but good soul." She perused him and again smiled. "And so you seem. I'm glad she had a good friend here. It's nice to meet you, Guy."

"I'm very sorry for your loss. It was a terrible shock." Guy tried to be consoling but knew it was impossible.

"Thank you."

The mother became quiet, peering at the ground. Guy put a hand in his pocket and also looked down. He fidgeted. Tiny teeth gnawed at his mind.

The mother looked up. "Were you close to Anna?"

"Yes, very close."

"Can you tell me, Guy, was Anna happy here?"

She confronted him with a beseeching expression, pained and hopeful, that could only belong to a mother.

Guy did not have an immediate response. He knew Anna's experience in Los Angeles was complex, both light and dark. There had been destructive times and sublime times. Then he remembered her persistent spirit that like strong wings carried her above all, and the joy that she often radiated. He heard a word whispered in a woman's voice into his ear: "Yes."

"Yes. She was happy here. She had people who loved her, and she did her work. Anna had a special spirit."

"Yes, she did. Thank you."

Then the mother looked more intensely into Guy as if probing for a hidden truth. Guy shuffled, suddenly feeling guilty, although not certain why. He felt faint and his vision misted.

The mother's expression fell severe. "Did you make love to my Anna, Guy? Did you love her to death? Was it your love that killed her?"

Guy jolted, startled by the questions. In a disturbing moment, he could not find a truthful reply. Was it possible? Could their love, in some fateful way, have killed her? He tormented. Might it have attracted the boy who killed love, to her?

Guy blinked, focusing his vision, and saw that the mother was not speaking, nor was she severe. She was looking warmly at Guy and smiling.

"Mother." He heard Anna's voice speak in his mind. Guy felt enormously saddened, and confused. He turned his attention to the father.

Anna's father was a tall, about six-feet-four, and hearty man with short auburn hair, graying at the edges. His face revealed the wrinkles of encroaching age and yet was handsome. Guy imagined him standing before his traffic lights on the city streets, monitoring to a tenth of a second their essential changes, green to yellow to red, with committed passion. A peculiar passion. And he imagined him with little Anna, the child, perhaps on his lap, or she watching him at work with a look of curious fascination on her angel's face. The father and his daughter.

"I'm very sorry, sir," Guy spoke, his voice hushed. He shook the father's hand.

The father nodded and partially smiled. He looked pained.

"Anna's light turned red," was all he said.

"Father," Guy heard Anna's voice speak.

Anna's sister stood quietly beside the father, observing. Guy smiled and offered his hand. They shook. Her hand felt soft but cold.

Guy struggled to see her features behind her obscuring veil that lay like a gray film. Her face was less lovely than Anna's, yet gentle. Its hazel eyes conveyed sensitivity.

"I'm Guy."

"I'm Terry."

"I loved your sister."

It seemed important to Guy, at that moment, to convey those words. In the face of death, love must be affirmed.

Terry smiled. She had the same bright, comforting smile as Anna, capable of transformations.

"Yes, I know. Anna told me. I'm glad you were in her life. Thank you, Guy. She loved you."

Guy looked down as if beseeching the earth for comfort. He had never heard that said to him from another person than Anna herself. A terrible grief swamped his heart.

"I'm sorry. I have to go. I need some time alone," he said softly.

Terry again smiled, her face gracious beneath the somber reality of her mourner's veil. That image penetrated Guy's mind like a brutal yet sublime painting.

"I understand," she said.

Guy thought that she, like Anna, must be a lovely person and that she shared Anna's heart.

"Sister," he heard Anna's voice speak in his mind.

"Sister," Guy said to Terry.

Terry tilted her head and then nodded. "Yes, sister, and I'm happy I got to meet you."

She removed a card from her purse and handed it to Guy. It had her address and phone number on it.

"If you are on the East Coast visit us, or call me, especially if you are having difficulty. I would also like to hear more about Anna's life here."

"It was a mad but beautiful dance in the City of Angels," Guy replied.

Terry flinched and then regained her composure. "Yes. That sounds like Anna." Her eyes looked into the distance.

"Anna, I'll . . . ." Her face became profoundly saddened, and she stopped speaking.

Guy placed his hand on her shoulder. "Anna's all right, I'm sure."

Terry smiled, dimly.

"I'm glad to have met you, Terry, and I'll speak with you again. Goodbye."

Guy walked away. *They would have been my family,* he thought, and he cried, not with tears but with something, somewhere, deeper.

Guy saw the little girl standing alone beside a bush, a winsome figure dressed in black. She looked familiar, and he approached her.

The sun was behind him, and as he stood before the girl his shadow enveloped her as if embracing, or consuming. *Peculiar,* Guy thought and extended his hand.

"I'm Guy. You knew Anna?"

She took his hand and shook it gently. Hers was so petite and fragile in his; he was careful not to squeeze it too tightly. It had been a long time since he felt the hand of a child, and in that moment, he realized a foolishness that pervaded his life. She appeared about ten years old. Her complexion was pale and her hair and eyes ebony.

She smiled. "I met Anna once, at Forest Garden. I'm Sage."

Guy then remembered the girl, macabre and intriguing, in the cemetery gift shop, with whom Anna had established an immediate rapport.

"I liked her," Sage continued. "I heard about it, about her, on the news. I was very sad." She looked down. "I asked my mom to bring me here."

She nodded toward a woman who was quietly standing, waiting, yards away. Then the girl looked into Guy's eyes.

"Last night, Anna, her ghost, visited me in my bedroom."

Guy's eyes widened.

"She was standing in front of my window. I could see trees outside, through her, but she was there. She told me she was my friend, and I should work hard to be an artist." Sage smiled radiantly. "She knew what I want to be. Then she told me I should find love and," she stopped, struggling to recall the words, "and cherish it." Her eyes scanned Guy's face. "You know she's still here." She glanced across the cemetery grounds.

Guy did not respond immediately but stood silent curiously examining the mysterious yet lovely girl. He imagined she was like Anna had been many years earlier, the child Anna. He chose to believe what she spoke.

"Yes. I believe she's here. I'm glad she visited you, and I believe you."

The girl again smiled and nodded. "I'm trying not to feel too sad. Death has a dark but kind heart," Sage stated with surprising wisdom.

Guy thought it was as if Anna had spoken through her to him. He had a powerful feeling that he should take the little girl home; that they should be together.

"Yeah, but my mom's waiting," Sage said with an intuition reminding Guy of Anna's. "Bye."

The girl returned to her mother.

Anna's ghost? Guy felt a distant but comforting relief. *That would be extraordinary!* And yet, he knew, not.

He strolled to a nearby slope and sat. Away from the voices of the mourners, the cemetery was quiet and serene, a green and lovely haven.

He would wait—wait for the people to leave. He needed to be alone with Anna.

Anna's ghost, he kept thinking.

The city, and the world, vanished. The blue of the sky blended into the green and browns of the grass and trees creating a soothing, pastoral palette. Gentle, intermingled sounds floated through his head: the coo of pigeons, the breeze sweeping through the trees, the hushed hum of distant traffic. The air smelled like the freshness of the country. Guy's spirit became light, caressing and comforting him as a mother holding a child. Again, the world seemed beautiful.

The dark mourners left and the shadows vanished. It was time, and he was ready.

Guy walked back to Anna's gravesite. He removed a small boombox CD player from his shoulder bag, placed it on the ground and pressed a button. Violins and cellos enchanted the air.

"A Mozart concerto, as you wished, Anna," Guy spoke aloud, standing before the humble block of her gravestone. Now he could read the inscription:

ANNA

'ANNA SPIRIT PERSONA'

I LOVE THEE, ALL.

Guy realized that Anna had dictated in her will what should be inscribed on her tombstone. She was sharing their love with the world. He touched the stone.

"You are a majestic soul, Anna," he declared, "and that is one of many reasons why I wish to offer you this gift."

Guy walked around her rectangular grave and kneeled at its edge. He looked into its depth. He did not permit himself to imagine Anna dead and cold, lying in the wooden casket. Instead he envisioned her alive and vibrant, her eyes gleaming and her smile affectionate, as was her spirit. He spoke tenderly.

"Anna, I love you. I have since first we met. I've loved you every day and moment since our lives wonderfully intersected." He paused, recalling some of their times together. "I read a passage in your journal. Forgive me if I violated your privacy, but I needed to read your words. I believe, and trust, that I know how you feel. So, with the greatest truth of my heart and soul, I ask you this. Anna, will you marry me?"

Guy waited, silent. He thought he heard a soft sound, like a whisper, rise from the pit. Then he felt a gentle touch on his shoulder. He smiled and nodded and then removed a folded paper from his pocket.

"I have written a marriage nuptial, Anna. It's simple. I'll read it to you." He spoke the words into the pit. "Two souls can meet, and their union changes all. The promise of the heart and spirit, and God's design for life, is fulfilled. It is the truest and purest of things: love. It is why they are.

"And forever they are joined, in spirit and in flesh, on Earth and in heaven, in life and in death—their breaths one breath, their dreams one dream, their lives one life. They should be wed. We are two such souls.

"Guy, do you take this woman and soul, Anna, to be your spirit wedded wife, to love and cherish in all, for eternity?"

Guy looked at Anna's casket. "I do."

"Anna, do you take this man and soul, Guy, to be your spirit wedded husband, to love and cherish in all, for eternity?"

Guy waited, quiet. "Give me a sign, Anna," he whispered.

A moment passed. He heard a bird's song. He looked up and saw a lone white pigeon circle above him against the opulent blue of the sky. Its form and flight expressed a grace and beauty. He smiled.

"Thank you, Anna." For the first time in days, Guy felt the warmth of the sun on his skin.

"If there be any living being in this universe who has a reason why these two should not be wed, let him speak now or forever hold his peace."

Guy listened. In what seemed not only within the cemetery but also throughout the entire universe, he heard a silence more profound and peaceful than he had ever before experienced.

"You, Guy, may present the bride, Anna, her ring."

From his pocket, Guy removed a ring he had purchased on the way to the cemetery. It was modest yet pure, a gold band with one diamond, now sparkling with radiance and color in the afternoon sun. The diamond represented him and Anna, joined as one, and the gold band the universe. He tossed it into the grave. It landed with a clink on the top center of her casket and remained there.

"With the love and right invested by God in me as a living soul, I now pronounce you husband and wife. You may kiss the bride."

Guy bent over and kissed the earth before Anna's grave. He felt both the cool of the ground and the warmth of Anna's lips on his.

"I love thee, Anna, my wife."

He then sat silent. It felt so strange and wonderful to be married to Anna, as if all things were now, at last, right, and would be forever. *Such a Beautiful, Winged Madness!*

"Take my and Anna's heart and soul on a delirious flight of love into eternity," he spoke into the air.

"And now, Anna, my wife, my love, tonight for our honeymoon, I will join thee."

Guy stood and looked one last time at her casket that now appeared peaceful and regal, with the gold diamond ring on its top. He felt behind him the wind of flapping wings. He smiled and then turned and left.

As Guy trekked through the cemetery, across its grassy fields, between its twisting trees, past its delicate plants, and through its light and shadows, he knew he had crossed some line, a line between sanity and madness, life and death, reality and illusion. Which was which he no longer cared. It felt good, a freedom, and he knew that soon much more would change.

"Merrily we stroll along, stroll along, stroll along," he sang jauntily. "Merrily we stroll along, my bride and me. Merrily we stroll along . . . ."

The Dark Yet Gentle Beast left the cemetery and followed Guy home. It observed the people and buildings and cars of the strange, fated world; a world always in waiting. As it treaded slowly and silently above the streets, no one saw or sensed its presence except Guy and a few aged or enlightened souls. No one else felt anything unusual or looked up. Guy, and the Beast, went home.

Chapter 26

"'How OLD IS the night?' The man asked.

"'How many hours has the moon shone bright?' The shrouded Angel of the Night replied.

"'Alas, many!' The man answered, exasperated. 'If I must live by night so I cannot see, when day arrives, if I lack the courage to see, will I die?'

"The Angel both smiled and frowned, a feat only a transcendent being can achieve. 'Dark to day and light to night. As day needs night to be, perhaps one must die to see.'"

Guy stood as a spectator, detached, a physicality with eyes, improvising a monologue while looking out his living room window. He observed his city in the enchantment and danger of night.

Tones of gray. A faint, burnt odor—ash, fumes, and exhausted souls. Rectangular forms, many. Squares of light like rows of glowing, captive eyes. Palm tree silhouettes.

There seems to be a simple order and logic to the city, and the world, Guy thought. *Perhaps there is. Perhaps it is not complex and confusing, but too simple to comprehend. Perhaps all things are.*

A police helicopter flew into view and circled, its spotlight a burning-down heat, the pounding of its rotors a forced assault against the cloaked quiet of the night. Police car sirens screamed, becoming louder and closer. *Sounds of Hell.*

"More violence," Guy mumbled.

He had never quite believed that the violence he knew was always there, waiting, would so touch his world. Yet, he should have known, for it was his world.

"Goodbye Los Angeles, City of Angels, and demons; risen and forsaken gods; those of a thousand breasts and borrowed flesh and feet that dance above death. So abstract and yet too real! What have we created together? La de dah and little more. Except perhaps love and art and dreams and all, if that accounts for something. I love you, L.A., and I hate you."

Guy wondered why there could not be cows in the city, moo-cows, whose milk could nourish the children of the streets, children who sometimes smile, and give to them the gentle hearts of pastoral fields, so they would not kill.

He pondered. How many drug addicts were in Los Angeles, in euphoric destruction? How many lovers? How many poet suicides? How many souls?

"The City of Angeles is my home. I, its ego. Illusion. A poem."

Guy watched two people, a man and a woman, like tiny toy shapes, walking down a sidewalk as to a lovely rhythm, an urban waltz, or the current of a stream, or the eternal flow of life.

"No, Los Angeles, I don't hate you. I understand. You are us."

His eyes perused the jagged, indifferent cityscape.

I wish I became the streets of L.A., became the dead, naked angels and dancing children and smiling moo-cows that did not exist. And I could just be, whatever, and it would be fine. And all would be a Beautiful, Winged Madness.

Guy laughed and then was silent. He sensed the presence of the Dark Yet Gentle Beast, outside, waiting. But now it seemed more gentle than dark.

He did not wish to think about what he planned to do. He just wanted to do it. It was an act of the heart and soul and should be simple, immediate, and pure, not contaminated by worldly thoughts, illusions of bleak foreshadowing, or rational contemplation. *It must be as Anna and light,* he affirmed.

All I want is to be with Anna, he felt, but did not think or speak.

Guy went to his desk. He ran his hand across the varnished surface of the aged and sturdy wood. He always liked its feel, like a physical universe reassurance. At the top of a sheet of paper he wrote 'My Will'. He stated that his collection of poems was bequeathed to the L.A. Library System, from where he borrowed books that had inspired him. *Perhaps they will publish my poems,* he speculated, *and someone will read them.* His paintings he left to a local city art museum that he had often enjoyed visiting and from where he had derived concepts. *Perhaps they will be exhibited and affect someone.*

He considered whom to leave his property to—furniture, stereo, TV. He thought of Raphael and the impoverished and homeless people he struggled to help. Guy left it all to them except for Anna's Woman in the Ghost costume which he wrote should be given to her sister, Terry. He requested that the naked statue of Anna be buried with him and that his modest funds be used to bury him beside Anna at Good Heavens Cemetery. Then he wrote, as Anna had, an epitaph to be inscribed on his gravestone: 'Guy, Poetic Guy Being'. A funny line came to him that he added, called 'Ode to My Death'. It felt correct to leave this desperate and confused world with a touch of humor.

Guy could think of nothing more. There was little in his life, especially with Anna gone. He penned the simple line, 'I have gone to my love,' and signed and dated the will. He left it visible in the center of the desk.

"Goodbye, venerable desk, upon which I have written so many words from my soul. Thank you for your service."

"Goodbye, my friend," he believed he heard the desk reply.

Guy went to the kitchen and obtained a bottle of wine and a glass. Then from his bathroom cabinet he removed two bottles of medication.

"Not for madness, but for love," he spoke as he examined their labels to confirm their contents. "This will more than suffice."

He considered playing music but decided he preferred the peace of silence. He sat in his faded and worn chair that had so often given him comfort, as again it did.

"Thank you, chair."

He poured a glass of wine, a burgundy, slightly tart, as he preferred it, and drank it quickly. He looked around his apartment at his plants and sculptures and his own paintings.

"I have done some worthy work," he critiqued and felt pleased.

He drank a second glass. Already he felt mellow, experiencing the wine's euphoria. "One of the more sublime pleasures of this world," he proclaimed.

He considered drinking heavily and becoming drunk, but chose not to. He wanted to act with consciousness and will. He poured a final glass.

Guy looked into his heart. How strange that he, a loner, a man who walked through life seldom blessed of heart, of love, would now follow that heart, so filled and yet so pained, and his greatest teacher, to his death and rebirth. Such is the wonderful irony of life!

"Let now my will be all, master of that heart that grants me life, yet servant to that same heart that grants me love. Let it act to one end alone, as to be never alone, nor never to end. My love Anna, and our spirits, are eternal.

"Love makes us mad and yet so sane and dear."

Simple, quick, and pure, he remembered. *All I want is to be with Anna. Do not think. Act!*

He raised his glass in a toast. "To you, Anna, my love and wife. I join you now."

Guy heard her voice speak in his mind, like a poet lover reciting into the night. "I love thee, Guy." And then the line she often said to him. "Good night, sweet prince. May flights of angels sing thee to thy sleep."

Guy smiled and brought the bottle of capsules to his lips. He closed his eyes. For a moment, all was a tranquil silence.

"No. Not yet, Guy."

It was Anna's voice, but not from his mind. It was outside, somewhere.

Guy opened his eyes. She was there. Vague. Real? Standing before the Garden of Eden wall painting, in front of the empty, painted space. A beautiful, ghostly Anna Eve, surrounded by trees and flowers and plants. Her paradise.

Guy jolted in a surge of confused excitement. He thought he should close his eyes and then reopen them to test reality, but he was afraid to. She might vanish.

"Anna?" He spoke toward the image.

"Yes, Guy, it is I, Anna, your wife. I am here."

Guy smiled more deeply from his being than ever before in his life. Whatever she was, she was there.

"But . . . how, Anna?" He stopped. "No. Don't answer. I know."

The ghost of Anna laughed, a haunting yet charming laugh. Guy stood and walked slowly to her, as a man lured by enchantment. Her image was semitransparent, the greens and browns of the painting dimly visible through her. But she was three dimensional, not flat like a film image, but rather like a hologram, and was draped in a golden gown. He remembered what Sage had said at the cemetery, that she saw the trees outside her window through Anna, but that she was there. Likewise, Guy saw paradise through her. He knew it was true. He reached out a hand to touch her shoulder. It passed through her and his joy ebbed.

"No, Guy, I am here. I'm not a hallucination or a dream," Anna spoke assuredly.

Guy's expression lifted. "This is incredible, and wonderful! Anna, listen, I want to tell you quick, for this may end. I love you, a thousand, a million times over! I don't know how I can even express it!"

"Yes, my love, I know, and that is one reason I came."

She smiled the warmest smile, not the smile of a ghost but of a woman in love. Her cocoa, mirage eyes, more wonderland magical than ever, glinted.

"And you know about the marriage?"

"Yes, I was there."

"And, you are happy?"

"Yes, absolutely! It's what my heart had decided, and I wanted. I am your wife, and I love the ring."

She held up her left hand. On her wedding finger was the gold diamond ring. Guy could not determine if it was the actual ring or an illusion of it, but he did not care. Seeing the marriage ring that he had intended for Anna on her finger was a joyous vision.

"May I kiss the bride?"

The Ghost Anna waited before answering. That was a question she wished she could hear a thousand times.

"Yes, you may. But it might not be as fine as I wish it could be."

Guy leaned toward Anna's lips.

"You may have to use your imagination," she whispered.

As his lips met hers, it was like an exquisite kiss in the air, and yet each believed they felt the moist, soft warmth of their joined lips.

"Our first marriage kiss," he said.

"It was beautiful," Anna replied.

Guy felt deliriously faint. His legs weakened. He did not care in the least what was of this world and what was not. *Mad or not, I am at a greater, and wonderful, truth.*

"Is love ever truly of this world?" Anna the ghost, with astute perception, commented.

Guy took some steps back and fell into his chair, more sprawled along it than seated, his arms hung over its arms, as a man dropped into a long awaited rest. Then he just looked at Anna.

Her flesh was paler than before and possessed of an ethereal quality, delicately unearthly. Her phantom brunette hair hung loose and free, as if just washed, tumbling around her shoulders. She wore no makeup—he smiled at the concept of spirits applying make-up—and she looked uncannily fresh, as a woman after a shower. She was clothed in a sleek, gold dress with her usual deep cleavage revealing divinely pallid breasts. The shimmering dress nicely wrapped and delineated her curves, descending to above her knees. She was barefoot.

"Your afterlife persona?" Guy smiled. "It's lovely."

Anna raised her arms and spun slowly, as a model, a ghostly model, on a phantasm walkway.

"Yes. At first I wasn't sure what to wear." Her eyes looked up and rolled in bafflement. "What would be appropriate. It's been a while since I've had to make such a fashion selection for such an occasion. But natural," she laughed, "as natural as a ghost can be, in a golden gown, felt correct."

"You're beautiful. Alive or . . . ." He stopped and glanced down. "You're always beautiful." His face tensed. "How do you feel, Anna? Is there pain?"

She shook her head. "No, not at all. It's like being in a peaceful dream, or a gentle, vast space, generally white or light gray. I can experience feelings by putting my attention on something, like the grief of loss."

She looked into Guy's eyes, entering deep and probing gently.

"But right now my attention is on my love for you, and I can feel it profoundly. I . . . never expressed it fully. This is important and one reason I've returned. I love you, Guy, totally! Do you know that?"

"Yes, Anna. I know. That's why I married you."

"And you will not forget it? Ever?"

"No, Anna, never."

Anna smiled. "Nor will I!"

They were both quiet for an extended moment. It was like the quiet they used to share when both were having the same, special feeling.

"Anna, the girl, Sage, you visited her? I spoke to her in the cemetery."

"Yes, last night. I felt I could help her."

"And you did. She'll remember that, for sure! She's unique."

Anna nodded. Then she turned and walked behind the branches and leaves of a painted tree, which became visible in front of her form.

"To me, Guy, this painted garden seems real. Dimensional. I create it and can feel it. I chose to feel it." She touched a leaf.

"And to smell its floral fragrance. It's odd but wonderful! It's real and yet not real, both illusion and reality, like being in a dream."

"Or in the world, in life," Guy interjected.

Anna grinned and nodded, strands of her hair dangling across her specter face. "Yes, that is true. I realize it more now than ever."

Her apparition form, like a perfect ghostly special effect, returned to the space at the front of the painting.

"And you can see me, and everything, fully?" Guy queried.

"Yes, fully. I can see whatever I put my attention on. You, seeker, would find it wild." She peered into the distance. "I will demonstrate it. Right now I'm putting my attention on the eastern U.S. coast. I can see the Atlantic Ocean, off the shore of Maryland. It's late night; there's a partial moon leaving delicate white slashes on the water, which is rolling gently. It's cool, 36 degrees. Somehow I know that. I can feel it. I hear a car now in the distance, inland. I have my attention on it and can see it closely. It's a Chevrolet Impala, dark blue, with three people inside." She paused. "Now I'm looking at the shore again. There are two people, men in long coats, walking on the gray beach. One is pointing to something on the ocean. It's . . . the lights, red and white, of a ship passing in the night. The name Lorielle is in white letters on the ship's hull. Inside, in a small cabin that smells of oil, a man, a sailor, is lying on a bunk. There is a bowl of fruit candy beside him. Ugh! They taste sour." Her face compressed. "He's reading a magazine about UFO's, an article about alien visitors hidden among humans." Anna chuckled. "I can see and feel and smell and taste it all, vividly."

"Damn, that's amazing!" Guy tried to imagine her experience.

"Most pleasing of all, I see you, Guy, fully. And I can always see you if I chose." Her apparition form swayed gently as if blown by a breeze, in an expression of pleasure.

"And I see you, Anna, a little ghostly, but there." His face suddenly tortured. "You are there, aren't you, Anna? This is not a hallucination?"

"Yes, Guy. I am here." She grinned. "In my Ghost Persona. And Guy, I'm learning things. I become excited and wish I could share it with you. Do you know that every moment, and every experience we have, is basically the same? There is only one moment and one experience. Listen."

Anna's form lifted a few inches above the floor.

"Imagine a man sitting in a movie theater. He's watching many movies. One is a romance, one an adventure, one a crime drama. He thinks he's having a wonderful romance, living a thrilling adventure, experiencing an exciting crime drama. But he's actually having only one experience—sitting in a theater watching movies.

"Life, and reality, is like that—one moment, one experience. It's now and spiritual being." She looked around. "I see that so clearly now! And there is only one Spirit, which we are all a part of. It is what we call God, and it is us. Isn't that so simple and beautiful? One Spirit, one Moment, one Experience. Everything is One! And to experience that, that oneness, is what every human being is always trying to do, in relationships, in love, and in pursuit of God. I want to share that with you like we used to during our talks." Her eyes saddened, appearing weightier. "I miss our talks. I hope we will keep sharing things, Guy. It doesn't matter if my body is alive or dead. It's basically all the same."

Guy grinned. "Anna, my love, my wife, returns from death a greater philosopher. It's what I expect from you. You are the same, Anna." He stared admiringly.

Anna smiled, ethereal but real. "Always! And I know now, for certain, that I am and always have been, Spirit. It's what we thought, Guy. The person, Anna, the human, not the body, was created by me, Spirit. As I created all my personas. Do you see?"

She became more animated, waving her arms.

"Anna was a created persona, my greatest and most perfect one, yet still an illusion. As Spirit we are great artists. We, as part of all Spirit, create everything perfectly, even our insane flaws, for a purpose. They are part of our game. It's all wonderful and funny. We create ourselves, then search to find ourselves, and it's all based on love."

The Anna Spirit laughed, lighter and freer than the air.

"You as Spirit are creating you as Guy. And it's doing an excellent job! It's a trip, Guy. But it's sad that one may have to wait until death takes one's body to see it, and then only if they chose to." Anna looked plaintively into the space above Guy. "To see Spirit—God."

"I will not have to wait, Anna. Now I know." Guy was half serious and half facetious. "And I promise, I won't forget. At least not for a few minutes, until TV calls."

Anna smiled in the tender manner Guy remembered so well, and missed.

"Good, my love."

As Guy looked at her, a lovely ghost, so real and yet so surreal, and so delighted, he was afraid to ask the question, but he did.

"Anna, can you stay? Can you stay here, every day, every night, in your garden, or somewhere, here?"

Anna perused the garden. "This painted world is real to me. It seems alive. But if you tried to place a plant from your apartment in it, could you? Would it grow? I think not, for it is where, and what, it should be. No, Guy, I cannot stay. It wouldn't be correct. In the spirit world one just knows what they must do. I don't know how, one just knows, like a profound intuition. And I am not meant to be back in the other world yet. There are things I must do here."

Sorrow obscured Guy's vision. Anna's ghost form became bleary, as if being dissolved by tears. He looked down, seeing nothing, and was quiet. Anna felt his sadness in her spirit heart. Then his expression brightened, and he looked up.

"Then I will join you, as I planned."

Anna's eyes reached gently. "Perhaps. That you must decide from what you know. But not yet. There's something you must do. Something I am asking of you."

"Yes, Anna. What is it? Anything!"

"Guy." She paused, a delighted expectation in her expression. "Guy, one reason I returned is to tell you this. You must write our story, everything, as you can remember, from the moment we met on the rooftop of this building."

Guy's eyes widened, but he did not speak.

"You can write it in any form you chose, but I believe it would be best as a novel." She looked into spirit thought-space. "Yes, a novel! That would be an artwork, and we are artists! It would be aesthetic reality, or an illusion of fact and creation, like our lives." She smiled, inspired. "And that is an important part of our story, such as you sitting there now, talking to Anna the Ghost." She chuckled. "It will be a story of love and Spirit, of artists and dreams and ideals, of reality and illusion, and of struggles, of yours and mine. It will be of us. And the story is not over."

Anna closed her eyes and swayed as to the rhythm of a gentle dance.

"We can dance again through the pages of a novel. What do you think?" Her excited eyes reopened.

Guy's face became a mask of concentrated focus, as it always was when he examined a vital issue. The idea pleased and intrigued but also confused him.

"But why, Anna? Would anyone read it? Would anyone care? Would our little lives mean anything to anyone?"

A smile lit her spectral face. "You must trust me on this, Guy. They will. This involves our purposes and ideals and a greater, unfolding spiritual design. It's a strange universe, almost as strange as we seem. And sometimes beautifully mad! Things can happen in surprising ways. But it is correct."

Anna did not need to say anything more. She seemed to Guy the essence of some wild truth that he did not understand but delighted in. He trusted her.

"Yes. I will write it." Then his expression became grave. "But Anna, I may not be able to. There's something I haven't told you."

"You mean the hallucinations and voices?"

"You know about that?"

"Yes. I saw it all. When I left the world. I'm sorry you've been suffering."

"Are you angry that I didn't tell you?" He pouted like a repentant boy.

Anna thought it was cute. "No, not at all. I know you were being kind. Thank you. But you should not worry. You'll be fine. There's a greater power and design at work."

Guy stared at her curiously. Her statement seemed enigmatic, but so did all else.

"I live and die for our truth, Anna. And thus it is with all worlds."

Anna stared at him, finding his statement enigmatic. But so seemed all else. Mysteries upon mysteries. She followed her own advice and trusted.

"But Anna, there are things I don't know, like what you thought and felt at times. How can I write it?"

"You are an artist. You can imagine and create. You know me very well, how I think and feel. Trust your intuition and Spirit. They will help guide you. But write it as truthfully as possible."

Anna brightened, her demeanor one of an encouraging coach.

"So don't worry, my love, my husband. All will be well. Be happy that you are alive. Trust Spirit, and keep awakening."

Those familiar words surprised Guy. His eyes narrowed, and he peered with an inquisitive, and probing, expression.

The ghost Anna, surrounded by the beautiful foliage of the garden, raised her arms in an expression of 'who knows?' Then they both laughed.

Guy's despair of the past days lightened. Anna was so lovely and real, his wife ghost, like a poetic dream. He wished he could stay in that moment forever. Then another question haunted.

"And then what, Anna? After the novel is completed, then what?"

"I don't know, my love, but you will." She observed his handsome, and questioning, face. "It's simple. It will be the ending of the story."

Guy grinned. "Yes, I understand."

"And now, my love," Anna spoke softly, "the only true love of my heart, I must leave. If I wait longer, it will be too painful."

For the first time since her appearance, Guy perceived torment in her expression.

"It already is painful. I don't know if I'm choosing it, but I feel it."

Guy felt it also. Anna had to leave, again. For an excruciating moment, they were both silent, feeling each other's presence intensely, and it was a tortuous joy.

"I know I'm leaving and yet I never leave you, Guy. But still it hurts. I think we never truly leave your world."

Guy walked to her. Watching him approach, Anna's face gladdened. He reached out, closed his eyes, and placed his hand on her cheek.

She did not seem to be a ghost. He felt her cheek's warmth, and she felt his touch. Her cheek flushed, surprising even her.

Guy felt coolness, like moisture, on his hand and opened his eyes. A tear was streaming down Anna's face.

"Ghosts cry?" He touched the tear on her cheek.

"This one does."

Guy felt the profound hollow of that sadness. He struggled not to block the echoes of that empty space opening. He wanted to feel all.

"It's OK, Anna. We will be together again soon. That *I* know."

Anna smiled. "Yes."

Nothing existed in that room, or the world, or the universe, at that moment but them. Not a man and a ghost, but two in love. It was all.

"And now, my husband, I must leave," Anna repeated. "And you must begin your work." She gazed across his apartment. "I always loved it here. It was like home. I'll miss it." She noticed the small statue of herself on a table. "The statue."

"Yes. Thank you, Anna. I love it."

"Perhaps it will help keep you company." Anna peered into Guy's eyes. "Before I leave, will you recite to me a final poem?"

"Yes, a poem for my wife." Guy considered. "OK, it's my simplest and truest poem." Guy's face concentrated, and he cleared his throat. "Uhhhm." He placed his hand behind one of Anna's and although he could barely feel it, as he lifted his arm, she lifted her hand so he was holding it in the air.

"Are you ready, my love?" He asked.

"Yes."

"Are you sure you're listening?"

"Yes, I'm listening."

"I don't want you to miss one word. This is my most important recitation."

Anna laughed. "Recite the poem, Maestro!"

"OK. Here it is. It's called Anna's Poem."

Guy waited, building drama, and then spoke.

"I love thee."

Anna the ghost smiled as her ethereal form became more luminous and substantial. She had never felt more present.

"Thank you. It's beautiful and perfect. With that, I now leave. One final kiss."

Guy leaned forward and kissed her. It touched the universe.

"Goodbye, Guy. I love thee."

Her form dimmed like an exquisite mirage vanishing in the air. Her hand in his became vaguer.

Then Guy had a wonderful idea. "Wait, Anna! Don't leave! Not yet!"

Anna sensed in her spirit consciousness that Guy was about to request something critical. She remanifested into her former illusion reality, like a woman called back by her lover.

Returned after that moment of near departure, she became disoriented. Anna wanted to deny all and hold Guy in her arms, close, and never let him go. But she knew she could not.

"Yes, my love. What is it?"

"Sorry I called you back, Anna. I don't want to make this more difficult, but I have an idea. A request." The excitement in his voice suggested intrigue. "Anna, remember I told you that I left this empty space in the painting," he pointed to the space behind her, "to be filled by the image of my truer and purer love, when I find her?"

"Yes, I remember. I thought it was sweet."

"Well, I have found her. That truer and purer love is you." Guy smiled, and then the smile inverted. "I'm embarrassed that I haven't already painted you into it. But perhaps I was waiting for the perfect moment, this moment." His smile restored. "Before you leave, may I paint you into the painting? There is an easy way I can do it."

Anna replied immediately. "Yes, I'd like that! And after you do, paint yourself beside me, holding my hand, and we can be together in your painting. It's a fabulous idea. You must do it!"

Guy nodded. "So be it! Wait here."

"Always, for art."

Guy went to his bedroom and returned rolling a wooden table of painting supplies: brushes, tubes of paint, rags, solutions. He placed it before the wall mural.

"Assume your pose, my lovely model."

Anna's expression became provocative, with a grin and a cocked brow. "I also remember you agreed to one day paint me," she paused and grinned, "probably nude you said, and you haven't done so yet. Shame! Sometimes you are such a fool." She sighed. "Well, you can do it now. You have an Eve, and Eve must be natural in her Edenic Garden. Although I realize this was not quite what you intended."

Anna reached behind her, unzipped the gold dress and allowed it to drop to the floor. She was wearing nothing beneath.

"Your naked, ghostly Eve. Only for you!"

She hooked the dress with her left foot and flung it behind her. Like a peculiar illusion, it vanished behind a bush.

"And I understand now, Guy," affection flowed from her eyes, "that every time you looked at me, or spoke to or touched me, you made love to me. You do it now. It's what a woman wants, and I've wanted, although it took me a time to realize. I, too, can be a fool. So paint me, and we can always be together, in love and in art, two happy fools, as it was always meant to be."

"Amen," Guy exclaimed.

For a moment he just stared at Anna, the spirit Anna again appearing very much the woman Anna. Her translucent, ethereal nude form looked fragile and vulnerable, like a dream one might attempt to hold onto when awakening only to have it vanish at the moment of desiring it. And yet, she appeared complete, a sensual, natural woman, and very erotic, standing naked in her primal garden. That strange duality, both woman and ghost, transformed Anna into a metaphor, a symbol for all women; a transitory, delicate, and lovely presence, a perfect model. *Anna.*

"You look beautiful, Anna, ethereal yet real. Death is kind, and very cool!"

Anna laughed, and her laughter charmed the garden.

"Now, take one step back so you're in the space correctly," he instructed.

Anna complied and extended an arm partially out, its hand open to receive another's. She glanced over her phantasmal body and then moved her left foot to the side one inch so her pose expressed a finer balance.

"Perfect!" She proclaimed.

"Yes, perfect," Guy concurred. Her provocative presence and confident nakedness reminded him of the night in the hospital.

"Anna, the hospital. Did you visit me that night?"

She grinned teasingly. "What does your heart and Spirit tell you, my love?"

Guy did not answer aloud, but they told him, yes.

With a stick of charcoal, he traced Anna's body and features onto the painted wall. It seemed an inexplicably strange experience to be so close before the woman he loved, drawing over her as she appeared so real and present, yet so immaterial and transparent. He had difficulty comprehending that Anna was dead and yet alive. That paradox expressed the unique experience they were sharing.

"You know Anna, I fear I've gone mad. I can no longer differentiate what is real and not. In an odd way, it is both wonderful and disturbing."

"No, Guy, you are sane, and I am real. Just accept."

"Yes," was his only reply. He took a spray can of fixative. "Close your eyes and hold your breath."

"My breath is me. I don't believe it will disturb me."

Guy lightly sprayed over the drawing to prevent the charcoal from later blending into the paint. The dark tracing of Anna's form on the wall reminded him of the outline police draw around the body of a slain victim on a sidewalk or a floor. A chill trembled him.

He examined astutely the color hues of Anna's rarefied flesh, so ephemerally lovely, and mixed several ivory-flesh variations of paint.

I wish I could paint her slowly, as a lifelong work of passion, never quite completed, so Anna would never leave. But I know she must, and I do not want to cause more pain. I will paint over her only once, in one layer of paint. It will feel like I am painting fate.

As Guy brushed over the spectral image of Anna's smooth and paled thigh, he saw how the process would work. Her form vanished beneath the paint. Anna would leave incrementally as he painted her, in a process one might view as either kind or tormenting. In attempting to preserve the image of his love, he would paint her out of his world. But he accepted that it was Anna's way.

"Can you feel the brush strokes, Anna?" he asked as he painted down her illusion legs.

"If I chose to, and I am choosing to. It feels like a soft, teasing massage. It's nice." Her legs vibrated, and she laughed. "Poltergeists can be sensual! What would it be like for a ghost to make love? I will not even think about it."

But she did. "I sense there would be a transgression of boundaries, like a misalignment of worlds, and the consequences would be severe. Still, it might be fun." She chuckled and then felt embarrassed and quieted.

Guy grinned. "But we're always transgressing boundaries, Anna. It's a part of who we are."

Anna knew his point was valid, but there was also more she knew. She looked into his loving but confused eyes and felt the passion that was her husband.

"Yes, my love, and I always liked that about us. We were born to defy boundaries and expand being and culture. But something more is involved here. We must proceed correctly. I am trusting Spirit." She paused. "It is all I am now! And you must trust also. We are creating a greater love." Then her face tensed. "Our society and culture put people into this terrible, blind hypnotic state, and we must do our part to help awaken and free them."

"Yes, Anna, I agree. Perhaps it's our destiny."

He applied paint to her toes, and she giggled. He finished painting Anna's shapely legs and petite feet. Next he moved to her pelvis region. He painted the soft cushion of her belly and then lower to the sublime manifestation of the woman, adding a small scarlet flower, an iris, by its side.

"It's lovely and delicate," he said.

"A truth," Anna replied with a euphoric smile. "An artist must paint truth."

"Miraculously yet sadly, it disappeared beneath my brush," Guy bemoaned, and Anna laughed.

Guy moved up to the smooth curves of her shoulders and painted over them with luxurious strokes. Anna moaned. Then to her arms and the hands he had always loved to touch. They vanished beneath the paint. He painted her trunk and sleek neck. As he developed the image, he applied shading by softening and diffusing tones, transforming them into gentle abstracted shapes that complemented the flows of Anna's body. The painting of Anna was to be an aesthetic vision.

"I attempt to paint an aesthetic and sensual perfection."

"I trust the Master," Anna replied. "Now paint my ethereal boobs."

Guy brushed in her rounded breasts, glimpses of which had so often pleasured his vision. He knew they were disappearing beneath his strokes. He took a couple of steps back, examined his work and then stepped forward and added a few touches, and then back again for assessment. They looked like the bosom of a goddess.

"Goodbye, sweet breasts," he whispered.

He painted Anna's long, flowing hair, like a visual poem of a waterfall. Only her face remained undone, and thus remained. The face, common yet lovely, which had lifted his heart to a place he had not known could even exist; a face and place he would never forget. Before he painted it, he touched her on the cheek, again feeling its warmth, and Anna smiled. He leaned forward and kissed her lips.

"I love you, Anna."

He painted her face, so wonderfully sculpted and gracious, and knew it was gone except for her eyes and mouth that he had worked around.

And in an instant, Guy realized a remarkable irony. When he first met Anna, on his roof on the night of The Event, she was a ghost, and now, when he last meets her in this world, she is again a ghost. Like a perfect circle.

"It's almost finished," he assessed softly, and Anna's eyes saddened. As he painted with subdued rose hues the sensuous shape of her lips, he saw them move. Anna whispered her last words to him.

"Goodbye, Guy. I love thee."

He smiled, nodded once and, with a labored effort that he concealed from Anna, completed the lips. He added a moist highlight in white. Only her eyes remained unpainted and not yet lost. At first he felt afraid to look into them, and then he did. They were dark and fathomless and possessed of Anna's mysterious enchantment. She moved them minutely, reminding him that she was still there. Guy knew he was looking deep into Anna's very existence and soul, and he saw her there.

With hues of dark brown, black, gold, and white, he painted over one of the eyes, slowly, carefully, adding a final highlight that gleamed like a mystical beckoning. He moved to the final eye. He looked into it, into the woman he loved, *my wife*, and knew she was looking into him. For a moment, they both existed together in one pure, shared space, the mad but beautiful space of love. "I love thee," they spoke with one silent voice.

I will not paint it, Guy thought. *Then Anna will stay.*

He heard her thought. *No, my love. That is not meant to be. You must complete the painting. We cannot be trapped in an illusion. Trust.*

Guy nodded. Before he could again think or feel, with his heart numbed, he applied his finest artistry and painted over the eye, and then added the final, singular dab of white, the highlight, like a lonely star in a dark universe.

"Goodbye, my love," Guy whispered. "I love thee."

Anna was gone.

All seemed simple. One reality. He just wanted to cry. There was nothing else to do. He again felt the unbearable sadness and loss, and it was all that he now was. Not a man, not a spirit. An empty space that wanted to cry. Deep, but in a peculiar way, also dear.

But he did not cry. He believed everything Anna had said, and was, and he wanted to have faith, for her. *All is correct.*

Guy laid down his brush, walked to his chair and sat. The room seemed peaceful in the quiet of the night. He wanted to sit in the dark but kept the light on so he could see the painted image of Anna in the lush exotic garden. It was sublime, not perfect, yet perfect, the painting over of death with the love and beauty of life. *It was Anna.*

He closed his eyes and cried.

*   *   *

His eyes opened. Some time had passed and Guy had drifted to sleep, but it was still night. He smelled the pungent odors of paint thinner and oils. The room had an empty stillness, as in waiting.

He knew he must complete the painting now. He did not want Anna to feel alone in her illusionary painted world, certainly not on their honeymoon. Guy went to the bedroom and brought out a full length mirror and laid it against the wall painting. He removed all of his clothes and looked at his nude body surrounded by space in the rectangle of the mirror reflection. He looked like a stripped, lonely man, although he was not. And yet he was.

With charcoal he drew his form and features onto the painting to Anna's left side, holding her hand. He painted it in, occasionally stepping before the mirror to examine his features for accuracy. He paled his flesh to better duplicate Anna's hue. *We must be a pair.* He painted his hair tousled so it appeared loose and free, like hers. When working his pelvic region, in a moment of both humor and male ego, he depicted his male organ, that most peculiar feature and symbol of man, somewhat larger than reality. He trusted Anna would enjoy that, spirit though she be, and he believed he heard her laugh.

On his portrait face, Guy created a serene smile. A temptation to paint himself looking at Anna, as he probably actually would be, was resisted. Instead he depicted himself as he had drawn it, looking toward the viewer, or the future, as was Anna. They looked together, it being a time for resolve, faith, and courage.

In a relatively short time, the painted portrait of himself was completed. He stepped back to view his work. His image appeared masculine and protective beside Anna's feminine figure. He thought the portraits were lovely, a resplendent blend of spirit and flesh. They looked natural and noble, standing as both Guy and Anna in their private, shared space and as Adam and Eve in a universal garden—a Garden of Life. The artist, the lover, and the husband were pleased.

An idea impinged. On Anna's opposite side, holding her hand, he would paint a small boy, giving Anna and him a son. It would be a gift to them and their love. From memory he drew the figure of a child, about ten years of age, also natural and nude. He sketched in a generic boy's facial features.

"He will be called Wake," Guy spoke into the air and to Anna. "For he was created from a celebration of both life and death, a wake, and he is to awaken all."

Then something happened inside himself, in his soul, as if he awakened, and he knew what he must do. He found a newspaper in his apartment that carried the story of the Cupid Killer on the front page, his identity now released. There was a picture of the boy, who resembled an adorable, brunette cherub. Guy painted the features of the Cupid Killer, the little boy, the stranger who killed love and had taken Anna's life, onto the painting of their son. Guy knew Anna would understand and agree. With the love they were blessed to share, they could forgive, and accept, all. The family was redeemed.

He and Anna had their child. The work was complete. Guy sat in his chair and then realized something was missing. Returning to the wall, he painted the white highlight in each of the boy's eyes, the glimmer of the transcendent, the spirit. He returned to his chair and re-examined the work. He loved it. Anna, he, and the boy appeared alive and beautiful, as they truly were. An Edenic family in the lovely Garden of Life, at peace.

In a world without murder, or pain, or death.

Perfect, he thought. Perfect, he knew Anna agreed.

But all was not perfect. Experience shifted. Guy suddenly again felt tormentingly alone. Anna was gone. And yet, he realized he was not really alone. All seemed strange. *Profoundly strange!*

He heard birds singing cheerfully outside his window, heralding the dawn. It was that mystical, otherworldly transition between night and day, dark and light, when it was not truly either and yet was both. *The proper time*, he thought.

He had painted three portraits in one night. A notable feat! Guy realized he was exhausted. It had been a full day, one of both pain and joy. And there was much work yet to be done. He sank deeply into the cushion of his chair. Experience again shifted. In an unexpected moment, Guy felt blessed. He closed his eyes and, fearing no nightmares, floated with the silence of the room and the stillness of the dawn. He fell into a serene sleep—the sleep that one is given when one is more awake.

Chapter 27

GUY AWOKE LATER that morning lying on his side on the living room rug, the muted luminance of morning light enshrining the room. At the first moment of consciousness, he thought it was just another day.

Then he remembered. He felt the assaulting darkness of death, then the elevating hope of eternal spiritual being, then the hollow dread of loneliness, then the joy of beauty and love—redeemers. He smelled the stinging odor of paint thinner and looked at the wall garden painting where Anna's pale yet lovely ghost portrait stared at him. The terrible sorrow returned.

"I should just die and join Anna," he muttered. But he could not, something inside him believed.

The novel! I have to write the novel! Anna requested it and in an assertion of faith, he knew it must be done. He felt guided.

"Probably by madness," he spoke hushed. "Lunacy and hallucinations."

But possibly not. *Something carries me. Spirit? Love? Maybe just being.* Guy pondered a fundamental question. *Could just being be enough?* He suspected not, and yet yes, it could be. If one just knew, just knew. *What?*

But now, he needed to know, or think, no more. Confusion vanished.

He drank his morning French roast coffee and wondered how he had ended up on the floor when he recalled falling asleep in his chair. *Carried by ghosts?*

He took a shower, warm and baptismal. Still naked, as it felt correct to be, he went to his wooden desk in the living room. Nudity—it had become a primary metaphor in his life and seemed the dress code for critical affairs. Was that what it was all about? To just be naked in this delusional, cloaked world?

He turned on his computer and created a file titled 'Chapter One'. He stared at the blank, *naked* screen. At first its pure white blankness intimidated him, like the fear of being nothing, or a challenge to one's substance. After a few minutes, a poetic passage came.

'If women were sculptures, he could enjoy just sitting and watching this one be.'

The novel had begun.

Several hours of writing later, the first chapter was complete. It seemed a peculiar and enigmatic process. The story flowed out of him, a gestalt of his captive memories and his creative imagination, all sculpted by an artistic sensibility, and perhaps Spirit, *that knows.* He understood immediately that love was to be its core and reality and illusion a theme.

Guy the loner, the misfit, the child of aberration and lunacy, was to write a novel of love and Spirit, artists and madness, beauty and ideals and purposes. *The strangeness of life, especially for artists and lovers,* he reflected, *never ceases to surprise. It is, indeed, a Beautiful, Winged Madness.*

Guy realized he had the title of the novel.

*   *   *

That night seemed especially quiet and lonely. After completing more writing, Guy did not know what to do. Those would be the difficult hours, between his sessions of work. Things no longer held meaning. Television was anemic distortions, devoid of the truths and discoveries of a struggling life. Music seemed oddly coarse, not as sublime as, say, a beautiful ghost. Books were sterile concepts and images. And the outside city and streets seemed to be just city and streets. The City of Angels desperately needed its angels.

He had his memories, his artistic vision, his perplexed emotions, and little else. Except, of course, his metaphorical naked body.

*　　*　　*

Passing hours and days. Slight, very slight, variations on a theme. Writing—two sessions, morning and evening; chapter after chapter. Staring transfixed into space, the consummate but meaningless space of nothing. Thoughts—both friends and enemies, some sweet, some mad, often sad. Meditation—a pursuit of meaning in spirit and an eradication of time. Terrible, amplified, crawling time. Guy did not want time. It had become an enemy. Time might bring feeling.

That was the reality of Guy's days.

The words Guy typed spoke of Anna and him, and something more. He saw the novel slowly evolving as if possessed of its own life and fate. It excited and frightened him, much as when one walks through life never quite knowing where he is headed or how it will end.

He felt excruciatingly lonely. Each unoccupied moment invited the loneliness. No, it was not loneliness. Loneliness was kinder. It was aloneness, when one is alone and knows he will remain alone, like being stranded on a vacant planet, somewhere, nowhere in deep space.

One evening he suspected something was very wrong. The prophets were false, the prophecies lies. As he sat in his old, companion chair, in the scant light of a lamp, and the sonic booming of a helicopter passing over his building hammered the quiet, he received a new visitor, powerful and severe: doubt.

Perhaps this is all bullshit! Sometimes fantastic, yes, but bullshit! He assessed the events that had occurred. Anna's ghost—a hallucination. Her ghost with the girl Sage—a lonely child's fantasy. The wall painting's new figures—just more paintings.

And him? He was what he seemed: a demented and grieved failed artist. And Anna? Dead. And the glorious purpose? To be alone, till death, alone and mad.

"Mary had a little lamb, its fleece was white as snow," Guy spoke aloud, for no reason than it felt right. He blinked and then had an unexpected and contrary thought: *it is often in aloneness that one finds the greatest truths.*

So what truth might he discover? Perhaps one that was also a solution: just accept all and be grateful, *even if it be madness.*

Chapter 28

THIRD STREET WAS, as always, a density of people and city, of urban reality and illusion—ethnic shoppers, primarily Hispanic, scouting for bargains and a softening of the harsh edge of scant survival; men with black, slicked hair committed to chores and pleasure hunting; blooming, sexual women, dark and earthy, the pleasure hunted; colors, cosmetics, tattoos, and commerce.

Music, an ethnic-defying synthesis of urban rap and Mexican rhythms, blared from speakers hidden in the front of family owned discount stores. Street carts sold enchiladas, corncobs, tortillas, and emerald green avocados so large they raised suspicions of genetic mutation. Venders barked pirated cigarettes, DVDs, and CDs.

Guy liked it. Noise, color, motion, scents of food and sex, and ethnicity. Simple passions of life.

Between writing sessions Guy retreated to the streets to shop and walk and see, a new ritual he vowed to perform each day, escaping to the world, the air and sun, and the people; a simple strategy for maintaining sanity and anesthetizing pain until his writing was completed. Afterward, it might not matter.

Threading his way through the swamp of pedestrians, a bargain store window displaying a cluster of colorful, shiny novelties enticed his vision. Red letters above the window announced: 'Enrique's Bargain Emporium'. Guy entered and was engulfed by a menagerie of enameled coffee table figurines, vacuous trinket gifts, and lamps with plastic rainbow shades, all offering the peculiar appeal of cheap, cloned art—the aesthetics of the people. Ceramic Virgin Marys, miniature toy

Ferraris, tiny glass cats and swans. *Pop culture junk,* Guy assessed. *Anna would be delighted!*

After a discriminating survey, he chose a four-inch long wooden manger cradling a porcelain baby Jesus. The little Messiah smiled with enameled joy. Also deemed worthy was a miniature book, a couple inches long, colorfully illustrated with Mexican gods and princesses, a tiny celebration of their mythology. He bought it because it made him smile.

Strolling home, jauntily step, step, stepping down the sidewalk, gazing dreamily at the lapis blue sky and the women in body-contouring jeans, Guy picked up several fronds, green with dried, brown edges, fallen from the towering palm trees. Symbols of Los Angeles. Little wings of the city's angels.

He was tempted to include a dented Coors beer can, but refrained. It was not to be a junk pile. Delight and love would be its themes; it was for Anna.

Guy touched the beer can with the sole of his shoe. Then two more times. It had to be thrice.

Returned to his apartment, he surveyed his gallery of paintings and selected one of a nude woman resembling Anna seated on a branch of a tree. He had painted it in monochromatic blue tones to create a contrast and tension between the warm sensuality of the woman and nature and the cool detachment of the artist's, and beholder's, viewpoint. The image might stimulate a viewer, but its coolness negated that seduction, conveying an unavailable fantasy.

Unavailable fantasy. The phrase perturbed him.

He moved the painting to the wall in the corner of the room behind a table displaying the statue of Anna. He arranged the gifts around the statue and included the Cadillac model and the small, artist studio tableaux with its skeletal painter that Anna bought him at the Day of the Dead celebration. Then he added to the wall the painting of Anna as a ghost that she left him in her will, an image disturbingly prophetic.

The Shrine to Anna had begun.

Guy sat on the floor before the statue and its adornments. It was time for the next ritual. He bowed to the statue and then meditated on its image; it was his burning candle, his inner light, his mantra. It was sacred.

In and out of the meditation, the placid absence, he drifted into feelings experienced with Anna, deeper and more profound than he remembered. Exquisite pains. Little deaths and rebirths. Ghosts that floated in delirious hauntings. There would be nothing, then there would be love. No one, then Anna, even more beautiful than ever. Nothing, then everything.

Guy had an unexpected thought: *beauty is the expression in the physical universe of the innate, formless beauty of Spirit.*

*   *   *

Guy watched the dimming light gradually transform his apartment into a stage of subdued shapes. Sounds from the outside city hushed from daytime business and play to evening repose.

Everywhere metamorphosis, he reflected. *Time to write!*

At his desk, on his computer, Guy wrote from his memories, his soul, and his artistic vision. Then he suddenly stood and walked back and forth across his living room seven times. It had to be seven, he knew, perhaps because seven represented spirit or luck. Or perhaps because he was mad.

He turned. Something there. *What the hell?* He could not comprehend and then could not believe. It was a white, wooden door in the center of the wall, a door that had never before existed. On it, in gold letters, were words:

'Exhibit: The Art of Love'

A hallucination, he quickly reasoned as he stared at the phenomena. It could not possibly be real, unless . . . Anna had created it, she as spirit possessing the ability to alter the physical universe. It might be an intriguing game presented for his entertainment or to teach him a vital lesson needed to complete the novel. Fun!

The mysterious white door waited, beckoning.

"What lies behind the white door? What truths? Or game?" Guy spoke in a resonant, supernatural voice. "Or horror?"

He knew it could be an illusion of madness, a door to terror. He stood, unable to act, rubbing the back of his neck, for anguished moments.

"Come! Enter my door! The Art of Love awaits." It seemed to speak.

What are you afraid of? Something in his mind asked. *Do you, artist and lover, fear the Art of Love?*

Guy walked slowly, slowly to the door. To open or not? The room was disturbingly silent, its light appearing to dim. Finally, he could not tolerate the indecision, the agonizing paralysis. His hand reached toward the doorknob, hesitated, and then grasped it.

An eerie squawk sliced his body. He looked behind him and saw a black bird, a crow, outside his apartment window, perched on a ledge. Anxiety heightened.

Guy turned the knob, and then stopped. *I can release it and walk away. Perhaps it will vanish.*

No! He opened the door, its hinges creaking. The crow again cawed, screeching, and its wings thrashed the window. Spears of ice stabbed Guy's flesh.

But he was not struck dead.

Before him was a narrow room, all white, like a deep closet. An illumination radiated from an unseen source in its ceiling. About fifteen feet in front of him, at the end of the space, stood a life-size statue of Anna. It was exactly as his little statue but larger and Anna, nude on its base, appeared real, of flesh, in the same pose with a partially outstretched arm. And she was beautiful. Guy stood captivated and stared.

Then she moved, lifting her other arm, and rolled her head once. She looked at Guy and smiled effusively.

"My love, you've come," she spoke in Anna's voice. "I've returned to you, not as a ghost, but as a living statue. As me!"

"Anna? Is it really you?" Guy was still outside the room.

"Yes, my love, it is I."

She swept her hand along the front of her body, as Anna often had. She looked fresh and sensual in her nakedness, the ceiling light bathing her in a gentle aura.

"I decided I must visit you once more, but only once, as a living statue, life-size. It's a gift, a love fantasy and artwork. The Art of Love! It is us, Guy."

Her arms reached toward him. "Come to me, my love. Come! Make love to me. My base is large enough for us both. It can be our honeymoon bed. Join with me. Come to me, Guy."

One hand waved him forward, the other touched her breast.

My love! Guy thought. She looked so erotic and waiting. He suspected she would be and feel real. He could again hold his love, his wife, close in his arms.

"If women were sculptures, he could enjoy just sitting and watching this one be." She recited the passage from his novel. "But you do not have to just look. You can make love to this one. Now, here. Come to me, Guy, my husband."

Guy was about to step into the room when a shadow foreboding halted him. Indecision revisited, and he did not move, standing like an inanimate, frightened statue confronting an animate, lovely one. Thoughts conflicted.

"Come to me, Guy," the seductive statue beckoned. "I am waiting, my love. Please, come to me!"

A hallucination, probably a trap. But never before had he been aware of a hallucination while experiencing it. Either he had changed or . . . it really was Anna, as she said. She was visiting again in a new and witty scenario, a new persona, just as Anna would do.

"Anna," he spoke aloud.

"Yes, my love. It is me. Come to me, my husband." She rubbed her breast. "Please, make love to me. I've missed you!"

A surge of heated yearning consumed him. *Anna!* Guy stepped into the room.

A terrible stench assaulted. The flesh on Anna's body began rotting. Her eyes became milky, their sockets black and hollow. The teeth behind her smile yellowed and decayed, some dropping from her mouth. Her hair grayed and then whitened into dry clumps, falling to the floor. And her entire nude body wrinkled and decomposed into a putrid death, strands of flesh peeling and hanging.

Through her chest, in her exposed, trembling heart, appeared an arrow.

Guy staggered backwards, horrified and nauseous. His face paled. He trembled and watched Anna, or whatever demon she was, decay into a corpse. Guy gagged, almost vomiting.

"What is it, my love?" The rotting abomination spoke in a now low and hollow voice that dripped from the bony jaws of its skull head. "Don't you still love me? Come to me, your wife. Please, Guy! I've missed you. I love you!"

She stared into Guy's horrified eyes and dropped her outreached arms to her side. Her head lowered and a tear fell from the black pit of her eye onto the statue base.

Guy had never witnessed such sorrow. For a moment, the revulsion he felt turned to a torturous grief, the deepest he had yet felt since Anna's death. It seemed unbearable, a black, infinite ache rupturing through him.

He wanted to go to Anna, his love, despite her abhorrent presence, and take her in his arms. It was still her and seemed a challenge to his love. He tried to move, but the horror kept him paralyzed.

She looked up and into his eyes, entering deep and probing desperately. Guy had never seen Anna in such pain. One of her decomposing eyes rolled out of its socket, dropped, and bounced off her base. Guy felt death killing his heart and soul.

She again extended her skeletal arms. "Come to me, please, Guy. I love thee."

Then, suddenly, Guy realized something lucidly. There was no possible way Anna would do something as cruel and tormenting to him, and to her, as this. *I know her heart.* The putrid decay before him was not Anna. It was a hallucination, a horrible, sick illusion.

Flee! was his thought. Then Guy's face hardened, and his chest inflated. *Screw you!* He faced his antagonist.

"Yes, my love," he spoke affectionately. "I will come to you. I love thee." He smiled.

Guy walked to her and extended his arms so they enveloped her rotting form. The odor was so horrendous, like a hundred dead rats, he almost fell ill. His arms closed to embrace her.

She vanished; the abomination that spoke as Anna, the hell in her dying form, vanished, as did the space and the door. Guy stood in his living room, only a beige wall before him.

Sent home to hell! He thought with both pleasure and pain, even if it be only the hell of his mind. He stared at the blank wall. It seemed so innocuous. Just a wall.

He heard a pigeon perched on the ledge outside his window cooing. He looked. Its white shape and extended wings reminded him of a petite angel. Guy smiled, but his heart still pounded, and pained. He was perspiring and his stomach hurt. The profound sadness he had felt moments earlier lingered, regardless of what the abomination had been.

"Will this ever end?" He questioned the universe.

A miniscule light gleamed in the darkness. Never before had he had such awareness about, and power over, a hallucination. Perhaps the haunted has some control over the haunting.

But it wasn't enough. Guy walked to the corner of the room and knelt before the statue of Anna that now seemed more beautiful and pure than ever, like a redemption.

I see too well, he thought.

*   *   *

The next afternoon, on his sanity excursion, in a discount store, Guy purchased several items: a miniature Grecian vase containing tiny, synthetic flowers, a model of a red Audi TT sports car, a favorite of Anna's, and a plastic but surprisingly realistic ice cream cone with a cherry on top, perhaps intended as a metaphor. He also selected metal ornaments in the shape of angels and fanciful animals—birds, deer, a rabbit—and a six-inch glass reproduction of the classic statue of Venus de Milo with cracked breasts and missing limbs.

Walking home he absorbed the environment, a critical part of his excursions. *All must be absorbed,* he avowed. The approaching winter breathed an invigorating chill across the city. Los Angeles was basically seasonless, never seeing the mystical beauty of carpeted snow, that winter enchantment. Guy always regretted that; glistening snowflakes fell only in his mind. But he had learned to enjoy the moderate variations in temperature and nature that indicated passages through the seasons, and time, through the journey.

He made certain that afternoon to feel the sun and wind on his skin and to enjoy the urban expressions of nature—the palm trees, bushes, plants, and birds. Minimal, but meaningful. He hoped nature might rescue him from the horrific images of death and beckoning corpses that persisted in assaulting his mind.

He stopped before an inky, splashy stain on the sidewalk and stepped on it three times. *One must avoid dreadful fates,* he reasoned. He looked up and observed a filmy cloud streaking the sky. *So delicate and lovely!*

Suddenly, he could not remember where he was. A hazy light appeared before him and then gradually cleared as an unmeasured period of time passed. *In a city,* he surmised. He looked around at the buildings and palm trees and at the plastic bag in his hand. *Los Angeles. Yes, on my daily excursion.*

Guy worried.

*   *   *

Back home in his living room, Guy cut the tiny plastic red, blue, yellow, and white flowers off their stems, like colorful little heads being decapitated. With a thread, he tied them together in a ring and placed the flower tiara on the head of the statue of Anna. *A crown of nature on my love.*

He took the tiny vase with its painted Grecian design and set it on the table, turned upside down. He placed the glass Venus and the additional purchases around the statue with the other novelty items. The collection was growing daily. With small nails, he hung the metal ornaments on the walls surrounding the altar.

Guy surveyed his apartment and selected a plant with luxurious emerald leaves and violet and white flowers and moved it to the statue's table. He then chose a four feet high white sculpture of a hermaphrodite, an alluring creature with features of both a man and a woman. He always thought the sculpture's gender duality gave it a transcendence of the body and a spiritual presence.

"To you, Anna," he spoke formally and placed it beside the shrine table.

Guy examined the arrangement, an ordered menagerie of peculiar and colorful items.

"A lovely and unique home for Anna," he spoke. "An evolving altar to the goddess."

Guy suddenly felt an impulse and knocked three times on the wood table. Then two more sets of three knocks. It needed to total nine.

How ridiculous! he chastised. *I have now become prey to obsessions. More madness!* Guy laughed, and then more vehemently, *cruelly*, he thought. And then he had an unexpected cognition: *It is the best of worlds, and the worst of worlds. It is all worlds.*

Chapter 29

TIME PASSED PASSING times. Clocks wore and weary moons slept. Suns ascended, stretching with luminous arms across the awakening city, and then descended behind an eclipsing wall of darkness, again and again. Children played on sidewalks and streets, then sidewalks and streets were emptied. In bedrooms couples made love in the dim of final hours, and then slept, night after night. Temperatures rose and fell, shadows appeared and vanished. People were born and people died, and then were born.

Life proceeded in the City of Angels, real and illusion, aware and unaware, day after day, week after week.

Guy wrote, morning and evening, and sometimes between. Lives voyaged across a computer screen, imprinting their digital trail. It was a serial drama of love and pain, magic and comedy. Guy twice lived his life with Anna.

During those long weeks Guy did not have a single visitor. He decided not to examine that lonely reality, for where could it lead but to a conclusion of failure, or at best, the choosing of isolation? Sometimes Guy forgot that he was part of a human race, and more.

Instead he made some phone calls, connections, to be. He called the woman Anna had met in the restaurant, Camille, a fan and saved shadow person.

"Hello, Camille. This is Guy, friend of Anna. We met in the restaurant. Anna is dead," was basically his communication, although with more sensitivity.

"I'm shocked and deeply saddened," Camille responded.

"Yet Anna still lives. It's all about purpose," he basically explained.

"I think I understand," she basically responded, and Guy suspected she did. "But you still live, Guy, and I find you interesting and inspiring."

Then she told him her business was doing well, and she had a newly designed line of clothes she called Shadow Dresses, inspired by Anna's play. On the front and back of the full length, monochromatic dress was a smaller image of the dress in dark gray, like a shadow of the dress within the dress. Camille said they were popular.

"I'm glad," Guy replied although he thought the design peculiar.

"Can we get together?" Camille basically asked.

Since she was an attractive woman, Guy entertained some delightful thoughts, but he belonged to Anna, no matter what her reality.

"I must decline," he said.

"Call me if that changes," she replied.

Guy also called Anna's sister, Terry. They spoke of Anna's life in Los Angeles. "She contributed her spirit to the city," Guy said and then was perturbed by the statement. Terry did not respond.

He told her the bitter as well as the sweet, like Anna's one night liaison with the part cybernetic professor and her ensuing depression. It was a painful memory, but Guy felt that Terry, as Anna's sister, should know. Sisters cherish sharing all things. It's why sisters are special.

"Thank you. I like knowing," she replied.

Guy told Terry of the writing of the novel, in which she would appear. She expressed immense interest in reading it.

"I hope you do," he replied, although he warned her. "You might be a little surprised."

"Now I'm even *more* interested in reading it!" she responded, and Guy was pleased. He told her he wished he had a sister such as her.

Several times Guy also called a number he knew had been disconnected. He liked hearing the soothing voice of the recorded operator explaining the error and offering a solution. It reminded him that such people were out there, everywhere.

And he called God. He dialed 8888 and spoke.

"Hello, God. It's nice to speak with you . . . Yes, I am good . . . Writing the novel. It is proceeding well." Guy laughed. "It is a little strange . . . I hope you do . . . Yes, I know there can always be meaning . . . Thank you, God. I like you, too . . . and from Earth to heaven, goodbye for now."

Guy bought a colorfully illustrated book of *Alice in Wonderland* and added it to the altar. It seemed correct. Sometimes he read passages to the statue of Anna and chose to believe that Anna heard. Guy suspected that in a previous lifetime, Anna had been the girl, Alice, who inspired the story. He especially enjoyed reciting the rant of the Queen: "Off with his head! Off with his head! Decapitate him! Abbreviate him!" It seemed appropriate.

Guy also added items discovered in the streets—twisted, gleaming pieces of chrome and discarded parts of toys—symbolic fragments of their culture. Tourist postcards in tinted color of Santa Monica Beach in the 1930's, with bathing beauties reminiscent of Anna's beach persona, were tacked around the wall. Photographs that Guy had taken of Anna or them together, including his treasured first picture of her shot on the roof of his building and the beach photos, were added, given special prominence.

He placed on the table a toy figure of a warrior princess, a small plastic replica of a hill with the Hollywood Sign, a herbal tea box with a pretty scene of a Japanese garden, and more and more such novelties and mementos.

Dried twigs and leaves embellished sections of the shrine contributing accents of earthy brown and orange. Guy broke a mirror and attached the tiny fragments throughout the wall and table, each reflecting colors or a glint of light, adorning the altar with sparkle and myriad hues.

He wove a string of blinking white lights through the shrine. When plugged in the entire altar lit up, twinkling like a hundred glimmering stars.

"I've brought the spirit radiance in Anna's eyes to her tribute. It becomes an artwork!"

Each day it grew more elaborate, decorative, and to Guy, sacred—the Altar to Anna.

And Guy suspected he had gone mad.

*   *   *

Early one morning, a splendid golden sun awakened the City of Angels, and Guy. After semiconscious morning rituals and elements—water, soap, caffeine, increased oxygen and pulse—he sat at his computer to write. He recalled his startling encounter with the Supreme One at Forest Garden Cemetery. Be that experience real or hallucination, a question now innate to most of his experiences, it had helped him, especially the simple advice: 'Be happy you are alive.' On this day especially, he was. Guy wrote the very words he was thinking at that moment.

Which, reader, you are now reading, he thought, amused at the strange alignment of realities. *Hello, reader. I hope you are enjoying this novel,* Guy smiled and typed.

When the final words of the chapter were inscribed to file, Guy felt he should return his attention to present realities, and he meditated before the statue of Anna in its splendid altar, a triumph of passion! An unexpected thought entered his mind: *love in the flesh can be as sacred as love in the spirit if that spirit love is embodied in the flesh.*

Guy felt behind him the wind of flapping wings. He did not turn to investigate. *Let it be what it is.*

*   *   *

'In a vision, mad, can be All—
A verse, a voice, love—that reasoned mind
Can never see nor hear.
So fall into that winged madness,
Till madness makes us sane, and dear.'

Guy wrote that simple verse one afternoon when the room was in a mystical ambiance of gentle light and color. He was trying to accept fate.

*   *   *

One morning, Guy sat on the floor before the altar to Anna and drifted into a dreamy muse. Statues and ghosts and Anna and him, all united by an embrace of love into one passionate flesh and object form, one being, endowed with one pure spirit. Never alone.

Guy had an unexpected thought: *one can love an illusion, in an illusion of love. But if one's truth is love, his love is true.*

*   *   *

That night, as Guy slept, flowing through a stream of subconscious images and voices and touches, he heard, either in a dream or from another world, Anna calling to him.

"Guy, awaken! Awaken, Guy!"

He awoke. His hand grappled for a lamp beside his bed and clicked it on. The room was quiet in the sober illumination. The statue of Anna was on its table, hard and still. Then he saw motion and jolted.

The statue now moved in a slow, exotic dance reminiscent of Egyptian dances he had seen in movies, perhaps performed by Cleopatra, although with more graceful motions.

"What the hell?"

He rose from bed, turned on another lamp and walked closer to the sculpture. Confusion skewered his expression as he watched its cryptic, sensuous dance. Then the statue, the miniature Anna, changed to flesh and continued its movements, its body surrendered to delirious flows as in a narcotic rapture.

In a moment of magic that further confounded his vision, it transformed into a different woman with graying hair and a maternal body. Guy felt a plaintive sadness when he realized it was his mother as she appeared in the last years of her life. She continued the enigmatic performance.

Her figure on the pedestal grew smaller, to half her size, and her features became younger, her body and face that of a little girl. It was his mother as the six-year-old girl, in the age of her greatest happiness, whom she had regressed back to in the final year of her life. With amazement and sorrow, Guy watched his little, lost child-mother deliriously dancing in her own world, as she had for much of her life.

Then her body enlarged, assumed curves, and Julie Not Julie—no, Guy remembered—Julie was the dancer on the pedestal stage. It was wonderful to see Julie, while still of a plain and unpretentious demeanor, lost in such rapturous abandon. Although her face revealed little expression, Guy suspected she was happy, so naked and free!

Her body thickened and muscles grew. Her hair became shoulder length. The movements of the figure were more assertive as Raphael, the mad humanitarian, was now enraptured in the dance. Guy suspected that in Raphael's mind he was dancing before a harem of beauties, all of whom he had rescued from destitution on unforgiving streets, and all of whom adored him and intended to repay their debt.

"Dance on, my friend!" Guy encouraged aloud.

The figure shrank into his new little friend Sage, a nude and innocent child, performing her dance and awakening to curious tides in her being, a smile gracing her face. Then the dancer was again a woman, Camille, Anna's Shadow Play friend with whom he had recently spoken on the phone. Guy remembered her as an attractive woman, but he was not aware she had such a lithe and fine body. It was not a darkness of shadows that now spirited her form, it was a dance of beauty.

That beauty coarsened. With some amusement Guy witnessed Dr. B. Willard, his therapist of many years, whom Guy had sat with in his conservative office relating his tribulations and tales of madness. Now naked with a paunch stomach and flaccid body tone, he danced merrily, and Guy laughed. The good doctor seemed to relish his fantasy.

The practitioner morphed into a young boy, about eight years of age, sprightly with wavy locks of light auburn hair, hazel eyes, and a pleasant face, dancing whimsically on the pedestal. Guy did not recognize him. Perhaps one whom he had not yet met? A visitor from his future?

Peter. The name drifted into his mind. *As in Peter Pan.*

The boy grew feminine and lovely, gracing curves sculpting his body. Anna the fleshed statue reappeared. For a moment the pattern of the performance changed. Anna stopped dancing, stood straight and smiled at Guy. Then she flowed again, returned to the exotic dance of rapture. Her movements were absolutely sensual and gracious, as Anna's often were. Guy smiled and laughed.

Then she morphed into a man—himself. It was with the greatest intrigue that Guy watched his own body, nude and two-feet tall, performing the charming dance of the living forms. He thought he moved rather well and had not realized that he was capable of such grace of motion, and of being.

His diminutive dancing self slowly transformed back into the form of Anna, which Guy perceived as a truth. He sensed the performance was nearing its end. Anna flowed through the dance for a few moments and then stilled. She stood straight, facing him, and partially raised her arms assuming the statue's pose, a look of dignity on her face. Her flesh paled, and she incrementally became the shiny, resin marble.

Guy touched the statue. It was solid and cold.

He sat on the floor and reflected. He did not know if it had been a hallucination or a creative visit by Anna or something else entirely, but he believed he understood.

I was visited by what I must remember: the people in my life. They are part of me and my experience, and I of them and theirs. We are all one, joined in the extraordinary dance of life.

*   *   *

The next day, Guy reached the passage in the novel where Anna was killed on that night following their lovemaking at the hospital. It seemed a terrible irony that the horrific tragedy followed an event of such wondrous happiness.

He felt profound fear and sorrow. The writing required that he not only remember that night, but that he employed all of the powers of his imagination to recreate the horrid scene. At first he thought he could not do it. Then he did it. The imagery appeared vividly, as if being communicated from another source. *Perhaps it was,* he speculated.

A chill shook him as he watched Anna walking alone down a dark street leading to her encounter. It was as if he was in the scene, walking beside her. They both saw the cherub boy standing in the illumination of a street lamp. Guy listened to Anna's thoughts and felt her feelings, her concern for the 'darling boy', and the words she spoke to him. Then he listened to, or imagined, the boy's thoughts.

'A pretty woman. I'm sorry, but there's too much pain. It hurts too much. It hurts us so! I'll go with you.'

Then the boy spoke aloud. "Do you believe in love?"

Anna, after a moment, answered. "Yes, I do. Ultimately, it is the most important thing."

Then the foreboding words. "I don't. I kill love."

The boy removed the bow and pulled back the arrow. Guy saw the arrow enter Anna and felt it in his own chest. There was not much immediate pain, but instead the feeling of being hit hard in the chest by a fist. Then a sharp, piercing feeling, then numbness.

Anna was on the ground, looking up. Her eyes appeared confused. The boy looked at her for a moment. He felt sad and whispered. "You'll be all right now." Then he walked away.

Guy envisioned Anna in her last moments, and after, and it was tortuous. He wanted to take her in his arms and comfort her, but he couldn't. He imagined her visions, and her process of making amends, and her acceptance.

And Guy realized: *what happened that night was not a terror. It was a grace.* Then he saw a beautiful thing.

Guy's imagination closed the scene and he wrote the words. *Anna is very well,* he thought and smiled.

Chapter 30

CHRISTMAS — WHITE. COLOR LIGHTS and smiles. Children being times never lost. One glimmering, glorious star—even the moon gifts it with a beam! A red suited man with a winter-snow beard transported from some other, Never, Ever land, once a year arrived. Gifts and hearts opened. The snow is so beautiful, it blinds the sight! (A vision of Christmas night). Bells toll joy for all. Jingle bells!

White wings and festive rooms of precious things. It is the time of peace. Rejoice! Christmas is now.

There was not a flake of snow or crystal of ice, but Christmas was in sight.

Guy smiled. He knew Christmas existed more in the heart and spirit than in the world, more in dream than reality. And that he welcomed. He was, after all, just another guy, especially at Christmas.

One snowflake in the mind, one gift in a thought, one love-touched heart, and Christmas will be. Guy sensed a Beautiful, Winged Madness Christmas, and he felt something, something other than the profound pain of loss or the mania of mad hopes. Some excitation, subtle but real, *Christmas,* and for that he was appreciative. Something to help him traverse the innumerable writing days until the purpose was completed.

Walking the city streets on his sanity excursions, day by day, Guy witnessed the celebrated arrival. Like a transcendent and dazzling UFO, it descended upon L.A.. Colorful blinking lights wrapped buildings and homes. Gigantic white words proclaiming 'Seasons Greetings' or 'Merry Christmas' strung the boulevards. Dogs on leashes wore cute Santa caps and red collars with jingling bells. The delectable scents of cookies and pies wafted from bakeries and homes. Missionaries with signs and kettles rang red bells soliciting holiday charity. The air was enchanted and people smiled.

Peace on Earth, goodwill to men, Guy kept thinking. *Perhaps it will be so.* Cynic though he sometimes was, Guy enjoyed Christmas.

And he prayed he would not find a demon in his Christmas stocking.

*   *   *

A couple days before Christmas, Guy took a bus to a shopping center to buy Christmas items and gifts for Anna, his love and wife, whose spirit he believed would join him on Christmas. The Metro bus rattled and moaned down Wilshire Boulevard beneath strings of white holiday lights and signs.

In a Toys R Fun store Guy threaded the chaotic crush of children and parents, a Christmas phenomena, scouring for a suitable present. What does one buy a ghost wife? He examined a Ghost Busters Weapons Kit, a toy based on the film. Although it would be humorous, he rejected it quickly. He surveyed toy cars and action figures of mythic heroes and funny stuffed furry creatures. He almost selected Ellie Angel, a stuffed elephant with angel's wings and a halo.

He heard a Christmas carol sung by a scratchy, electronic voice. On a nearby display was a plastic green Christmas tree, about eighteen inches high, with some of its branches flapping like the lips of a mouth. In an annoying, distorted computerized voice it sang, "Joy to the world, the Lord is come! Let Earth receive her King." Being so humorously absurd and tacky, Guy knew Anna would love it. Her gift was found.

He next visited a thrift store and bought a string of Christmas lights, silver tinsel, snow spray, tree ornaments, and a gift card. His holiday shopping was completed, and he had not waited until the very last minute. He had been an excellent Christmas shopper, almost like a normal person.

A normal person. For an instant the idea felt consoling, and then only ludicrous.

The next morning, after writing, Guy decorated the altar with the new Yuletide adornments. When he plugged in the lights, the altar awoke, glimmering with colors and sparkle. The Altar to Anna became a dazzling Christmas shrine and its aura effused the room.

Christmas harkens everywhere, in joys that light the air. The lyrics to a Christmas song sang in Guy's mind.

He stood before a mirror and looked at his reflection. He had the smile of a little child excitedly awaiting the arrival of Christmas. It was a smile he liked and had not seen for a long time.

Then, in a flash instant, a thought. *Absurd!*

* * *

Past meets future. On the morning before Christmas, Christmas Eve day, Guy reached a critical point in the writing of the novel and, he surmised, his life. Seated at his desk, Guy typed the passage about the moment he was currently in, the transition point between the past and the future. The novel was brought to present time. It provoked a peculiar but gratifying sense of truly being present, in his being in the moment. Events leading to a destiny seemed to be reaching that destiny, which would now be fulfilled, whatever it was. And more than before, Guy felt that he was truly the writer, the story character, and the actor performing the character, and both the creator and the creation. It felt very familiar.

He wrote a nonsensical yet meaningful line. 'Now, now, now to future, future, future now.'

And Guy (I) realized again that at some time in the future, the reader would be reading what he (I) wrote at that (this) moment, and he (I) decided to address the reader.

'Hello, dear reader. It is a pleasure and an honor to present to you Anna's and my story. It is my sincerest wish that you learn something from it, or at least enjoy some moments of pleasure. And with the highest of intentions, I wish for you a Beautiful, Winged Madness.'

So how are this story, and his life, to be completed? was now the primary question. Perhaps he will live out the ending, writing it as it occurred, history following life, life creating history, as it often does. Or Anna the ghost spirit might transport him into the future, revealing it, which he would then write and afterward live. Or perhaps it would be done in another, mysterious manner. He wished it would be a strange and inverted reality, such as being shown the future, which he would then write and live, only to have it produce an entirely different outcome, which would include him going back in time to again see the future, which would be different than both.

The present influences the future, yet can never be what the future is, Guy mused, amused. Whatever it be, or not, he was soon to know. Guy saw that the most exciting story of all is one's own story.

In the evening, Christmas Eve, Guy celebrated its arrival by turning on the altar lights that in an instant became a Technicolor spectacle. *Behold!* he thought with modest pride and then sat before the statue of Anna, his love, to wait. *For what?*

He meditated. In the silence of the room, lit only by the blinking lights, in the stillness of his mind, in the nothing-something, minutes passed, then many, many more. Anna entered his thoughts.

"I'll be with you for Christmas, in heart if not in all," she sang softly to him with the warmth of a Christmas hearth, and then vanished.

And Guy wondered why he was alone on Christmas Eve. Slowly he understood. It was a time when he must be alone, to remember and to prepare for his transition into the future, be it life or death or both. It would not be the same as the past, or the present.

I must be certain the past is completed, as the last word I have written in the novel completed that portion of the story.

He thought again of Anna and their times together, and her spirit, *my second soul,* never lost. And of all of his life—his mother and friends, his madness and visions and purposes and work.

I should not be afraid.

He remembered: each moment is equally valuable and meaningful, as is the one he was now in—a moment of reflection. As the ghost of Anna said, there is actually only one eternal moment and one experience. All is one. One never arrives or leaves.

Lives and destinies were about to be fulfilled. Or perhaps all might simply end, without a grand significance. Merely an end to lives of madness and creations and pleasures and loves. And pain, sometimes excruciating. Should one expect anything more?

No matter what happens, it will be correct, he told himself, again and again.

*   *   *

At midnight, Guy watched the Christmas Midnight Mass broadcast from St. Peter's Basilica at the Vatican in Rome, delivered by the Pope who resembled a science fiction priest in his luxurious white and gold robe and peculiar peaked hat that suggested a huge folded napkin. It was a grandiose affair with the Holy Father on his white throne beneath a golden dome, like a person of royalty. On the dome was one colored window depicting the Holy Spirit as a white dove.

Guy thought it both foolishly wasteful and beautifully perfect, a marriage of man and God, material and spiritual, both worldly and otherworldly. The Sistine Chapel Choir sang rapturous carols, and the Pope spoke his Christmas blessing.

"In the name of the Holy Spirit, peace be with you . . . . First Creation began with light.

Christmas is the feast of light . . . ."

Holy, spirit, peace, creation, light. Words—powerful! Guy thought. Although not Catholic, nor of any religious denomination, Guy joined the Pope in prayer.

The past was completed, Guy concluded. *A new Christmas arrives!*

*   *   *

Sleep, perchance to dream. Later that night, in the fantasia of sleep, Guy sat alone in a white chair on a white carpet in a white room without other furniture or windows; a room emptied, a pure space. In the corner of the room was a green Christmas tree with exquisite ornaments, glistening gold and silver tinsel, and twinkling colored lights, the most beautiful Christmas tree he had ever beheld. It had an invigorating fir scent, and its top was crowned with a star, a *real* star, of gold luminescence with extending beams of light. A spirit being appeared before him. Its features were amorphous, like a ghostly form, and Guy could not determine if it was male or female. But it was illuminant, radiating a soft field of white light, and it was lovely.

"You may think of me as the Spirit of Christmas," the spirit spoke in a melodious voice. "I have appeared in this dream to help you."

"This is a dream?"

"Yes, Guy. And yet it is as real as you and I." The spirit grinned and held out its hand.

In an odd perception, Guy saw an area of empty space above its palm, as if it was designated by boundaries, although there was nothing there.

"Take it. It is yours," the spirit instructed.

Guy reached out his hand and received the space. It felt like he was holding nothing that was yet something.

"You will fill it, as you always do," the spirit declared.

Guy understood. He sat silent within the space of the white walls. He twitched, apprehensive, as one about to dive into waters far below.

The spirit being laughed amiably. "Relax, Guy! You have done it every day of your life, and you have shown your courage. You are not given anything you cannot do. Trust Spirit! You have written the novel, have you not? It is almost complete. You were apprehensive about it, but was it not a wonderful experience?"

Guy nodded. "Yes, it was, although also difficult. All the memories and feelings. It's been a strange but fabulous voyage."

"So it is when you do your purposes." The spirit's expression was gracious. "And thus shall be the future. Enjoy it! And now, Guy, I have a Christmas gift for you."

The being waved its arm and a space opened on the wall, filled with a pale, golden light, a radiance.

"What is that?" Guy stood.

"Come. You will see."

The spirit took Guy's hand. Its hand felt delicate, only half substantial, like a form composed of energy. It led Guy through the wall, into the light.

The moment Guy entered he experienced a powerful sense of serenity. All of the world's problems vanished, and there was an absolute faith in events that would follow, events he knew would be correct, and a grace permeated it all.

"Spirit, this is the space you exist in, right? The space of true love and serenity. What we at times feel, but what you are?"

The being nodded. "What we, as spirit, are. This is the space of my spirit, but it is also the space of yours. That is why you can experience and comprehend it. We are all the same."

Guy realized that he did understand the wise spirit's words. He thought of Anna and wished that she was there to share his experience. Immediately, to his amazement, Anna appeared before him in the light dressed in her Aesthetic Being Persona, looking glorious, like a work of art. Then Guy realized it was not a persona. It was her.

"Anna!"

She smiled, lifted an arm, and waved. "This is where we have always been," Anna decreed, mildly enigmatic.

Guy wanted to go to her and embrace her in his arms, but he intuitively understood this was a different reality, and their love transcended any and all realities, with or without touch.

He did not even have to say anything. Anna nodded and again smiled. She knew. Then she waved goodbye, turned, and walked away in the golden light, vanishing.

Guy felt surprisingly happy. He comprehended. Anything he placed his attention on manifested. It was pure creativity. A miniature Earth, about a yard in diameter, vividly blue and brown and green, appeared in the air, a fine layer of clouds floating around it. The planet rotated very slowly and across the United States land mass Guy saw areas of dim lights.

People in cities arising early on Christmas morning, Guy surmised. He looked at Los Angeles and imagined his tiny self there, sleeping in his bed, in a wondrous dream.

Guy knew that for those moments, while Earth was in the illuminated space, all the people of the planet felt the same serenity and love and peace that he was experiencing. It would be real to them. He chuckled, realizing they would probably attribute it to the spirit of Christmas, which, in a sense, it was.

"Guy, breathe slowly and deeply," the spirit being instructed.

When Guy shifted his attention to the directive, Earth vanished. "You just eliminated Earth."

The spirit grinned. "Sorry. Now breathe slowly and deeply."

Guy complied and felt the wondrous serenity profoundly penetrating all of his body, flooding every cell. "Wow!" was all he could say. He closed his eyes and surrendered to the experience, even more astonishing and pervasive than before. *I know what life is seeking.*

"Thank you, Spirit, for this amazing gift!"

"You are welcome. Now, close your eyes."

Guy complied.

"I leave you with love and serenity. Hold it dear, for it is you. Now see and feel Christmas! Let it fill your mind and heart. Awaken blissful, for it will be Christmas morning. Merry Christmas, Guy."

*   *   *

Sugarplum fairies dancing in his head to a melody of Tchaikovsky tickled his consciousness, and exquisite angels flapping their luminous wings awoke Guy, blissfully, early Christmas morning. He remained still for a moment, enjoying his returning consciousness.

Then he remembered his dream, and an exhilarating hope permeated him.

Christmas! The thought surged through his mind. He quickly rose, showered and shaved and then dressed in a black T-shirt with a white dancing Zen skeleton on its front, one of his favorites, clean jeans and a casual blue-gray sport coat. He brushed his hair, twice, and dabbed on cologne.

I must look and smell good for this special day, he resolved. *And for Anna.*

He made some potent coffee, looked out the window at the golden-orange sunrise, *the Christmas sunrise,* and then sat at his desk. Guy wrote the passage of his previous night, Christmas Eve, and his surprising dream encounter with the amazing spirit into the novel.

"Back to present time. How might the future be revealed?" Guy knew he must stay receptive. "Perhaps Anna will bring it."

He plugged in the altar lights. The shrine burst into a kaleidoscope of colors and sparkle, like a visual ode to Christmas. He brought out his gift and placed it on the statue's table.

Guy put a CD of Christmas music on his stereo and sat before the statue of Anna.

"Merry Christmas, Anna. I bought you this gift."

He pressed twice a button on the base of the plastic Christmas tree and it sang in its synthesized voice, its branch mouth flapping.

"O Christmas tree, O Christmas tree,

Of all the trees most lovely.
O Christmas tree, O Christmas tree,
Of all the trees most lovely."

"Do you like it, Anna? It's rather humorous, don't you think?" He smiled. "I had hoped we would be spending this Christmas together." His voice trembled. "I was . . . so looking forward to it. But sometimes events crush our wishes." Sadness surfaced like a gray tide. "Where are you now, Anna? In a beautiful place, a space of love and caring, free from sadness and pain? Perhaps the space we visited last night, in my dream." He peered at the little statue's face. "I hope so. Or perhaps you are here." He glanced around the room. "Wherever you are, I believe you are also here."

Guy became silent, listening to the Christmas songs. He always felt comforted when hearing Christmas music. It evoked a fantasy of faith. An instrumental came on. Guy knew its lyrics and sang along to the music, and to Anna, his love and wife, wherever she was.

"O come all ye faithful,
Joyful and triumphant,
O come ye, O come ye to Bethlehem."

An unexpected thought entered Guy's mind: *Christmas surfaces the dormant joy that always waits in one's soul.*

He read a gift card. "Wherever you are, Anna, I love you and Merry Christmas. Guy."

Yet, his eyes alone beheld it.

Guy decided to read some of Dickens' *A Christmas Carol,* hoping it might assuage the threatening sorrow. *Besides, there should not be a Christmas without Ebenezer Scrooge and Tiny Tim,* he declared. And he had already been visited by his own Christmas spirit.

He read some chapters aloud using his most theatrical voices to bring the characters to life. "Christmas! Bah! Humbug!" was recited with great relish.

"I am a perfect Scrooge." Guy chuckled, paused, and frowned.

In a harrowing passage, the Ghost of Christmas Future revealed a gravesite: Scrooge's. But in Guy's mind another name was inscribed on that tombstone: his.

The concept of visiting ghosts advising Scrooge seemed at that moment eerily ironic. Guy kept speaking the words into the air.

Alone.

*   *   *

Evening arrived. The light in the room dimmed, accentuating the chromatic effect of the altar's Christmas lights and tinsel. Guy sat quietly in his old chair as time passed. He stared at the statue of Anna, thinking of her. *I have been blessed.*

Then he felt profoundly sad with a deep loss welling in his chest like entombed tears. He stopped it. Guy knew pain was not what it was all about. He accepted that Anna was well, and all was purposeful. He had been graced to be with her.

And then he had a vision.

Guy saw what was to be the ending of his and Anna's story, which also was a continuing. It surprised him, for all elements connected, and that felt redeeming. He was pleased; more than pleased. He was accepting of all.

That night Guy wrote in the novel the events of the day, Christmas Day. The story was again brought to the present moment, but he did not write what his vision had shown him.

"Tomorrow I write the future." He resolved aloud. "Then I will create it."

Guy looked at the clock. It was one minute past midnight. *Christmas is over. The future proceeds.*

He felt behind him the wind of flapping wings.

Chapter 31

GUY AWOKE EARLY the next morning in a sinking delirium. He was descending rapturously into the earth while ascending into the sky.

Form is but a play of shadows, he thought.

"Now I die into the flames of a primeval sun."

He smiled, amused by his mock-epic dramatics. Guy always had the fantasy of being a grand Shakespearean character. Perhaps today, at the end of his odyssey, he would be.

"I rise as the man-god of the earth requesting consumption into its torrid sister. I will burn in a fatalistic rapture!"

He hastened to the rooftop of his building. He was naked, as an epic character should be when facing creation. No one else was there. The air was chilled and pristine, but he did not feel cold. The dawn streets were quiet. With a mystical grace, a gray-blue luminance gave form to the contours of the city, like a silhouette awakening. A pale golden-orange wash appeared over the horizon into which an amber sun slowly surfaced. With a primal power, it proclaimed its beauty and dominance over Earth, heralding a new day.

Yes! Guy agreed.

He witnessed a new universe being created. The sun drowned him in its bleeding, orange sea. A preparatory death.

All begins and ends!

He returned to his apartment to take caffeine. Still no constricting clothes. He sat at his desk and typed into the novel a few comments and the birth of the sun. Then, from his previous night's vision, he wrote the final passages of his and his love's painfully euphoric story—the future.

All that follows, dear reader, is the future I have seen, and will live, he (I) addressed that reader, you.

"Anna," he spoke. "Can you hear? The novel is completed!"

I love virgins, Guy mused. *They carry a strange, mature truth. At this moment, Anna and I are virgins.*

It is a beguiling horror, sometimes the story of life, when virgins are sacrificed.

Guy knew the Spiritual Universe was listening. It always listened to lovers, to life, and to death. He and Anna were in the All. And it understood.

He created a page with the novel's title and subtitle: 'The Beautiful, Winged Madness, A Story of Love and the Reality of Illusion'.

Then comes me, the mad, beautiful author: 'by Guy, Poetic Guy Being'.

The creator and the created.

Guy decided to write a poem for the reader. It would be his farewell following the novel's ending.

He then found his will and added and initialed an appendage. It stated that the manuscript of the novel, which he would copy onto a CD, should be given to Sage, his and Anna's child friend. He knew she would do what was correct with it. She would know.

Guy finished his French roast coffee, its taste and stimulation seeming euphoric. *Such wonderful little pleasures fill my life,* he thought. *Perhaps I should live.* For the slightest instant he considered that. Anna *was* dead. He could go on and just complete his life. That would be normal. The instant ended.

Guy went to the room's expansive window and looked at the city. *How many times have I looked out over L.A.? For what do I look? For a moment and a memory.* It was now fully daylight and the streets were alive.

Guy decided: *I will walk through my city one last time, at least in this reality. It will be as my first.*

Showering was next and then shaving, that most masculine of rituals.

*   *   *

In the mirror appeared a man, whom Guy recognized immediately. It was the Mirror Man from weeks earlier. He was older and thinner than Guy with unkempt dark blonde hair, a trimmed beard, and a character etched face and dressed in a plain black T-shirt and a brown leather jacket. His head was turned partially to the right, and he smiled at Guy slyly.

"You have returned, stranger in the glass, who looks at me with such purposed intent." Guy paused his razor in midair. "I do know you, don't I?"

The stranger smiled. "How old is the night? How many hours has the moon shone bright? When it dims, does the night die?" The mirror spectator challenged.

Guy was not vexed by his question. He looked with comparable intent back at his questioner.

"The night is as old as it is, and the moon has shined as many hours as it has. And if night dies, it is reborn into day." Guy grinned, pleased with his response.

The man in the mirror smiled fondly, his earth-brown eyes gleaming, and he nodded. "I have created you, and you have created me. Do you understand that the creator and the creation are the same?"

Guy peered into the stranger's eyes, seeking a proper reply. "Yes, we are both. You are that creator, aren't you?"

The Mirror Man nodded. "Yes, and I live through you, as you do through me. I am, you are, we are." He glanced upward into mirror thought-space. "A writer creates a character who is the writer, and the writer is the character. One creates the talk the other speaks, and what the other speaks creates the talk he writes."

Guy's look reproached.

"You appear now, vision of me and not me, to confuse me? Haven't I had enough confusion?" Guy took some shaving cream from his jaw and dabbed it onto the mirror stranger's nose.

The image man looked down his nose and wiggled it. "It's actually quite simple, my friend; a question of spirit, illusion, and reality. I created me then that me created you that now creates me. What could be purer, or simpler, or more beautiful?"

Guy returned to shaving. "Yes, I understand. Beautiful and mad. The Beautiful, Winged Madness."

The stranger in the mirror rolled his eyes and compressed his face into a lunatic expression, goofy and light as the air of a drunken euphoria. Then he relaxed it and stared at Guy kindly.

"We are one, Guy. You know me."

Guy aborted his shaving. "Yes, I know you. I will dedicate my novel to you—reflection of me who reflects you. We will both be."

"Ah, yes! The first purpose of all. To be. Excellent!" The mirror man beamed, his eyes brightened. "And by what name will you call me?"

"I know your name. But I will refer to you as the Man in the Mirror."

Guy resumed shaving, being careful not to nick his chin. The Mirror Man vision dimmed, but he dimmed into Guy. Vague words trailed.

"When day looks into the darkness of its night self, does it see the dark, or does it see the light of the day that it is?"

The Mirror Man laughed in a fading, fading, fading voice.

Guy finished shaving and splashed cool water across his face, tingling his skin.

"It sees either, depending on which is purposeful," he answered aloud into the mirror. "Hello, and goodbye, stranger and friend."

*   *   *

I dress, for the millionth time.

Favorite attire: jeans, T-shirt, and a sport coat. My first spoken words in white letters across the front of the black T-shirt: 'To Be or Not To Be'.

A musky cologne, because it smells like life and sex.

Guy left his apartment and walked the city streets. The City of Angels seemed enchanted, its buildings and sidewalks washed in white and pale colors, pastel blues and greens and gold. It had an oddly baptismal, innocent feeling to it, as if on that day all mortal angels were freed from dark disillusionment and vain dreams.

The cars seem alive, Guy observed cheerfully. *Jauntily bouncing down the street like animated objects in a Disney cartoon.*

Guy wondered if Humpty Dumpty might have been real but was too extraordinary for anyone to believe. Like the ghost of Anna. Maybe all the bizarre childhood characters were. Perhaps Humpty had rolled into Los Angeles one day and really had fallen off a wall and broken into pieces. How sad!

He would ask Anna. She would know.

The scents of the city, a trace of acidic fumes from cars fused with the ambrosial nectars of gardens and flowers, played on his senses, defining a city.

Guy would miss Mexican burritos, the ones with the melted cheese and red sauce, served with sour cream. And seeing the new model cars, especially the sports cars.

Guy saw, or hallucinated, a jester dressed in red spotted tights and a floppy Elizabethan hat, merrily strolling down the sidewalk. He stopped before Guy and, using mime, put his hands together in the form of a bird. He flapped his fingers like wings and raised his hands toward the sky.

"Birds, or angels, or souls, flying into heaven? Ascension?" Guy both thought and questioned.

The jester nodded and smiled, then strolled away.

Guy looked at the palm trees, their fronds stretching above him before the vastness of blue sky. They stood like tall and proud guardians of a city they never understood and yet loved. *I be a palm tree,* he thought.

Guy knew he was in a rare and higher state of being. It seemed as if a blanket of grace had been laid over the city. *How bright are the colors and pure the air. I feel its vibrancy!* He observed carefully each person he passed. It seemed so simple and clear.

Whether they are wealthy in fashion designer attire or a bum in tattered rags with the odor of refuse, each walked his path of truth. They were not lost. They were going home. All seemed redeemed.

All my life I have been blind, Guy critiqued with a humbling chuckle. *I see the sea, said the blind man to the mute. I will sing its praise, the mute replied.*

Guy had an insight he took most seriously: *this must be how great spiritual masters like Christ and Buddha perceived the world. All beautiful and graced. The creation of the world by Spirit.*

Suddenly Guy looked to his right. His expression became curious, and then he smiled. *Another walks with me,* he thought. *Yet, also, strangely within me. One with whom I am intimately connected.* But he could not identify his visitor. *Whoever you are, welcome!*

Guy returned his attention to his surroundings. He felt saner. As he walked, he realized what the uniqueness of Los Angeles was. It was a city without an established identity or self so it continually recreated and redefined itself. And that endless metamorphosis, those infinite incarnations, was its identity. It was like Anna with her menagerie of personas, each fun and metaphorical. It made Los Angeles interesting.

No wonder Anna liked L.A., he thought. He decided to nickname L.A. 'The City of Anna', believing there was no finer tribute that could be given it.

Do you, spirit of Anna, walk with me today through your city?

The city exploded with greater light and colors and vibrancy. *It was so!*

Guy again chose, and became, beautifully mad, for it is best to be mad in love and in death, *and I be both, as I be both sane and mad.* He sensed the Dark Yet Gentle Beast hovering over the city, waiting. It moved stealthily as a gray and stalking form, like a primitive but essential beast risen from the depths of man's primordial consciousness. But this day the beast did not seem threatening. It even seemed compassionate. It was just waiting to complete a purpose.

"Soon, my mysterious friend," Guy spoke to the lurking presence.

"What is will be our world. It is what is will be."

Guy heard the lyrics of a 1960's song and saw down the street an anachronism of a man, in his fifties, tall, bearded, hair to his shoulders, dressed in a burgundy T-shirt, fatigued brown leather coat, and Levi 501 jeans, faded. He sat on a low garden wall singing his illusionary reality and strumming a guitar. Guy approached him.

"What is will be our world," the estranged prophet continued.

"Do you really believe that what is must be? That we can't change our world," Guy questioned.

The singer paused his song and looked at Guy. "Well, man, it seems that way, often. Don't it?"

"Do you know," Guy replied, "there is something, something that exists, far, far greater than any of our inane considerations that can change our world, infinitely?"

He placed his hand on the man's shoulder.

The minstrel startled. "Wow! Yeah! I know what you mean, man. I've felt it before."

He grinned like a child, looked at his guitar and resumed his performance. Guy nodded and walked away. Behind him he heard the song. "Something greater creates our world. Something more is what will be."

One block later. Guy's vision scanned the city landscape, assimilating it all at once. The endless streets and concrete apartment buildings and palm trees and gardens and cars and humanity.

"Show me a final truth," Guy spoke into the air.

Moments later. A person, whom Guy believed to be a woman, her gender was not fully discernible, about thirty, robed in an old, musty blanket, her face soiled and yet still lovely as an angel's, walked toward him. She appeared homeless. She looked around, then into the sky, then directly into Guy's eyes, as if searching. Her look scratched at his sight. Guy thought he heard the question, "Why?"

He felt compassion for the woman and wanted to present her something nice. He stopped her on the sidewalk and gave her twenty dollars from his wallet.

"What's your name?" he asked, placing a hand on her shoulder and ignoring her disagreeable odor.

"Ruth." Her voice was timid and her eyes continued probing him.

"Well, Ruth, today I'm going to write and dedicate a poem to you. It will be my final poem, about one of the angels of Los Angeles."

"Thank you."

Ruth displayed a meek smile on her orphan face. Then she muttered something incomprehensible, turned, and walked away.

Guy watched the walking human rug continuing on her journey. He knew she, too, was moving toward her truth. It was impossible for her not to. When she vanished from sight, he strolled the city several minutes more enjoying its mysteries and intrigues.

"Goodbye L.A.," Guy spoke as he walked into his apartment building.

*   *   *

Returned to his living room, Guy wrote the poem for his new friend, titled, *Ruth, A City Angel.*

> 'A woman (I believe I perceive the gender), in a
>   moldy, blanket robe,
> Hair and flesh grayed from city air, scented and crusty
>   as an unwashed, unwashed sock,
> Promenades on her street home, impeding my path
>   and scratching my sight.
> She looks left, then right, then up.
> Still, arrested, musings aborted,
> She enters my eye and bares to my psyche

A scathed angel with a dazed child's face, searching
    and lovely still,
Amongst bottles and cans, musty, abandoned couches,
    paper sermons, and urine spills.
She shouts her question for me,
Looks, waits, then walks out,
A muttering, divine marionette—unstrung, alone,
On her familial street home.'

"For you, dear Ruth."

Guy saved the poem into his novel. It felt correct that his last poem was to be written not about himself, or even Anna, but a stranger, as to the world. And he knew that, in spite of all, Ruth was blessed.

Guy added to the novel a couple omitted passages about the day's events and the dedication to the Man in the Mirror.

Now Guy (I) have faith that all will proceed precisely as the vision showed him (me), and as he has (I have) written.

"*Now,* it is done!" He (I) smiled.

Guy put on some music, low. He chose one of his favorites: Mahler's *Ninth Symphony,* that anguished and sublime work about love and despair and death and acceptance, both brooding and beautiful, like a soul's journey through life and beyond.

Fatal and eternal, he thought. *Perfect!*

He looked at the clock, watching the second hand. For precisely one minute he swayed and danced around the room in an expressionistic, free form dance. A dance to life! All is one.

He viewed the wall painting of the Edenic Garden with him and Anna and their cherub son, like a naked and innocent first family. Anna looked especially captivating, a fusion of goddess, spirit, and woman.

"Very soon, Anna."

He was not afraid. *After all that has happened . . . .* He was to be spirit walking a new road through a foreign yet wondrous land, with Anna. He felt rather euphoric, his soul light and free.

"Make sure you go to the bathroom before you leave, while you have a chance," he remembered his mother saying when he was a child. *Mother,* he thought and smiled. Guy went to the bathroom and returned.

In his vision of the future, now written in the novel, *that I now live,* he had not hesitated. It was done that day, the day after Christmas, and so it would be. Guy was ready. There would be no noble, tragic Hamlet-like indecision. This was not such a drama. It was about purposes and love and destinies, and his awaited.

Besides, I am no Hamlet. I am just Guy—poet, painter, and spirit in love, and that seems more than I ever believed I would be.

Guy sat in his aged, venerable chair that was, as always, a comforting friend. He remembered his conversation with Anna when he asked if she believed that one could simply will one's death, as he thought his mother had. They both agreed one could.

"We will the continuation of life every moment we're alive. We could choose not to, as in suicide," Anna said.

And so it would be. There would be no overdose of pills. He would will it, and it would happen, because it was correct.

Guy had a peculiar impulse. He went to his phone and dialed E-A-R-T-H. A message came on. "I am sorry. The number you dialed is not a working number." Guy laughed.

"Hello Earth," he spoke into the phone. "I just called to tell you goodbye, and that I will still be around. Thank you for all you granted me, and I sincerely apologize for any difficulties I may have caused you. I will speak with you again. Goodbye."

He hung up and felt a comforting relief. *All must be complete.* Then he made a second phone call, to his apartment manager. An answering machine came on and Guy left his message.

"Mr. Courtney, this is Guy in 504. Could you please come by my apartment in the morning? Just come in. The door will be unlocked. Thank you."

Guy wanted to make certain he was quickly found. It must unfold correctly.

He took a blanket and a pillow from his bed and laid it on the floor before the Altar to Anna. The afternoon sun streamed through the window onto an area of the carpet, so he moved the pillow into that light. He opened a window to allow in some air from the outside world. He lay on his back on the blanket. The warm sun on his face seemed an invocation of purity.

Guy looked at the altar. It was a lovely and inspired creation, a tribute. Obsessive, perhaps, but can anything be excessive if an expression of love? The marbleized statue of Anna stood regal and sensual in the altar's midst, glistening white in the sunlight.

"The time has arrived, Anna. I love thee."

I suspect I am mad, though not totally. Half mad and half . . . inspired. Of course! I am an artist. It is my fate. And this is The Beautiful, Winged Madness!

He concluded there was nothing more that needed to be said or done. He knew what was ahead and simply closed his eyes.

The man becomes the ghost, Guy thought, *for the ghost of the woman he loves.* Then a sensation of warmth penetrated his heart. *How peculiar and nice!* The sensation became a delightful excitation that swelled and extended through his body and being. He opened his eyes.

Guy had a magnificent realization. What he had been searching for, the purer and truer love, was his. It was within him, in his heart and soul. And it had always been there.

He instantly understood. He had shared that love for a time with Anna, as she had with him. And he knew they would continue sharing it together, somehow, somewhere. It was a simple, but profound happiness. The best!

But it was much, much more. He now knew that even if he had never met Anna, even if nothing in the world or the universe had ever responded to it, he would still have had the pure and perfect love he sought. It did not depend on anything or anyone else. It was him. And so it was with all his other ideals and purposes, as an artist and a man. They were in him; he was a true and pure lover and artist!

Guy laughed at the sublime irony. He had sought all his life for what he had always been and always had.

He lay quiet for some moments enjoying his feeling of peace and completion. Pure and perfect moments. A rustling sound from outside the window pulled his attention. Perched on its ledge was a glistening black crow.

"Hello, my friend. You look familiar."

The bird shook its head and lifted its feathered wings.

"Why yes! You are the crow from Forest Garden, who perched on David's shoulder."

The majestic crow stared at Guy with its dark and enigmatic eyes, eyes like Anna's.

"So now you have come to take my soul? Well, that is fine, but may I ask something of you?"

The ebony bird cocked its head.

"If you take my soul, will you deliver it to Anna? She awaits me."

The crow spread its wings fully, like an unfolding black cape, and then slowly closed them.

"I'll take that as a yes. Good. So be it!"

Guy smiled. The crow cawed and remained contentedly on its ledge, possessing its territory, waiting.

Guy looked into the sky beyond his window. Its vast, calm emptiness provoked serenity, and Guy floated. He was a few inches below the ceiling, yet he could still feel his resting body below and the sun's warmth on his face. The music of Mahler faded and delicate sounds from the outside city drifted in through the window, surrounding him. He heard birds singing melodically and the yells and laughter of children at play. A dog barked four times. A song played by chimes sounded from an ice cream truck cruising the streets, hailing its customers. The melody was the old song *Pennies from Heaven*. It evoked a charming memory of Anna in her 1930's Bathing Beauty Persona, looking sleek and playful, standing on the sand in the toasty sun on that delightful, and daunting, Sunday at Santa Monica Beach.

Guy heard the faint whirring sound of a motor. He saw in the pristine azure sky outside his apartment window, floating majestically, the silver surreal blimp with the illuminated gold letters on its shell spelling 'Trompe l'oeil'.

The reality of illusion, the illusion of reality. How true. My life! Guy also perceived, with lucidity, that what is often considered true and real, the physical universe, was but an illusion, and what is often considered an illusion, Spirit, is the only thing that is real and truth. One of life's great ironies.

"I release the illusion and become the truth," he spoke aloud to any who would hear.

He looked at the statue of Anna.

"I love thee, Anna."

There will be stars out tonight, and romance. Let's face the music and dance. The lyrics of a song from a decade past serenaded in his head.

Then a verse he wrote spoke in his mind: "In the end, as in the beginning, all things are as fine as love and illusion."

He felt extremely drowsy and closed his eyes. *It will be easy,* he thought. *Far more so than living.* He recalled Anna's comment about Peter Pan spoken long ago in a cafe.

"I believe. I believe. I believe," he whispered.

A gentle moment passed. It was so, so easy. It felt just like he was falling asleep, falling asleep, falling . . . .

A drifting through soft landscapes of gray. A peculiar little man, dressed in striped tights and a floppy, three-pointed hat, stood on a stage before an audience of thousands. He bowed, and a curtain behind him closed. The house lights dimmed.

*　　　*　　　*

There was a loud knocking on a door, startling Guy awake. He opened his eyes and looked around. He did not understand. He was sitting in his old chair. The apartment was quiet, a morning light filtering through the room.

"What the hell?"

More persistent knocking pulled him to his feet.

He opened his living room door. Anna stood in the hallway, smiling provocatively. She looked exquisitely lovely.

A blissful disorientation overtook Guy. "Anna? How?"

She swept her hand down the front of her body. "My Aesthetic Being Persona. I wore it just for you today."

A light infused her eyes. She looked to her left and adjusted the fall of the black dress over a shoulder. "Perfect! Like it?"

Guy's expression erased. He looked behind him to the corner of the room. There was no statue of Anna and no altar, only empty space with a painting hung on the wall. A packed suitcase was on the floor beside his chair.

"What's going on?" Anna questioned. "I came to go to the hospital with you."

"The hospital?" He looked at the clock on his wall. It read ten o'clock.

Anna saw the suitcase. "I see you're ready to go." Her eyes turned down. "But still, I wish you wouldn't. I have a bad feeling about it."

Then Guy understood. He had not yet gone to the hospital. There had not been a Raphael or Julie Not Julie, or a night of extraordinary lovemaking. Anna had not died. They were all a creative visitation to his dreaming mind.

He had fallen asleep in his chair awaiting Anna. Falling asleep—that was all the tragedy and adventure.

"A dream!" he shouted and took Anna in his arms and held her tight, kissing her twice on the forehead and once on the cheek.

"I thought you had died. In a dream. It was terrible! Then all these things happened." He kissed her again, on the lips.

Anna smiled and looked into his eyes. "Bummer! But I'm still quite alive and intend to remain so for a while." She laughed her delightful laugh.

No words could have made Guy happier or any sight thrilled him more. He hugged her tighter.

"I love you, Anna."

Then he released her from his grip and for some moments just looked at her. Her presence seemed incredible. A miracle!

Anna waited patiently, apparently sensing the importance of those moments for Guy. "I love you too, Guy," she finally spoke. "I don't mean to break the sentiment of the moment, but are you ready to leave? We can have breakfast on the way to the hospital." Her expression became ambivalent. "That is, unless you've changed your mind."

Anna grinned and nodded several times.

The hospital, Guy thought. *It did not have to happen. None of it had to happen. He and Anna could create the future. They could choose.*

"I'm not going. I'm not going to the hospital!" Guy announced with conviction. "To hell with it all! I'm leaving the disability program and therapies. No Room B. Let's just be together, Anna."

Her face illuminated like a door opening to the sun. "I'm so glad! I know that's right!" She kissed him quickly on the lips. "My courageous Guy! I have a lot to talk to you about. Things have changed. I was going to wait until you returned from the hospital, but it's better now. I think you'll be pleased." She considered for a moment. "Think of wings lifting from our beautiful madness!"

She laughed and then ran her fingers through her hair, tousling it wildly.

Guy, strangely not surprised, understood and knew he would, indeed, be pleased.

Anna walked to the suitcase by the chair and kicked it over.

"Great! Settled!" She exclaimed. "But first, let's get some breakfast. I'm hungry."

She took his hand and pulled him toward the door.

Anna, let's make love together, tonight, Guy was about to say but suppressed the words.

"And most of all," she added, "make sure you keep tonight free. *All* night."

They looked at each other and a tender anticipation passed between them. *Yes, things are to be different,* Guy mused with a grin. Anna had never seemed so lovely and promising and perfect as she did at that moment, captivating Guy.

His attention evoked a smile in Anna. "Yes," she said.

Guy closed the door behind him and locked it.

Then his world went black.

Then his world went white and light.

That was the last dream Guy had in his life.

Chapter 32

SEVERAL DAYS LATER. Two small gravestones were tiny gray dots in the neutral vastness of the cemetery grounds. Guy was buried at the bottom of a grassy swell in the picturesque serenity of Good Heavens Cemetery, his grave placed beside Anna's as requested in his will. A black crow, perched on the branch of a nearby tree, watched the interment with an interested stare.

On the day of his funeral, television news announced that there was a moderate 4.7 earthquake in Japan, a flood in Mississippi that destroyed scores of homes, and rulings in Washington, D.C. by the Supreme Court on the constitutionality of a method of execution in capital punishment and the rights of states to define pornography. In Los Angeles nothing emerged as sensationally newsworthy. The humidity was lower than normal and the Los Angeles Zoo announced the addition of a new annex to house exotic birds. There was no mention of Guy's passing or funeral, and no article on him in the obituary section of the city papers.

The day was mildly overcast. Seven people and one black crow attended the funeral—several patients from the hospital who Guy knew from group therapy sessions, his long-term therapist, a city appointed Protestant minister, and Sage, his and Anna's ten-year-old friend. An additional person, a cemetery attendant who cared for the plants—he liked plants because they were natural and non-judgmental—stood in the distance beside a twisting Cyprus tree.

Another sad life ends, he thought and wondered how many, or few, people would attend his funeral when he died.

Sage, incongruously attired in a sweeping white dress, evoking an angel, with skin delicately pale like that of an exquisite doll, stood alone among the mourners. The others, preoccupied with companions and death, did not notice her presence. She felt as the air that blew in a gentle breeze across the hills of the cemetery, softly touching the bushes and trees and black shadow mourners, present but unacknowledged. *Here and not here,* the girl mused, *like a spirit. Like Guy and Anna. We are all spirits.* She rather liked that idea and smiled. If any had observed her, they would have concluded there was unusual nobility in her comportment.

Sage's memory returned to the previous evening when the ghost of Guy visited her in her bedroom, as Anna's had previously. *Or perhaps they were dreams,* she thought. Either way, she cherished the experiences. When she saw and identified the vague specter before her, semitransparent and dressed in gauzy jeans and T-shirt, she felt profoundly sad for she knew what it meant.

"Do not be sad, dear Sage," Guy's ghost spoke in a voice that sounded as if it had carried from another room, or world. "I like seeing you happy, and it's good where I am now. It's like being in a wild dream."

Sage, dressed in her pajamas, forced a smile. She kind of understood what he meant.

"Why you and Anna? You're my friends."

"It's purpose and destiny, Sage, and Anna and I accept it."

"Can I be dead and join you? We could fly around together."

Guy's ghost, hauntingly visible before her bedroom window, laughed. "Not yet, my little friend. You have great things to do. Be happy that you are alive."

Sage saw the ghost's face become radiant, which looked peculiar on one so vague, and she knew he had imparted a vital truth.

"OK."

Guy's ethereal form, like a filmy mirage, lifted higher above the floor.

"I feel like a balloon."

Sage giggled. "Have you met God?"

He smiled. "Yes, I have, and he's the same as he is in your world. He says, hi Sage!" Guy waved a specter arm.

Sage smiled brightly. "Hi, God!"

"Sage, soon you will receive a novel I wrote. I am entrusting it to you because you will know what to do with it."

"I . . . don't understand. But I'll do what I'm supposed to do. I want to help."

The ghost nodded. "You will help, and I deeply thank you for that. And it will also benefit you. Tomorrow my body will be buried in Good Heavens Cemetery. I suspect it will be a humble affair." The spirit of Guy grinned. "I would be pleased and honored if you attended. Not to mourn, but to celebrate."

His atmospheric hand touched her on the head, and she felt the touch.

So she was there, at the funeral, dressed in white, and she tried not to mourn. Waiting for the minister to give the eulogy, Sage placed blue roses, donated by a neighbor, on her two friends' commonplace graves. The vivid color of the roses next to the drab gray of the headstones looked like a determined assertion of life against a threat of nothingness. Sage liked it. She knew there was not a nothingness, ever.

She examined Guy's grave. The gravestone was a nondescript stone slab, about two-feet wide and one-foot high. On it was a simple acknowledgment of his life, with his name as requested.

'Guy, Poetic Guy Being', and the year of his birth and death. Below it was an ode.

'Ode To My Death.

Hail to thee, corpse of me!'

Sage laughed. *Guy was funny and wonderfully mad,* she thought. She wanted to grow up to be like him and Anna and yet still be herself. She knew how important they were. She, too, would be an artist, and they her inspiration. And she, too, would love and live past death.

"Thank you, Anna. Thank you, Guy," she spoke, not to their graves, but to their spirits.

Sage returned to the line of mourners and stood quiet, listening to the minister who seemed like a peculiar creature from an alien planet. She thought he spoke without speaking, presenting a confusion about Guy returning to somewhere to be with something named God. But she knew they were always with the true God, and they were moving ahead, not back.

I will have to help the minister, Sage resolved.

As the ceremony proceeded, she felt both deeply sad and immensely happy. Her eyes teared as her lips smiled. A thought came into her young mind, from somewhere. *Be happy that you are alive and keep awakening.*

Guy's therapist, Dr. B. Willard, stood at the end of the queue of mourners, listening to the eulogy. He was a black-suited man in his late fifties with receding, gray hair, silver framed glasses, and a paunch belly. It always pleased him that people said he looked like a TV soap opera doctor. He enjoyed the fantasy of being a celebrity psychologist.

He thought the minister's words were suitably reverential and comforting, yet as he listened he kept fidgeting and shuffling, irritated. The doctor had long ago decided that he could never know whether God existed, and he would stop trying. It had little relevance to the real world anyway.

But death, that was real.

One should never deny death or one lives in an illusion, he felt like speaking aloud to the bereaved mourners. He enjoyed helping people who pained. Human pain was his specialty.

Although Guy's death certificate declared 'cause of death unknown', the doctor believed it was suicide. He thought about the years of therapy with the strange young patient. The good doctor felt confident that he had helped Guy live a more directed and meaningful and, yes, happy life.

He looked at his patient's grave, considered, and then looked at it again. He felt confused.

"Damn funerals!" he mumbled. "Morbid affairs. I deal with enough morbidity with my depressed patients."

He considered whether it was appropriate to permit himself to feel sad. He believed suicide was a self-determined and irresponsible act and to respond with sorrow would imply sympathy and thus agreement with the act. That would be an inappropriate position for a therapist to take. And yet, the loss of a human being, especially one of his patients, was regrettable, and he did feel a degree of affinity for Guy, as peculiar as Guy was.

The doctor concluded there was but one proper response: *I will embrace the concept of sadness but not the emotion. I will be sad without feeling sad.* The doctor smiled broadly. And he would not consider Guy's suicide a tragedy. That denied the self-will of the act. He preferred the term 'consequential reality'.

All was decided. The doctor was pleased. *Perhaps funerals are not so bad after all,* he reflected. *If one responds correctly.*

He noticed the cemetery smelled nice with the sweet nectar of flowers. *A positive,* he assessed. People were beginning to leave, so he assumed the affair was over.

Exiting the funeral site, he made a mental note: *I must remind my assistant Susan to move Guy's folders to the former patient file.*

The good doctor looked at the sky. It was gray and overcast and he assumed that was why it was especially chilly that day.

"I will have to remember to bring my overcoat," he muttered, "to the next patient funeral."

Epilogue

A LONG TIME later, or perhaps it was a short time, Guy the Spirit had a vision, or perhaps it was real. It may have been him, being again both creator and creation. He was uncertain but did not even care for the boundary between reality and illusion had long ago vanished. Those two seeming incongruities now existed as one in a playful harmony, as in a superb artwork or the magic of a novel, as did he as Spirit with all else.

A boy, about eight-years old, with a face of precocious innocence, wavy auburn hair, and penetrating hazel eyes, walked across the rolling grass of Good Heavens Cemetery. He was dressed in floppy blue jeans, a black T-shirt displaying the image of a wizard brandishing a magic wand, a tan jacket, and a crème straw carnival hat, its brim and top round and flat. He was visiting, as he often did, the graves of the two souls, the artists Guy, Poetic Guy Being, and Anna, Anna Spirit Persona. He had been told their story by his parents who read about them in a fact-based novel.

"Tons of people know," he thought and smiled. The two artists now seemed his friends.

After their deaths, a journalist published a feature article about them in a national magazine, focusing on Anna who had been a victim of the notorious child serial killer, The Cupid Killer. Interest in the two artists with the enigmatic monikers burgeoned. Then a young girl announced on the news that she had in her possession a novel written by the man known as Poetic Guy Being. In it was the key to the mystery of their remarkable lives and creations. A small but committed publishing company purchased the publishing rights. The book, titled *The Beautiful, Winged Madness, a Story of Love and the Reality of Illusion,* incrementally became a popular seller, especially in the Los Angeles area. Some of the profit from the sales was kept for Sage's future education and development as an artist, as she believed her two friends, Guy and Anna, would have wished. The remainder was donated to libraries and public art and theater schools.

One person at a time, month after month, year after year, in a vibrant city in California or a literary café in New Orleans or an artist loft in Greenwich Village in New York City, or somewhere in American suburbia, awakened to the idiosyncratic tale of the two artists and their odyssey of art, spirit, and love. Books of Guy's poetry and reproductions of his paintings sold. DVDs of Anna's performance pieces, many of which she had filmed and others that were recreated, played in homes and art schools to varied reactions, sometimes embraced and sometimes denounced, but always provoking.

Some romantics considered Guy and Anna the Romeo and Juliet of Los Angeles, estranged souls who sacrificed all for their love and art, and to that public a faith in love and romance, dreams and ideals, and sacrifice was reborn.

It was not unusual to see a fan of the novel resurrect a persona that Anna had worn or create one from his or her own inspiration. Elegant Death Mistresses strolled the grounds of Forest Garden Cemetery enjoying the sensuous statuary. Beauty of the Everywoman Statues appeared in the pews of Catholic Churches to the startled stares of worshipers. Techno Pop Cyber Punk Extraterrestrial Futurists possessed the floor of hip dance clubs. A few bold souls even recreated the Dust People Persona.

Some found it easier to deal with the intrigues of the body and flesh than the depths of the soul, but others, inspired by the examples of Guy and Anna, explored both.

And more and more, the cherished words were spoken: "I love thee."

Some saw the Cupid Killer, the child who killed love, as a metaphor for the very conditions in society that Guy and Anna sought to resolve. People spoke, and listened, to their children more.

And people went naked. Nude Adams and Eves appeared in lush gardens, living metaphors of some elusive truth.

Adventurous fans tried to locate the decrepit shack on the vast desert where Guy and Anna played The Game. A few did.

Critics, including psychiatrists, repressed conservatives, and religious fundamentalists, denounced Guy and Anna as delusional fatalists, dangerous role models, socially and sexually estranged neurotics, and goofballs.

Guy and Anna gradually influenced the world, not monumentally, but to a consequential degree. Somewhere, someone embraced spirit more, or put their faith in a bold artistic creation communicating their soul, or made a commitment to truer and purer love. Somewhere, someone transcended.

Once a year, a modest but expanding Beautiful, Winged Madness Festival was held on the grounds of Good Heavens Cemetery. Attendees donned their favorite personas while enjoying a Mozart Quartet, readings of Guy's poetry, presentations of Anna's performance plays, and adventurous works by other artists. Guy's poetry books and painting reproductions were sold, as were, of course, Beautiful, Winged Madness T-shirts.

The boy, who always attended the festivals, thought it a peculiar phenomenon for so much love and beauty and art to exist in a cemetery, a home of death. But so the two artist lovers had intended for the world.

Guy and Anna became new angels for the City of Angels. But the little boy, standing in the cemetery on that warm spring day with flowers blooming and the air infused with nectar fragrance, had not read the novel and did not know all the details.

"Too adult," his parents had judged. "When you're older."

If he had, he would have discovered, to his surprise and in a unique experience of converging realities, that he, too, was a part of Guy and Anna's unfolding story. But soon that would change since he planned a clandestine reading of the book.

"I must," he resolved, "for I, too, am an artist and artists must try to see all!"

I am a spirit and have a purpose, even if it seems mad. He was already experiencing visions, surprising and wondrous, including him one day writing a beautiful and mad book. And the boy knew that he, too, would help to create a better world.

He accepted without reservation that he loved Guy and Anna, and many others he could not see or touch, and all spirits. He was awakening.

His attention startled, *awakened.* Like an eclipsed sun emerging from a penumbra moon, a little girl appeared from behind a nearby tall tombstone.

I think she's a girl, he surmised, *for she also is a ghost!*

The mysterious girl, her entire body covered by semitransparent gray veils, raised her arms straight out from her sides, creating herself into a cross. She stood perfectly still for one, two, ten seconds and then spun and swayed in a haunting, spirit dance. Captivated, he could not refrain from staring. In the middle of a graceful spin, her veils flowing like a shadow dance, the girl suddenly stopped. For a moment that transcended moments, indeed all time, the two children looked with profound intrigue at each other. Then she glanced down and tugged gently at her specter gown making certain it fell straight along her body.

"Excellent!" She declared.

Through her veil he saw a smile. She walked to him.

"Do I . . . know you?" Her voice was deep and gruff to sound haunted.

"No, yes. I don't know."

His eyes melded to her presence. The girl phantom slowly pulled up the veil from her face, and the boy beheld a sight of beauty! Not perfect, yet perfect. He saw that she was about his age with a cute, rounded face, crème complexion, cascading red hair, and eyes of blue-green, like the dazzling sea of a magical dream.

A ghostly angel, he thought and felt a strange and delightful sensation in his heart, a feeling that seemed familiar from a long, long time past, but he could not remember when.

His young poet's mind, which was struggling to rise from some place within him, a place of grace and spirit and wings, recalled a verse he had written recently when thinking about someone lovely who he believed was somewhere thinking about him. For no viable reason but that he knew he should, he spoke the words aloud, to her.

"Sun kindly wait; you must shine on she who brings your soul. Ignore the night.

I am but a lost boy, my dreams untold.

I need her light!"

The girl looked deep into his eyes. "You're a poet," the pretty specter spoke with a now not so haunted voice.

She extended a black-gloved hand. Immediately he shook it.

"I'm Ambrosia," she stated. "Like the drink of the gods. I'll intoxicate you." She smiled.

"I'm Peter. Like Peter Pan. I will never grow up." His chest heaved. "I believe, I believe, I believe."

They both laughed.

"I like to dress like a ghost and haunt the cemetery." She waved her arms and made eerie sounds. "Ohhh, uhhh. Some people are spooked. I think they believe I'm a real ghost." She grinned. "But others get all wide-eyed and smile, like they've seen something wonderful. I think I help them. It's fun!"

"I think you're pretty," Peter blurted and then looked down in embarrassment. Timidly he looked back up.

Ambrosia smiled, but her eyes darted as if wanting to touch his and yet avoiding. Peter thought she looked even cuter.

"Do you like Shakespeare?" she asked, her eyes now focused.

"He's a good friend of mine."

She glared out of the corners of her eyes. "I'm going to be an actress, and I just learned my first Shakespeare. Would you like to hear it?"

Peter nodded like a bobble head.

"OK. It's from A Midsummer Night's Dream, the ending. From Puck. He's a sprite, a mischievous spirit. Like us! But think of me as a voice in the air."

She walked a few steps away and then turned toward Peter. For a moment she stood quiet, her eyes closed in concentration, and the cemetery hushed around her. Then she opened them and spoke.

"If we shadows have offended, think but this and all is mended. That you have but slumbered here while these visions did appear."

Listening to the enchanting, fanciful girl reciting the splendid words, Peter had a feeling he had never before encountered. It was a wild stirring in his heart and a call to his spirit. He knew nothing would ever be the same again.

"So goodnight onto you all. Give me your hands if we be friends, and Ambrosia shall restore amends."

Ambrosia held out her hands, and Peter took them in his. She smiled and bowed.

Peter had a vision and the scary but wonderful experience of falling into the Beautiful, Winged Madness.

THE END
NEVER ENDING

A POEM FOR THE READER

(To be read or scanned)
By Guy, Poetic Guy Being

(To scan, read only words in **bold**.)

Vision! **I be**seech thee!
A poem for our readers, please.
Light as **spirit**, profound as **soul**.
As formless vision designs its form
to transcend design and form. Now
greater Vision sees
its sole (soul) **creator**.
Beneath the That
I be you and you be they and All be God.
I (like the metaphor object eye—vision—perception,
    consciousness, awareness. Self Spirit God.)
See? With I and eye.

*This is, and always is, **The Poem**.*

This day to find a love and beauty, **I** cannot reason or see,
Spirit whispers to my soul,
"Die to live, then create what you **be**."
Only NoOne can be what you are.

Let **Spirit** possess the **flesh**, its mirror of **beauty and being**.
The Earthly Vision.
And let it not be too long unloved.
A glimmering is in the spiral center's black.
Tiny with feet and mouth it moves and speaks,
Creating being created.

One word only does it know, and it only needs to know.
BE

A thousand colors and myriad forms,
Dance and love and cry.
A celebration is born—alive and still.
Perfect and torn.
I am there, as are you, and all who ever lived and died.
And are yet risen. Creators!
Life and Art, **Madness and Beauty.**
Even Dark Masters who kill.
All wonder. Is this it?
And they know. *This is* **The Poem.**
The Vision.

A character, of persona and spirit, foolish and wise,
Struts and dances upon the Stage.
"**I am** a jester. My name is **Game**. Can any guess my game?"
A girl, of emerging Age, prepares to possess the Stage.
"Thy **game** be to create to **be**, thy game which be thy
    name—Jester."
The Jester bows and surrenders the Stage, but leaves behind
    the Prize.

Behind all frail and fated forms—this Something,
I feel **Spirit** and **Eternity**.
The wind of flapping wings.
Be happy that you are alive!
God asks you for this Dance.
Keep **awakening**!
Follow the A that leads **To Be**.
We are nothing and **All**.
mystery upon Mystery.

Mary had a little lamb—a shadow lamb.

Once upon a time, in the beginning, was the Word—**the Poem**.

All truth can be found in a grain of sand.

The sound of one hand clapping.

Stay! Play the Game and you will see

A Vision. ***The Beautiful, Winged Madness***.

And know that All be in **fun.** The soul's grand **Play**.

The Jester's first and last purpose.

For **We**, human spirit mortal immortal, gods of **God**,

In **loving** and **creating**

To Be, and Be.

Poetics 0-1:

The Poem should be as the Creation—simple, balanced, perfect:

God be We be God

Poetics 8:

*The only true Poem is the Poem that is the **Poet**.*

Now, at last, The Poem.

POEM